THE SIGHTLESS CITY

By
Noah Lemelson

A Tiny Fox Press Book

ISBN: 978-1946501-33-2

Library of Congress Control Number: 2020951240

Tiny Fox Press and the book fox logo are all registered trademarks of Tiny Fox Press LLC

Tiny Fox Press LLC
North Port, FL

To Dolly,
For teaching me what it means to live a good life.

To Bessy,
For making that life so much fun.

The United Provinces of
The Æthmach Republic

(As Well as Some of the Lesser Regions of the World)

1603 AD (After Diedrev)

The Välkmaa

ANKLAF

VIDEK

KAIMARK

TOR

BASTILLIA

SULCOSTA

TYRISSA

The Interra Sea

El Helmaud

Utarra

Prologue

Before he had come out here, before he had traded in his bespoke leather brogues for military boots and marched out to the edge of civilization, Marcel had never known how strong the wind could taste. In its whipping midnight gales, the wind carried the flavors of the Wastes, rust and dust and æther-oil. But it brought more to the palette this grim night, hints of blood, smoke, and humiliating defeat. The remains of a battle Marcel had survived only through luck and circumstance.

"A gift," came Desct's whisper. The soldier handed Marcel a gas mask, his sardonic smirk disappearing as he slipped on his own. Marcel holstered his Frasco six-shooter and studied the mask. It looked not unlike a skull, bug-eyed and painted black.

"It shall banish all melodious odors," Desct said, as if a salesman. Behind him two more masked soldiers, members of their squad, worked to cut open the bars of a large sewer pipe, taking care to step over the blue-uniformed corpse of the lone Principate scout they had had to eliminate. The pipe, just large enough to squeeze into, dug into the side of the hill, and deeper still, sloughing out the industrial muck of the city beyond.

Huile. Bright in the night, a beacon at the edge of the Wastes, girded with ancient walls and split in two. At the far side was the city-proper, its civilians cowering under the oppression of the occupying army. Peaking up from the closer half stood the smokestacks of the æther-oil refineries, where the Principate now camped, sleeping in their victory, unperturbed by the blood they had spent the day spilling.

"Remember," their captain whispered, "we're here to plant our explosives and run, not trade bullets with imperial idiots." It was strange to see Captain Alba like this, her golden hair covered by black leather, the cerulean gleam of her eyes hidden by dark glass, her voice, boisterous and cocksure, muffled by mask and caution. She glanced Marcel's way. Not at him, he realized, but at the satchel hanging from his arm. Silently, he opened it, the clockbomb still clicking inside, its payload the last hope for their beleaguered cause.

Marcel had never thought his military service would come to this. The stories he had been raised on were those of front-line gallantry and noble last stands. Not sneaking through sewers to plant bombs under sleeping soldiers. This was the part of the story often left out, the less glorious side of military heroism.

With a slight clunk, the gate to the sewer fell. One by one, the squad started to crawl into the cramped dark, Alba leading.

"I can still take the bomb," Desct whispered. "This is not what you enlisted to do, no one would judge you for returning to camp."

Marcel realized the mask was still in his hands. Somehow, putting it on felt an immense challenge. Once he tightened the leather straps he knew he would not loosen them until the Principate army was dead, or he was.

One last breath. He let the acrid taste of the wind settle on his tongue. It was somehow now comforting, as familiar as the sea-salt breeze of his home. Yet there could be no waiting, not anymore. Not if Huile was to be liberated, not if his fellow soldiers were to be avenged.

8

He lifted up the gas mask and slipped it on. It was a natural fit, tight, the air stiff and sterile. Desct stepped forward, over the corpse of the soldier whose expression was mercifully hidden by the night, into the maw of the pipe. There was a cost to being a hero, Marcel knew, but as he followed his squad into the dark, he was determined to pay it.

...Wedged, as it is, between the wild, Ferral-haunted forests of the north, and the shattered Wastes to its west, an ignorant person might well discount the Border States as just another rural backcountry, unworthy of tour or travel. Yet, it takes only a few hours strolling the streets of any of the independent cities of the Border States to understand why they remain the most popular travel destinations for Bastillian tourists on a budget. They are the perfect compromise for adventurers eager for the frontier excitement of the Wastes, but who still demand the comforts of civilization. From the lively Bell Day festivities of Ordone, to the rich old-Vastium cuisine of Tascula, to the perfectly preserved pre-Calamity architecture of Anres, each city offers its own unique gifts, wonders hidden behind wind-worn walls or within scrap-ornamented market halls. Even the lesser States, such as Petram, Vatil, and Huile, bear a unique Waste-rustic charm, and are worthy of a few days' detour.

Yet, I'd be remiss to leave my recommendation as fully glowing, for the smart traveler must also strive to be a wary one. War is no foreigner to these ravaged lands, and the wounds of the past century fester still. For every marvel and bedazzling sight these cities offer, they also shelter hidden perils, bitter mercenaries and errant raiders wandering the roads, hungry mudlions and toxic cockatrices resting under untended ruins. This close to the Wastes, there is always something dark and dreadful hiding just beneath one's sight...

—Introduction to "A Tourist's Guide to the Border States" By Matas Joubert

Chapter 1

"It was a scraprat."

Marcel Talwar sat, real leg on the floor, mechanical leg on his desk, sharing the details of his investigation with the middle-aged Miss Dobis.

She furrowed her brows. "A scraprat?"

"Yes," Marcel said. "Scraprats often like to eat trash. That's sort of their thing. No one is spying on you, you just have scraprats."

Miss Dobis mulled this over. "But Miss Paquet is always shoving her nose in other people's business. It would be just like her to go through my trash."

Marcel had known from the beginning that the life of a private investigator would be different from how it was depicted in the pulps. Fewer shootouts for one, though he considered that a mercy after his short military career. Marcel had expected some drudgery, some misunderstandings, even occasional stupidity. Still, he had not expected Miss Dobis.

"Why don't you run me through what you saw?" she asked, a slight accusation in her voice.

Marcel shrugged. "I waited up all night in the alley behind your apartment, hidden, watching your trash, *as instructed.* By three in the morning I saw movement. I tiptoed closer and found a small, scabbed, fuzzy form. A scraprat. On the second night, same deal, a scraprat. And on the third night?"

"Miss Paquet?"

"No, Demiurge-be-damned, a scraprat!"

The woman shifted her gaze around the small office. It was a shabby thing, Marcel had to admit, chipped walls threatening to splinter, bookshelves overflowing with useless guidebooks and browning novellas, a pre-war voxbox with a broken speaker, a single plain desk, and a pair of even plainer chairs. The only decoration of note was a crinkled photograph framed on the wall: Marcel marching with the other surviving members of his squad in Lazarus Roache's post-battle parade. There he was, waving as he stumbled forward on his new, æther-fueled leg, frozen mid-stride alongside Heitor Desct, whose impish grin was lost in the blur, Lambert Henra, whose rotundity had somehow survived the austerity of war, and Alba Rosair.

Alba Rosair. Her image was faded and distant, but he could still make out the look of disquiet on her sharp face. He often wondered if it was that moment, after the battle, after his hospital stay, Huile aglow in a Resurgence victory, if that was when their relationship began to sour. Alba was a woman of war, and in peace her smiles had become sneers. He could imagine her now, shaking her head as he wasted his time with civilians' inane blabber, asking if this was the future they had traded their friends' blood for.

"I would have expected more from you, *young man,*" Dobis said, interrupting his thoughts.

Marcel sighed. It was true that the common stereotype of a private investigator was someone middle-aged and gruff, not a man in his mid-twenties with an awkwardly genteel accent he couldn't quite kick and faint, lazy stubble. Still, most people respected results in the end; Miss Dobis seemed determined to ignore anything that threatened her sturdily built preconceptions.

"I did what you paid me for," he said with weariness. "I spied and puzzled out the mystery of your stolen trash. What else do you want?"

"How do you know that it wasn't Miss Paquet looking through my trash before I hired you, and scraprats only now?"

"I mean..." he tapped his desk and sighed again. "Look, it's just common sense. I can't prove it, I don't have a time machine."

"A time machine?"

Why was he making this harder on himself?

"Just something from a pulp I read, never mind. The point is, it was scraprats. Now stop worrying about it."

She crossed her arms. "Reading books instead of doing your job! You know if the Principate were still here, they would have interrogated Miss Paquet and gotten to the bottom of this."

Marcel considered himself a reasonable person, not prone to shouting and tossing papers. But there was a time and a place for everything, so he chucked the surprisingly thick file on the Dobis case at its namesake's feet.

"If the Imperial Principate were fucking here, they'd line everyone up with a suspicious name and shoot them in the back of the head! Is that what you want? To lick the Imperator's boot?"

"How dare you!" she said, her large, unscarred cheeks shining red.

"How dare *you!*" Marcel shouted, cogleg clanking to the floor. "Look out the window! You ever take a walk outside this city? See the cracked land, the ruins, the oozing trees, the Demiurge-damned Wastes? Whose fault is that?"

"What?" she shouted, throwing up her hands. "Who cares?"

Marcel sputtered on his words, temporarily stunned by the woman's boneheadedness. The Calamity wasn't even a century gone, living memory if you found someone's great grandparent, and yet people like her treated it with a shrug. "The Principate's fault!" Marcel finally shouted.

The woman scowled. "The trolleys ran just as timely with them in charge," she said.

"Good men and women of the Resurgence died to keep the Imperator's hands off this city," Marcel said. "They died to free Huile!"

She scoffed. "Not sure why that's such a fuss. I heard all they did was open the pipes in Lazacorp and let the gas do the rest."

Marcel took the banded clump of four-hundred-and-fifty frascs that the woman had given him just minutes before and threw it back at her with all the force he could muster.

"Get out!" he said. She stumbled, then picked up the crumbled wad, seemingly unsure of what to do with it. "I don't want the cash of some Principate sympathizer! Were you a collaborator? Is that it? Do you miss the blood you could suck from good Citizens, like some sort of autocratic ghul?"

"I do-don't need to take this!" she said. "I'll report... I'll report!"

"Say whatever you like," Marcel said. "It's your right! One we fought for! Get your Inferno-cursed ass out of my office, or I'll investigate you, see if any of the skeletons in your closet wear Principate blue."

Ms. Dobis tried to say several things at once, but gave up and made a snort of contempt. She stood and started to walk, nearly tripping in her too-tall shoes. As she opened the door, she turned.

"You're nothing more than a gunman for cash," she snapped.

Marcel opened his mouth, but the woman hurried out, eager for her words to be the last. He swallowed his insults as the door slammed, and started to pace around the perimeter of his office, fuming.

The gall some folk had, the complete apathy for the sacrifices of others. The city was not even three full years free and still some were eager to spit on the graves of those who had paid for that freedom. Marcel hadn't needed to take the job; it was below the dignity of a war hero. But he had taken it anyway.

What Marcel did, he knew he did for the average citizen, the sort of folk the United Confederacy of the Citizens' Resurgence was supposed to stand for. He could have made mountains of cash selling his war hero's reputation, or by working a cushy job in City Hall, but what good would that do? A hero didn't stop, couldn't stop, just when the battle was won, when the oppressors were slain. Marcel had lost his damn leg freeing this city, lost most of his squad, had served Huile for more than two years rooting out the last Principate collaborators, and yet for some troglyn-headed idiots that wasn't enough.

He pulled his canteen from his hip and took a long sip. If this were some cinegraph show, Marcel mused, the canteen would have been filled with whiskey or rum, but alcohol never dulled much for him. If anything, booze darkened Marcel's dreams and made his nights more fitful, so instead he sipped twice-boiled and three-times-filtered water. He wiped his lips, the acrid taste still stinging his tongue. Life in Huile wasn't all that much worse than in more developed cities, but he missed the simple joy of clean water untainted by the Wastes.

He sat down and slowed his breath to calm his temper. It had been stupid to threaten her. Not that her complaints would reach anyone's ears. City Hall knew what sort of man Marcel was, and the gripes of a civilian busybody wouldn't sway them. Still, his outburst had been unbecoming of a Citizen of the UCCR, betrayed, in its own small way, the values of the Resurgence. His Confederacy had been founded to protect the rights of average folk, even rude ones, from those who would wield power as a cudgel. Let the idiots be idiots. As long as they didn't turn Principate, their thoughts were their own.

Marcel picked up the notes he had scattered and tossed them in the bin. A distraction was in order, perhaps a pulp. He glanced over his disorganized collection. Though he had some tolerance for the fantastical tales that seemed the popular fare these days, ridiculous fables about dragons and sorcerers; he preferred those older pulps which were more grounded in reality, stories about men and women, autocars and æroships, scraprats and griffons. Real things. Yet he didn't always have a choice in the matter, he had already read most of pre-Calamity pulps that had been scavenged from around Huile, and merchants from more civilized lands beyond the Border States rarely carried novels of any kind.

He studied instead the tower of unopened mail that occupied the far corner of his desk. Not greatly entertaining, but he supposed it had to be dealt with at some point.

The pile was a familiar mix: bills, ads, the new issue of *The Huile Gazette*, a missorted letter for a "Marcus Talbert," and then a large envelope.

This last one was strange. Quite fat, with no stamp or return address. It had his name in quick-scrawled letters on its front, and beneath it were the instructions:

Show To An Engineer!

The package was heavier than it looked, and when Marcel cut it open, a flurry of paper cascaded onto his desk. His picked up one document, then another, then more. Each was a convolution of organized lines and abstract symbols that to Marcel's eye might well have been the chaotic scribbles of a madman. These were technical drawings, clear enough, and written on the margin or on free-floating scraps were dense, minute notes, whose words Marcel could only recognize as some form of highly technical mumbo-jumbo.

The instructions had been prescient; Marcel had no hope of making out what these dozens of drawings of cylinders and linework represented without the aid of a Guild-trained ætheric engineer. In truth, he could only make out one clear fact. These papers were from Lazacorp. This he deduced from the simple observation that each page had *Property of Lazacorp* printed in mechanical typeface on its bottom corner.

He sat down and organized the mess, both on his desk and in his head. Someone had clearly stolen technical documents from the company that was the beating economic heart of Huile and tossed them at his doorway. Why hadn't they taken them to an engineer themselves? That was easy to answer: because if there was even a single engineer in all of Huile they were certainly on Lazacorp's payroll.

His thoughts ran in ten different directions, but after a minute he shook them out of his head. As intrigued as Marcel was, this stranger, who had not even bothered to knock, was not his client. Even if he was, it wouldn't make these schematics any less stolen. If Alba were here, perhaps she'd search for an angle, a way to use the pilfered papers as leverage or blackmail. Such was her mercenary instincts, but Marcel had taken his career path to mend tears in law and order, not poke more holes in them.

He tapped his desk, stared at the papers a minute, and then shrugged and continued to dig through his mail.

The next letter from his stack was an æthericity bill, from Lazacorp itself. Beneath that he found a menu for some newly open bistro serving *"Exotic Meals From The Verdant Fields of Utarra."* Then there was a note with a job offer to spy on some rich bastard's wayward son. Pitiful work. Below that sat a decorated letter that invited him to the funeral of—

Marcel nearly dropped the letter as he read.

"Desct," he said to himself. "Demiurge's grace... Desct."

Chapter 2

The roar of the skyrail train woke Sylvaine Pelletier up that morning, as it had every morning. 5:35 exactly, one could set a clock by it. A city run by engineers would accept nothing less. Her apartment simulated an earthquake as the traincars roared over, her cot swinging back and forth, her few possessions bouncing on her shelf, struggling against the custom restraints she had welded onto the walls. Hers was a student apartment, a small metal box hanging precariously off the frost-decorated bottom of Icaria. On the few maps where it was labeled, the neighborhood was called the Underburg, and it attracted half the students in the city for the same reason any neighborhood attracts students anywhere: rent was cheap.

Sylvaine got out of her cot and stepped over to the corner that served as her kitchen. As she brewed tea, she reminded herself to check the bolts above her home. It was an extra precaution all Underburg residents took. In most apartments, failure to perform proper maintenance only resulted in blocked up toilets or burst light bulbs, but for Sylvaine, a few rusting bolts were all that stopped hers from plummeting off the bottom of the city down 200 metres to the junk-strewn mountainside below.

The automatic teakettle whistled steam. Fifty-four seconds to boil, twice as quick as when she had bought it. *Introduction to Practical Mechanics* had paid off in this little way; it had taken her less than an afternoon to double the efficiency of the kettle. The little machine always brought the hint of a smile to her face, its existence evidence that despite her academic troubles, despite her physical appearance and the prejudice that it brought, Sylvaine was an engineer. And for an engineer, nothing was impossible.

She drank her tea and ate her breakfast, a piece of day-past-stale bread, as she stared out the hole in the wall that served as her window. The outer Wastes of the upper Border States stared back; rocky, brushy, with patches of green in the distance where independent farmers grew palewheat and waste-bred tubers, and blocks of grey concrete and iron closer, where the Guild had financed agri-factories.

She took some pleasure in this growth of industry. More efficient to mechanize the farming, even if, admittedly, the Calamity had opened up more than enough space for simpler crop plots. In the back of her mind, she wondered if she just hated the green. She had come to the capital of the Engineer's Guild to get away from all things natural.

Sylvaine washed up in the corner sink of her apartment. She was glad the trains woke her up so early, it gave her enough time to wash her fur. *Hair, damn it, hair!* Years of schoolmates calling her a beast had formed habits that were hard to break. She had once, in a childish fit of inspired idiocy, tried to shave off her hair. But a shaved ferral still didn't look much like a human, which her classmates had been eager to remind her.

There was never as much mockery for her teeth, despite her elongated canines and knifepoint incisors. Perhaps it was because the children never saw them, Sylvaine hadn't had much to smile about.

6:09, a minute ahead of schedule. Schedules were pieces of craftwork that Sylvaine cherished, a manifestation of mankind's control of time itself. In other cities, in wasteland towns or forest-edge villages, people might wake at dawn, close shop during storms, and meet at sundown. Weather and the other barbarities of the natural world were given little respect in Icaria where life was a matter of controlled clockwork. That suited her fine.

Sylvaine wasted a moment of free time to manage her reflection. Brown hair sprouted from head to toe, a thick mat of it, which she patted into place. She studied the ends of her ears, which were better suited to a cat or coyote, with eyes that reflected moonlight if she stayed out late. Her nose was not overly hideous, but it harassed her daily with the detailed knowledge of every oil slick, pollen grain, or sex-laced sweat drop staining a student's undershirt. When she stared too long at herself, she couldn't help but forgive her bullies' cruelty; the jokes and taunts came so easily. Instead she gazed to her clothes, her tight-fitting shirt, her workwoman's coat, with the hammer-and-gear pin of the Engineer's Guild on the lapel. It was the machines you made, not the blood you bled, that were the credentials of an engineer. She told herself this every morning. Maybe one day she'd be able to believe it.

The selling point for Sylvaine's apartment, besides pocket-change rent, had been its proximity to the rickety Underburg skyrail station. She clamored through the short maze of catwalks that hung below the city and jumped onto the first traincar that rolled in. The Q-line, a straight shot to the Icarian Guild Academy. A golem attendant hung welded into the train's wall. No, *auto-homid,* she chastised herself for her imprecise slang as the mechanical mimic of a man stamped her ticket. As she sat, it whirred and groaned, turning on rusting gears towards the next passenger.

The nice thing about an Icarian traincar was that there was always someone even stranger looking than Sylvaine. A salvi dipping her head down to fit in the train car built for human-sized passengers, sitting beside the usual batch of engineers spouting extraneous metal arms and lenscraft eyes. Her skin was a deep gray and her long horns riddled with decorative carvings. Sylvaine wondered if the salvi was a runaway slave from a Malva Ironship City, or if her family had lived in Icaria for generations. The tattoos that peeked from holes in her sleeves suggested the former; grids of flesh-carved serial numbers, in Malva script.

The salvi caught her gaze and winked. "Icaria!" she said.

"Tourist?" Sylvaine asked.

"Immigrant hopefully." The salvi smiled. "Icaria! If they won't let you make it anywhere else, you can make it here!"

That's what Sylvaine had heard, before she had left her family to live in the city-on-the-mountain. Perhaps it was even true. Unlike in the Principate, there were no laws here against Salvi, or Ferrals, or Mutants, and unlike in the legally safe but socially hostile cities of the Resurgence, the Engineer's Guild's love of bodily augments and additional metal limbs left them with comparatively fewer discriminatory views on those who differed from the physical norm.

Still, three years out and Sylvaine was no closer to "making it." Gear's-grits, she hadn't even been able to pass *Applied Æthermantics* on her first two attempts despite near perfect grades in all other classes, so the state of "making it" was just some mystical land beyond the horizon, as real as the dragon empires of Xue-leng she had read about in some trashy fantasy pulp.

Sylvaine sat back on her uncushioned seat and turned to the window. The train ascended from the Underburg through the interior of the city, past layers of pipes and rotating machinery, hollowed-out engine rooms and cargo holds turned dense tenements, up to the surface. A great metropolis, one of the largest post-Calamity, stared back; towers of iron and glass built in orderly grids, smaller factories and workshops crammed into every free nook. Autocars rolled over the metal streets, alongside stranger vehicles with clanking legs or chain tracks. The sidewalks bustled with folk of all shades, sizes, and head adornments, whether hats, horns, metal-implants, or just well-trimmed hair. Merchant hocked exotic wares, mostly fakes, while showy engineers marketed their inventions to skeptical crowds. Beyond the city-proper stood the snowy mountainside, covered in great metal tethers that prevented the unnatural city from sliding down into the dust and ruins below. No one on the streets paid any mind to the season, the frigid mountain winds were blocked by skyscrapers and the heat of the Icaria's uncountable engines burned away the late winter's chill.

Sylvaine glanced up to study the largest structures in the city, the negative-density towers. They were her favorite sight in the city, massive bulbed pillars that loomed like gods. Even the æroships were careful to give birth to these titans. Before the Calamity, they had lifted Icaria far above the clouds, a nomadic capital for the Engineer's Guild. Sylvaine enjoyed imagining what it must have been like to live in the floating city, before the ætheric ripples of the Calamity mutilated its internal machinery and sent crashing the remains into the side of the Atsol Mountains. Only the most ancient of engineers, those whose metal replacements had let them live several lifetimes, held any memories of Icaria's glory days.

Sylvaine reached her lecture hall at 6:57, three minutes early. At seven precisely an old kortonian hobbled over to the stage. His height, average for his kind, was just above that of a human child, but his squarish forehead, heavy wrinkles, and clunky brass-bordered spectacles dispelled any notion of youth or human blood. He walked to the human-sized podium and cranked forward a kortonian-sized lever, the platform lifting him to a presentable height behind his lectern. He began speaking as the gears groaned into place.

"Welcome to Applied Æthermantics 101. My name is Professor Gearswit."

He coughed.

"Now that pleasantries are out of the way, let us begin. What is æther? If you're still asking this question, you probably shouldn't be in this class."

He laughed at his own joke. A few students chuckled politely.

"Still, I must educate a depressing number of first-year students who come here with an excess of imagination that, no, despite what some fools claim, æther is not 'magic.' It is simply a form of trans-material energy not bound by the same laws that govern most physical objects. For those who possess an inborn biological predisposition for æthermantic manipulations," he coughed again, "or to use the common parlance, 'The Knack,' æther allows the creation of mechanisms and machines capable of far more than what a simple mechanic can produce."

Sylvaine hated that phrase, "The Knack." So many engineering students seemed able to lift an ætherglove and instantly start infusing machines with almost supernatural properties, all because of this "Knack." When Sylvaine picked up her glove all she got was snickering, pitying glances, and failing grades.

To comfort herself she watched the late students trickle in. Many were other-folk, like her. The bulk of this minority were the short and square-headed kortonians, but there were also some slender, metallic-haired malva, a few massive salvi (who tended to sit as far away from the malva as possible) and a handful of mutants, red-skinned, some with twisted horns or lizard eyes, others with patches of boils and cog-like spikes running down their backs. The humans came from all lands, the Torish coasts, frosty Anklav, the isles of Tyrissa and some even came from the Kingdoms of El'Helmaud, across the Interra Sea. It was known throughout the world that an engineer trained in Icaria was worth ten from local academies. These human classmates were rarely only human. There were nearly as many metal limbs as flesh ones, and Sylvaine often overheard her classmates comparing and bragging about their "upgrades."

Still, she was the only ferral. She was the only one with fingers that ended in retracted claws, the only whose tufted ears flicked by instinct, the only one who looked like a fur carpet that had decided to grow limbs.

"Since this is a sane class, we'll be working with stable æther. If you want to work with raw sangleum oil, then take Professor Stelhan's class on ætheric transformations. Unstable æthermantics is not demoncraft, whatever your priest might have said, but I do recommend you watch yourself around the stuff. There's a reason sangleum weaponry was able to blast the heart of our continent into a scrap-strewn desert, though I think any sensible person would put the blame for the Calamity on the politics of the Severing War, not the tools those fools happened to use to resolve their internecine bickering."

Sylvaine glanced idly around the repurposed lecture hall. Lodged in one of the negative-density towers, it looked like a hobbled-together student project; metal chairs welded directly into the layers of pipes that constituted the floor, scaffolds bolted onto the walls to provide extra seating space. The roof was merely a large tarp stretched over the room to hide the gaping emptiness of the tower above. There was something inorganic about the lecture hall that excited her, as if the building itself defied its own origins.

"And, to preempt any of you too ambitious for your own glove, no we won't be using elemental æthers, trust me, better engineers than you have tried. Nor will we be performing any church-sanctioned 'miracles' with the 'holy æthers,'" he snorted the two terms. "And we're not beastmen, so natural æthers are out."

Sylvaine shrank down into her seat. She knew her professor did not mean it as a slur, but she could feel the eyes of her classmates shift over to her. It wasn't her fault she was born into this body. She had never even been to the Nemori Forestlands. She was an engineer, damn it! Why wasn't that good enough?

"So, we will continue using good, old-fashioned stable æther. And, as this is an applied course, I think a demonstration may be in order."

Sylvaine's mood flipped instantly, and she scooted a few centimetres forward on her seat. If her desire to avoid notice hadn't been so great, she would have sat in the front row.

The short man pulled from under the lectern a block of iron, a small engine, and a glove covered in a small web of tubing and brass chambers. He put the latter on.

"Who here has tried to manipulate wood or stone? *Tried* is the key word. If your materials were processed thoroughly, then maybe a few of you might have found some minor success. Unlikely even that. Metals are the ideal medium, and if you open your textbook to the Appendix C there should be listed different metals' resonance frequencies."

He tossed the iron block in the air. As it reached its apex, he thrust his gloved arm out and the block stopped in midair, then rotated and morphed, as if putty.

"You see, by burning a small amount of æther-oil in my glove, I can utilize the ætherlines in the earth, and thereby alter the mass, density, and structure of resonant objects."

Sylvaine held her hand to her mouth to hide her smile. She didn't want to appear the stereotypical ferral, gawking at technology, especially since many of the other students seemed more interested in whispered conversations than watching the wonder before them. Yet every demonstration still left her in awe, and few engineers outside of Icaria practiced their craft as theatrically as Gearswit.

The professor moved his fingers, and a piece of metal separated from the block, which fell, solid, clanking onto the podium. This smaller bit he manipulated and morphed into a minute cog, which he placed in the small engine beside him. He touched it with a spark from his glove, and the machine burst into life, a small light beaming from its top, fed by the work of the engine.

"There you have it. Some simple engineering. Now, how many have you taken *Introduction to Ætheric Theory?* This next part might be a refresher..."

The fun over, Sylvaine opened her notebook to a page dense with diagrams, letting her professor's words fade into a mechanical drone. Hand-drawn gears, engines, and belts made up her intricate vision, intelligible only to the trained eyes of an engineer. It bore a simple title: "prototype mobile negative-density generator Ver. 3." The basics of her design had been lifted from old textbooks on the inner workings of Icaria and related ærocraft, but there was an addition at the bottom of her schematic, a tiny module that was all her own.

She'd heard Gearwit's lecture twice before, so, tuned-out, she set to work. Her current designs utilized the powerful, but potentially explosive, power of pure sangleum. Stability, the constant concern with raw sangleum, would be maintained by an internal feedback system measuring off an inert sample. To the layperson it might sound like engineering fiddle-faddle, but Sylvaine knew if her system had been in the city's towers at the time of the Calamity, Icaria would still be airborne.

It would prove her a true engineer worth her pin, if she could get it to work, but without the Knack, it remained nothing more than fancy drawings.

Class ended at 8:33, three minutes late. Gearswit's lectures invariably decayed from the mechanical precision of the very material he taught. As Sylvaine walked to the door she heard a gentle voice.

"Ms. Pelletier, may I speak with you a moment?"

She turned to see her professor gather his notes and step down from the podium.

"What is it, sir?"

He stepped towards her and straightened his dusty brown jacket. He was just over waist-high for her, but stood as if they were equally tall.

"I can't help but notice this is the third time you've taken my class," he said after a moment. "To be frank, I was surprised when you enrolled the first time."

Sylvaine shifted her gaze.

"You've done quite well on my tests," he continued. "Unfortunately, this is *Applied Æthermantics*, and I'm afraid your workshop constructions have been, well, nonfunctional."

It was true. Without the spark of æther even her most ingenious designs sat as immobile hunks of metal. She took a deep breath. "I know sir, but this quarter I can make it work, I just..."

"That is the problem," he interrupted, "you keep trying. There's no shame in not being able to manipulate æther. Not everyone possesses the Knack. The Academy offers a very prestigious mechanics program for folk like you. Professor Grayratch is teaching an excellent advanced class in that very sequence, on classical energy sources. The man's a genius, even built an engine that runs on coal. A pure curiosity of course, no practical use, but still fascinating. I know you've been trying up the engineer's path, but I'm sure my recommendation would be all you need to get into his class."

"But I want to become an *ætheric engineer*," Sylvaine said. It was why she had come to the city in the first place, not to muck around with the same sort of work that a corner mechanic could do. She knew ferral mechanics, had met friends of her father who had worked on autocars or with other repair jobs. Some people would smile as the furred men worked, act impressed with the most infuriating sort of friendly condescension, the kind you would give to a child who finally managed to tie her shoes right. Sure, ferrals could move a few bolts around, even fix an engine or sketch out some gearwork, but that didn't prove anything in most folks' eyes.

Gearswit gave an exasperated sigh. "To be honest Ms. Pelletier, while a few who do not innately have the Knack develop it later in life, I have never heard of such a case in a ferral. I've not, in my long years teaching, ever seen a ferral capable of manipulating mechanical æthers to even the smallest degree. It might just not be in their biology."

He used the right term this time, but she still hated it. *Ferral,* because the first humans who found her kind thought they looked like feral dogs.

Gearswit seemed to notice her discomfort.

"I've been theorizing about why you keep coming back to my class. I believe it is because you are afraid of being different."

Sylvaine didn't respond.

"I do understand how you feel. Kortonians are not what might be called standard."

She tried to appreciate his concern, but she knew that she really was different. People didn't stare open-mouthed at Gearswit. They didn't ask to pet him. They didn't wonder out loud if he might go berserk. They didn't whisper among themselves, "Is it dangerous?" *It.* Kortonians were never an *it.*

"I respect your... experiment," Gearswit said, cleaning his spectacles. "Few ferrals try the path of æthermantics, so I suppose it was worth a shot to see if... repeated exposure might somehow awaken your Knack. But with experiments you must respect the results."

"Years ago it was thought that Salvi lacked the Knack," Sylvaine offered. "Before Vtel—"

"I am aware of Vtel Starning." Gearswit's exasperation snuck through his deep sigh. "And the thousands of other Salvi engineers since. It worked for them, it didn't for you. I am sorry Ms. Pelletier, but reality is such."

Sylvaine knew her professor was most likely right. But ætheric engineering was the reason she left her family, left everything. She couldn't just give it up, even if the dream was as impossible as her parents had warned her.

"Listen," Gearswit said, "I think I can get the negative marks removed from your transcript for the previous two times you've taken my class. But removing a third?"

"I just..." Sylvaine said, searching for an explanation she didn't have. "...just need more time. Give me some outside assignments, chances to prove myself."

Her professor sighed again, softer. "Workshop starts at the end of the week, if you want to try, try. But there is no shame in giving up on the impossible."

Chapter 3

The funeral for Heitor Desct was scheduled for that weekend. It was a large, bombastic affair, completely removed from the character of the man, who, though charismatic, had always been private and modest in his personal affairs. Marcel considered it doubtful that the late Editor-in-Chief of *The Huile Gazette* ever had the cash to finance such a funeral. This mystery was solved by the small text on the back of the funeral notice, which stated that the funerary service was to be hosted by none other than Lazarus Roache.

Marcel had to respect Lazarus. Even for Huile's resident sangleum tycoon, the funeral was more than a generous affair. With no living relatives, Desct could have ended in a pauper's grave; instead he was given the hero's sendoff he deserved.

Still, while staring at the gold and white banners, the imported Tyrissian silverware with intricate filigrees, and the diamond-speckled chandeliers, Marcel could not help but feel out of place. A few Vidish beers shared in the back of a reasonably priced café would be closer to the celebration of life the deceased likely would have planned. Marcel's gut felt hollow when he thought of how many months (years, even?) it had been since he had shared such a night with his friend.

There had been no explicit reason for their distance, no moment of falling out, but as the months had passed after the war, each of their conversations inevitably fell back to the battle, to shuddering memories of choking chaos, to painful reminiscences of comrades who did not make it back. It had become easier then for Marcel to see Desct less, to focus on his own career, safe in the knowledge that his friend would always be there, that there would always be the chance to reconnect and make up for lost time.

But now there was no time.

Marcel slowly picked at the plate before him. It was covered in greenberry salad, Torish squash pasta, and beef, real beef. He tasted the meat and was surprised to find that it came from a cow. An actual, full-blooded, cow, not their Calamity-mutated, ornery and cheaper cousin, the taur.

He chewed, watching the other guests mingle. He supposed he should, perhaps, join them, but he could only recognize a couple faces.

Few of the guests, if he had to guess, were native-born residents of Huile, but instead likely came from one of the nearby, wealthier Border State cities, or, like himself, hailed from the more developed southern interior of the UCCR. Huile's post-emancipation rehabilitation had made it a very popular site for investment and immigration. Most guests were human, but Marcel did notice a kortonian or two ambling about. It was easier to spy the hulking figure of a visiting salvi diplomat, his decorated horns poking above the crowd.

Many funeral-goers wore the bright flashy getups that seemed the norm at all Huile gatherings: Bastillian red-mixed-yellow dresses or overcoats decorated with Utarran baubles. Some men did wear less ornamented and more properly somber black and white suits, which Marcel recognized as imported Phenian brands. Such seemingly humble outfits were in truth the most extravagant on display, considering the immense cost of transporting luxuries from the heart of the Confederacy to the edge of the Wastes. Marcel, in his simple coat and work pants, looked almost a pauper by comparison, though he couldn't imagine Desct would have preferred that he compete with these faux gentry.

Some of these men carried canes, for show more than use, and a few women had brought bouquets of waste-touched flowers, which they tossed in a pile beside the urn. How many had actually known the man well, Marcel wasn't sure, but he could guess it was only a fraction of the crowd. Some fool had even brought a small dog, which dashed around the guests' feet, yipping incessantly. By Marcel's measure it all seemed inappropriate for a memorial, but perhaps such was the style of Border City folk. He had still not fully adapted to his new home.

A hand suddenly clasped Marcel's shoulder. He flinched instinctively, breath quickening.

"Marcel! My good man!"

It was the ever-chipper voice of Lambert Henra. Marcel calmed, it wasn't... well, he didn't know who he thought it would be. A Principate soldier come for revenge?

"Lambert. It's uh, good to see you." Marcel stood and shook the hand of the stout-stomached Minister of Justice. In Lambert's other hand was a tall glass of champagne, and standing beside him was a thin, blonde-haired woman Marcel had never met.

"Ah, this is Evelin. Evelin, Marcel. He's my old war buddy I was telling you about."

She smiled. It was all teeth.

"You see, my dear Evelin, we were both in the Huile Sewer Rats. Dreadful name, I know, but it was a dreadful battle."

"You fought in the Battle Under Huile?" the woman asked.

"Well, I mean, I *meant,* you see..." the man stuttered.

"He fought in the Battle of Huile Field," Marcel corrected. "Not the famous one. He couldn't make it, foot problem I think."

Lambert flinched, and Marcel felt a twinge of guilt for dismissing him so.

"War injury, actually," the man said. "In the first battle I was shot right through my boot. It was horrid I assure you; I was in terrible pain. Perhaps that misfortune saved my life in the end. I'll admit that it wasn't nearly the injury Marcel received later on. Oh, Marcel, do show her your leg."

Marcel silently swore, then pulled up his right trouser leg to reveal shining brass and twisting gears.

Evelin nodded. "My cousin has an arm like that."

"Yes," Lambert said, "but Marcel's is a true battle scar. Got it in the Underway, undertaking Lazarus's plan, you see. Released sangleum gas on all those nasty Principates. Won us Huile, wouldn't you say?"

Screams echoed through Marcel's skull, images of red fumes, bodies bleeding, melting away at the caustic touch, gas mask too tight, leg burning in agony, friends disappearing in gunshots and pink clouds. A corpse wrapped in imperial blue, staring up at him, pain blurred through blood, seeming to accuse, 'You did this.'

Marcel grabbed the table to steady himself. His cogleg burned, but he managed to keep upright. Lambert offered a worried glance, and the woman seemed distracted by something in her drink.

"Yes, right." Marcel nodded quickly, recovering his composure. "A necessary victory."

"So," Lambert nodded, "still working hard then, investigating and all that?

"Work's slow," Marcel admitted.

"You know, Evelin, my dear friend here uncovered, just last month, a Principate spy, still working within the city!"

"Oh," the woman said, pulling a long hair from her cocktail and tossing it away.

"Just a corrupt mail clerk, trying to sell some stolen letters," Marcel said. He had nearly forgotten about the Steinmann case. He hadn't felt the usual rush sending the squat, cleft-lipped clerk away in chains. In fact, Marcel had almost felt bad. The man seemed more a desperate idiot than a true-and-blue traitor, but the evidence had been clear.

"You undersell yourself, as always," Lambert tutted. "The scum would have escaped clean if not for your keen eye. Ah, you would have done so well on the force, but I suppose an independent spirit must find its lone way."

The woman sipped her drink languidly, while staring Marcel up and down. "You're not from here, are you?" she asked, as if she just noticed the tan of Marcel's skin.

"No..." Marcel began.

"Are you one of those, uh, Elhemmade guys?"

"El'Helmaud," Marcel corrected reflectively. "And *no*. I'm from Bastillia. Phenia to be precise."

The woman stared with a blank expression.

"The capital of the United Confederacy of the Citizens' Resurgence," Marcel added, worried that this woman somehow lacked even basic geographic knowledge of anything outside of the city's wall. Her soft nod did not much dissuade his fear. Lambert drank in the awkward silence.

"Great soirée, eh?" he asked. "Just like our old victory celebrations."

"Sure." Marcel looked over at the distant band in full tuxedos, pulling up their pristinely kept instruments, including what looked like an ætheric guitar. "Desct would have enjoyed it."

"Yes...Yes, I think he would have." Lambert's indefatigable smile fell. "A terrible shame. Wastelung is what I heard. That can sneak up on a man fast. To think..." Lambert glanced down a moment, silent. "After everything we survived, you two especially, to have to... the world simply isn't fair sometimes." Lambert sucked in his breath and placed a somber grin on his face again. He slapped Marcel's shoulder, who responded in kind, albeit weakly.

"Well," Lambert continued, "then I guess that leaves us two left to carry the banner, eh Marcel? Oh, and our Captain Rosair, I suppose, wherever it is she ran off to."

Marcel tried not to react to the name, but pain must have been visible on his face, because Lambert mumbled an inaudible apology.

"It was very good catching up with you, Marcel, but I must go make the rounds. Let us get you out of your apartment one of these days, yes?"

Marcel sat back down and pushed his now cold food around. It *was* good catching up, though Lambert's inexhaustible energy reminded Marcel why he so often stayed home. The man was far better at managing social frivolities and burying the past.

Guests mingled and talked around dozens of white tables. Marcel was glad he had chosen one in the corner. The band played a few forgettable tunes, and he slowly ate, mind wandering the ætherscape. His thoughts drifted back to Alba's smirk, the first time they met. How stern she had seemed to him as a new recruit, her face that of a hardened Resurgence mercenary, a fiery gaze under a UCCR cap. Yet, with time, Marcel discovered that his captain held a secret softness, rarely shared.

The other soldiers had laughed at Marcel's aim on the firing range, a rich cityboy trying to play at war, even Desct had thrown in a lighthearted barb. Then Alba had stepped from her position, silencing all mockery with her gaze, as she walked toward Marcel. She leaned down and, arm to arm, aimed the rifle. The head of one target disappeared, and then a second, and then a third. Wordlessly they fired together at the faux Principate soldiers, their blue uniforms ripped with holes. She taught him how to be a soldier through grit and discipline.

A week later, on the eve of battle, she had led him out of camp on a moonlit night into the scrap-strewn Huile Field, to practice softer arts.

The band cut off suddenly.

By the funerary urn and the monochromatic photograph of Desct in uniform, stood a raised platform. A priest of the Church of the Ascended climbed to the podium. He was an older man, dressed in a bland suit, and he gave a correspondingly bland address. He meandered on about the deceased's immortal soul, how it would rejoin the world, live again in a new vessel, and how Desct's sacrifice and struggles brought him, and the rest of the world, one step closer to reunification with the eternal Demiurge himself.

Marcel paid the speech minimal attention. Desct had been agnostic in life, and Marcel shared the man's religious indifference. True devotees of the Demiurge were a rare sight among the respectable circles of the UCCR, religious fervor invoked images of Waste-wandering hermits or Principate bootlickers. The audience seemed equally disinterested, many whispering among themselves, continuing their conversations, now just in slightly hushed tones.

As the priest left the stage, the musicians tuned their instruments. Marcel recognized the notes and watched as a man in a military uniform presented a wrapped banner at the base of the urn. Marcel could see in it the folded visage of the Phoenix, and rose with the crowd as the Ode of the Resurgence began:

"By hammer, blade, and rifle,
The Citizenry marches forth!
Tyranny laid to silence,
A people in Rebirth!
The Phoenix flies above us,
From south to stolen north!
Not slaves, no more,
Let liberty warm our hearth!"

Marcel belted the words from deep within his chest, forcing them out and himself up, lest he bend over and weep.

"So go on! Go on! Brave Citizens take your freedom!
Go on! Go on! Death can't stop our drums!
Go on! Go on! We light the flames of revolution!
Go on! Go on! Born from the ash of destitution!"

Desct had had a spirited voice, shared in the singing bars of Phenia, or with silly limericks over campfires, or in his own rendition of the Ode as they trained in rank.

Marcel blinked away the mist of tears and glanced around the room. Not all were as enthusiastic; a few in the back seemed only to be mouthing the words. A young man whispered some joke to his partner, who giggled. Even Mayor Durand, the once-general of the Huile campaign, gave only a perfunctory performance.

But next to the Mayor stood another man, singing with ardor. He was a striking figure, with short-cut wavy blond hair, a sharp striped suit, and a short-brimmed hat that he held to his chest. Lazarus Roache bellowed with all the gusto befitting a patriot, which made sense, as he was one of the few in the room who had risked his own life for the future of Huile. His voice rang over the crowd as the Ode reached it end:

"As Citizens, not slaves,
As Citizens, not subjects,
Hand in hand...
We watch the Phoenix rise!"

As people slowly sat back down, Lazarus strode to the platform. The man had handsome features, cutting blue eyes, a strong but not overbearing chin, and teeth like carved marble. The audience quieted their movements as the man graced them with his smile, and he strolled on as if he owned the place, which, technically, he did.

The sangleum tycoon mounted the podium and waited there a long moment before speaking.

"Hello, all. I am pleased to be here to celebrate the life of a good personal friend of mine, a true war hero, Heitor Desct. Now, I am often credited with saving Huile from the Principate menace, and while yes, indeed, it was my plan that saved the city, plans are worth nothing more than the breeze if not for men with the courage to carry them out. Desct was such a man, and so much more. He was a man dedicated to the values of the United Confederacy. Liberty, without limits, freedom, to pursue one's own destiny, and, of course, virtue. The common man's virtue, the Citizen's virtue, the virtue needed to fight for what is right.

"Here, my friends, was a man willing to risk his life, to give all his body and spirit could provide, in order to break the chains with which the Principate had bound this city. Chains I myself once suffered in, until I was able to slip out and bring to my saviors in the UCCR the blueprints for our glorious victory."

The speech continued along such lines, inspiring praise of Desct's heroism along with general extolment for the Resurgence and its republican values. At one point the man digressed to personally thank Mayor Durand for his service. The thick-chested mustached man bowed to the applause.

There was always something hypnotically attractive about Lazarus's words, and though the speech was not unlike many Marcel had heard him give in the past, the crowd sat transfixed. He wished Desct could have heard the eulogy. Though his friend had preferred the poorest and most downtrodden during his life, there was still some honor in being praised by one of the greatest and wealthiest members of society.

Soon Marcel's turn came to speak, and with it, the requisite applause. He walked to the stage as slowly as was acceptable, preparing himself. He had written a speech the night before, full of his pain, his loss, the years left alone, unwilling to face his friend and remember what they had gone through, what they had had to do. That speech was now at the bottom of his wastebasket. The speech he gave was the one he knew was proper, on heroism, valor, with affirming anecdotes and even a joke. Huile didn't need broken men; it needed heroes.

Afterwards he could talk through his truth. Once he was alone, away from the needs of the city, it would be better that way.

It was near midnight when the funeral started to peter out. Most guests had left, taking autotaxis or the recently renovated trolley. Of those who were left was a kortonian, neck craned, talking to a man in a business suit and a woman in an imported Tyrissian dress; a long multi-piece, tiered gown giving home to half the rainbow. Besides them, there was only a small smattering of dazed drunkards, the one closest to Marcel passed out, hair soaking in his lobster bisque.

Marcel sat in his chair, waiting out the last stragglers. He opened his satchel and glanced through the diagrams again, underneath the table. It was at this point a mere practice in time killing, as the notes had not enlightened Marcel one bit on their meaning. He had half-expected to have spoken with Lazarus at some point during the night, perhaps mention the diagrams or even return them, but instead the man had dashed off to some urgent business. Bagging the documents, Marcel glanced around the near empty room, and in the dimming light, walked over to the urn.

Desct's smile in the photograph was small and mild, just a slight bend on his face. Perhaps it was no smile at all. The photograph was taken soon after their shared victory, and Marcel could not remember any smiles after their fight under Huile.

Marcel stared at the urn. How odd that he decided to be cremated in the end. The man had always joked that he planned to leave behind a beautiful corpse.

"I'm sorry," Marcel said. "If I had known you were sick... I should have seen you more anyhow. Huile's not Phenia, the city's not that large. It was difficult... I guess it was hard for you too. Only thing anyone wants to talk with us about was the war, and well, some memories don't sit well. We did right, I know, we sent the Principate packing, got ourselves a whole parade, a new life. You finally got that paper off the ground. Before the war you would never shut up about it, going to 'shine light on the darkness of ignorance' or something. I might have laughed, but I never doubted you. I guess I should have congratulated you, brought you out to dinner, sent you a fruit basket, Demiurge, I don't know. It just hurt too much to remember, sometimes."

He paused a moment, sucking back his breath. Breaking down here would not befit a soldier's image.

"If the Church is right, and you do see Danel, Rada, Henri... if you see them all up there waiting for their new life, tell them that I'm sorry. I'm sorry they ended up martyrs. I know it worked out as it should, the city is breathing free, independent, it is everything we were promised. I'm just sorry they couldn't see it, and that you..."

"Mr. Talwar?"

Marcel was suddenly very aware that someone was watching him talk to an urn. He collected himself and turned.

"Yes?" he asked to the tired-looking man whose light, wheat-hued hair thinned at the edge into greasy strands. It was Lazarus's butler, whom he had met on at least a dozen occasions, and whose name still escaped him.

"Namter, sir," the butler said, reading his expression.

"Yes, I know," Marcel said.

Namter gestured with his gloved hand to a door in the back of the room.

"Mr. Roache wishes to speak with you."

Chapter 4

Namter led Marcel towards a lift in the center of the building. It was an old iron thing, a remnant that had survived not only through the recent battle for Huile, but also the Calamity. A century's worth of repairs were visible in the sealed cracks and layers of chipped paint. As Namter lifted the lever, the whole box shook and clanked, bulbs bursting into æther-oil fueled light.

"The power that flows through the veins of Huile," said Namter without emotion, "a gift of sangleum from Lazacorp to you."

"Does Roache require you to say that?"

"Yes." He paused. "To every guest, sir."

Namter dropped Marcel off by the entrance to Lazarus's office at the top floor. Marcel stared out the lone window as he waited, shouts echoing from behind Roache's gold-leafed door. The building was by the edge of Blackwood Row, and Marcel could see the wall separating it from the rest of the town. Beyond it peered the fuliginous iron smokestacks of the Lazacorp refineries, vomiting their red-black smoke that melded into the pitch dark of the night sky. Alba had liked to refer to the Lazacorp neighbor as

"Huile's scarred asshole," but then again, the woman took on an irrational hatred of anything Lazarus Roache.

Marcel allowed his ears to tune in to the angry fracas. The door was too thick to make out details of the disagreement, but he was able to identify the other shouter as the hoarse, bitter voice of Lazarus's business partner and on-site foreman, Verus.

Verus's identity was confirmed when, after one last half-discernable insult, the door swung open and the haggard mess of a man stormed out. He had a patchy beard and wore rough scars. His coat was black taur- leather and heavily stained, his hands were covered in hole-poxed gloves, and his boots were smeared with industrial ash. Even by wastefolk style, it was rough. The man's demeanor matched his clothes, hunched posture and twitchy fingers. His sharp face was accentuated with an eyepatch, and his mouth wore its usual scowl. He stared his one good eye in the direction of Marcel.

"Hello, Verus." Marcel feigned politeness.

The foreman grunted. "What you here for?"

"The funeral."

"Right." His single eye hardened into a squint, as Verus picked at Marcel's expression, though for what, Marcel couldn't guess. "Sad business that. A. Good. Man."

He held each word a second too long. Marcel was quite sure he had not seen the foreman at the service, not that he'd missed his presence.

"And with Roache?" Verus gestured back towards the door.

"Can't say. He called for me." Marcel was finding it increasingly difficult to keep up a cordial façade.

Verus stared a few more uncomfortable seconds, then walked past, towards the lift, muttering something about a lap dog.

———————⌒∞⌒———————

Lazarus Roache stood up from his leather desk chair and split a grin as Marcel walked into the room. His smile was wide and warm, and his youthful eyes had morphed from the innocuous crowd-wandering gaze he had displayed during his speech, to an exacting focus, like that of a hawk.

"My favorite war hero," Lazarus said. "Come, take a seat!"

Lazarus had changed little in the two-and-a-half years since Marcel had first met him. He could remember the moment, as they sat in a wind-torn tent on the outskirts of town. The Huile Sewer Rats had been huddled together, Marcel one of a squad, all listening to the crazy plan of some sangleum tycoon, as Principate shells shook the remains of the camp. Lazarus still wore that same combination of a snug, striped suit and a short-brimmed hat, still had the same confident laugh, the same quick gestures, as he now motioned for Marcel to sit, which he did.

"Having some spat with Verus?" Marcel asked.

Lazarus waved the idea away. "You know the man. Good at his job, but rough, waste-bred."

"I'm surprised you still haven't bought out his shares," Marcel said.

Lazarus shrugged. "I need someone who can speak with wastefolk traders and day-laborers in the coarse manner they're accustomed to. Such is the price of operating so close to the Wastes. Verus keeps the refineries running well enough, and it's not like I have any evidence of malfeasance."

"What was your argument about?"

Lazarus paused and smiled, teeth blocks of white with no empty space. "Always on the job, aren't you Marcel?" he laughed. "Just a disagreement about an employee. Enough gossip, it's been a long day."

Lazarus gestured to Namter, who Marcel had not noticed enter. The butler poured a steaming cup of tea, and then left with a bow.

"Fresh import from Isles of Tyrissa. Beautiful blend, a little exotic, mixed with my own special ingredients. Have some."

It wasn't a question. The fumes emanating from the teacup wrinkled Marcel's nose. Tea always stirred up something unpleasant in Marcel's stomach, and this was not the first time Lazarus had added his special blend, an almost metallic-tasting powder that tinted the water a pinkish red. Tea was one of the businessman's eccentricities. Marcel could recall that whenever the drink had been thrust under his nose Lazarus would smile and claim that:

"No truly civilized conversation has ever started without a cup of tea." The blond man winked, on cue.

Marcel lifted up the teacup to his mouth. He glanced for a convenient potted plant, but finding none among the imported art pieces and gilded furniture, snuck out his half-empty canteen with his free hand and undid the cap under the table.

"That one new?" He pointed to a painting of a yellow blob behind Lazarus. The man turned, and Marcel sucked in the tea. It tasted worse than it smelled.

"Ah! An Antonine Moreau," Roache said. "Good eye. Painted before the Severing War, actually predates the whole Principate. Don't know the exact date, but at least a century back now."

Marcel spat the mouthful into his canteen and hastily screwed back the lid. He swallowed his spit trying to get rid of the damned drink's aftertaste.

"A mercy I managed to recover the old thing. It had been a gift by the old Mayor of Huile, LuGouffe, before, you know, the Principate got to him," Lazarus continued, turning back. "Thought they got to this, but I finally found it in a factory basement, of all places. Beautiful thing really, office felt dreary without it."

Marcel had read about Moreau back at Phenia University, but had never really been taken in by abstract art. Still, Roache had been sufficiently distracted, and as Marcel placed the teacup down with a clink, the man smiled.

"Good, no?"

"Excellent as always, Lazarus."

Lazarus held his smile a moment, and then dropped into a somber expression. "Tragic, what happened to Desct. You two were the last of your breed."

Marcel scratched at his chin and avoided the man's gaze. "We did what was needed."

"Don't retreat into false modesty, Marcel. I knew you two were heroic material the moment I set eyes on you." Lazarus gave a soft smile. "Such sacrifices are not quickly forgotten. Were you in touch much before he passed?"

Marcel tried to hold the shame back. "Not much, no. I didn't even know he was sick."

"Truly? Not even a letter?"

Marcel shook his head.

"I suppose he was a private man." Lazarus nodded. "And here I thought I was the only one given the cold shoulder. Well, we must forgive a man his solitude and let the matter rest."

He tapped on the desk to bury the topic. "There is one manner I wished to discuss with you. An unfortunate incident I thought you might look into while I am away."

The offer grabbed Marcel's attention, and pulled him some from his regrets. He took a notepad from his bag; Roache had always been a fertile source for leads. Even the recent Steinmann case had begun with the tycoon's suspicions about missing correspondence.

"Away?" Marcel asked. "You're traveling?"

"Tomorrow. To Icaria," Lazarus said with a grin. "Need Guild talent to help rework Huile's water purification plant. Can't have a true democracy without water."

45

Marcel's eyes flicked back to his bag, where the schematics sat. "Is the incident related to the water treatment plant?"

Roache's eye's narrowed, and he spoke slowly. "In fact it is." He waited a moment, watching Marcel's face, who kept his eyes straight and avoided another tic. "It involves the theft of some important schematic documents. Experimental filtration techniques and the like. Cutting-edge industry stuff, boring to the layman, to be truthful the details sometimes fly over my own head, but I have friends in Icaria who I know will be fascinated."

Marcel tapped his pen, trying to map out in his head all possible ways those notes could have made their way to his desk. "Suspects?"

"One." Lazarus nodded. "A man who is... well let me avoid ambiguity, he is unhinged. A bald Torish brute, built like a giant, usually wears a mask over his left eye. Goes by the name Kayip. Though, who knows, maybe he goes by something else now."

"Sounds like some wasteland nutter," Marcel observed.

"Yes, nutter, that's a fair description, man's as insane as a taur in heat. He is quite dangerous, though. He often carries around a damn sword, like some wannabe warpriest. A public menace." Lazarus shook his head and stared out the window, at the dimming lights of the small metropolis.

"You know how it is," he continued. "As soon as you do something worthwhile out come the naysayers, the hairsplitters, people who want to knock you down. Before I set foot here, this city was little more than an old crumbling wall and some half-inhabited tenements. Look at it now! You could move it to the heart of Bastillia and it wouldn't look shabby among its neighbors. Yet still some mad fool seeks to tear away what he can."

He turned back to Marcel, sighing. "I have had more than my share of issues with this Kayip before. He would come by Blackwood Row claiming to be a tourist or a journalist, if *that* could be believed, would try his darndest to sneak into my refineries. When he failed he would take out his rage by instigating fights with

46

my workers, or else fish around the bars for gossip. Sold lies to newspapers for half-a-frasc, threatened dear friends of mine."

Marcel opened his mouth to ask for possible motives, but Lazarus continued.

"He's obsessive. I can't say for certain why's he's targeted Lazacorp, but I believe he's ex-Principate."

"A soldier?" Marcel asked.

"Out for revenge, no doubt, hateful that I helped cast off his kind's foul yoke. Can't get close enough to hurt me directly, but can cause problems in others ways." Roache sipped his tea. "I think it's likely the man has fled town, but I can't be sure. All of which, of course, leads to the question of what he did with those schematics."

"Here," Marcel said, lifting them out of the bag. Lazarus's eyes flashed with surprise, and Marcel couldn't help sharing in it. In truth, he hadn't even realized he had decided to show the plans until he already had, but then, how could he not? Lazarus was a client now, a long-standing colleague, and friend to the city. There was no sense in keeping a vital piece of the case, and the man's property, from him, especially not for the sake of a possible Principate thug.

Lazarus shifted the notes about, inspecting them, then straightening them into a clean stack with a smile. "Impressive, one step ahead as always, Mr. Talwar."

Marcel laughed. "Not quite. Someone left them at my door. With the instructions to 'show to an engineer.' Now what do you make of that?"

Lazarus let out a soft chuckle. "I take it he didn't know your history. Thought you were just some amoral, self-centered detective. Maybe he was hoping you might toss them into the hands of a Principate-sympathetic engineer."

"That seems a mad hope."

"He is a mad man. And there are unfortunately still some who hold such sympathy, even within this city." Roache hardened his expression. "There were many who were quick to flock to the

Principate banner after the mayor was murdered, many who would toss roses to their occupiers. Perhaps the man remembers that."

Marcel nodded along, mouth closed, trying to swallow away some lingering bitterness. "But I don't understand how this madman could have snuck away valuable Lazacorp documentation. Blackwood Row isn't exactly the easiest place to sneak into."

Lazarus folded his hands together, eyes flickering in thought. He tilted his head to glance around Marcel at the door, silently, seeming to listen for footsteps that never came. He inched forward and spoke with an almost conspiratorial air.

"There was... one other person I thought you might look into. The employee Verus and I were... disagreeing about. The engineer, who in fact, made these very diagrams."

"What's the man's name?" Marcel asked. "Height, look, features?"

"Corvin Gall," Lazarus replied, listing off a description of a tallish, brown-haired and tanned man, augmented with several metal prosthetics. "A man of the Wastes, no Guild certification. Verus picked him out, since we lacked any ætheric engineers in Huile. Now Gall hasn't done anything wrong, per se..."

"But you have a bad feeling," Marcel finished. Lazarus's response was a simple smile. The tycoon seemed to have a near-supernatural sense for people, and just about anyone he had pointed out as suspicious Marcel had later found clear evidence of criminal activity or treason.

"In truth," Lazarus continued, "I'm hoping to find his replacement up in Icaria, but until then..."

"I'll keep an eye out." Marcel bagged his notepad.

Lazarus nodded and stretched, "Yes, I'm sure you will, Marcel, you haven't let me down yet." He reached into his striped jacket to reveal a gold pocket watch. "But it is late. Do you need an autotaxi back?"

Marcel stood. "If we're done then I'm good to walk, if it is all the same."

"Very well." Lazarus smiled and gave a casual salute from his chair. "Always a pleasure, Mr. Talwar."

The night was cold, and the city was asleep. Now and then an autocar or 'truck passed by, a pre-war artifact or one of the new breed from some local Border State city. One fairly ragged traveler trotted over cobblestones on a waste-toughened horse, but aside from these occasional night owls, Marcel was alone among darkened windows and dimmed lamps. He normally preferred solitude, where he could appreciate the city he had saved in its quiet abstraction, without the complication of its waking inhabitants.

But tonight he could use the company. The buzz of a new case, the excitement that came with future work, had fueled his step and occupied his mind for a few blocks, but then the groan of the past droned back. Perhaps it was the shock of Desct's death, or the sight of Lambert and Roache, but war thoughts now crept into his mind, and his cogleg ached.

He pulled his jacket closer and tried to focus on anything else. The buildings he passed were of a pleasant enough architecture, though they ran a strange gamut of styles. Some were ancient, old piles of brick or wood maintained for over a century, discolored by hasty patches of post-hoc masonry. Others were modern monoliths of granite or ironwork behemoths, whose numbers seemed to grow each month, construction sites as common as corner side cafés. Odder to walk past were those apartments which had been cleaved down the middle, blasted by the Severing War or during the Principate occupation, and just half rebuilt in a new style.

Huile was a fine enough city, though nothing compared to the Tyrissian metropolises Marcel had visited as a child. Here he could feel the lingering scars of the Severing War, that great war which had birthed the Calamity, of which all wars that followed, including Huile's own siege, were mere echoes. That war, and the devastations that followed in its wake, had shaped the city, ravaging its outer districts to ruined fields, polluting its natural aquifers, and forcing its men and women back behind ancient walls that had not been used for centuries. Even in peacetime the scars were clear, nothing the war touched could forget the impression of violence it left.

Grim thoughts again. His metal leg sent shivering aches. Two and a half years a phantom and still his amputated wound cried.

He turned down a side street, trying to trim a few minutes from his walk. The streetlights were fainter here, but still hummed with the energy of æther-oil, Lazarus's gift, extracted as sangleum from the grounds around Huile, which had burst with a sudden bounty of the red toxic goo in the years after the Calamity. Marcel could not help but wonder if the UCCR would have rushed so quickly to the aid of Huile had the city lacked this key resource. He had never realized the value of æther-oil growing up in the rich heart of the Confederacy, but here, at the border of the Wastes, it was a necessity, as much as water or bread; the only thing keeping Huile safe from the barbarity of the Wastes or the cruelty of the Principate.

He followed the large wall that separated Blackwood Row from the rest of Huile. The refineries of Lazacorp's own district poked out a little above the wall, like a great metal skeleton. It was strange to live in bisected city, where life among the quiet streets felt like a separate world from the industrial clamor just metres away. Indeed, as his squad mates had often joked, Huile seemed less like a city with a refinery, and more like a refinery with a pet city attached.

Marcel took a moment to catch his breath, and with it got an acrid whiff that sent him retching. The shortcut was a mistake. Work must be going late, and sangleum fumes had snuck over the edge of the wall, not enough to be dangerous, but the smell overwhelmed him. Marcel pulled his shirt over his nose, but it felt like a gas mask. He could feel the edge of his vision dim, imagine himself back there, under the clanging machines, within the cacophony, among horrified shouts and gunfire.

Marcel held his breath and dashed back down an alley. He steadied himself against the side of a tenement house, breathing in the modestly clearer air, and glanced up past the lights and the scrap-tiled roof. He stared at the moon, its bright ivory glow, its geometric perfections. It reminded him of Alba, of her face, snow pale to his waste-dust brown. He wished he could pull that face down, pull the whole woman to him, walk with her, let out his churning thoughts and hear her boisterous laughter. There had been a time when that laughter came quick and loud, even over the whistle and shudder of artillery. Problems seemed smaller then, when he was with her, the war a simple game, the impossible merely an inconvenience.

The years had not marred his memory nor altered single perfect detail of their first night together. The two of them had lain naked outside the Resurgence Camp, behind an abandoned agri-factory, his head in her lap, her smile the curve of the moon. Her breasts were small, hugging onto a chest more muscular than his own. His pants lay half-trampled across the roots of an olive tree, her coat had hung from a leafless bush, and he never did find his underwear. The only thing to hide their nakedness was the darkness of the outer-Waste sky. Their escapade could have gotten them court martialed, not for the sex necessarily, but for the unnecessary foolishness of leaving camp in the middle of a siege. Still, the risk had been preferable to the lack of privacy in the overcrowded town of tents that made up the Resurgence camp, and with a brief break in the artillery fire, they wanted to make use of the sudden silence as best they could.

"What's that look?" Alba had asked with a smirk.

"I was just staring at your eyes," Marcel said slowly. "They're like sapphires, stars of blue glistening bright in the night sky."

She laughed, it was a deep and free-flowing. "They teach you poetry at university, scholar-boy?"

He shook his head. "Mostly focused on medical classes."

"Makes sense," she mused, "since that was pretty shit for poetry, Mar. Then again, you're pretty shit at medicine. The fool I was thinking we were going to be sent a university-trained field medic. You'd just as soon send a man to his death for a knee scrape than know how to set a proper bandage."

"That's not... entirely fair," Marcel said. "Anyway I left first year. Barely got to the theoretical stuff."

"Oh yeah?" She smiled and started to play with the curls of his hair. "Got tired of university girls?"

"Not exactly," he said.

"Don't tell me *that* was your first time?"

He smirked and snorted away the idea, as if it were completely ridiculous. It hadn't been his first time, but in truth, it might as well have been. Of course, there had been university flings, but everything felt meaningless in the heart of Bastillia, where people were born into wealth and freedom, kilometres away from where soldiers died to protect that comfort. Marcel had hoped it would be different out here in the Border States, but people here were still people. Merchants gouged prices when soldiers came around, soldiers threatened townspeople for kickbacks, and townspeople hid behind their walls rather than fight for their own independence. But Alba was real, she was genuine.

"Ahh, what a disappointment," she said. "I was hoping I had deflowered you."

"Why?" he asked.

"It was a joke, Mar."

"No, why did you... I mean, what made you..." He paused. He knew it was a strange question, an awkward one, but he had to know. "Why are you interested in me?"

She stared, quizzically, into his eyes. They were like sapphires, shit poetry or no. Finally she shook her head. "Fuck Mar, I don't know. Because you care, I suppose. You don't have to be here, you could sit rich and fat in Phenia, Demiurge knows plenty do. But you decided to fight for your words."

"You care too, you fight too."

She shrugged. "We all fight imperials in the Border States, that's just what we do. Born with a rifle in our hands, there's never a choice. Freedom, independence, Citizen's rights, these are just words for us, an excuse to fight. Inferno, I bet you've written papers on theoretical models of *liberty,* or some other nonsense."

He kept silent. He didn't want to call her a liar, but he knew that she cared. She kept order in her squad, demanded that soldiers treat the Huile folk with respect even when they didn't return it. She trained with a fierce energy but a cool head, and resolved camp disputes with a stoic equanimity, keen for justice. Maybe she didn't know the exact definitions of what Phenian academics determined to be "Resurgence values," but she lived them.

Alba noticed the look on his face. She dipped her head down towards his. He closed his eyes, and let his lips touch hers. They held it for but a moment, yet it was a moment he could live in forever.

Marcel tripped suddenly on a misplaced cobblestone, catching himself on a streetlight. He turned and stared at the café facing him. *The Little Imp,* read the darkened sign, a familiar image of a crimson infant, dance frozen in painted wood, and Marcel realized he had overpassed his apartment by several blocks. He cursed, shook away the haze of memories, and turned around. These reminiscences of past dalliances did him no good.

Alba was gone, he needed to remember that. She had abandoned Huile, had abandoned him. Two years hadn't been enough time to purge her from his mind. Still, the pain had dulled some, and given time, he hoped, she might be gone forever.

...but calculations and planning are only ever the half of it. So many look at engineering and see with narrow eyes its utility alone, its end products. Autocars and æroships, toasters and turtle-tanks, motorguns and monowheels. For those outside the Guild, engineers are just the means to that end, a group of eccentric, often oddly-dressed, tools to produce the goods needed to grow crops, build cities, or win one of their endless asinine wars. Alas, even students come to me with a similar vision of themselves, believing their future to be one of a well-paid cog in a lifeless machine.

Well, my dear reader, I can assure you that machine is not lifeless!

For in all this we forget the æther, that wonderful force which makes the impossible practical, which bends those troublesome laws of physics and gives them a good spanking! To mold with æther is not a science, and is more than an art. It is a joy! One does not see the machine as a diagram, or even as the disparate metal pieces before you, but instead one feels the machine as a system, as an organism! An engineer does not work a machine as a carpenter does a piece of wood. Instead, they inhabit the machine, become the machine, feel it as one feels their own body. This is a universal joy among engineers, whether Man, Kortonian, or even Malva. All boundaries fade away within the act of æthermantics, and from this act of profound creation, we are made more than mortal.

For those readers who lack this gift, I can only offer my apologies, and I hope, that within these pages I may let you live through vicarious imagination the craft I engage with everyday at my workshop. And to those beginning their journey into engineering, I ask that wherever you end up, whether in Icaria, or at your hometown, or even at the frontlines of some puerile battlefield, that you never, ever, forget the joy of engineering...

—"The Engineer's Joy" By Lewalt Screwspline.

Chapter 5

Work calmed Sylvaine's nerves. Not that it wasn't stressful to thrust her head into an anarchic mob of pipes and ducts, to try to force a semblance of order upon a ventilation system no doubt designed by a half-paid engineer dreaming of revolutionizing the industry with their fully-mad designs. It was, however, the stress of something achievable. Sylvaine had not met an airshaft she couldn't unclog, nor a heater she couldn't fix. Admittedly this job would have been done a half-hour earlier had she the "Knack" to alter the mechanical structure of the ventilation system from a distance with a bolt of concentrated æther. But that's what she had her partner for.

Well, normally, at least. Today the laggard Javad hadn't shown. She actually liked the man, but his occasional apathy had recently evolved into habitual truancy. Maybe with his engineer's salary he could afford to miss a few jobs, but for her every hour's worth of a pitiful mechanic's wage was one more proverbial bolt keeping her home latched on to Icaria. Still, complaints didn't fix systems, so head went to dust-filled duct, and wrench went to pipe.

The building she was working on that day was a fancy new apartment complex, built for Icaria's life on the ground. It was constructed in a faux rustic architectural style evoking pre-Calamity rural townships. The nostalgic romanticism was lost on Sylvaine as she squeezed her torso further into the ventilation pump. The filthy musk overwhelmed her fine-tuned nostrils, and she wished, not for the first time, for the scent-numb noses of her peers. How nice it must be, she thought, to work with oils, molten metal, and binding liquids and not have to smell each one with nauseating intensity. Now every bestial instinct in her mind was shouting for her to get out of that hole awash with odd chemical smells and covered in several dozen layers of dust. Luckily, Sylvaine had a lifetime of practice ignoring those instincts.

She searched around the crawlspace, her eyes adjusting to darkness. Her hair flicked in the drafts, and she followed the movement until she reached the blockage. She had to stare for a few seconds, for it was pure, numbing, stupidity. Whoever installed the pump had placed it backwards! It must have been installed by some out-of-towner or an Academy reject hired for low costs, it was impossible to imagine a Guild engineer being so incompetent.

There were a couple ways to rectify this, and she cycled through her options, all either labor-intensive or workplace safety violations, or both. Except for one.

She pulled her ætherglove from her belt and inspected it in the dim light. The glove was a thing of beauty. Flawless craftsmanship, made of tough leather and polished brass pieces. A small æthermeter graced the knuckles, the numbers in silvered cursive, with tiny tubes of rubber connecting the æther-oil canister to the sparkpoints at the end of each finger. It cost her half a month's earnings, forcing her to take a second shift of maintenance work at Wheelston's, but it had been worth it. Or it would have been worth it if she were at all capable of using it.

All it would take was a simple spark of æther, basic entry-level æthermantics to morph the pipe quickly and safely into shape. A flash and she'd be done. She had tried such on her own, desperately despondent, or in the workshop, crushed by the gaze of dozens of classmates. But here she was in the moment, among the pipes and gearwork, confident, focused. If the Knack was ever to come, why not now?

She knew how stupid she was being, even as she slipped on the glove.

Just do what your classmates do. She closed her eyes, breathed in and out, just as she had been taught. *Focus,* she told herself, with all the faith that came with repeated failure. *Envision the spark, find it in your mind, and lead it out of yourself.*

She searched each corner of herself for something, anything.

Nothing.

She pulled this nothing as far as she could manage, hoping, nearly praying despite her engineer's atheism, that the spark would come.

Thirty seconds later she let her hand drop and removed the glove.

Her disappointment was deep and familiar, so she shrugged past it as she took out her wrench and tried to funnel her frustration in the direction of the machine itself. She sweated and grunted, brute forcing the piping out past layers of clinging dirt and rust, before fidgeting around in the dust and damp grime for the better part of twenty minutes getting all the pieces in place. A rush of stagnant air signaled her success, flinging her out into the hallway. She coughed violently as the system discharged two months' worth of dust.

"Well then, I see you've got the air flowing."

She looked up with a swallowed yelp, to see a soft-faced man staring down at her. He was almost tall and looked not far from thirty, though his clothes were that of an older-generation's style: a clean striped suit, with a short-brimmed hat and black leather shoes, all spotless in a city of dust and industrial ash. His half-smile highlighted an otherwise perfectly symmetrical face, topped off by neatly cut dirty-blond hair. He looked at her in a way she wasn't used to, warmer, yet piercing. His smile grew complete as he offered his hand. She took it, and the man helped her to her feet.

"I guess I have you to thank for finally being able to breathe again."

"It's my job." Sylvaine shrugged as she tossed her wrench into her bag and grabbed the straps. "I have to earn my tuition somehow."

The man burst out laughing as if she had told the best joke he'd heard in years. Sylvaine gave a nervous chuckle to play along. Why was this man talking to her? Most people either gave her suspicious glances as she worked, or simply ignored her altogether.

"My name is Roache," the man said, shaking her hand. "Lazarus Roache."

"Sylvaine," she replied, as a mote of dust fell from her hair into her nostril. She turned and sneezed, her face flushing with embarrassment.

"Sorry, excuse me. Sylvaine Pelletier."

Lazarus's smile widened. "Sylvaine, that's a lovely name." He looked her up and down. "But you're covered in dust! I can't have that. Come to my apartment, we'll have you cleaned up, get you some tea. It's the least I can do, I insist."

Sylvaine tried to protest, she had just met this man, but before she could get out a coherent thought he was already leading her up the stairs.

Lazarus's apartment was the penthouse. The main room extended to each side of the tower, its width half that length. It was open and airy, a space far larger than Roache's furniture and decorations required. Its size was further exaggerated by wide windows, the northern ones displaying the frigid slopes of Mount Icaria, half-covered by the suburbs of the city, and the southern windows overlooking the rumpled bedsheet hills of the Border States. The furniture ranged from red velvet Phenian chairs beside a pre-

Calamity Vastium wood table, to an El'Helmaudi rug adorned with roaring griffons and twisting serpents, which lay underneath a gold-bordered vitrine stuffed with shining antiques and filigree knickknacks whose origins Sylvaine couldn't even begin to categorize.

Three men were milling around the table. They turned as Roache entered.

"Gentlemen, this is Sylvaine, an engineer," Lazarus said. Sylvaine felt her cheeks flush with the title.

"This bulky fellow," Lazarus pointed to a broad, blond statue of a man whose multicolored waistcoat fit the ornate furnishing, "is Ewald Kauf, running for the Icarian senate. I dare say he'll make a name there big enough to fill his suit."

Ewald laughed and grabbed her hand. "It is a pleasure, madam. I consider it an honor to meet one of the hardworking women who keeps our grand city running."

Sylvaine nodded, dumb. No one had ever declared the act of meeting her to be "pleasure" or an "honor."

Lazarus gestured to the sitting man, lanky and gaunt, whose gaze was locked onto the book in his hand. "And this is Gath Melikoff, a gadget merchant."

Gath did not look up, but instead simply growled a "hello."

Sylvaine nodded, and glanced at the final man, who looked like a butler.

"Oh yes," Lazarus said. "And Namter," he addressed the man directly, "why don't you start boiling some tea?"

The man left the room with a curt, "Yes, sir."

Lazarus took her bag, and Ewald pulled up a seat. "Please Sylvaine," Lazarus said, "make yourself at home."

"Thank you," Sylvaine squeaked out. She had never been invited into a client's apartment before, she felt out of place. She could smell the dust on herself, mixed with sweat dripping from her fur.

"It's uh, so nice to meet you all. I'm sorry that I'm so dirty entering your beautiful home. Please let me wipe myself off." She walked across the room and tried the door. It was locked.

"Not that one," Lazarus said. "Wrong door. Place is still under construction, so we keep that locked. Just metal and dust, I'm afraid. The other one."

She made the short walk as fast as would be appropriate, hoping her fur hid her abashment.

Sylvaine splashed cold water from the marble washbasin onto her face. The now grime-infected liquid swirled down the drain. Her fu— no hair, was sticking out in all directions. Bags hung under her eyes, her face worn from weeks of late-night studies.

It was unusual to be treated with such hospitality. She considered herself lucky when she received even basic professionalism, and not thinly veiled fear or disgust. Something in the back of her mind told her it was all wrong, that she needed to leave, but when she pressed her instincts, they couldn't give a reason why. The situation just smelled odd.

But nice. She realized she liked the way Lazarus looked at her, as if the hair and teeth and claws didn't even register in his mind. Was this how other women felt?

She left the bathroom to find the butler pouring tea. Lazarus took a sip and closed his eyes, savoring it. Then he gestured her to an open seat.

"Utarran white, please have a taste. No truly civilized conversation has ever started without a cup of tea. It's pleasant to have some company here. I just moved into town, you see."

Sylvaine smiled. "It's pleasant to have a client bring me tea." She took a sip. It tasted like distant mountain air, natural and fresh, free from the smoke and smog of industry. She didn't really like it.

"I take it you're still in the Academy," Lazarus said. "Otherwise, I can't imagine why someone of your talent is still working maintenance."

"Third year," she admitted.

"Ah, so you must have taken æthermantics," Ewald said. "My cousin just went through that sequence."

Sylvaine avoided his gaze. They could see what she was, they must know, but then, why did he ask? The three had lifted her up with compliments, and she didn't feel like popping her own balloon.

"Well, I have been working on a project that involves a lot of æthermantics." She pulled her notebook from her bag. "Just an attempt to design a new negative-density generator. Nothing too special, I know every other student tries a crack at it at some point, considering the history of the city."

"Nonsense," Lazarus said, taking the book. "It's a fascinating subject."

He stared at the esoteric scribbles, then passed it to Gath. "Too much for me. I'll let our gadgeteer have a shot."

Gath seemed irked to be involved, but he opened the book and stared. Finally, a smile forced its way onto his face, and for the first time he looked at Sylvaine with interest.

"Novel way to modulate æther frequency," he said. "Very, *very* interesting. So, this section here, it equalizes the frequency of the inflow and the sample?"

"It's a read-match system," she explained. "The sample remains steady, the inflow is altered in real time, to maintain a consistent, precisely modulated outflow."

He thought on this a moment, then nodded. "Have you made a prototype?"

Sylvaine paused, then sighed and shook her head. "I haven't managed to."

"There's plenty of engineers in this city who would jump on an exciting new project," Ewald said, "and if you're looking for financers, I know people."

Sylvaine tried to come up with an excuse, but her expression prompted Lazarus to speak first.

"No need for explanation Sylvaine, a project sent to another engineer is no longer your project. I understand, to most folks a designer is just a name on paper. I am sure you poured your soul into this, and you deserve the full recognition for creating it." He looked her over. "But you can't. Because you lack the Knack."

There it was. Sylvaine avoided the man's gaze and kept silent.

Lazarus laughed. "No need to be bashful. The Knack is one of the stupidest ideas under the Demiurge's sun. Elitist hogwash. There is no Knack. It's all just confidence and skill. You know how many lifelong mechanics I've seen turn into æthermancers?"

He pulled out a vial of scarlet powder, clumps of which stuck to the glass.

"This is Slickdust. Boosts creativity, heightens energy, and—" He paused, lifting the vial up so the sunlight glinted off its red. "—helps to spark æther. It's an experimental wonder drug, I tell you, used by half the engineers I know. Here, have some."

He poured a pinch's worth into her drink.

Sylvaine eyed the tea; the pale-tinted translucence swirled with veins of red that slowly congealed into a vaguely brownish liquid. She had heard of some students experimenting with deepshrooms, or cog-loosening pills, but never something called *slickdust*. Then again, if anyone would have been left in the dark, it would be her.

"Is it safe?"

"Of course," Lazarus laughed, "see?" He poured some into his tea and drank.

She sniffed it as subtly as she could manage. It smelled faintly of iron mixed with something she couldn't place. It seemed too perfect, a drug that could solve all her problems, give her the

Knack? It was like a dramatic turn in a pulp novel: a young girl trodden by everyone, given magical powers to save her town and earn the respect she deserved. In fact, that was the plot to *Maiden Firehands and The Troll Lords*, which was sitting under her bed back home.

She lifted the cup slowly. It was odd how much she wished to be at her dingy shack of an apartment at that moment, despite the luxury and outward cordiality of Roache's penthouse. But no one was nice without reason, at least to her. She was just some student, some *ferral* student; why would he want to help her? The whole idea was ridiculous, a medical cure for a lack of Knack? Then again, if it was a simple problem of biology, why shouldn't there be a simple solution? There was no reason for Lazarus to lie. Unless he was trying to sell her some waste-snake oil, but then, no price had been stated. What did else would he have to gain? Genuine concern, she reasoned, was the only logical explanation.

Her hand shook slightly, tiny waves dancing from one side of the cup to another. She could sense them watching her, not directly, but subtly, side glances, polite stares, the kind refined folk would give, those who would never *gawk* at a ferral, but neither would they miss their chance to study the oddity.

She placed the glass down with a clunk.

"I have to go."

Lazarus gave a look of concern. "I didn't mean to scare you off, of course if you don't want to take it..."

"I'm late." She grabbed her bag, embarrassed she couldn't think of a better excuse. As she ran out the door, she caught a distant, "It was nice to meet you!"

Sylvaine stopped and gathered her breath half a block from the apartment. She leaned back on the side of an alleyway, trying to quiet her mind. Some instinctual sliver of her brain was relieved, but the rest of her cursed itself. A man had been kind to her for the first time in, well, a very long time, and she had fled.

Maybe he was going to try and use her. But he hadn't asked for money, or favors, or anything. He had drunk the liquid himself, so it couldn't be toxic. Even if the possibility of slickdust working was minute, it was everything she had ever wanted, wasn't such a chance worth some risk?

She stared up at the window, now distant above her, half hoping to see Lazarus again, beckoning her back. No, she couldn't go back, she'd seem even more foolish. But then, why should she let being a fool stop her now?

Her regrets, fears, and second guesses battled it out in her mind as she turned down the alley, and nearly ran into the chest of a large man.

"Sorry" she muttered, as she tried to move past him.

"It is not your fault," the man said, making himself an obstacle. "May I ask you something?"

He was thickly built, completely bald, his face tanned and etched with scars, some barely visible, others deep cuts. On his face the man wore a smooth metal plate, a strangely unadorned mask that covered his left eye, sunlight dimly reflected on its dirtied surface.

Sylvaine shook her head, muttered something about being late, and sidestepped him.

"You are an engineering student," the man said, following her. "Do you know a Professor Gearswit?"

She glanced at him, and quickly regretted it, as it was clear he took it for a yes.

"I need to speak with this Gearswit, would you be able to send a message?" he asked, as they both turned an alley corner, an open and busy street not far ahead.

"He has a mailbox with the Academy," Sylvaine said.

"Yes, I am aware. I sent him some important documents, my only copies. I was hoping to discuss them in person."

Sylvaine increased her pace slightly, and the man grabbed at her arm. She recoiled, and the man slid to her side, hands up as if to say he wasn't a threat, but standing too close for her to be confident in that sentiment.

"I do not wish to bother you, but did you meet with that man, on the top floor?" He stared at her. "Mr. Roache he is called. I just need to speak about him a quick moment."

A siren blared out from the street ahead. Sylvaine glanced over to see a police autocar zip by, on call to some distant corner of the city. She turned back to face the stranger, several choice words on her lips, only to find the strange man had disappeared.

Sylvaine hurried out to the main street, for once happy to be among crowds. *Demiurge's Hammer*, she thought as she walked, *Icaria is a city of freaks.*

Chapter 6

"Corvin Gall... Yeah I think I know him, he's that gearhead, right?" the drunkard said, shaking his empty mug.

"Another one for my buddy here," Marcel shouted to the bartender, who shrugged and poured half-a-litre's worth of cheap waste-brewed beer into the stained cup. The drunkard, who had given his name as Vik, took it and drank with clumsy enthusiasm, spilling more than a few drops onto his wrinkled and oil-stained Lazacorp uniform.

"Yeah, that sounds like the guy," Marcel said, "an old friend of a friend. You speak with him much?" Marcel tried not to let his excitement leak into his words, lest his new "buddy" realized the value of his gossip and demand a price greater than just a few beers.

Vik scratched at a sore on his chin, and sipped. "Yeah, he's not the chatty kind. Seen him working on some projects round Blackwood Row, fixing the piping and the like. Had to deliver to him a good many parts, I tell you. Just about whenever I finish one shipment, I get a call for another, so he must be hard at work, I guess."

Marcel tried to etch every word into memory, wishing he could simply take pen to paper and transcribe the conversation in his notebook. He'd had considerable trouble these past two weeks uncovering anything of substance concerning the two men Lazarus had asked him to look into. The name "Kayip" had led only to looks of confusion, the madman seemingly a myth, if the stares of most folk he asked were any indication. Gall, at least, Marcel could confirm existed, and lived in Blackwood Row, but that's about all he could manage to find.

Most Lazacorp employees had tightened their mouths as soon as they figured out that Marcel was a private investigator. The Lazacorp guards were the worst, most lacking even the dignity to toss some excuse, instead responding to Marcel's questioning with loud, surprisingly inventive, strings of curses and insults. This was... unusual to say the least. Normally at least a few Lazacorp employees had been pliable in the past, but with Lazarus out of town, lips sealed themselves.

As limited as Marcel's overall success had been, "The Drunken Taur" was still the best watering hole for listening in on booze-loosened words. Marcel chose his own carefully.

"Yeah, I was just wondering how Gall was taking to his new job," Marcel said. "Do you get a chance to talk to him at work?"

Vik shook his head. "They keep us busy. If he talks much with anyone, I guess it'd have to be with those skinsick fucks."

"The mutant workers," Marcel said, catching the irritation in his tone. It seemed an unfortunate habit among many Huile-folk to refer to mutants with casual slurs. Such waste-infected prejudice was certainly unseemly, but there was no sense sinking an interview over some loose talk.

"Sure, whatever," Vik said, sipping. "Doubt he talks to them much. Nobody talks to them much."

Gall was clearly an obsessed craftsman. A useful tidbit, Marcel supposed, but it didn't bode well for an easy investigation. "Does he drink much with the other workers?" he asked.

Vik seemed to mull on this a bit, staring into the puddle at the bottom of his mug. Marcel glanced around. The barroom was in an old, unrefurbished building, an increasing rarity in Huile. It was about as grimy and rundown as the city got, which, since its uplifting by the UCCR, wasn't all that grimy or rundown. The furniture was mostly waste-style, scavenged junk held together by welding or tape, but at least kept relatively clean. The walls were covered with faded advertisement posters. One was older, by a century at least, pre-Severing War. It displayed, on a cracked browning sheet, a smiling soldier in the now defunct Republican Guard uniform. In one hand he held a bayonetted rifle, and in the other a bottled drink. *"When fighting under the El'Helmaud sun, our boys can't resist a cold bottle of Sted's Sugarized Pop!"*

Marcel had never heard of Sted.

Over the past few hours the bar had been a mix of waste-merchants comparing scrap, off-shift Lazacorp workers drinking loudly, old men playing flickerdiscs, and a gaggle of bored teenagers who argued about nothing. A fairly usual crowd judging by the bartender's demure expression, as she languidly smoked a clope, back against the wall. One metal-armed man had returned Marcel's stare, though in the dim lighting Marcel couldn't guess if the look was friendly, a threat, or if the man was simply lost in some drunken stupor.

Finally Vik nodded, and tapped his glass again. Marcel forced himself not to roll his eyes while waving down the bartender. Only after Vik had taken another long sip did he answer.

"Nah. Never saw him drink."

Marcel glared, letting a hint of his frustration through.

"I mean, he doesn't drink with us, you know, the cargo-pushers and the paper-signers and the like," Vik continued. "The guards keep to themselves, that's how wastefolk are, so I don't know if he does anything with them. Honestly, I never saw Gall off the job. Inferno, I barely saw him then. He mostly worked hidden in the monolith."

"The... monolith?" Marcel asked.

Vik waved his hand. "Nothing strange, just what we call that... whatsit ... that water filtration thing they're building. Covered it up in a big box of a building, looks monolithy. I guess it's to keep out the fumes."

Marcel nodded, more for politeness than anything. There was little useful the man had told him that Marcel hadn't already heard in the few miserably short conversations he had already managed to wring out of other workers.

"Did Gall... get into any trouble?" Marcel offered. "Find himself in fights with any other workers, feuds, misunderstandings?"

The man chugged the rest of his beer, and stared at the glass. Marcel couldn't figure out if the man was lost in memory, or if Vik was calculating how many more drinks he could stretch this interview out for.

The door flew open with a clatter, the entrance of someone who desired a whole bar's worth of stares. Marcel provided his, squinting up past the blinding midday light at the brick wall of a man he recognized as Dutrix Crat. Crat was one of Verus's many hires, though to what exact position he held, Marcel had never been sure. The man strode over, his long, swaying coat covering all but his buzz-cut head, which was decorated by a collage of tattoos: eyeballs and scarred men interspersed with abstract letterwork. He looked down at Marcel and Vik with a glare usually reserved for piles of excrement found unexpectedly on one's front porch.

"Vik," he said. "You're supposed to be on shift."

"Shift?" Vik said, breaking his gaze away from his drink, "but I'm not on..." He slowed his speech as he realized who it was he was speaking to, and then just let his mouth flap open, unwilling to commit to any specific sentence.

Crat did not give the man time for discussion or excuses. He grabbed Vik's arm and pulled him out the door.

"Wait!" Marcel shouted, running after. Despite dragging the drunkard, Crat moved with impressive speed, having already shoved Vik into an autocar by the time Marcel caught up.

"Inferno do you think you're doing?" Marcel asked.

"Returning a worker to his work," Crat replied.

"He doesn't look like he's coming willingly."

Crat turned to Marcel, his tattoos seeming to join in the hateful glare. He opened the car door. "Are you coming willingly?" he asked, eyes locked on Marcel.

Vik nodded, slumped in his seat. "Yes sir, of course, sir."

Dutrix Crat slammed the door again. He stepped forward slowly and leaned over Marcel, abusing every extra centimetre of height he had over the man.

Marcel's hand instinctually went to the pistol on his belt, but he fought the urge to draw it, even as Crat tried to swagger his bulk over him.

"And what is it you think you're doing, Talwar?" Crat asked.

"I'm running some preliminary inve—"

"You are harassing Lazacorp employees and mucking around for gossip," Crat interrupted. Marcel tried to respond, but was half-shocked. He had seen this man out and about many times. He hadn't thought much of Verus's quiet assistant, who the foreman liked to walk around like a muzzled guard dog. With Lazarus away, the hound was evidently off its leash.

"I'm doing my job," Marcel recovered, taking only a small step back.

"Keep your job out of Blackwood Row," the man said, taking a large step forward.

"Excuse me, gentlemen."

Both turned as a young policeman walked up. He looked Crat up and down, and the man slid back towards his car, retreating under the gaze. The policeman turned to Marcel and nodded.

"Lambert sent me, said he had a case he wanted to talk to you about." Then his eyes flickered back to Crat. "Is this man bothering you?"

Marcel shook his head. "Just having a friendly chat," he said, allowing himself a little smugness in his tone.

Crat bowed his head, muttered some inaudible excuse, and ducked into his autocar. It actually impressed Marcel how quick the fight left the man. He watched as the car groaned to life, and Crat puttered down the street, past the main gate. The retreating autocar kicked up dust in the noon sun, growing smaller and smaller as it disappeared down the road.

Marcel smiled at the cop. "So that case you mentioned?"

As was his general manner, Lambert had scheduled his meeting away from his office in City Hall. Marcel found himself pointed in the direction of *The Piglet and The Scone*, a pleasant café on the main thoroughfare of Huile, Viexus Avenue. *The Piglet* was decorated with a carefully manicured pre-Calamity charm, a pretense that it had survived a century of warfare all while retaining its cheerful quaintness, instead of opening its doors a mere half-year ago, just another one of the many new high-end bistros that rode in on the wave of Phenian investment.

Lambert had evidentially double-booked himself, as Marcel found the man sitting and smoking across the table from a blonde-haired woman Marcel recognized from Desct's funeral. The Minister of Justice smiled and waved Marcel down, ordering a cup of coffee and a redberry muffin.

"Marcel, a colleague and old war buddy," Lambert explained as Marcel sat. "Marcel, this is Sophia. I was just relating to her some of our war tales."

"Yes, we already me..." Marcel started, before realizing that this was *not* the same blonde-haired woman from the funeral. He forgave himself for the mistake, Lambert clearly had a very specific type. "Nice to meet you."

"You were in the Battle for Huile as well?" the woman asked.

"For and Under," Marcel said.

"That must have been rather frightening."

"Oh, I wouldn't say we were frightened, would you, Marcel?" Lambert gestured with his lunchtime cigar. "No, no, we had a rush of patriotism in our blood that day."

"You could say that," Marcel offered, hoping that would be the last of it, but Lambert continued:

"It was our duty to free the city, you see, after the Principate had pulled their silly little coup. We had ourselves a grand army: Huile patriots, men from General Durand's northern army, and plenty of volunteers, from the Border States down to the heart of the Confederacy. It was exhilarating to be amongst so many patriots. So, I'd say it was more of a fevered anticipation than fear."

"You said you had a case?" Marcel asked.

Lambert smiled and spoke with his gaze, eyes flashing back and forth quickly. Marcel suppressed his sigh.

"Yes, it was a glorious day," Marcel agreed.

"Our squad was known as the Huile Sewer Rats. A dreadful name, I know, but it fit our Resurgence spunk that served us so well. We were one among many, courageous freedom fighters against Principate tyranny!" Lambert narrated, as much with his hands as with his voice. "Our camp was on the outskirts of Huile Field, though when we first arrived the field, as it were, still held many of the buildings from the old outer city, blocks of decrepit ruins squatting outside Huile's walls. The Principate had dug themselves in deep there, rows of trenches and motorgun nests, mazes of mines and booby-traps. Imagine facing all that!"

Marcel didn't have to imagine, and in truth, the air in the camp had not been one of dread or even apprehension. It was pure confidence. General Durand had brought in heavy artillery from

Phenia, and the resulting bombardment had forced the Principate headquarters to retreat into the refineries of Blackwood Row.

UCCR shells played symphonies throughout the night, leveling any and all structures larger than a doghouse that had the misfortune to sit outside of Huile's walls. The barrage had been a source of inspiration, soldiers had sung smug songs about "Poor General Agrippus and her boys in blue," and some had even joked that the coming battle would be more like strolling over a graveyard.

The only complaint had come from their captain. Marcel had overheard Alba shouting in the command tent that they needed to just fire straight onto the refineries. It wasn't like there were many civilians in there, she had yelled, it was just the æther-oil.

Alba had lost that debate. The next morning their squad was given only hardtack for rations, despite the abundance of taur and spikefowl meat most other squads had received.

"We waited for days," Lambert continued, the woman nodding politely, "on edge, eager to get into the fray. When the last shell fell, we screamed, 'For Freedom, let the Phoenix rise again!' and charged."

Actually, the only one who had spoken, as far as Marcel could recall, was Alba herself, who had shouted, "Move, you idiots!"

"Our job, you see," Lambert said, "was to take the ruins of the æroship tower halfway to the wall." Lambert flicked his cigar up, as if to indicate its height. "Good vantage point. I was the comm-man, had a great ætherwave voxbox strapped to my back, to call back everything we saw."

Marcel ignored his coffee and Lambert's narration to watch people pass by the open café. The majority were Huilians, dressed in a mix of colorful styles that had been already fading out of fashion when Marcel left Phenia. There were some outsiders as well, in rougher garb, all leather and patchwork. Autocars drove beside rusting wasteland buggies, and even a few horses trotted down the cobblestones. Most of the shops and cafés were open, and there were even a few permitless street vendors, hawking scavenged knickknacks, cooking strange-smelling dishes, and arguing with police.

But despite his best efforts, it was impossible to filter out all of Lambert's words. He had heard Lambert's telling of the battle so many times that he could almost believe the account's accuracy. But when Lambert described a frenzied assault up to the æroship tower, Marcel couldn't help but remember the stunning quiet of the battlefield that morning, the eerie absence of Principate soldiers. When Lambert described his wounding, Marcel could only recall wondering how the man had managed to get a bullet in his foot without any enemy troops in sight. When Lambert narrated their heroic assault up the æroship tower, Marcel could only relive that strange unease he felt climbing the abandoned spire.

"We could see the whole battle from the top," Lambert said. "It was a glorious affair, our fine men and women pushed the Principate brutes to the walls of Blackwood Row, which our artillery had blasted to rubble."

Alba had reported back to command, through the voxbox, that the Confederacy lines advanced without resistance.

"It's too easy" she had said. "The Principate bastards aren't cowards, they could force us to bleed for every metre, yet they don't." Marcel got the sense she would have preferred a bloody fight, a painful push through the rubble. He had convinced himself that all was as it seemed, that this was victory, one where he hadn't even needed to unload his rifle, for why shouldn't a noble cause give birth to a noble end?

Then he noticed the dust clouds.

"They were crafty," Lambert said, "I'll give the Principate that."

Marcel had grabbed his binoculars. From around the bend of the city a storm of dust appeared, and in it, dozens of motorcycles, autotrucks, warwalkers, and dathkreis rode. The back of the Resurgence line burst into clouds of debris and bodies. Marcel spied a tank, then two, then eight, some treaded, others crab-legged. Alba shouted their observations with a controlled mania through the voxbox, but the details didn't seem to matter much. Within a few minutes the host of Principate war machines had crashed into the UCCR army.

"Yes, well, it was an unfortunate thing," Lambert said. "They were throwing their own men away, really, but I will admit it foisted upon us a great cost. We hadn't expected such barbarism. It was a hard-fought battle, but they barely managed to squeeze out a small victory."

It was a slaughter. Marcel could only watch, as they hadn't brought any scoped rifles or small pieces of mobile artillery that might have been of some use. The motorcycles and trucks skimmed by the lines, peppering the unprotected backs of the Resurgence soldiers. A few days earlier the ground would have been uncrossable for all but infantry, but the continual pounding of the artillery had created massive open spaces that the Principate army used as highways.

"Still, it was a heroic struggle, it set up our eventual triumph. Good men spilled their blood, but not in vain, wouldn't you say Marcel?"

'Walkers clambered over the rougher areas, firing from above, and dathkreis flung themselves straight into the Resurgence ranks, giant metal balls with motorguns and blades, slicing through dozens of men before turning and firing upon the rest. Alba shouted through the pandemonium, yelling into the voxbox that they needed to pull back.

"I mean just look at the city now. Yes? Marcel, are you with us?"

The screams of artillery sung through the air, one shell skimming the tower itself. They landed where the Principate war machines had been minutes before, but rarely on the enemy's current position. Marcel saw few tanks in flames, but he saw many Resurgence squads disappear under the fire of their own artillery.

Alba didn't wait for instructions, or possibly she ignored the ones she was given. "We're getting out of here," she said.

"Marcel!"

"Yes! What?" Marcel shook himself from the grip of memory, before swearing as some of his coffee spilled from his still-shaking hand onto his lap.

"Are you all right?" Lambert asked. The woman had an eyebrow raised. Marcel put down the coffee and wiped himself with one of the café's embroidered napkin.

"Yes, I'm fine. It was... a fine battle. Yes," he said. His pants were going to be stained, and Lambert's rendition of their shared history had more than irked him. The man reveled in the heroism, as if it were all good fun. The war was heroic, Marcel had no doubts, but not in its victory. The heroism lay in the sacrifices it demanded. Lambert had only had to sacrifice a toe and a few days sick leave, not even a cost compared to what it spared him from. For Rada, Henri, Danel... their glory had not come so cheap.

"Good man," Lambert said to the woman, "a bit of a daydreamer. I have some business I need to discuss with him, but if you wish to grab tea in, oh, say an hour?"

The woman took out a decorated bronze watch. "I can't. My father's caravan is heading out of town in... well I should be going now, actually."

"Already? I didn't know you were leaving today," Lambert said, his face aghast.

"Yes, it was nice speaking with you two." She got up and finished off her drink, before walking away.

"If you're interested in history, why Marcel has his own..."

But she was already on her way, a prompt waiter strolling in to remove the remains of her meal.

"Ah damnations," Lambert muttered. "Always the pretty ones. They get you on a rope and drag out what they can." He tapped ashes off his cigar. "Perhaps that's what makes it fun."

"You certainly tell our story in a... fun way."

Lambert chuckled meekly, "You know how it is, Marcel. Start with the funerals and the grieving widows, people go white in the face. We let the misery color everything, let anger muddle every mind, how can peace ever return? So we put on a bit of a show. A soldier's duty never ends, I suppose."

"I suppose," Marcel repeated, shaking his head. Lambert wasn't wrong, it was the pulps and the heroic stories in the papers that first got Marcel interested in joining up. If he had known the cost...well then he might have suffered less, but where would Huile be? Or the UCCR? If it took sacrifices to keep the Principate at bay, then sacrifices needed to be made. Perhaps it was easier for his friend to put on the proper face, since Lambert was in his hospital bed when the Huile Sewer Rats had been sent to earn their name...

"So, do you have a case?" Marcel said, knocking on the table as if to startle away the past.

"Oh, indeed," Lambert said, reaching into his briefcase. "If you aren't too busy."

"Could always use a distraction," Marcel said, thinking of the empty calendar book sitting on his desk.

"I hope this is more than that," Lambert said, pulling out an envelope. It was of brownish paper, cut open, with a folded letter poking out. "A mailroom mix-up got us sent this." He passed it to Marcel.

"From Gileon Fareau, to Lazarus Roache." Marcel read off the front. "Since when does City Hall read private mail?"

Lambert laughed. "Not normal policy for the Office of Justice, no, but Mr. Roache gave me explicit permission to open his mail in unusual or emergency situations. Considering the name, I thought it reasonable to check it out. Know him?"

Marcel shook his head. "Should I?"

"I would have thought people in your business would scour the obituaries for jobs, no?"

"Must have missed him," Marcel said. In truth he hadn't read any of the *Gazette* in the two weeks since Desct's death. He saw the first issue with a new name in the Editor-in-Chief section, and he let the other issues simply stack in the corner of his office. That made it less real.

"You needn't be embarrassed." Lambert shrugged. "He was some Lazacorp worker. Died three—no four days ago. Fell into machinery. Unpleasant. I sent a few men down, asked some questions, the story seemed straight, apparently an unfortunate accident." He watched his smoke rise. "I don't want to send in more men and simply cause a scene with Verus, you know how that man is, but..."

"But..."

Lambert pointed to the letter.

Dear Mr. Lazarus Roache,

Sincere apologies for bothering you, as I am aware you are quite a busy man, but I know not where else to turn. I am honored that you took me in to your fine business, few in Huile would give a poor scrap-merchant such as I, without wealth or friends, a chance, let alone a job transporting valuable machinery throughout your refineries. Your generosity and kindness has lifted me up, your example proved to me the beneficent glory of the United Confederacy of the Citizens' Resurgence...

Marcel skimmed over a few more paragraphs of histrionic praise.

Still, I find myself in a quandary. There is a man I have worked with who I fear may not be acting in good faith with Lazacorp. I do not wish to besmirch the integrity of your hiring process, but I worry that perhaps some facts about his past were withheld from you. As I do not desire to have this letter descend into simple gossip, I would much prefer to speak with you on this matter in person. Sooner rather than later, as I admit, I have some fear about the possible intentions of this man.

Forgive my impertinence, I hope that I am not insulting your beneficent generosity with excessive requests, but I have one more plea. Would it be possible to have my shift changed so I no longer have to work alongside this man? I have requested such a change to Mr. Verus, but since I was not willing at that time to explain my full reasons, it was denied.

Please, good sir, please fulfill these requests for me, and I will be eternally thankful.

Yours in gratitude,
Gileon Fareau

Chapter 7

Marcel glanced through an old newspaper as the trolley rumbled its way out of town. He read Gileon's obituary, then reread it, and then stopped to think, and reread it again. It stated that: A) Fareau died in a "workplace accident" at Lazacorp. B) He left no living relatives. And C) … Well, there was no C.

Still, this did little to dishearten Marcel. If the case was easy enough to unpack by reading a simple obituary, then it would never have been thrown to him. Assuming there *was* a case, but that was an assumption Marcel felt safe in making. Coincidences did happen, but not very often. Gall was an obvious suspect, sketchy enough to have warranted Lazarus's attention: he fit perfectly into the story. Others were to be considered no doubt, some unmet guard, or bureaucrat, or cart-pusher, or even a mutant worker, though Marcel was hesitant to assume the latter, considering how many false accusations beset Mutants, based on the universal bias against the grotesquely featured.

The trolley stopped and a kortonian got on, the only other-folk in a slowly dissipating mass of transit-goers. There were few people who took the trolley to the very edge of town. Most people who worked the agri-factory drove themselves or took the autobuses that made daily routes. This left the denizens of the small neighborhood by the southern wall and out-of-towners, those Vidish lumber haulers, wastefolk scrap-merchants, and Border States tourists, whose caravans parked at the gate.

It would have been easier for Marcel if the inner wall of the city separating Blackwood Row from the rest of Huile had a few gates itself, but safety regulations blocked it, meaning the only way to get to the Lazacorp refineries was to leave the city proper and re-enter from outside. This circuitous system was to protect the people of Huile from sangleum fumes and Lazacorp's mutant workers from the possibility of violent human bigotry. Lazarus had recounted dozens of unfortunate incidents that had plagued Blackwood Row before the Resurgence took over. His decision to hire Mutants had satisfied all humanitarian inclinations, and no doubt saved lives considering Mutants' natural resistance to sangleum poisoning, but the influx of such workers had sparked bitter words, thrown rocks, and even a few riots.

It was an unfortunate reality that while the people of Huile might be comfortable with Kortonians and even the occasional salvi, Mutants were a step too far. Considering the grim fact that most mutants were born of the ætheric storms of the Calamity, combined with their kind's general... look, Marcel could understand these misgivings, even though he couldn't, in all Resurgence righteousness, endorse them. Conflicts between non-mutated wastefolk and independent mutant clans were so commonplace that it had even become a cliché in Phenian cinegraph shows, with mutants usually playing the villains, worshiping ætheric aberrations like gods and committing every sort of atrocity. Marcel had been out here long enough to know that the reality was a bit more complicated, that the horned men and women were just as often the victims as perpetrators.

The trolley rolled into the edges of town, where some buildings were still not yet fully occupied, and a few had even been left ruined by generations of scavengers; husks of brick or concrete, where scraggy grass now grew. Those that were filled tended to be the cheapest of overnight inns, small bars, scrap-houses, and other petty business to sate the needs of wastefolk merchants. Still, Lambert's men kept even these areas clean and safe, so that even the closest thing Huile had to slums were innocuous enough. One could walk even these streets safely at night, could speak freely without fear of paranoid ears leading Principate shadows to your door, could sleep comfortable, belly full, behind walls that kept out the raiders and troglyns and all the barbarism of the Wastes. How many cities in the Border States, or in the whole of the world even, could offer that?

It seemed madness to recall how Alba had been willing to throw this city by the wayside, just weeks after saving it. He remembered arguing with her at a café, Desct playing an uncomfortable third wheel. Her plan, so she explained, was to head into the Wastes, to take up the bounty hunter's trade, to fight for herself for once, and leave this, what did she call it, "mudlion's shit-pit."

Marcel had asked how she could think of leaving just as the town was about to become something, a bastion of UCCR freedom, a bulwark against Principate imperialism, a place worth the blood spilled on it. She had suffered as he had, and yet hadn't the guts to stay and steer the city on, to make sure what they had sacrificed, what they had had to do, was worth it in the end.

Alba had said that life wasn't like the pulps, and if he was a damn enough fool to believe any of Roache or City Hall's promises then she had a griffon in Vastium to sell him.

Yet here the city was, everything that had been promised to him.

The trolleyman cranked a lever, and a recording crackled from the brass speaker of the automated dictaphone at the end of the car.

"Last Stop. Renaud Street," a feminine voice said.

Marcel satchelled his notes and hopped off, jogging through the gate and past a small crowd around a Wastes-bound caravan, and an even smaller crowd waiting for the armed autobuses that traveled between the more civilized cities of the Border States.

Outside the walls, Huile's history was written clear in stone and dirt. The ruins of the older districts of the city had been leveled into a wide field, marked in spots by the graffiti-decorated ruins of long-collapsed buildings, sinkholes of stinking muck, recently sprouted groves of thick-barked saplings, patches of finger-cutting shrubs, and small splotches of red ooze: overeager veins of sangleum that hadn't the patience to wait for Lazacorp pumps. Beyond that the landscape shifted into sharp hills marked in strange whites and blacks, dried rivers decorated with swaying grasses, groves of wild, æther-tainted olive trees, and overgrown skeletons of settlements whose names existed only on out-of-date maps.

The deciding conflict out there was not the recent Battle for Huile, but the now centuries-past Calamity, and its wounds healed slowly into scars. Much had died, but what remained, from the agri-factories to the taur herds to the flocks of skraggers searching for an afternoon meal, trudged on after their own manner. In a way Marcel was almost thankful for the Wastes, harsh, wild and even sickening as they could be. At least they kept at bay the Principate, who even in their recent invasion had had to take the long way around.

Still, as Marcel glanced around in the midday sun, he could not find what he was looking for. There sat not a single independent autotaxi idling, nor even a scrapper-folk clunker looking for city-folk cash. He could wait around, but the fresh new case raised in Marcel a restive impatience.

He'd normally gone to Blackwood Row in the back of a Lazacorp 'taxi, a necessity since the road that left Huile's main gate didn't directly connect to the road leading to Blackwood Row, except at a crossroads by an agri-farm complex a good two kilometres south. His eyes followed the city's wall west, through the brush, piles of old bullet shells, and dense rustgrass towards Blackwood Row's main gate. He didn't intend to take the long route, and the gate didn't look all that far.

Half an hour later Marcel emerged from the grasp of razortwig bushes and rustgrass, covered in dust and half-sunstroked, fantasizing about the petition he would send to City Hall demanding a more direct, paved road.

"Hey, who in Inferno are you?" came a shout.

Marcel found himself faced with a firing squad's worth of armed men. Lazacorp men, rifles raised, wearing blue-tinted metal helmets, some with sun visors covering their eyes.

"Marcel," Marcel said, a bit quicker and in a far higher register than he'd meant, "Marcel Talwar."

"Who?" shouted one of the men in the back, near the opening of the large gate. Several autotrucks loitered near the entrance, backs covered, and those guards who weren't holding up Marcel were caught up in an argument with some metal-armed man leaning on the side of an autotruck. Marcel had seen plenty of Lazacorp guards before, but usually in the company of Lazarus himself, where they tended to be more amicable and professional. The man in front of him wasn't even wearing a shirt, and his tanned chest was a canvas for long tattoos of naked women and stone-faced trolls.

"Marcel Talwar," he repeated, annoyance overtaking his initial fear. "War hero?" he offered. "Fought in Huile Sewer Rats. I was in a fucking parade with Lazarus."

"Oh!" said the closer man, fully dressed. "I know you, you're that—uh, you're Mr. Roache's friend."

"Yes, sure. Just put those down. Please."

The man waved away the other guards, and business continued as the nearest guard checked through Marcel's identification papers, investigator's license, and even the warrant Lambert had written up. A tanker-truck rolled out of the gate, hauling gallons of æther-oil, likely to Resurgence friendly city-states nearby, perhaps Quorgon or Dechetville. Marcel knew he shouldn't be annoyed at the guards' failure to recognize him—he hadn't joined the army for the fame. Still, it had only been two years. Had the sacrifices of his friends been forgotten already?

"What is it you need, Mr. Talwar?" the guard asked, gun slung over his shoulder, staring at the warrant as if it were in El'Helmaudi script.

"I'm investigating the death of Mr. Fareau."

"Fareau?" The guard scrunched his forehead. Marcel nodded. "You know any Fareau, Remus?"

Another guard walked over, helmet hanging on his belt. "Yeah. He's uh, had an accident. Collapsed walkway." Remus stared at Marcel. "Didn't think he had family or friends or nothing."

"Investigator," Marcel said.

"Invest..." Remus scratched the bald of his head. "Police already came through."

"*Private* investigator. I'm just here to look around, talk to a few people. If you know anything..."

The man shook his head, then grabbed the shoulder of the other guard and the two whispered out some nervous conference, glancing back every few seconds. Marcel put his papers back in his satchel and began walking towards the gate.

"Wait!" Remus said, "You can't just..."

Marcel stopped and stared. This had never been a problem when Lazarus was around, but without their boss, even simple tasks seemed like legendary feats of logistics. Or perhaps this was Verus's hand, Marcel mused.

Remus gestured, "I'll contact Verus. You can talk to him, okay?"

Marcel nodded. He had planned to speak to the foreman at some point, anyhow.

As he waited, he tried to interrogate the first guard, but got little out of him, only that he "didn't share a shift with Fareau," "didn't see much," "didn't hear much," and "never really talked to the man." Marcel tried a few others, but they could give nothing more than the first, often less, though with more swearing.

Twenty minutes passed and an autocar drove through the front gate. The ever-haggard visage of Verus stared from the driver's window. The mesh of scars on his face reminded Marcel of cracked waste-dirt, and his black leather eyepatch only further accentuated his scowl. The foreman got out and stared death through his one good eye at Marcel.

"Roache send you?"

Marcel crossed his arms and shook his head. "What makes you say that?"

Verus laughed a growl. "Doesn't trust me? Thinks he can't leave Blackwood Row for a few damned weeks. Is that it? Needs to have his dog thrust its nose into my behind, smell where I've been sitting?"

"Inferno are you talking about, Verus? I haven't talked to Lazarus since he left."

The man chewed on his tongue. "What you here for then?"

"Gileon Fareau."

"Eh, him?" Verus said. "Fell."

"So I've been told. What's this about Lazarus Roache and spying?"

Verus narrowed his eye. *"Workplace disagreement."* The words seemed ill-placed in his mouth.

"What, you don't agree with his choice of going off to Icaria or something?"

Verus turned his head, seeming to pick at Marcel's face with his gaze. "He doesn't need to be mucking around up there. And you don't need to be mucking around here neither."

"It's my job and my right," Marcel flashed the warrant, and Verus grabbed it, muttering furious nothings as he read. "If you keep me from my work, that's as good a reason as any to bring in a few officers with me. I'll get in one way or another."

Verus scowled, tossing the warrant back. "I'm not keeping you. What is it you want?"

Marcel gestured past the gate. "To see where it happened."

"That it?"

Marcel nodded.

"I'm not keeping you from that." Verus threw his arm to the car. "Well, what's keeping you?"

Verus drove him through the gate, into Blackwood Row. It struck Marcel, whenever he visited, how the neighborhood looked far more pleasant than the looming smokestacks would suggest. The buildings were well-maintained, old brick things with only a thin layer of soot. The streets were clean asphalt compared to the inconsistently maintained cobblestone of Huile, and it even boasted something of a park, the wide-open Liberation Square, re-named and re-dedicated after the liberation of Huile. It boasted geometric paths interspersed with small plots of plant life: flowers, bushes, and trees, not one of them a waste-touched breed, though even these arboreal imports could not escape being colored black by the smoke. In its center stood a de-commissioned tread-driller, a fat tank of a machine, with several long mechanical arms, drill bits polished to gleam. Marcel had some notion the Guild-imported machines were used in digging new sangleum wells, but the last he had seen them in action was clearing up the battle rubble outside Huile.

Mutant workers, dressed in denim uniforms and reddened skin, pushed dollies of machine bits and carried crates throughout the neighborhood. Others worked repainting the outside of a pale-white building, or repairing a sunken pothole. A few blocks in a large fence cut off the route, manned by several guards, making languid rounds, rifles strapped to their backs.

"High security," Marcel mused.

"For the workers' sake," Verus said in a disinterested monotone. "You weren't there for the riots, after we built up this place." An almost smirk worked up his face. "Back with the old taurshit mayor. I doubt you can imagine what the Huile folk can do, when worked up to it. *'Out to purge the skinsick.'* Their words, Talwar, not mine."

They turned down a small road, passing refinery towers ensconced in scaffolds. Marcel tried to ignore the growing acrid taste of the air as Verus slowed his 'car in front of a massive concrete block of a building.

"That was a long time ago," Marcel said.

"Depends on your measuring stick," Verus got out, and Marcel opened his door. "Not even seven years, fully."

"Well, we have UCCR rule of law now."

Verus pulled out a snake's-length rope of keys and after a few seconds picked out the right one. "So they tell me." He waved Marcel over without looking up, "Come on now, it's right through here."

Chapter 8

'Right through here' meant over twenty minutes of wandering down hallways, into basements, through underground passageways, and up and down a series of lifts and narrow stairwells, and that didn't even count the ten minutes Verus left him waiting in a hallway while the man ducked into a side office to make some vocaphone calls.

"I was in the middle of quite a few things," he snarled.

Marcel was not eager to linger long down in some subbasement of Lazacorp. In fact, even the thought nauseated him. The cramped, dimly lit hallways still had a burning hint of sangleum wafting through. They were as labyrinthine as his war memories recalled, and he kept jumping at shadows, though he knew there was nothing to fear.

An investigation, an investigation, he had to keep reminding himself why he was there. He sucked in his breath and tried to keep away memories of that final grim battle. It was hard not to imagine the grasp of the gas mask, hear the muffled gunshots through it, the whizz of the gas, feel the burning in the leg he no longer had. He caught himself wishing Alba was here, to pull him out again, but he held his breath a moment and suffocated the thought.

He was becoming more than half-sure that Verus was wasting his time, had taken detours, to disorient and enrage him. Marcel bit his tongue and tried not to show his discomfort. He couldn't afford to appear weak.

Mutants passed by every minute or so, some hauling, some just walking. They eyed him, moving forward quickly, responding to his weak waves and smiles with vague mirrored facsimiles. Marcel tried to converse with them, but most were busy, or possibly, made themselves busy. Perhaps if he pushed harder he might get more than a sentence, but he wasn't sure he had the strength down here to do anything more than keep his wits in some loose order.

The mutants who passed by bore the marks of sangleum mutation across their whole bodies: red chitinous skin, patches of scabs, yellowed eyes, and very often small, or not so small, horns, jutting at odd angles from their head. Some had more idiosyncratic mutations, elongated or twisted limbs, hard knife-edged ridges, long back-stalks that oozed bile, nails that sharpened into claws, and great boney growths on their joints that gave the impressions of giant gears.

One hunchbacked mutant bumped into his shoulder. Marcel stumbled, nearly falling, catching himself on the wall. The mutant didn't stop, but hurried on, mumbling something, though if it was an apology it was a vague one.

Marcel rubbed his forehead and tried to massage away a headache, now entirely certain that Verus was wasting time. He pressed his hands into his pockets to force a nonchalant air and brushed his hand against paper.

He took out the crumpled scrap of newsprint, which he had certainly not put there. His mouth opened to shout to the mutant, but decided against it, instead uncrumpling the message. What he found was a piece of an old issue of *The Huile Gazette*. It was unmarked, aside from a stain that suggested it was recently trash.

One side was a blank crossword puzzle, the other a snippet from the old issue.

"*...when completed the new Lazacorp facility should be able to provide the whole of Huile with water as clean as that which pipes in Phenia, according to the words of Mr. Roache. The operation, beginning next week is expected to...*"

The door slammed open, and Marcel thrust the newsprint back into his pocket. Verus stumbled out, glared at Marcel, and thrust his thumb up.

"A couple floors that way," he said. "Come on, now, don't waste my time."

Marcel inspected the catwalks that weaved between half a dozen other catwalks among the towers of machinery in the windowless block of a building. He could see a faint line along the railing and part of the walkway where it had collapsed and been re-attached.

Sweat dripped from his forehead and splattered down, hissing into steam on the machinery. It was easy to see how rust could build up here, or how someone could become dehydrated and disoriented, trip and plummet. He leaned his head over the rail and glanced below. Four floors to the bottom—a clean fall, straight into some dense growth of grinding mechanisms that Marcel couldn't hope to identify.

Mutants continued to work below, their footsteps muffled by the constant clang of metal and screams of steam. He glanced around for the hunchbacked mutant, but he was nowhere in sight. That the paper snippet was a message was clear enough, but of what?

"You done?" Verus was leaning on the opposite handrail.

"How'd it happen?" Marcel asked.

"Man was drunk," Verus said. "We had the section roped off, but he wandered onto it on shift. Crack, smash, you get it."

"So you knew there was a structural problem?"

Verus walked over and slammed his foot down. The catwalk shook but didn't give. "Yes, these things happen, which is why we had it roped off until we could fix it."

"So, no fault of yours?"

Verus gave his impression of a smile, "None."

"But you had a drunk man on staff."

Verus shrugged and crossed his arms, "Roache's hire, not mine."

"Any witnesses?" Marcel asked, wiping his forehead with his sleeves. "Seems a busy place."

"Late at night," Verus said simply. "We keep a strict curfew."

"One which Gileon broke."

Verus rolled his single eye and stretched his shoulders. Marcel kept up his stare. Finally Verus snarled: "The man was wasted, what about that confuses you?"

Marcel flipped through his notebook and tapped his pen. "Were there any signs something was wrong before the accident, unusual behavior, unexplained requests?"

Verus shook his head.

"He didn't ask to be reassigned to a new shift, anything like that?"

Verus freed one arm to wave the question away. "No, nothing like that. Just some drunk idiot. Maybe you desk-job folk don't realize it, but when men are doing real work, sometimes accidents happen."

The letter claimed Gileon had asked Verus specifically for a change in shift. Why would the foreman lie about that? A misremembrance? Possible, but Marcel doubted it. Still, despite his detestable airs, Verus was not the primary suspect.

"I have some questions about the structural integrity," Marcel tapped the guardrail with his pen. "You have an ætheric engineer on staff?"

"I can get you a mechanic," Verus said simply.

"That's not what I asked," Marcel replied.

"It's rust. I can find you a child to explain the concept."

"But you must have an ætheric engineer on staff." Marcel dragged his foot along the line where the section of walkway had been attached. "Smooth work here, this doesn't look like welder's, strikes me as æthermantics."

Verus shrugged.

"It might help if I had some other parts of the refineries to compare to," Marcel said, thinking back on the mutant's note. "Places a little more stable, maybe somewhere else Gileon worked around. Perhaps the water filtration plant?"

"No," Verus said.

"It's an easy request, Verus. I don't even need you to come with me if you're so damn tired of my company."

"I said no." Verus stepped forward, and Marcel could feel the sharpness of his stare. It occurred to Marcel that it had been several minutes since he had last noticed the man blink. "That project is a private Lazacorp venture. There's dozens of buildings here. Why in Inferno do you want to shove your nose in that one?"

Marcel gripped the railing as the man pushed towards him, gaze cutting. He steadied himself, sucked in his chest. He wouldn't allow the brute to simply intimidate his way out.

"Schematics were stolen, were they not?" Marcel said. "Of that facility. I don't know what exactly happened here, Verus, but if it wasn't just an accident, I need to see all that I can."

Verus softened his stare but didn't relent, anger morphing into a wary curiosity. "How do you know about that?"

Lazarus never told him. Odd, but it seemed whatever feud the two were having now spread to intelligence breaches. A topic he would need to discuss with Roache. Perhaps this explained some of Verus's paranoia, if he was not even aware that the documents had been returned.

"Lazarus mentioned it before he left," Marcel said, the simplest explanation, not even a lie, technically.

Verus nodded. "Figured as much. So he has you sniffing around, is that it? Using whatever excuse he can pull up? Listen, tell Roache that everything is how he left it."

Marcel slammed the rail. "Last time, Verus. I haven't spoken to Roache any more than you have. I don't know what kind of spat you two are having, but this is a simple investigation into Gileon's accident." He pulled out his warrant and shook it in the man's face. "Does this have Lazarus Roache's name on it? Anywhere?"

"Everything in this damn city has that man's name on it."

The enmity was complete. Or perhaps that was an excuse. Either way Marcel shook his head and thrust the warrant back into his bag. "Fine. I'll tell Lambert you're preventing a simple investigation and get some badges to rummage through here."

He turned to walk away, and as he did so, Verus grabbed the edge of his coat. "I'll get your engineer," Verus muttered.

"What?" Marcel said, pulling himself free.

"I'll get you your damned engineer," Verus snarled.

"I thought you didn't have one." Marcel couldn't help himself from grinning. It was clear enough that in whatever list of secrets Verus kept, the filtration plant ranked higher than Gall, but he didn't mind starting with the engineer.

"I never said that." Verus snorted with disgust and waved over a guard. "Grab Gall, I need some gunk cleared out of here."

"It fell, then I put it back." Corvin Gall ended his description of the accident in the same sentence that started it. The man resembled a bulky golem, not just in size and girth but also in material. His legs were metal prosthetics, his arms mechanical, his face marred by a great metal plate over what had once been his left ear and forehead. His back bore a long metal pole that appeared to be grafted into him, a work light and several tools hanging off its end. Layers of oil-stained leather covered his chest, but Marcel was willing to guess there was some metal in there somewhere too.

94

Verus leaned back on the sprawl of piping. Marcel had hoped that the man would now take the excuse to get back to work, but despite his complaints, the foreman stood and stared.

"And... do things often fall here?" Marcel asked spinning his pen on a blank notepad.

"Decay. Time. Accidents. Everything breaks. Here less than outside, but everything breaks. This was easy to fix. Boring."

"And what did you know about Mr. Fareau?" Marcel asked.

The engineer raised an eyebrow and scratched his chin.

"Gileon. The man who died," Marcel said.

Gall turned towards Verus, who avoided his gaze and waved him on from the perpetual lock of his crossed arms.

"I just fix machines," Gall said.

"He delivered you parts and such. You must have talked to him at some point."

"Don't like conversation," Gall said.

"How about before this job?" Marcel said. "You're from out west, so was Mr. Fareau. Any chance you two met up? Knew people in common? I'm just trying to get some sense of why he might have been drinking."

"The Wastes," Gall said.

Marcel nodded. For a moment it seemed like some memory or insight had bloomed behind Gall's eyes.

Then the engineer shook his head. "Didn't like conversation back then, neither."

"So what, you just work all the time?"

Below, two mutants lugged a large metal cylinder. The second one slipped, and the cylinder clanged onto the catwalk, shaking the entire structure as the first cursed out his scrambling partner, sending furtive looks upwards.

"I like machines more." Corvin Gall smiled. Not a single one of his teeth was natural. "They don't talk."

Marcel jabbed his pen. "I want a yes or no, flat out. Did you have any contact with the deceased?"

"No," the man said. Marcel scribbled out the simple answer. Gileon was taken by enough fear of this engineer to send a letter to Roache, but by the man's telling he barely knew Gileon existed.

Verus rubbed his head, and started to scratch at a scab on his arm. Marcel stepped closer to Gall.

"On another note," Marcel said, lowering his voice. "I heard some schematic notes of yours went missing a few weeks back. Is that true?"

He gauged the man's face for surprise or guilt. Instead he found rage.

"Damned thing to steal! Damned! Weeks of notes, progress, all gone! Was making my way on the modulation, just needed to get the resonance right, could have had it by now!" The dully-sedate man now paced back and forth, fingers flicking rapidly. Verus took quick notice and rushed over. "Damn skinsick mutants," Gall continued, "could have been any of them! Thieving bastards, sneaking around, you see them!"

Verus grabbed his arm and pulled the engineer back behind him. "All right Gall, you can shut up now." Surprisingly the man did, though he kept up his fidgeting. "You, Talwar," Verus shoved forward his finger, "Inferno do you think you are doing, setting off my employees, causing a damn mess?"

"Conducting my investigation," Marcel said. "And I would like to continue it."

"Continue with what?" Verus shouted. "There's nothing, you've found nothing. I don't know how many hours I'm going have to waste to explain that the man fell. That people fall sometimes. I could show you what happens to a body that falls from that height."

Marcel stiffened up. "Was that a threat?"

Verus's face didn't change a twitch. "Just offering anything that could help with your investigation."

"Well," Marcel leaned back, hand resting by his holster, a gesture he was sure was due to overactive nerves, but not sure enough. "Since you asked, I would like to see Mr. Fareau's room."

"Didn't," Verus said.

"What?"

"He didn't live in Blackwood Row," Verus said. "Never enough taur-fucking space here. Had a place in Huile, on one of Roache's properties." As he finished his sentence his eye flickered back and forth, and his smile faded a bit, as if he had not fully remembered that bit of trivia until just that moment. He stared down, and quickly muttered some complaint about the mutant workers who had just now begun to again haul the cylinder below.

...Sister, do pity me, for day by day the grim reality of my miserable reassignment strikes me with greater and greater force. I recant my complaints on the barbarity of the Wastes, oh fool I was for thinking those dead lands the grimmest corner of our Principate. Nay, Videk alone is the most miserable of all provinces, and the Vidish, the most perfidious lot. There are some in the East Vidish Extraction Co. that can be trusted (Kaimark and Anklav born for the most), but there are twice as many who are happy to sneak behind our back and sell our sweat-earned lumber to the highest bidder, Principate blue or Resurgence red!

I hate this land, sister, I hate the grasping shrubs and the miserable rain. I hate the endless forestlines and the thieving provincials. But most of all, I despise those damn Ferrals. Think of the fool I was just weeks ago, glad to be away from the open Wastes. Yet there were fewer places to hide in the openness of desolation, fewer holes for beasts to slumber. There ambush was a rare danger, not a constant nuisance! Raiders can be bribed, but these beastmen? Ah, the idiot I was, glad to be away from the stink of the skinsick, the misery of those mutated souls. Yet with them at least I can squint to see the humanity, polluted by oozing skin and twisting horns. What humanity do these Ferrals have? I do not care much for claims of common ancestry, these things have more in common with a rabid dog than anything that that should walk on two legs. They huddle amongst themselves, filthy, hiding between tree branches, or in muddy creek beds, arrows notched, eager to let them fly at my workers, barking and hooting all the while.

It sickens me to see how the Resurgence traitors try to use these animals, allow them to pollute their cities, to live among them. It is not love that guides their hands, a joke of a claim I can promise you, they detest the beasts as much as we, I can see it in their eyes. No, they suffer the Ferral presence just so they might have some foul ally amongst the forestlands with which to vex and nettle us. I do not know when the Imperator's victory will claim fully Videk. It is clear to me that such a blessed day is far further than those in Kaimark claim. Yet still I await it eagerly, when the last of the beastmen are hunted down...

—Excerpt from a letter bearing the signature of a "Darya Wagmer." Found during a Resurgence-funded lumber raid, deemed of no strategic import.

Chapter 9

Sylvaine sat leaning on the curved wall of rust, schematics in hand. The open mountain wind flowed past her, fluttering her hair and papers as it whipped through the inert engine that hung off the side of Icaria. The air was biting cold, but it didn't bother her much, one of the few benefits of her fur—*hair, damn it.* She shook her head and glanced up to watch a skragger fly over to land in its nest, a tangle of shrub branches poking out of caved-in section of Icaria's hull. She pulled her toolbox closer, away from the edge of the long drop, and wondered where in Inferno her partner was.

Javad had still not shown for a single day's work since the quarter began, and she had reached the end of the tasks that she could cover alone. Wheelston's Repair Inc. had assigned their combined morning to repair duty on one of the great engines that had once propelled Icaria through the clouds. A great browning cylinder it was, with sets of blades the width of a house that creaked behind her.

She knew it was a pointless project; even if the engines were restored to complete functionality they'd still be mere ornamentation. Most of the internal machinery of Icaria, even that which had not been destroyed by the ætheric waves of the Calamity, had been hollowed out for storage space, or else melted down and recycled. Still it was a common Icaria creed, spread by political slogans and grandiose speeches, that one day the city of engineers would grace the sky again. Damn the Calamity, damn the near century of rust, damn the mountainside suburbs that relied on the city, damn logic and damn common decency, Icaria would fly again!

This nonsense never bothered Sylvaine much, pointless jobs paid as well as vital ones, but without the spark of æther she had no chance of replacing the, admittedly functionally decorative, æther-circuitry that lay deep within. She could lie and claim the job done, it would hurt no one, but whenever the next repair team clocked in they'd report the failure, and she had no doubt fingers would be quickly pointed at the 'layabout ferral.'

She played with the thumb of her glove; it would be so simple if she could just slip it on, point, and poof! Then she could be out of here and at workshop where she could...

Panic gripped her a moment, replaced quickly by a now mundane despair. *Don't think about it.* There was no reason to ruin herself with dread, but she couldn't avoid it.

That night was to be the final night of workshop. Tomorrow she was scheduled to present Gearswit her negative-density generator in its complete, intricate, beautiful, and entirely nonfunctional glory. No doubt Gearswit would try to be kind about her project, as tactful as a kortonian could manage, maybe he would even hold off a full flunk and mark her as an "incomplete," with a polite but firm suggestion to finally give up on her fool's excuse for a dream. She dreaded looking into his eyes and seeing the thoughts behind them, those I-Told-You-So's, those meandering theories on why a ferral would try to be an engineer, try to act human.

The thought of Lazarus's drug came back, the painful possibility that the path to her happiness had been handed to her and that she had smacked it away, to live in fear and failure.

She turned back to her current distraction; some schematics Gearswit had given her. "Extra credit" was the official term, a reason to keep her on the class roll even as her project remained inert. An excuse to make her feel like a real engineer for just a little while longer, all while clearing out his slush pile. And these notes were clearly pulled from deep within said slush pile, Gearswit himself wasn't entirely sure who had sent the schematics, nor what they were supposed to represent. He had just said that he got it in some envelope dropped off at his desk with the simple instructions: *Show To An Engineer!*

These schematics were certainly intricate, pipework interwoven with precise care, a multitude of tanks fused within and about a massive central cylinder, each component sketched with exacting specifications. The components ranged from standard, but high-quality, Icaria imports to custom in-house machinery. The gargantuan device looked expensive, it looked sophisticated. It also looked like nonsense.

On the whole, the machineworks vaguely resembled the outlines for some sort of large-scale water filtration plant, perhaps for some massive military instillation or small metropolis, but any inspection of its internal design showed parts that seemed to lack a purpose within any sort of water filtration system. Extraneous modules filled every extra metre of space, piping twisted in strange patterns, dumping what should be clean water effluent into the influent tubes, and some of the pipelines had specifications she had only ever seen used in sangleum transport.

It was a mess, made worse by the fact that, by mistake or design, much of the schematic was mislabeled, with many of the stranger mechanisms designated as mundane filtration machinery that should have been half, or twice, the measured size and an entirely different shape. Then there was this strange module near the mid-point, which seemed to have even baffled the sketcher. Pages were focused on it, with abundant use of question marks. A good section of the module was drawn in only the vaguest of stretches, the author either unwilling to make a guess on its functions, or else having ran out of time.

The clangs of footsteps on rungs reverberated down. Sylvaine bagged her notes and thoughts to stare up and watch as a figure crawled down the long ladder from the city's surface. She was a malva, slender-built, copper-haired, wearing a thick, stained coat. Sylvaine recognized her as a fellow student from lecture hall.

"Sylvaine," the malva said, as she stepped onto the engine. It was not quite a question, but Sylvaine nodded anyways.

"You are?"

"Rostialva. We're partners," the woman said. She was a continental malva, that was clear from her ear and nose piercings, as well as the abstract tattoos on her cheek, all of which would be scandalous for the more common seafaring Malva of the Thalassocracy. Her hair shined in the alpine sunlight, shimmering copper, as if thin metal shavings had been welded to her scalp.

"Where's Javad?" Sylvaine asked.

"Where's Javad?" Rostialva repeated, with a more than a dash of mockery. "Where's my partner as well? Rusted pus if I know. Rusted pus if I care. Let's get started."

Sylvaine started to unscrew the most worn of the panels. After replacing her third, she noticed a lack of something.

"You planning on helping?" she asked.

Rostialva leaned on the curved wall. "Well, I figured since I have the luck of being teamed with an engineer with no Knack, you might as well handle the practical stuff, since I'll be doing double the æthermantics."

"The only æthermantics involved is fusing a few æther-circuits in the back."

Rostialva opened her arms wide. "Well if you want to handle half of those, I'll help you with these. No? Then I'm on my smoke break."

Sylvaine tried to stare her down, but the woman already had a clope in her lips. She considering arguing the point, but could tell when someone had chosen not to budge. The argument could go all the way to their employer, but even in Icaria, a ferral's side of the story was never the preferred one.

She worked for the greater part of an hour; as she would have alone, only with the additional misery of the stares of her partner, and her occasional, a bit too loud, mumble. As Sylvaine finished putting all into place, Rostialva walked over, snapped a spark into fresh circuitry, and then lit another clope, as Sylvaine started the inverse of her previous hour's work.

After she replaced the last panel Sylvaine walked past Rostialva.

"I'll request a new partner," she said.

The malva smiled. "Oh no, woe is me."

Trying to filter her fumes lest they condense into a cloud of rage, Sylvaine walked through Icaria, her anger now polluted with the fatalistic dread of her upcoming workshop session. It would be further embarrassment to come into workshop in a wild fury, so she tried to distract herself with the hour she had free. She turned by Zev Airclank Square, and headed towards *The Cogcrafter's Lunch*, a small café in which she had sometimes grabbed croissants with Javad after work.

She wandered through a main thoroughfare and past a crowd of Kaimark tourists, who gawked at the golem workmen, metal-morphing street-performers, and the uncountable variety of mechanical marvels that had become the prosaic decorations of Sylvaine's everyday commute. One child, still wearing his Principate militaresque school uniform (apparently out of pure habit) stared at Sylvaine with wide eyes, pulling on his mother's sleeve. Sylvaine was in no mood for a crowd of, at best, gawks, and quite likely sneers, and so took a quick turn down a side alley. A few dozen metres in she realized her mistake.

She glanced back and found that same bald man who had accosted her outside Lazarus's apartment, standing only three paces behind her. He smiled as if he hadn't been sneaking up behind her. If she weren't so unnerved, she'd be impressed that a man of that size could walk with such stealth.

"Hello," he said, "I was wondering if..."

"No," she said. "I can't get you Gearswit."

"It is of great importance, I gave him..."

She continued walking. With all the miseries of life, she didn't need a half-mad stalker as well. The man followed.

"Please, just a moment of your time."

She ignored him, taking a turn down a further sub-alley. The buildings here rose high, their doors back entrances to apartment complexes and first-floor shops. At a glance all looked locked. If she had the Knack, those locks would be formalities, but for now there was another block of narrow dim and another intersection before she could slip out back into the crowded sunlight. She focused her gaze forward and tried to ignore the petitions of the man.

Unfortunately, the crackpot would not allow himself to be so peacefully ignored. He dashed forward with such silent speed that Sylvaine didn't realize he had moved until he was right beside her.

"This is too important," he hissed. "I am sorry, but I *must* speak with you."

Sylvaine leapt back, and then ran down the alley as fast as her feet could carry her.

"Wait!" the man shouted. He didn't wait himself, but sprinted after her with equal rapidity. She held her bag close and put workshoe to pavement. She resisted the urge to get down on all fours and bound forward with every limb, despite the adrenaline pounding her deepest instincts awake.

She turned the corner with a skid, and found the expected open street blocked, a rectangular extension of the tenement complex to her right pushing out to cover the street.

Sylvaine froze. She had taken this shortcut just a week ago, but Icaria was a city of engineers. When construction required only a flick of the hand, every odd structure became protean.

There was another way, behind her, but as she turned she saw the man blocking her path, the hustle of the street a distance behind him.

"Stay back," Sylvaine said.

The man stepped forward, his words a fierce whisper. "I understand why you run, but you're in danger. He will only use—"

"Stay the fuck back!" Sylvaine hissed. She glanced around with a frantic fear. There were pipes near the man's feet, it would take only a small spark of æthermantics to burst them, distract the man with steam or knock him to the ground under a river of sewage. For any of the engineers in this city this would be a simple, dignified, escape.

Her heart pounded against its cage of bone, her visions sharpened, her nose took in every scent. Her ears twitched with inhuman precision, she could hear the man's sweat hit the metal floor, hear his hands rubbing against his bracelet, yet she couldn't make out any coherent meaning out of the words the man was speaking.

Sylvaine could escape, something inside her was sure of it. Fight then flight. A roar, a slash, a dash out, safe on the far street, with clothes ragged, fur on end, and blood decorating her claws. But how humiliating that would be, the ferral finally going berserk. It was a horror she had seen in many a cinegraph show, vile monsters that hunted the heroes, half-naked ferrals hunched over like animals, with wild eyes and stained fangs.

She sucked in her breath; trying to count her heartbeat, to calculate the distance that separated the man from herself, anything to bring back her mind into the realm of the sane and quantifiable. Whatever that man might try to do, could it possibly be worse than becoming *that*? A beast with no thought but survival?

His every step forward, his formless words, his outstretched hand, each pushed her instincts up, and up, through her shaking body, to her brain, where fear battled against reason.

A shout. Her pursuer paused and turned. Shapes in the distance, silhouetted by sunlight, all man sized, alike in color. It took her a moment to quite focus her mind and realize the shout had been "freeze!", the men police.

"That's him, that's the bastard!" A familiar voice, another man. *Lazarus*, she realized, standing beside the cops.

The line of the police stepped forward. The bald man raised his arms. Then he let out a whisper, which, despite her now focused sobriety, she still couldn't understand. In the span of a second the bracelet of the man reforged itself into a long blade, and as it did so the man jumped to the left, the fresh blade slicing through a metal door. He disappeared into the shadow-strewn hallway beyond.

"Shit!" shouted one of the cops, and a trio of them dashed forward into the building. Lazarus Roache ran up with them, coat flapping, but stopped as he reached Sylvaine.

"Sylvaine!" he said. "Are you all right?"

She nodded, slowing her panting. She glanced down and was glad to see that her clothes were not excessively messed, and that her hair was still mostly in place. "Yes, I'm all right."

"I know that man," Lazarus jabbed his finger, "A real piece of work. When I noticed him following you into that alleyway, well, I'm glad police were nearby is all I can say."

Sylvaine tried to gather her words together, thoughts now slowing back into a sensible pace. She managed a "thank you."

The man smiled, teeth gleaming even in the shaded alleyway. "Come, let's get you somewhere more pleasant."

Lazarus led Sylvaine to *The Cogcrafter's Lunch*, which he had, quite coincidentally, also been heading to. He grinned and asked if she had ever been, and she nodded as he ordered chocolate croissants and tea. A woman played a bandonion by the passing crowds, a couple exchanged laughs a table over, and Lazarus spent a moment to banter freely with the waiter. It was strange how quickly calm returned sitting alongside Lazarus. The police were still only a few blocks away, but here, resting on a faux-rattan chair, basking in the aroma of rising bread, it all seemed to her a past life.

"Has that man been bothering you?" Lazarus asked as the waiter left, concern etched on his forehead.

Sylvaine shook her head. "Not much. I mean, I ran into him once before."

"Before," he asked. "You talked with him?"

"No, no!" Sylvaine said, with some embarrassment. "It was obvious enough to me the man was crazy, but he wasn't so disturbingly persistent."

"He's a creep, scum," Lazarus said, taking a nibble from his pastry, "but don't worry, Icaria's finest are on him."

"He had a strange weapon," she said, "Did you see it? That bracelet-sword. It looked like some pre-homid autochthon machine."

"A what?" Lazarus paused. "Oh, one of the... what does the Church call them, the Ascended. One of their artifacts. Forgive my illiteracy in the proper terminology. I can assure you I am no churchgoer, no, too sharp for that. Not as sharp as you, I suppose, at least not as well educated. I obviously have much to learn from engineers like yourself." He chuckled, and Sylvaine felt herself blush.

"Yes, I believe he stole it," Lazarus continued. "From a chapel or museum, perhaps."

Sylvaine regretted not getting a closer look at the object, not that she had a good chance in the circumstances. Those time-forgotten gadgets were rare enough, and despite their scientific value the Church of the Ascended hoarded them greedily. She couldn't help but feel a twinge of guilt that some madman thief could not only possess such a machine, but use it, while she couldn't even get her ætherglove to respond to her entreaties.

"How is your project progressing?" Lazarus enquired.

And at once her pleasant respite fell apart, the candid conversation and flaky pastries immaterial against the oncoming dread of her evening workshop. She chewed, trying to find the words to explain her upcoming failure, but couldn't manage to even meet his eyes.

She rummaged into her bag, seeking some distraction. "Well, I mean, I've been busy. I've been analyzing other engineers' projects," she said, lifting out the strange filtration schematics.

To her surprise Lazarus took them and looked them over with a focused gaze, one by one.

"You said the madman gave these to you?" he asked.

"What? No, they're Gearswit's, my professor. Not sure where he got them."

Lazarus shrugged. "Reads like nonsense to me. But I was curious about your negative-density... Ah, just a moment!" Someone on the street had clearly caught his attention. He smiled and shouted, "Javad!"

Javad? Sylvaine glanced backwards, but there he was, her wayward partner, walking down the street, short, black-haired with a youthful, almost naïvely wide smile. His style had changed, however, he was wearing a striped suit that almost matched Lazarus's.

"Mr. Roache!" he called out walking over, then: "Sylvaine?"

"Hello Javad. It's nice to see you," Sylvaine said, as the man sat down, his smile turning sheepish. "What have you been up to?" She tried not to sound too accusatory in front of Lazarus.

"Working with Mr. Roache!" he said.

"He's an excellent engineer, have him on a pet project of mine. Come! Let's take tea," Lazarus said, pouring out three cups of steaming water.

"I apologize I quit work so suddenly," said Javad. "Mr. Roache gave me an excellent offer."

"I'm not sure you told them you quit," Sylvaine said, *nor me,* she kept from adding.

"Ah right, well I've been kept very busy, must have slipped the mind."

"It's an excellent project," Lazarus said. "In fact, I think your skills would be invaluable. If you're interested, of course."

Sylvaine shrugged. "Does it have a place for a mechanic?"

Javad laughed. "Oh, still bothered by that whole thing?"

She gritted her teeth to hold back some choice words. Javad could be careless with his tongue, but it was something else to dismiss so easily her deepest source of despair. That the man could just laugh off her broken dreams... still it would do no good to berate the idiot in front of Lazarus.

She closed her eyes, and let out a breath, "Yes... I am still having some trouble."

"My apologies," Javad said to Sylvaine, glancing quickly at Lazarus. "I just mean, well, I think that could be easily solved. With slickdust."

Sylvaine raised an eyebrow. "You know about slickdust?"

"Of course!" Javad said. The waiter dashed by with a tray and started to serve the pastries and pour the tea. Javad sipped. "Mr. Roache hooked me up. My work has risen to levels I didn't know existed."

"But is it... dangerous?" she asked, pushing her croissant around with her fork. "I mean," she said, eyes towards Lazarus, "you said it was experimental."

Lazarus laughed with an unusually nervous tone, tapping his fingers together. Javad laughed without any reservation.

"Is that what he told you?" Javad said, "Gear's-grits, the man is a salesman."

"Forgive me," said Lazarus, "I may have embellished a little. I just thought it might be useful to you, and got a bit carried away in my description."

Javad shook his head. "No, it may be new to Icaria, but I've known people who have been using it for years down in El'Helmaud. No negative effect, so innocuous that I wouldn't have believed its influence on my æthermantics if I hadn't tried it myself."

"And you never mentioned it?" Sylvaine said, trying not to hint at her anger.

Javad paused.

"The supply only came in recently," Lazarus said. "I'm sure the man didn't mean to raise false hope."

"Yes," Javad said, "I didn't want you to get excited about something that was not yet available."

"Speaking of which!" Lazarus took out a red vial and added some to his and Javad's drink. He gave Sylvaine a wink and shook the vial. "Would you fancy a taste?"

Javad was already drinking, Sylvaine glanced at her own cup, a sad brownish tea stared back. She had been fantasizing about the drug since she had denied it, imagining a world where all of Lazarus's promises were true. She hadn't expected another chance, and now that it was in front of her, its seemingly magic powers sounded a tad more plausible.

"And you're sure it's safe?" she asked.

From both of them, "Of course!"

She nodded slowly, staring at the drink. The mocking grin of Rostialva danced around in the back off her psyche, hidden laughter echoing in from years of memory. She saw her machine sitting inert, her failures manifest, felt clearly the waves of shame that never ceased to break upon her.

"Well, I guess it couldn't make things worse." She tossed the acrid liquid down her throat.

Chapter 10

Sylvaine wiped the sweat from her forehead and the oil from her hands as she stared at her near-finished machine. The outer chassis was made mostly of cheap scrap-metal, but within its innards lay dozens of æther-circuits, mazes of wires, store shelves' worth of piping and compressors. This prototype was largely scavenged from the remnants of her previous design, but she was still proud of it. If given ætheric life the generator could turn pure sangleum into enough negative density to lift an object one hundred times its own mass. Still, that was a very large *if*.

The workshop itself was in a dense basement, once a minor engine-cooling station back when Icaria was skyward. Its ceiling was a nest of pipes that wormed up to the surface of Icaria, which shook down dust as the occasional autocar or engineering experiment drove on the streets above.

Besides Sylvaine, a couple other students still worked, tinkering with gizmos, gadgets, and ætherial-phase transistors. She lost all sense of time while working, but guessed it must have been late into the night, considering that most of the class had already left. Not Rostialva, unfortunately, Sylvaine could still sense the malva's stare. Sylvaine glanced back at her, but the woman didn't even have the decency to look away, to pretend she wasn't watching Sylvaine, waiting to see the ferral fail.

There wasn't anything to do about it. Sylvaine knew the script: close her eyes, breathe in and then, nothing. Except, maybe, distant laughter.

Still, there was the slickdust. The lingering aftertaste sat in her mouth, bitter, almost spicy. Besides that, there was no difference. She felt as she had always felt. There was no surge of energy, no gurgle of imbibed knowledge floating in her stomach. There was the machine and her.

No sense in delaying. She took her glove and replaced its small fuel vial with fresh æther-oil, as if that would make any difference. She closed her eyes and held out her hand.

Envision the spark. Envision the spark.

She looked into herself expecting nothing. Instead she found something. It was indefinable, a warmth maybe, or a vibration, an intense thought. It moaned and groaned, shook and rumbled. She felt heat in her veins, as if her blood had caught fire. This something flowed to her glove where it felt like a piece of the sun burning out of her fingertips.

The energy was painful, felt even a bit hateful, as if it was only grudgingly following her will, but what energy it was! She ignored these thoughts, just focused on the machine, on its inert circuits. Then, suddenly, her hand shook. She opened her eyes to watch a bright red bolt curve from her finger into the machine.

With a hum, her generator came to life.

She stared. Blinked. Stared again. It wasn't possible.

A fellow student walked by, nodded a vague congratulations, then stopped and turned back, realizing who had sparked the machine. His eyebrows turned to a question, and Sylvaine couldn't answer. Slowly she turned the dial on her machine. It shook, and for a moment she was afraid it would shoot smoke and die out on her, but then, it stilled itself. Æther-oil from the tank on the side poured into the long cylinder of the negative-density generator, and the machine started to creak, then hum, then lift off the table.

"What in all infernal assery?"

It was Rostialva's voice, and with her curse those left in the room turned to stare at Sylvaine's machine. The negative-density generator was working! Too well, she realized suddenly, as it floated up and up to bump against the ceiling. She hadn't attached the proper safety chains; she never had the faith she would need them. It was too far up now, wedging in the pipework of the ceiling. Unless...

She raised up her glove, sucked in, searched for something, and again found it. Reacting to the sparks of her glove, the chains sitting around desk flung themselves up and welded themselves to the machine.

No, she chided herself, nothing flings itself, welds itself. *She* welded it, *she* pulled it down with a pull of æther, *she* repaired the scratches on the hull of the machine with a wave of her hand, and let it float up the height *she* desired.

"Amazing," a student said.

"I would have never believed it." Another.

They were as blown away as she was, unable to believe that a ferral could...

"I had a similar design, you know," the first voice.

"Liar," the second. "You would claim to have built Icaria itself if no one would correct you."

"Yeah, well, I have to admit this is going to make my auto-miner look a bit underwhelming."

Their words weren't focused on her. All thoughts were on the machine.

Sylvaine heard laughter. It took her a moment to realize it was her own.

A few days later Sylvaine accepted an invitation to lunch with Lazarus Roache. They met at *The Cable*, a restaurant built in the shadows of one of the gargantuan suspension cables that tethered the city to the mountainside. It was more upscale than Sylvaine was used to, Bastillian cuisine, full of rich creams and towers of tiny pastries, all far beyond the wallet of a student.

"On me, of course," Lazarus said.

The pastries weren't the topic of conversation, though Sylvaine savored the custard tarts. Instead they went on about the workshop, Sylvaine's machine, and the miraculous effect of the slickdust.

Lazarus took a sip of tea and smiled. "What did I tell you? You should have more faith in yourself, Sylvaine. You need to see the things in you that I see."

She blushed. "It really impressed Professor Gearswit. Not just because I had made something functional, but he was impressed by the generator itself. He said, well, he had the same opinion your friend had."

"Gath knows talent when he sees it," Lazarus said. "Your professor is wise to look past the details of the slickdust."

"Well..." Sylvaine said. "I didn't actually mention that. It's just..." she wasn't sure why she had kept it a secret, but it just seemed unthinkable. As if it would stain her first true engineering victory.

"It's just that you are bright enough to know how people would react," Lazarus said, pouring her another glass. "They'd use it as some excuse, as if it should matter. Slickdust does nothing but heighten the potential you already have, it would be foolish to let another use it as some pretense to undermine you."

Sylvaine nodded, sipping, wondering if she would agree with them.

"Sylvaine," Lazarus said, "talent is talent, every engineer uses tools. If you must keep yours secret, don't feel guilty about it. Your work defines you, not how you came to it."

She swallowed, feeling the warmth in her stomach, and tasting the wisdom of the man's words. "Yes. It just all happened so quickly. One day I was a pen's dash away from failure, the next that very same professor is introducing me as his greatest prodigy."

Sylvaine looked up at the great negative-density towers that loomed over the city, and then at the cable that gave their table shade, its far ends installed deep into the mountainside.

"I think he has that stereotypical engineer's dream," Sylvaine said, "that someday Icaria will fly again. I can't say I share it. But at least it'll get my project some attention."

"Yes. Yes." Lazarus nodded. "But leave the old dreams to old fools." He sipped. "You know, there's a job working for me if you're interested. Javad is already on board, but we could use someone with your talent."

Sylvaine twisted her hair, an act more of anxiety than flirtation. "I'm not sure. I need to finish my studies."

She felt cornered, afraid to disappoint Lazarus. It surprised her how important impressing him seemed to matter, but she also couldn't leave before she had proved herself officially as an engineer. She took in his gaze, a mask without clear emotion. Sweat formed at the pores of her fur, had she ruined everything? Would Lazarus leave her, and take the slickdust? Could she lose it all?

Then he laughed, and all was right again.

"Of course. I wouldn't want to interrupt your studies, or worse, have you think I just introduced you to slickdust to get an employee. No, you're more than that, Sylvaine, and the fact that I can help push you the extra step is enough for me."

Sylvaine smiled back, not even hiding the sharp tips of her canines.

"You know," she said, taking a nibble of her tart, "Gearswit said he was going to sponsor my project at the Academy Exhibition in three weeks. Half the engineers in the city will be there." She knew that when they saw her with her generator they wouldn't see a ferral, wouldn't see a beast. They would see an engineer, same as any other.

"Wonderful!" Lazarus clapped. "Which reminds me." He presented a yellow paper bag. "A gift for you."

Sylvaine opened the bag and pulled out an indigo cloth. It was a dress, embroidered with abstract shapes and designs, giving the impression of an engineer's drawing. In its neck sat a pin in the shape of a hammer centered among the teeth of a gear: the Insignia of the Guild, in greater detail than she had ever seen, covered in gold leaf.

"Oh, I can't, I mean I don't..." Sylvaine stammered, staring at the dress. She had tried wearing dresses when she was young, but all it did was increase the mockery, 'Look, the monkey's playing dress-up!'

"...I'm not sure something like that would work on me," she finally concluded.

"Nonsense," Lazarus said, "it would look great on you."

Sylvaine glanced at the busy street to her right. Even in the bustle of Icaria, where everyone had three things on their mind at once and were jogging because they were five minutes late, some still took the time give a confused glance to the ferral holding a dress.

"People would think..." she began.

"Who cares what people would think!" he interrupted, grabbing her hand suddenly. "People are idiots who only see what they want to see. It doesn't matter what they think, they don't matter, only you matter." Lazarus smiled perfect marble teeth. "So come on, try the dress."

His words were as silky as the cloth, and Sylvaine found herself examining the dress again. Perhaps he was right, she had spent her whole life worrying what random strangers would think, how they would see her, and it hadn't helped her a moment. They saw what they wanted to see. She had brought life to metal, a task said impossible for Ferrals, but now it was easy as opening a door.

Lazarus was the only one who understood what she was capable of, and she had proved him right. Those people on the street, those people who had mocked her, they could think what they want, because they didn't matter in the end.

"Okay!" Sylvaine said, with confidence that she didn't know she possessed.

Chapter 11

It was long past evening by the time Marcel made it back to Huile proper. A junker autocab took him to the gate just in time to make the last trolley ride. It was largely empty, only night workers and half-wasted Huile-folk back from a night of cheap booze and cards.

Marcel's muscles groaned, and his head felt stuffed with dust, which the fresher air of the city was unable to clear away. The short expedition had worn him down, with its claustrophobic hallways and sharp discourse. He found his head bobbing in dyssynchrony with the rattling trolley, his juggled theories dropping from his mind as it slumped towards the black borders of sleep.

He leaned his head onto the window, and found himself, in panicked jolts, back in the darkened passageways under Lazacorp. Memories once stomped deep grabbed up at him. He could feel the gas mask, hear the screams. Blurry pain rushed over him as he felt his leg burning away to nothing.

A stone in the track was able to knock him back into coherence, and he gripped on to wakefulness. The meandering corridors and acrid-scented machinery had dug up more than he realized, but he wouldn't let himself fall back into old terrors. With this lingering fear came a hint of embarrassment, he was still in his twenties; had his vigor abandoned him already?

On a normal night he'd be in bed by now, and his squeaking mattress called for him. It would be so easy to take an early stop, stumble home, fold into his bed's worn sheets, and let the mystery sleep.

Peacetime's monotony had in two years starved away his night owl youth. After classes in Phenia University he would spend hours drinking and singing at Madame Vin's Cinderbird, swapping exaggerated tales of drunken exploits or overwrought political diatribes while watching the exotic twirls of dancers hailing from all corners of the explored world, from Vidish forests valleys to the distant plains of Khulizwe. Or, if not that, then he would wander the endless dockworks, where great iron behemoths spewed out both steam and workers long past midnight. Or he would hit up a show, live or cinegraph, artistic or bawdy, or just pass out on a friend's floor.

Even when he had been trekking the Border States with Desct, before the two had heard about the brewing conflict in Huile and decided, on an inebriated oath, that their destiny lay to the north, he would hike through abandoned hilltop ruins well past nightfall, or explore tantalizingly perverse midnight quarters of cities whose official allegiance with the United Confederacy had not deterred them from opening their gates to the more spendthrift of raider-folk.

Desct would have given him Inferno for napping now, and Alba... thinking of what she'd say spun his guts in a knot.

As the trolley turned down Viexus Boulevard, Marcel pulled the chain and hopped out. He jogged the last metres to City Hall, where all but the lights of the grand atrium sat dim. There, at a desk beneath the story-tall Banner of the Phoenix, he found a young policeman, who informed him that Lambert had gone in for the night.

"If it's an emergency," the man said, "I could ring Mr. Henra up. I mean, it might take a minute to get a warrant."

"He already got me one." Marcel waved the document, too tired for patience. "I just need access for the apartment complex on Twelve-Fifty-One Durand Street."

The cop looked over the paper, his eyebrows furrowed.

"Well, I should probably get my captain, I think."

"Never mind," Marcel muttered, taking the papers back. He grunted out an empty thanks and jogged down the steps out into the street.

After searching around the street for an idling streetcab that wasn't there, he walked the half-kilometre to Fareau's apartment. Maybe it would matter, most likely it wouldn't, but he wasn't going to wait the night. He held down a shiver of thrill that he hadn't felt since Desct's death, and to be honest, a good while before that.

Perhaps he would have had more excitement in his life if he had remained closer with Desct, if the two hadn't let their separate careers and sour memories of wartime push them apart. Perhaps the memories wouldn't have been so painful if they had only fought in the Battle of Huile Field, if the Sewer Rats hadn't been assigned to Roache's eleventh hour plan. Perhaps then Alba would have stayed, and perhaps the others would have lived and...

No, he was on business, regrets were for personal time.

Fareau's apartment was housed in one of Lazarus's new complexes; seven stories tall, almost a skyscraper by Huile standards. The darkened leadlight that arched over the front entryway displayed a discordant scene, bellowing shriekbirds, weaving grapevines, great oak trees, and men in antiquated autoarmor.

Marcel pulled out a military grade lockpick. One of the rewards of urban-recon training was a practical expertise in breaking and entering. And one of the benefits of a war hero status was that no one had ever confiscated Marcel's equipment. It took him a few minutes, but soon he prodded the tumblers in place, and the door slid open.

He strolled through the well-lit but unmanned foyer and took the far stairway up. He wasn't sure exactly what he'd be looking for, but his luck had always held strong during previous investigations. Documentation was a common hook; more than one Principate spy had been found out with a stack of letters, or detailed logbook. One idiot had even kept a personal journal, a moronic feat of self-incrimination.

As Marcel reached the sixth floor, he noticed a flash of light from under an otherwise darkened door. *62*, read the copper letters. Marcel slunk slowly up. He pressed his ear by the keyhole. Footsteps, a single pair, heavy, and the clatter of objects tossed to the floor. Someone was making a mess in there.

Marcel put down his bag, pulled out his Frasco six-shooter, and loaded it. The door was wooden and didn't look all that strong. He braced himself with one arm against the stairway banister. There were upsides to having a metal leg.

A quick kick. The door splintered and flew open, Marcel stumbling in after, pistol out.

"Get down on the ground!" he shouted.

The handtorch light flashed towards him, blinding. A chair was flung past his head, and Marcel jumped for cover, firing off two bullets, as he landed behind a couch.

"Gall! If that's you, come easy. It'll be better for both of us that way," Marcel shouted.

There was a crack and what sounded like a mechanical groan or a distant scream. The couch burst into a strange vivid darkness. Marcel jumped back, suddenly aware of an intense heat. The couch was on fire!

He dashed around it, to the back of a small table, and aimed. The figure was running out a broken window, smashing the last pieces of glass as he leapt down the fire escape. Marcel couldn't get a good glance at the man; he was large, with a hooded jacket covering up his features.

He thought about chasing for a moment—he had his pistol, and a glance was all he needed, but the flames demanded his attention.

The living room lit up from the crackling light. He rushed past the nearby kitchen nook and into the small bedroom where he found a taurhide leather duvet on the unmade bed. He grabbed it, sprinted back, and tossed it onto the couch, pushing it down to snuff out all air.

Half a minute later, Marcel peeled off the leather to reveal a couple burnt cushions but not much else.

He kneeled down and sniffed, shuddering. Sangleum. He hadn't seen what lit it, and there was no sign of a match or lighter. The only plausible theory he could summon was that a spark from an ætherglove had done so. The strange thing is, he hadn't even recognized the flames as fire for a moment. It had seemed briefly to burn *black*.

Marcel rubbed his forehead, perhaps it had just been a burst of smoke, or the manifestations of weary eyes, he was damn tired. He got up and grabbed the light his assailant had dropped. He wanted to label the figure as Gall, but he couldn't be positive, all he had been able to make out was that the intruder had been generally largish.

A few waves of the handtorch made it clear that whoever the man had been he had torn up the place in a frenzy. It wasn't a large or well-furnished apartment, just a cabinet, a couch, some cooking utensils, a closet-sized bathroom, and a bedroom, but the place looked as though some wild animal had been set loose. Two metal boxes lay on the floor, one still locked. The other had its padlock shattered, the papers it had been holding sprawled out. Those closest to the couch were burnt, a few more pages had been scattered by the scramble, fluttering about by the broken window. It was clear enough what the intruder had been looking for.

Marcel holstered his pistol and searched the apartment. The man's living quarters were sparse. Gileon clearly had not been much of a reader, judging by the empty shelves. Nor, despite his supposed inebriation at death, was there much evidence of the man being a drinker. Marcel was only able to find a lone, half-filled bottle of "Trolltears" pale ale on the side of the kitchen sink. The trash was mostly rotten foodstuff, and Fareau's wardrobe held only a couple of hanging garments.

There was another box of the same design under the man's bed. These two still-locked boxes were easily picked, and like the smashed box, each overflowed with documents and stationery.

He gathered the papers up and took the pile downstairs, where he was able to find a vocaphone in a back office. He made a quick call to Lambert, whose voice cleared from a relaxed grog at the news of the flame-tossing burglar. Lambert hung up to call his men, while Marcel sat down to inspect his prize.

A good third were damaged fragments. Of those remaining many were technical drawings, schematics, and notes, of which a good number did not seem to be in Gileon's handwriting. Marcel squinted at the esoteric drawings and realized what seemed so familiar. They were near identical to those that had found the way onto his desk a few weeks back. They were blueprints of the water treatment facility.

He put those to the side, best to leave them to one who could read them, and started on the letters.

"...know a scrap-trader, associated with the Taur Maw gang. Get the pipes in from him, and they'll burst within a week. Can make that last at least a month."

Marcel compared the handwriting to Gileon's original letter. Mismatch. He lifted up one of the schematics. He was no expert, but the rough slanted l's and the general harshness of the writing seem to fit. As he suspected, the bottom of these notes were labeled, in the same scribble: *C. Gall.*

Among these were receipts written on browning waste-paper, with Gileon Fareau's signature. Marcel didn't know how much complex machinery cost, but the prices listed were in mere handfuls of frascs, the value of scrap-metal. Combined with these were receipts of transactions in the other direction, with Gileon playing salesman.

It hit Marcel quick. Fareau had been selling the real parts and replacing them with scrap.

He dug through the documents at a fevered pace. Lots of back and forth, between Gall and Fareau, starting friendly, with a bit of an eagerly conspiratorial air, holding quite a few references to *"bleeding these idiots dry"* and *"making a fortune enough to embarrass a caravan-lord."*

Then the letters took a grimmer, more hesitant, tone. *"...could get people hurt..." "...beyond what we agreed..." "...not sure about this..."* all in Gileon's hand. Gall responded with fury: *"...don't need you..." "...gutless coward..." "...keep your damned mouth shut!"*

Beneath these were drafts of the letter Lambert had shown to Marcel, for Lazarus, signed Gileon Fareau, with words crossed out, rewritten in anxious script. Some referenced to imminent danger, other made mention of the water treatment plant by name.

Marcel pushed aside a few more drafts to find a notepad. Here too the man was indecisive, scribbling down simple sentences in oversized letters. *Bring To The Police* with a line through it. *Sabotage!!!* scratched out.

Then beneath them, circled and underlined: *Show To An Engineer!*

Marcel could hear the shouts in the next room, Corvin Gall's violent incredulity echoing over the dispassionate words of his interrogator. Lambert looked through the letters, which he splayed across his heavy desk, beside his steaming mug of maroon tea.

"A scam," he muttered, "switching in broken parts and selling the good ones."

Marcel nodded. "Seems that way."

"Keep the profits off the stolen goods, maintain Gall's job security and healthy paychecks." Lambert rubbed the corner of his eye. "You know Mr. Roache had complained to me privately about the costs of the water treatment venture. Necessary, of course, for the city's good, but it's clear now how it became such a money sink."

Marcel sat on the dark oak desk, spinning one of Lambert's intricately decorated, imported Tyrissian pens around in his fingers. "Until Gileon Fareau got spooked. Until it became too real, and he wasn't willing to bring in faulty parts that might get someone killed. Tried to find a way to whisper past the ears of Gall, sent Roache the note, sent me the schematics."

"Good thing he did." Lambert gestured to several pages of said schematics. "Imagine if the plant went to opening day in these conditions. Old pipes of sangleum leaking into the water, good citizens could have well been poisoned."

If only Gileon hadn't been too afraid of being found out himself, if only he had been brave enough to say it straight, then maybe the man would still be alive.

More shouts reverberated, Gall's muffled screams of "liar," "ass-licker," "griffon-fucker," and "stiffland-shitgorger" making it through the walls.

"I don't think the man will be all that helpful," Lambert said, sipping. "But the case is strong."

Marcel idly looked over the office while he thought. It was well furnished, though not to his taste. The walls were decorated primarily with framed photographs of Lambert standing beside the few people in Huile who could be considered celebrities, as well as several paintings of Kaimark landscapes, sharp hills and dense black-green trees, most likely left from the Principate occupation.

"It would have been trivial for an engineer to fake the collapse..." Marcel said, as he tapped the pen on his knee, uneasy, despite his words. There was clear evidence plenty, overwhelming reasons to be suspicious, but no undeniable proof.

"Well, we have the means and the motivation," Lambert said, organizing the scattered notes, "and you saw him break into Fareau's apartment."

"I saw *someone*," Marcel corrected.

"A large man who could ignite æther-oil from a distance. Anyone else in the city who matches that description?"

"You keep better track of that than me," Marcel said, lifting himself off.

Lambert chuckled. "The answer is no. And we found the man preparing to flee last night."

Marcel tried to smile. "Thanks for that."

"Huile's finest do their duty with speed." Lambert laughed. Then, studying Marcel's worried eyes, said: "Come now, you don't need to put on such a serious face. The case is strong, you did a damn impressive job."

Marcel paced a bit, ending up beside Lambert, where he eyed the notes. It all made enough sense as it was, but he couldn't toss aside the feeling there was something he was missing.

"I think Verus might have been involved," he said.

Lambert leaned back on his leather chair. "Why?"

"He..." Marcel tapped his fingers. "... acted suspicious. Rude, bitter, slow, had to squeeze every answer out of him."

"Nothing new there," Lambert chuckled. "I've dealt with him more than you, Marcel, and I'll admit the man keeps his cards to his chest. Combine that with his general incivility... No, I'm being too gentle, his ass-headedness...."

Both men shared a quick laugh.

"...I can understand your suspicions," Lambert finished.

But there was more to it than that. That mutant who had snuck him the scrap of newspaper. Just like Gileon, he had been unwilling to talk straight, afraid, presumably, to be overheard.

"You interview the mutant workers?" Marcel asked.

"Quite a number, in fact," Lambert said. "Knew nothing of use. As for Verus, well, no one *loves* the man, but he's professional and civil enough."

Marcel leaned back on the wall. "Could Gileon have sent away the schematics to keep them out of Verus's hands?"

"To avoid his own incrimination?"

"Well sure..." Marcel said. No, that checked out. "Roache never mentioned the fact that I returned the stolen schematics to Verus."

Lambert nodded. "They would have gone back to Gall, he told me of his suspicions of that man. Can't say I agree with the way he handles his foreman, but Roache has a good sense of character."

Marcel pushed himself up and paced again. All the pieces fit neatly in place, but Verus sat outside the puzzle. Perhaps that monk Lazarus mentioned... no, now Marcel was just grasping at straws.

"Don't think I'm dismissing your instincts, Marcel," said Lambert with a shake of his head. "Quite the opposite. I think Verus wants as few eyes on him as possible, more a pride thing than anything illicit, but it poses a problem. This case seems clear and clean now, but it can become something out of Inferno if he fights us on it."

"You think that'll be an issue?" Marcel asked.

The vocaphone rang, and Lambert grabbed the mouthpiece. After a few seconds of whispered conversation, he hung up. "Well, it's time for us to find out."

A minute later Verus opened the door. The foreman walked with his back straight, motions smooth and reserved, thoroughly unlike himself. He sat down across the table, and gave his approximation of a pleasant grin.

"I heard that there have been some... allegations made against one of our employees."

Marcel tapped his finger on the desk. "When I interviewed you yesterday you claimed that Fareau had not asked for any change in shift, yet I have, myself, a letter declaring that the man did exactly that, fearing for his life."

Lambert patted Marcel on the shoulder, "We don't need to start with accusations."

"It is all right," Verus said, smile unmoving, like a painted mask. "There was a mistake on my end. In fact, later last night I checked my records and found there was indeed such a request. Alas, it got lost in the paperwork. These things happen."

"And you claimed he was an alcoholic, that he was drunk the night he died."

Verus folded his hands, not letting his gaze leave Marcel's. "And he was. I can find you friends of his to confirm this."

"In the man's apartment, I found barely a drop of alcohol," Marcel said.

"I never said he was a... collector." Verus's laugh sounded like rusting gears struggling to move, "I would guess that he drank at bars."

"Now, now," Lambert said, "this is all good conversation, but we must get to the heart of the matter. Corvin Gall."

Marcel tapped the desk, staring Verus down. The foreman merely pushed his strained excuse for a smile to the wrinkled edge of his face. Marcel sighed. "Yes, Gall."

"You must understand," Verus began, "that I have some questions—"

"I have a few questions first," Lambert said, with sudden speed and force. He lifted up his notebook, pen in hand, and before Verus could respond, asked: "Were you aware that Mr. Fareau had been stealing equipment?"

"No," Verus said. "Treachery like that would never have been tolerated at Lazacorp."

"But the documentation is indisputable that such theft occurred," Lambert said. Verus blinked, and opened his mouth, but Lambert continued. "And did you have any awareness of ongoing sabotage?"

Verus's eye shot back and forth. "We've duly informed City Hall about the delays in this project."

Lambert raised an eyebrow. "And the reasons for it?"

"Well..." Verus stammered, glancing up at Marcel. "We haven't been able to pin down exactly—The details are Lazacorp matters."

Marcel tried not to smile, it was unprofessional and inappropriate to the situation. But there was significant enjoyment to suppress, watching Verus wiggle under Lambert's grilling.

"There is a clear reason here," Lambert said, gesturing to the letters. "If we are not certain we'd have to do a more thorough investigation on the Lazacorp premises."

Verus's fake smiled fell. "I see what you're doing. It is low."

"Then you concur with our assessment about your engineer?" Lambert asked.

Verus stared down at the floor for a moment. Then a second moment. He bobbed his head slowly, until it became a spiritless nod. "Yes. He must be the cause of all this. It seems the man tricked even I."

"And you'll sign an agreement of that?" Lambert thrust forward a form forward, offering his own pen. Marcel couldn't help but be a little impressed, his normally leisurely friend could move fast when on the hunt.

Verus took the pen as if it were discarded offal and read over the form. Finally, silently, he signed it.

"Excellent. I think the case is settled." Lambert smiled, leaning back. "We will have Gall sent south to Ordone for trial."

"Ordone!" Any last veneer of Verus's civility snapped, his face twisting into a snarl. "You're not going to try him here?"

"The extent and severity of Gall's crimes goes beyond the norm for a small city such as ours," Lambert said. "He must be tried in a court system better suited to handling complex cases such as this."

Marcel's smirk was irrepressible. Perhaps Verus had been planning something, but by the look on the man's face, he had been outplayed left and right by Lambert.

"This is an unusual decision," Verus said, in a tone that implied less civil words.

"It is an unusual case."

Verus stared Lambert down, single eye piercing with the same sharpness he had unleashed on Marcel. Lambert smiled, as if he didn't even notice, and the foreman finally relented.

"Very well," Verus said, "but there is one issue I must discuss. There are the documents. Records and notes about the water treatments plant, some you have gathered here, some that were on Gall himself, which your men... took for evidence, I believe the lingo would be." He tried to force one last smile. "I can assure you that these have no relevance for your investigation. If they could be returned—"

"I'm afraid that's impossible," Lambert said.

Verus tilted his head. "They are Lazacorp property. Without them our project will be delayed even further."

Marcel watched the two men. Verus's face projected calm, but his fingers writhed wildly, like a knot of worms. Lambert did not give any hint that he was perturbed, sipping his tea.

"Yes, I am aware," Lambert said, "and we have sent notice to Lazarus Roache up in Icaria. When he returns and we finish our investigation, we can get both your confirmations and then return the relevant documents."

"You have been speaking to Roache," Verus said.

"We were in communication."

Verus stood up suddenly, abandoning all efforts to maintain a composed demeanor. "Yes. Yes, I see how it is." He turned to Marcel, his smile a blatant sneer. "And you, Mr. Talwar. I must congratulate you. Such *vision* you had, to discover this all by yourself. Very impressive. You have done a great service, and I thank you for opening my eye."

With that the man was gone, door clanging behind him. The interview had been quick and precise, like a Resurgence bushwhack ambush. Marcel sat back down on the vacated chair, noticing the now-tired shouts of Gall murmur out, barely audible. His smirk dissipated slowly, as he waited for the thrill of victory to come.

And waited.

But it didn't come.

Lambert clapped his hands, "I think that went rather well!"

Chapter 12

The days seemed warmer in Icaria, the night sky silkier, the hum of the traffic more musical, the rhythm of Sylvaine's footsteps more soothing, all since the day she had met Lazarus Roache. Her schedule had not changed significantly—work, school, study, repeat—but now instead of passing out with a textbook as a pillow in her hanging shack, she slept in an apartment two floors below Lazarus's penthouse, rented out from the man for a mere pittance.

In between classes she would work in the penthouse itself, on both assignments and her own personal projects. Her extra credit for Gearswit fell by the wayside; in the frenzy of her new life, she had even lost some of the papers, but her professor did not care one iota. He agreed that her time was better spent focused on exploring the theoretical possibilities presented by her negative-density generator. On this matter, she was often supervised by Lazarus's gadgeteer friend, Gath Melikoff. Though the man was as gruff as ever, he did seem to take genuine interest in her work, which was a novel, but entirely pleasing, phenomenon.

At times, Sylvaine found herself struggling with the æthermantics. Her glove would not follow her commands, stubbornly inert despite her mental screams. Or worse it would take gears that were meant to be simply adjusted and instead melt them into a useless pile with an unintentionally forceful bolt of æther. At these times she'd slip back into old fears, that she wasn't meant to be doing this, that she was a ferral playing at a human's game. Then, sure as the ringing of an Icarian clocktower, Lazarus would appear, a vial of slickdust in hand.

A supplemented drink or a few sniffs later, and everything would be in order. How sweet the song slickdust sang in her veins. Its warmth flowed to her very core, heating her to flight. Floating, she felt like air, lighter even. She felt like the city itself as she worked, as if she too flew above all the mess and dirt of the world. Slickdust was the fuel for her destiny.

With Lazarus' hand on her shoulder and his wonder-drug flowing through her veins, Sylvaine performed acts that the ignorant would call magic, giving form to metal, purpose to scrap. Whenever she had doubts, or saw a beast in the mirror, she would take some slickdust, and then, standing in front of her, would appear the woman she knew she was: an engineer.

At the Academy, she found herself elevated from a near dropout to the focus of acclaim and jealousy. Her own creation caused all to marvel, herself included, and the machine easily held tight the attention of everyone who bore witness to it. Old men and tired-eyed students who would have never given her a second look, unless to gawk at her ears and claws, now huddled together to study her negative-density generator. Gearswit even pulled her aside after workshop to talk, with the closest the man could display to glee, about the updates and proceedings of the yearly Academy Exhibition, as well as the gossip of his peers. It was quickly becoming clear to all in the know that Sylvaine would be the star of the show.

Sylvaine never did mention the slickdust to her professor, or anyone else. She considered it, but whenever the topic of her sudden Knack started to flow its way into conversation, through idle talk, or burning curiosity, she found herself steering clear with a social adroitness she didn't know she possessed, bringing up some in vogue innovation, or bouncing away with a joke, or even half-feigning insult at the idea of the topic itself.

Lazarus commended her taciturnity when she sheepishly mentioned one such conversation.

"I know how people are; they will look for any excuse to dismiss the extraordinary," the man said, tapping the edge of his teacup, mixing tendrils of red and white.

"What do you mean?" Sylvaine asked, leaning back in one of Lazarus's large leather chairs, inspecting the sandwich platter on his luncheon table.

Lazarus sipped and shook his head, "You are the first ferral engineer in recorded Guild history. They may credit you with your discoveries, but if you admitted that you took slickdust? It would be seen as reason to dismiss your accomplishments."

"Gearswit isn't like that." Sylvaine took a bite, chewed, and put down the pulled lamb sandwich. "But is that true? That it is the drug?"

Lazarus laughed. "Trust in yourself, Sylvaine! Slickdust can't do anything but awaken what's already inside of you. And, unfortunately, I am quite sure your professor *is* like that, damn near everyone is in this city. Even if he's unusually generous, if you go talking, soon slickdust will be the story, not you, not your invention. So, trust me and keep it to yourself. For now."

Sylvaine thought on this, and nodded, "If you say so."

"Namter, some tea for our guest." Lazarus snapped his fingers. The middle-aged butler with the eye bags of a centenarian lowered the earpiece of a rotary vocaphone.

"Apologies sir, but your 'visitor' has been seen near Wrenchstern Station."

"Ah, well." Lazarus stood up with a grumble and walked to a cabinet. "Best you greet him."

"I just wonder, sometimes," Sylvaine laughed, all nerve and no humor, "why someone like you, I mean, someone so successful and busy, would spend so much time helping someone like me."

Lazarus laughed. "Haven't you heard of a patron? It's only right that a man like me should notice talent and cultivate it!"

She felt herself blush, but it was true, she was talented. That was undeniable, and even if she wanted to deny it, Lazarus' voice wouldn't allow it. It was so sure, so confident, so uncontradictable.

"That's right. I'm sure I'll make you proud with my project." It was a strange and intoxicating confidence that flowed through Sylvaine's veins. She liked it.

"I can drink to that," he said. And they did.

Her favorite moments, the ones she savored, were not her achievements at the Academy, or even her long hours of work, wrist deep in machine parts, which had previously been the few times in her life that she could declare herself happy. Instead, they were the quieter moments with Lazarus as they took gentle strolls around the city or long, meandering walks would wind up the carved slope of Mount Icaria. She would share her dreams, her ambitions, intricate plans of invention and creation, and in response he would tell her his own stories, dozens of them, of his journeys, his investments, his triumphs. If he were any other man she wouldn't believe the tales, but with Lazarus anything was possible. It was impressive that the man had accomplished so much in such a short time, considering that he looked like he could be no more than thirty.

Sylvaine wanted to do more with the man, walk further, alone, away from the eyes of the city. What she would do then... well, she pushed those thoughts out of her head; they were unprofessional. Instead, she contented herself with holding Lazarus' hand as they walked, sometimes his arm, though she never pulled too closely. At times, she desired to get as close to the man as she could, to feel her hair against his skin, but whenever she walked a tad too near, by intention or unconscious desire, he'd move back, laugh, change the subject. She'd blush but he seemed not to notice. It was, she knew, for the best; he had supported her as a patron, and she would use his support to create machines to rival all the creations of Icaria. It was only in her softer moments, that she wondered if a man like him could love a woman like her.

Chapter 13

As his master played patron, perused the political parties and dinner tables of Icaria's high society, and ingratiated himself with any he might take advantage of, Hieronymus Lealtad Namter worked.

Namter worked every minute of every hour of every day, apart from those necessary for the basic and unpleasant upkeep of life. So far today he had had to: prepare Roache's breakfast, organize a meeting for Kauf's colleagues, clean up the kitchen, send orders to his Unblind Brothers, prepare morning tea, organize Roache's notes on new opportunities in Icaria, pay the heating bills, send a letter reminding Roache's allies in the Crimson Eye raiders that dalliance meant treachery and treachery meant death, order pastries for a luncheon, tally slickdust supplies, sign forms requesting a leave of taxes from the UCCR (a mere formality), feed the prisoners, send an inquest into Unblind recruiting efforts in the outer Wastes, clean the bathroom, send for a plumbing engineer, greet the ferral, hang her work coat, and read a letter sent from Verus.

It was this final task that had distressed him the most. In this letter, with his characteristic straightforwardness, Verus accused

Roache of setting his engineer, one Corvin Gall, up on false charges via the person of Mr. Talwar.

Namter knew such a letter was a long time coming and had dreaded the righteous indignation he knew would fly from Verus's hand. It was a necessity that the engineer who worked on their upcoming Enterprise was indisputably loyal, Namter understood this clearly. The possibility of sabotage, or worse still escape, was not something they could risk. He had wished this matter of hiring practices might have been settled diplomatically between his two masters, but Roache saw diplomacy as a weapon, and Verus had never understood the concept in the first place.

The pair had been picking at each other for some time, chafing under their forced company and necessary alliance. In his letter, Verus insisted that this recent act had gone too far, that Roache would have to answer for his treachery when the man returned to Huile. It attempted to remind Roache, though Namter needed no such recollection, that they all served the same Master and that their actions were meant to function in harmony, not foment betrayal.

Namter had long been Roache's liaison to his "foreman" (as if the man were merely that!) due to their shared faith in the Brotherhood. It was a task Namter had once cherished. Verus, the great Awakener, had opened Namter's eyes to the perversity of mankind, their deep and fundamental spiritual rot. Verus had taught him the doctrines of punishment and subservience, the only road to reconciliation between humanity and their proper, pure, and truly divine sovereigns. This creed had spoken to Namter in a way the hollow words of the Church of the Ascended never had, with their banal and toothless insistence that humanity was, in its essence, divine. The world was rotting, anyone with eyes could see it, but only Verus could explain why.

It would have been easier and more pleasant to ignore Roache, and to speak with Verus directly, but one did not choose one's place in the order of the world. Namter had his obligations, and despite the long hours, despite the dismissive words of Lazarus Roache, despite the way everyone, even that foul ferral girl, looked at him as if he were a mere domestic, he would perform his duty. It was Verus' own teachings of complete obedience that forced Namter's hand on this matter, compelled him to treat his once spiritual mentor with cold distance. Namter did not miss the bitter irony of his position.

So he took pen to paper and wrote the necessary reply, a vague and useless denial, with the promise for further communication upon Roache's return to Huile. Their time in Icaria was almost complete, and Namter prayed that soon they would all be realigned upon their proper, divinely mandated, task.

"Namter, some tea please." Roache tapped his pen on the wood, his spread of notes covering an eighth of the long table. Beside him his ferral client worked away under the watch of Gath Melikoff.

"Of course, sir." Namter nodded and started the kettle.

"No, no, that's off-track," Gath said. "What you got to focus on is the æther modulation. That's what we... where *you* have opportunities for real innovation."

As the kettle bubbled, Namter wiped off the thin layer of ash-speckled dust that had formed since the morning upon the windowsill. Icaria being higher than the plains of the Wastes, he had hoped that the air here would be cleaner, but the smoke of industry meant Namter's lesser duties were without end.

He pocketed the rag and took a rare free moment to glance out the window. The city lay below him, each tower a monument to hubris, the streets open sewers of narcissistic bustle. Men drove multi-legged vehicles and overloaded autocars, each machine a vile manifestation of the metropolis' ego. Even the far mountainside was infected with the rusting growth of Icaria.

The sound of clanging metal echoed out from behind the locked door. The ferral glanced up.

"Mechanical issues," Roache said. "Damn pump in there, giving us trouble." He shot his eyes towards Namter, a silent order. Namter gave no reaction, as was necessary when the ferral girl was here. By his reckoning she was an unnecessary experiment of his master's, proof that Roache's gift functioned even on the beast-blooded, as if such knowledge was remotely necessary to their task.

"I could try my hand at fixing it," the ferral said, eager to shove her nose in other people's business.

"No, no," Roache replied. "You have more important work. Come now, don't fall prey to silly distractions."

Namter drifted to the small cabinet where they kept the key to the mechanical room and the extra syringes of slickdust. He had to wait until the woman was good and occupied in her writing before taking out the necessary equipment.

Just then the vocaphone smashed its hammers against its bell, and Namter stepped over to answer it.

"*The Unblinking Eye Bleeds*," came a hoarse voice, in the sacred tongue.

"*And Through The Blood It Sees*," Namter whispered, glancing to make sure the ferral was focused on her notebooks.

"Favor to you, Watcher," came the voice of his Unblind Brother. "The scarred heathen has been found."

The kettle whistled and the woman scribbled. Namter pressed in his open ear.

"Speak quickly," Namter whispered, hoping not let his excitement leak out.

"His nest was a small apartment in the Underb—"

"Where is he now?" Namter interrupted.

Roache tapped his pen, over the whistle of steam. "Namter, the tea is ready."

"We contacted Kauf's friends in the police. Together we chased him to an old workshop on Spline Street. He frightened out the few workers there."

"Do you have it surrounded?" Namter kept his voice quiet and calm.

"Namter…" Roache muttered, tapping his pen like a conducting baton.

"Yes, Watcher. The police have interrogated the workers, we know he has no easy exit."

"I'll be there." Namter clanked down the receiver, before running over, and turning off the kettle. He poured the tea as quickly as he could manage without upsetting decorum. Roache watched the steam with wariness.

"A bit hot," he said.

"Apologies," Namter replied, "but I think it might be best if I take a temporary leave. Sir."

"Hmm?" Roache raised his eyebrows "You haven't even handled the water heater, err, pump."

The ferral did not notice the error, face down in her writings.

"Your 'visitor' has one last request. I think it below your dignity to bother with him yourself. If it is acceptable, I shall provide the necessary hospitality."

"Oh, yes?" Roache nodded, "Well, I suppose that does take precedence. I'll be glad to be finally done with this whole affair."

Namter did not smile until he had taken his cane and left the apartment. He too would be glad to finally end the nuisance posed by the monk Kayip.

A red autocar hummed its engines in front the apartment tower. Ewald Kauf waited beside the door, hands in his red vest pockets. He scowled when Namter walked out.

"Lazarus is not coming?" he asked.

Namter shook his head. "Just I."

Kauf's driver, an elderly man in a blue suit, rushed out to open the doors to the autocar. Kauf sat himself down. Namter followed, taking the back seat.

"He's had me keeping an eye out for his stalker for weeks," Ewald said, "and he won't even give me half an hour?"

The 'car started down the street.

"I can assure you, Mr. Kauf, that I am better suited to handle the current situation."

The politician grumbled something impolite. His manner might have bothered Namter a lifetime ago, before his eyes had been opened to the truths of the world, which left the petty bickering of men like Kauf beneath his attention. He had plenty of experience with those who imagined themselves climbing the stairs to the highest seat of power, men who didn't realize the only reason they had been brought along at all was because they had been the cheapest to buy. Namter himself had calculated a lowball offer, in sangleum contracts, to purchase the politician's loyalty and secrecy, and the man had barely bargained.

Kauf glanced back through the mirror. "You hurt your leg?" he asked, gesturing to the cane.

"It will be of use," was all that Namter replied. He watched the city blur by, men and women walking, mutants and other useless offshoots crowding the streets, golems, those pitiful mechanical mimics of men, carryings goods and directing traffic. Somehow Namter detested this city even more than Huile. The latter was simply a pit with pretensions. Icaria had tried to fly, to soar beyond the restraints set upon man. It had crashed, and it would fall further still.

Such thoughts were simply background clatter in Namter's mind. More central was Kayip. The man had been a nuisance for over six years now, shouting his bellicose vows of vengeance, murdering Lazacorp members and Unblind Brothers, attempting to rally opposition from whatever corners he could manage. A series of failures, of course, but the monk's attempt three or so years ago had caused quite a headache. They had been forced to foment a Principate coup, and then, when that went poorly, a Resurgence countercoup, just to keep their investments in Huile secured. Kayip was worse even than those Vapulus mutants who kept harassing Lazacorp's Waste-bound caravans, an open sore which hemorrhaged away profits, and suppurated innumerable stacks of paperwork.

It would be a welcome relief, with all the bickering between his masters, for Namter to finally put a close to the book of Kayip.

The autocar stopped at the edge of Icaria—*edge* here more literal than in most cities. Namter got out and spared a second to glance over the handrail at the end of the street. It was a sheer drop to the snow and scrap-adorned mountainside, marred only by the occasional outcroppings of the Underburg.

The workshop was an awkward box of a building, and surrounding it idled several police autocars, the mechanically augmented policemen armed and milling, watching the few windows for any sign of movement.

Kauf marched straight towards them, but Namter walked towards the other group: half a dozen men in hooded jackets who stood by the double doors to the warehouse.

"Greetings, Brother Watcher," the foremost, Brother Avitus, said.

They were rough-featured to a man, and, like Namter, had seen the world clearly, and knew it to be diseased. Several wore their hoods down, displaying without fear their sacred marking of the Eyes, and the unreadable letters of Truespeech. Each held, on the end of a long pendant string, an orb of Oathblood. Namter ignored a muffled stab of envy. Despite his relatively heightened position within the Brotherhood, he had never himself been marked, nor was it possible for him to carry around his own sacred orb. It was too risky in his position, and further, the markings and orb would have made Roache uncomfortable, with its imagined implication that Namter's loyalty might have fallen to Verus.

"Where is the false priest?" Namter asked.

"Somewhere inside," another Brother, Tullius, answered. "We sent in Pyotr and Valens." The man paused, looking towards the ground. "They were not sufficient."

Namter tapped his cane on the metal paneling that was Icaria's excuse for a sidewalk. Another infuriating product of his master's feud had been Roache's insistence that he vet the list of Unblind they took to Icaria. If Brother Tacticus or Mateo had been allowed to come, then this madman with a sword would have been long dealt with. Still, there was no good in idle complaints.

"Underway exits?" he asked.

Avitus knocked on the half-rusted wall. "According to the workers, this was never part of the city-ship proper, just a few walls and some windows put up a couple years ago. No basement, no access to the sewers. Unless the man has taken up engineering, he has to come out one of these entrances."

Namter nodded. Kauf and two policemen walked over, the latter pair eyeing Namter's Brothers with an emotion somewhere between concern and bemusement.

"We've installed a Shaftsworth's Fifteen-Hundred," the leftmost policeman said.

"A Shaftsworth's?" Namter asked.

"A motorgun," Avitus said, with a tone more often used when discussing animal excrement.

The cop snorted. "It is much more than that, it is a state-of-the-art anti-personnel weapon."

"It's a useless piece of junk!" Avitus interjected. "It didn't catch the monk when he went for Brother Valens, and your," he jabbed his finger at the policemen, "trigger-quick friend was the death of Pyotr."

"Our fine police force," Kauf said with up-curved lips, "usually works alone. If there were some mistakes, I'm sure it is merely due to the unusual situation we find ourselves in."

"Who are these guys anyway?" the policeman barked. "You know, Kauf, we appreciate your donations to the department, but you never said anything about some cloaked weirdos and their—"

Namter slammed his cane with an echoing clang that silenced the man. "Thank you, officer," he said, giving a short bow, "but you will remove your motorgun. I will handle the situation."

Seeming to truly notice him for the first time, the officer looked Namter up and down. The butler's black vest, straight-lined undershirt, and worn face must have made him seem even more out of place than his hooded companions. The officer glanced towards Kauf, who gave a noncommittal roll of his wrist.

"It's the only thing keeping the man pinned," the officer protested.

"For now," Namter said. "But I know this criminal. He does not care for his life; your men do. There is a better-than-not chance he will outwait them and find a chance to get the jump on them. Then we will not have a madman with a sword but a madman with a Shiftsworth, or whatever it was you called it."

Namter gestured toward Brother Tullius, who unfastened his orb of Oathblood and handed it to him. It was warm in Namter's grasp, and the man cracked the rarest of his expressions, a smile.

"Keep your men steady at the exits. I will remove this madman."

The inside of the workshop was darkened. The lines of hanging light bulbs had been smashed, likely by some thrown lug nut, their shards decorating the floor. The only source of light came from a few hazy, yellowed windows, behind which Namter could just make out the silhouettes of the policemen outside. He positioned himself between two of these windows, so that the light behind him might blind the monk who was skulking in the dark.

Namter stood at the end of small clearing, beyond which sat a jungle of darkened crates, conveyer belts, and inert machines, many riddled with bullet holes. In a dim crack between machinework, he could spy the corpse of Brother Valens, left arm a metre separate from his torso with his head completely missing. Somewhere in there hid the errant anchorite, the last grief-maddened remnant of a past expedition.

The policemen groaned as they lifted away the interwoven mess of brass cylinders that was apparently a motorgun. They had trouble at first believing their orders to move, and by their glance alone declared the butler insane, but it when all was cleared up they were more than happy to exit.

As soon as they closed the giant doors, Namter removed his right glove. He took out the orb of Oathblood in his deeply scarred hand. He breathed in and tightened his grasp in a sudden motion. The vial shattered instantly, glass jabbing and cutting, piercing into his palm and fingers. It stung a glorious kaleidoscope of pain, the Oathblood mixing with his own. He felt divine life shudder through his pitifully mortal frame, a shock of agony and ecstasy.

Namter lifted his lacerated hand, and with a silent prayer a burst of black flame materialized from his open wounds. He kept himself from marveling at the pulsating fire, which flickered like a chained beast, this wondrous boon of pain and fury blessed by hidden divinities. The fleeting thought that such a gift as Oathblood was used to fuel autocars and form slickdust, that idiots gave the holy substance a name as crude as sangleum, nearly brought Namter down from his exalted euphoria, but even the sins of mankind seemed pitiful in the presence of hallowed grace.

He stopped his demonstration there; it was enough. He must not let himself get carried away, make the first move. He had displayed control of his territory, but Kayip still stalked, confident, beyond its edges. Namter knew, even with this gift, that if he allowed himself to wander within lunging range the monk would quickly take his revenge. This was a game of spikefowl. The first one to move lost.

Namter clicked a hidden button on the back of his cane and started to pace small circles between the blinding safety of the window light.

"This is what you wanted, Kayip? Just you and I alone." Namter laughed. "Very well, I know it, I am not your main prize. I would have thought the wise thing would have been to stay in Huile, but instead you followed us all the way here. Perhaps you finally learned that you have no voice in that town. Well, you are just as mute here, you will find no more allies, no more idiots for you to condemn to death in your crusade. The ferral rightly thinks you mad, and a deranged hermit like yourself will get no attention from men of good standing. This city, too, has no use for you."

He smirked and did his best to appear at ease. An overconfident foe was easy prey, and if he could convince Kayip he was that, perhaps he could lure him to make the first strike. He tapped his cane on the floor, as if to accentuate each point. Oathblood ink, oozing from a secret nib embedded in the cane's bottom tip, dried into invisible runes on the workshop floor.

"Then again, perhaps staying in Huile would have been too painful for you. A wiser man would have given in after their first failure. All your advocating, your warnings, your troublemaking, and what did you leave the world with? Two dead armies. Too many corpses to count. I'm sure you would say that the souls would live again, born back into our world, fresh lives to toil anew, but we both know the truth. They suffered for your failure."

Namter heard a small creak of movement off behind a bulbous machine in the shadows. He tried not to react to it, hoping his smile was bait enough, though he did move himself to the opposite side of the summoning circle, finishing the last touches on the Truespeech written along its edges.

"Why don't we have a practical theological debate, right here, right now?" Namter said. "Two thousand years your Church has poisoned the minds of men, hiding the truth by murdering those who discover it. Yet your supposed authority is your powers, is it not? Those blessings imbued into ancient metal, handed down by your Demiurge. Well, you've seen what I can do, without the need for holy gadgets and doodads, so why don't you try out some of these so-called miracles?" He paused. "Nothing? Has your Demiurge finally given up on you? Your all-powerful creator abandoning you in your time of need?"

Kayip had not moved. Six years could teach a man patience, and it had been amusing to watch a cocky young monk devolve into a worn-out fugitive.

Namter turned his head suddenly, in a direction orthogonal to the last sound that Kayip had made, as if he had focused in on a mistaken position. He muttered prayers, and black fire formed around his hand. His eyes stared forward, but his ears tuned to the side, where he could hear the smallest scuff of movement, and the slight, almost inaudible clinks as Kayip's sword formed itself.

"Let me see you burn, coward," he shouted, towards the empty shadow.

Kayip did not scream when he charged, but he could not hide his attack. He ran the metres separating them in a second, rags fluttering behind him, sweat streaming off past his faceplate and behind him in glistening drops, his sword forward in one hand, stripes of reflected light rushing up its blade.

Namter tapped his cane onto the floor, activating the trap. The circle screamed to life.

Kayip tossed something from behind him. A sphere flew through the air. A head. Valen's head. It soared in an arc, over the circle, which burst into life, a shout beyond human lungs.

Instantly a dozen elongated shadow-shaded arms writhed up from the floor, grasping up, grabbing the head where the man was supposed to be. Namter swore, a rare transgression for him, and jumped backwards, as the divine ink-black arms tore at flesh, ripping it from bone, grabbing at the bait and pulling Valen's remains back down with them.

Kayip dove and rolled around the twitching mass, jumping at Namter. The flame in Namter's hand was meant only to be a bluff, but now he tossed it out in a panic at the crazed monk, falling back to avoid the blade. The black fire blew a wall of smoke, and Namter, with both adrenaline and Oathblood running through his veins, pushed himself back, readying for Kayip's next vengeance-fueled strike.

It didn't come. As soon as he swung his fist, Kayip switched directions, leaping towards the light of the window. Namter understood now the man's plan and threw flame with a shout, but the warmonk was already through the glass.

Light burst in, blinding. Men screamed outside; gunshots went off. Namter pulled himself up and staggered out the front door. As he pushed through, he saw several police standing over a corpse, and the others, as well as his Unblind Brothers, leaning over the railing at the end of Icaria.

"Kayip!" Namter shouted.

"He jumped over!" Avitus said. "Ran into the Underburg or somewhere."

Namter slumped against the railing, searching the web of darkened scaffolding that hung above the cliff face. No sign of the monk. The monk who had had him at sword length but who had run instead.

Ewald dashed towards him, face white. "Dear Demiurge, that man's a demon."

Namter scowled at the twin blasphemies and straightened himself. Kauf glanced at his hand.

"Are you all right?"

"Get your men down there now!" Namter shouted. Pain rang though his palm, and he now noticed that he had left a trail of blood, and a few shards of red-stained glass. "And get me some damned tweezers and a bandage."

On Designations of Heresy and Their Evolution

Though the word "Heresy" may, to enlightened readers of the United Confederacy of the Citizens' Resurgence, invoke gruesome memories of the Church Wars or the fraught Schisms that decorate our history books, the concept itself is one that defies easy definition. Indeed, when the early Church was a mere cult of the Imperial House of Diedrev, it had no concept of "Internal Heresy" (Falsis Internum), that is, heterodox beliefs and practices within the Church of the Ascended. Instead, it was focused on the eradication of rival religious systems (Falsis Externum), primarily the pre-Imperium animistic practices common in Vastium, Kaimark, and other recently united regions. However, it was the practice of "gods worship," which seemed to be the focus of the early priesthood's greatest ire; in particular, those polytheistic faiths that held as dogma that ætheric aberrations were, in fact, agents of divine will. Church efforts in this front were clearly comprehensive, as these particular religious practices seemed to have all but died out by the time of the conquest of Irissia. Even so, paranoia about the return of such "demonic cults" was a key contributor to the later expulsion of the tribes of Kort and Malva, and the accusations of "demon worship" exacerbated the violent struggles of the Schisms. It could be argued, then, that fears of external religious competition in fact created the entire concept of Internal Heresy in the first place.

Now, before I continue on about modern conceptions of "Heresy," I must waste some ink on that interminable academic debate about the so-called "neo-cults of the gods." Despite claims made by some academics, priests, and members of this new and violent theology, there is no evidence to support the notion that these indeed represent a revival of the pre-imperial "gods cults."

Certainly these modern belief systems share with the older an emphasis on the divinity of ætheric aberrations, but there is no historical line to connect these two movements. These new cults are, at best, a loose attempt to reconstruct ancient beliefs but are not a direct continuation of them. These recent movements can be understood as a manifestation of the societal chaos created by the Severing War and the Calamity. Their focus on ætheric aberrations and their supposed "divine powers" must be seen only as a response to the increasing prevalence of ætheric aberrations in the inner Wastes as a result of the Calamity. Though occasionally violent, the threat posed by these cults is almost assuredly exaggerated due to their association with ætheric aberrations. Any caravan-lord worth their frascs will spend days preparing for the possibility of raider attacks before wasting a minute worrying about "gods cultists." Unfortunately, research into the beliefs and practices of these religious movements have been hampered both by the secrecy of its practitioners as well as the militant stance taken by the Church of the Ascended itself.

As for post-Calamity notions of "Heresy," the most in-depth exploration was laid out by Professor Asara Maturo in her 1729 essay...

—Excerpt of the dissertation of Hasim Bisett, entitled "The Church of the Ascended and Post-Calamity Theology." Accepted and published by Phenia University.

Chapter 14

Life had become better than all but the most ludicrous of Sylvaine's fantasies. Under Lazarus' eye and Gath's tutelage, she had pushed herself to the very limits of her skills, practicing mechanicurgy, æther-circuit programming, mid-distance metal manipulation, and just good old-fashioned engineering. Whenever she would reach a wall (metaphorical, or in one test of her advanced metal-warping techniques, literal) Lazarus would pull out a vial of slickdust, and she would break through. Once or twice she had asked if it was safe to up the dose. Lazarus would say, with his words grabbing her like gloved hands, that *of course* it was safe, that he knew what to do, and she should trust him completely.

So she did.

She kept on with her studies, her experiments, and her late-night practice sessions. At times, she wasn't sure what it was she was even practicing for, just that she needed to do better, be better, that she needed to hone her skills, to take more slickdust. Lazarus's words were true; with each sniff or drink she felt stronger, her mind honed scalpel-sharp.

She was not only shaping herself into the engineer and the woman that she always fantasized she would be but something more, something grander. She would not just become the first ferral to graduate as an ætheric engineer, but also the greatest engineer that had ever lived, or would ever live. The stares of others meant nothing to her anymore, the prejudices of an insipid civilization were to be discarded, their norms pitiful words. The laws of physics were now just mere suggestions, tools to be bent, or simple distractions, for even the sky might quake if Sylvaine should decide to tame it. Amidst her manic frenzies of genius, she knew now there could be no more limits for her potential!

Then the slickdust ran out.

"My supplier hit a snag," Lazarus said, "but it should be no worry, I'll find some in the city."

Sylvaine nodded, trying to take his words to heart and to avoid the pangs of panic as she noted silently that the Academy Exhibition loomed a mere four days away. Still, Lazarus was an intelligent man, a dependable man. He knew people, knew how to get things done; there was nothing to worry about.

She continued to work, but her confidence started to lag, her focus wavering. Her machines would break down suddenly or melt in a shower of æther-sparks. Worse still, at times her glove would lay inert on her hand, limp and disinterested in her orders, the deep fire inside her extinguished as if she were back in the damp pit of despair Roache had pulled her out from.

She kept asking the man if he had found a supplier yet, but Lazarus simply said to trust her, that the slickdust would be coming any hour now.

Those hours became days, and her mediocre performances collapsed into complete failure and then into a nauseating withdrawal. Sylvaine dragged herself around Lazarus's apartment, without even the energy to make the arduous trip one floor down to her own room.

"You said there were no ill effects," she moaned, lying from leather arm to leather arm on Roache's large armchair, watching the ceiling spin.

"Hmm?" the man said, looking up from a pile of paperwork. "Oh, well you have been using a very large amount of the stuff. Don't worry, it'll pass."

"When?" she asked. "Will my engineering be affected?"

"No need for so many questions," Lazarus tutted. "Just calm yourself. Namter, some water for our guest?"

Roache's butler would tend to her from time to time when he wasn't busy doing whatever it was that man did, and Sylvaine ended up spending most of her hours groaning on Lazarus' couch. She'd ask how long it was until the Exhibition, each answer somehow surprising her by being both too short and too long. It seemed an eternity had passed in her sickened stupor, yet it also felt as if the Exhibition date was running up to her at lightning speed. It didn't make any sense; she didn't have the energy left for sense. All she had was the gut-churning nausea, the aching muscles, the pounding headaches, and the horrible, growing fear that all she had built would now collapse.

It was the early afternoon of the very day of the Exhibition when Lazarus finally strolled through his front door and opened his briefcase to reveal a sloshing bottle of red. The smell hit Sylvaine instantly, and for a brief moment she felt alive again, just enough to pull herself up.

Lazarus pulled out a syringe and filled it with the crimson fluid.

"It's... slickdust?" Sylvaine asked.

"Yes," Lazarus said.

"It's a liquid?" Her vision was too blurry to even be sure of that.

"At this point, an oral dose might reduce withdrawal symptoms, but it won't be nearly enough to get you to your Exhibition. This should jumpstart your Knack, and keep it going strong, for weeks, months, maybe indefinitely. You'll be a true-blooded engineer, through and through. But if you're uncomfortable with the idea, we can wait and miss the Exhibition."

"No, no," she tried to stand, and fell back down. "Anything."

She thought she caught the ghost of a smile, but it was difficult to see through the haze.

"Very well; we'll have to do this intravenously. Don't worry," he winked, possibly, "it will all be okay."

Sylvaine nodded and held out her arm. Lazarus took it, a gesture of skin against skin that might have once excited her, but the most titillating thing in that room now was the red liquid.

Lazarus grasped tight, and Sylvaine felt a pinch. Then suddenly, a burst of life. The room leapt into sharp, vivid color, the drone in the back of her mind silenced. She nearly jumped up, but instead slowly helped herself to her feet with Lazarus' guidance. Her heart raced against itself, and she could feel her cheeks blush bright. She wanted to grab her glove, as she was as sure as anything that her powers had returned.

"Well, look at you!" Lazarus laughed and slapped her back. "Ready for your show?"

Sylvaine nodded vigorously and had to catch her breath for a few seconds before she could speak. "More than ready!"

She ran out of his grasp into his bedroom where Namter had already set up her dress. She was in it in seconds, and after a minute of frenzied work at the washbasin she looked as good as she ever had—better, in fact, by her own estimate. As she dashed towards the door, Lazarus grabbed her by the shoulder.

"A word of advice," he said.

She was late, but he wasn't asking permission. He pulled her close and put his lips to her ear.

Her breath stopped, the heat that flowed through her froze, the man's words worming into her brain. She could barely make them out, barely process the meaning, what insanity was Roache saying?

"Forget it," Lazarus laughed and pushed her away.

"Forget...?" Sylvaine said. They had been talking about something...what, she wasn't sure. She blinked around, her blood pumping at a sprinter's pace, *where was she?*

"You're late," Lazarus said

The Exhibition! Memory flowed back, and she held back a squeal as she rushed out the door.

"Good luck!" Lazarus shouted. "I'm sure you'll have an *exhilarating* time."

The hanging lights of the display hall were tiny suns, blinding Sylvaine with their fluorescence. Why did they have to be so bitterly incandescent?

A minute before, she had watched the world in intense focus, all sharp lines and saturated colors, smells overwhelming her, sweat and oil, exhaust and excitement; then, before that, it had all been shadows and confusion, a blur of grey; and on the train over, jittering over-energy and rapid, battering, sensations. Sylvaine had jumped back and forth between experiential extremes since she had left Roache's apartment, stimuli either needle-sharp piercing or rag-smothered soft.

Lazarus had told her that it would all be fine, and she knew that was true; yet, if anything, her swings had gotten worse. Now she was immersed in a deep mist, the room nothing more than an abyss of ill-defined dimness. Shadows darted around, and only when she focused could she recognize them as people. Around her there was a sea of indistinct murmuring. She tried to grab onto the conversations, but their meanings slipped by her, and the din of the whole thing felt like waves crashing on her skull.

She squinted for the short shadow that would be Gearswit. Technically, all she was obligated to stay for was his brief presentation. Then she could run off, to the bathroom or, perhaps, to a vocaphone to call for Lazarus. He would know what to do.

All she was waiting on was the tiny man's speech.

Gear's-grits, he's going to give a longwinded one, isn't he? she realized with an ache.

She had initially planned to use this time to wander around and inspect the other students' projects. In her manic phase she had rushed over to her own device, past dozens of fascinating works of machinery that even now, through the oppressive haze, called to her curiosity. Springson had on display a spider-golem, which he claimed represented a revolution in miniaturized multiped locomotion. Fifika had made a mechanical arm inspired by the Malvian whipblades, one that could shift between normal functions and a snake-like grasp. And though she had not seen it herself, rumors claimed that Gulizar had been working on a single-man æroship of some import.

Now she doubted she'd even be able to find any of them in the maze of fuzzy blobs that she deduced must be the other projects. Even her generator seemed to fade in and out of the world.

Sounds were no clearer, and among the indistinct murmurs and shouts, there was a buzz in her ear, some words that seemed to originate from the back of her mind, rather than from the deluge outside her head. They were soft, yet impossible to dislodge, piercing yet formless. Some snippet of a conversation, but she couldn't remember from who, or when.

A short figure started to grow in front of her. Sylvaine blinked; it was moving towards her, followed by a pack of ghosts.

Gearswit! She focused and could make out her professor's voice. He welded pride into each syllable he spoke. He described the work of his students, the progress they'd made, and his estimation of each project's practical worth. Or at least that seemed to be the gist of what he was saying; individual words were beyond her ken. He mumbled and pointed, pontificated and laughed at inaudible jokes.

His speech lasted a century, give or take, but suddenly Sylvaine noticed a lack of noise, and that the small blotch appeared to be pointing. *At what?* Sylvaine stared at his hand. *The machine!* Of course, she needed to start her negative-density generator.

Her glove was like lead as she lifted it, her head pounding with every heartbeat. Still, she managed to point her arm towards the generator. She looked inside herself for that energy, to spark the æther and bring life to her creation.

Nothing.

She panicked, searching every centimetre of her body for it. Then, deep down, she found something. It was hot, burning, caustic almost, a raging fire as opposed to the managed hearth that she expecting. There was something frightening about this power, something alien and vicious, and her instincts pushed it back.

"Take It," came Lazarus voice. He wasn't there, couldn't be, yet she heard it all the same. It was that once indistinct buzz, crawling out from a hidden corner of her mind, clear now as a dictaphone recording.

She concentrated on the force. It grew, infecting every ounce of her tissue with burning heat. She tried to bring it to her hand.

"Wait."

Yes, she must wait. *Why?* came a thought. Well, because...because she had to.

The power grew and grew, she thought she heard some murmurs from the shadows. It frightened her. She had to release it, get rid of it.

"Let It Grow."

No, it was better to let it grow. True, she only needed a fraction of that power to start the machine but... but the voice. It was clear and correct.

"Bring It To Your Hand."

She did. It felt like her skin was melting into her gloves. Pain shot through her arm, but she kept it steady. Around her she could hear the murmurs growing into full discussion. Someone even shouted.

"Destroy It," the voice said.

She didn't register letting the power go. Didn't even feel the explosion until she was already on the floor.

Her senses went black.

Shock. She was knocked away from herself. Blasted away into a nothingness. She felt neither body nor mind.

Then, after an infinite second, the world came back.

First came the sounds: Footsteps in a frantic cacophony, discordant thuds on carpet and metal. Shouts, violent words that full of terror but were otherwise nonsense to her. Ringing, like a bell tapped with a spoon, again and again and again and again.

Smell came back next: Oil. Smoke. Burning rubber, burning carpet. Burning skin, burning flesh. Above it all, the iron-tang of blood.

She pushed herself onto her arm, which screamed in pain, or maybe she did. Sylvaine fell back, kicking herself away from sharp shards on the floor. She tried her arm again, and it held her, but barely.

Was the overwhelming blood-scent hers? She felt pain but there was no clear wound.

Around her, the hall started to spin back into reality. A pillar of smoke billowed from the hulk of metal and flame that she recognized as her generator. Splinters of metal were lodged in the floor, like tiny arrows. Figures ran about screaming incomprehensible words, their features slowly coming clear even in the hurricane of motion.

In the eye of the maelstrom she found some relative calm, men and woman standing eerily still. They stared, as one, at a small figure laid flat on the ground.

Gearswit.

Demiurge be damned, it was Gearswit!

A burnt pipe was lodged in his chest, and blood flowed from it past his brown lapel onto the floor, where it pooled into a puddle. No, a lake. He did not move, he did not even twitch. One of the figures turned to her. She didn't know him, but she knew the look on his face. It was fear. It was disgust. It was hate.

"Run," Lazarus' voice said in her head.

So she did.

Chapter 15

The world had managed to pull itself back into focus as Sylvaine burst out the doors of the exhibition hall into the cool Icarian evening. Hyper-focused, in fact, as she could hear every shout from inside the hall, could see the minute twist in the face of each curious pedestrian, could smell her own fear.

Gearswit. His short body bent and bloody. His pride replaced with shock and agony. Sylvaine stumbled towards the stairs. *Gearswit.*

"Sylvaine!" A voice came up the steps at the street below. It was Ewald Kauf, beside the open door of a red autocar.

She rushed down the stairs, holding up her dress to avoid tripping over its ash-marred strips, and collapsed in the backseat of the 'car. Ewald got in the front and turned to flash her a smile.

"Don't worry, it was just an accident. We'll go back to Lazarus' and work this all out."

Sylvaine couldn't manage anything more than a nod between panicked breaths. Her head still pounded, and thick sweat ran through her hair. The sounds and smells of the hall stuck to her mind as if it were tar. The image of Gearswit, twisted in shock and agony, was like a photograph stapled to her forehead.

She had killed him; he had done nothing but try to help her, and she had killed him. Tears escaped, wetting her dress. She was no engineer. She was a hack, a cheating amateur who got her own professor killed through her incompetence. They were right about her, they had always been right about her, she was never meant to be an engineer. She was nothing more than a beast with pretensions.

Lazarus. He will sort this out. Sylvaine wasn't even sure what she meant by this thought, but she knew it to be the truth. Her professor was dead, but somehow, in some way, Lazarus would make it right.

Streetlights seeped in through the window as she watched the city flash by in numbed shock. Monuments to human ingenuity filtered through moonlight, a different world past the glass, forever separate from herself.

Thoughts were too painful, so she avoided them, even the deep ones, the long-quieted ones, the voice in the back of her mind which asked: *Why was Ewald waiting outside the hall? How did he know that she had had an accident?*

Lazarus would sort it out.

Sylvaine almost felt like herself again as they took the lift to Lazarus' penthouse, though she would have been happier feeling like anyone else. She kept seeing Gearswit's face—a fabrication, since she had run before looking close enough to make out his features. That made it worse, for it was not one pain she saw, but all possible forms of torment written across dozens of expressions.

She immediately noticed a difference in the penthouse, even if it took a few seconds to piece out its details. The atmosphere was grim, not comforting and warm, but threatening and imposing. The lights were dimmed, and the great curtains covered the windows. Lazarus was sitting at the table, dashing out some lines on a small notebook amidst his piles of papers. He did not pause his work even to glance up at her arrival. Gath leaned on the wall behind Roache, his slick black hair gleaming like oil. He held open the edge of the curtain, watching for something outside.

The ever-locked door was, for the first time, open, its inside's shadows. Sylvaine could see nothing more than some dimly lit industrial equipment. Then she smelled them, and focused her vision. There, in the dark between the machinery, were bent forms, their soft moans and cracked coughs now reaching her ears.

Finally, Lazarus jabbed a period then placed his pen in its vial of ink and raised his eyes to meet her. He did not smile. The sides of his lips were raised, yes, but it could not be called anything like a smile. He stared at her, a glare indifferent to her tear-wet face. He wore the curiosity of a lion inspecting a small, limping rodent, unsure if it wished to spend the pitiful effort to swipe its claws.

"I take it you've had a rough night?" he said finally.

Sylvaine stared blankly and nodded. Gath closed the curtains, while Ewald left Sylvaine's side to stand at the end of the table, wearing a strange, giddy expression.

"Tell me," Lazarus said, "did anyone die?"

"Die?" she mumbled. Then, "Gearswit."

"Your professor?" Lazarus asked, tapping the table, thinking for a moment. "Yes, that should work fine. Indeed it is fortunate for you, Kauf. One less loose end to deal with."

Ewald Kauf laughed, an awkward noise, shuddering from deep in his stomach. Gath merely shrugged. Sylvaine stared at Lazarus, trying to focus well enough to make sense of his words. He noticed her gaze.

"Oh, don't worry," he said, "the kortonian was already a liability enough, he wouldn't have been tolerated much longer. I'm not positive how he obtained those schematics that he shoved onto you, though I have some monk-shaped theories. Perhaps he didn't even understand their significance, but it is of no matter now."

Lazarus's words were nonsense, all nonsense, what was he talking about? Meanings started to connect in the fuzz of her mind, but they couldn't be correct; she *must* be misunderstanding. Some dim memory approached Sylvaine, some conversation she had had with Roache, before she had left, some advice he had given her, whose specifics now seemed vital, but its details remained foggy.

Something moaned and twitched slightly from within the open door behind the men, and Sylvaine squinted to see in the dark.

"What's in the room?" she asked softly.

Lazarus ignored her question and turned to sign some documents on his right. "You do know if they find you, they'll try you for murder," he said. "Oh, you'll say it was an accident, which is a half-truth, since from your point of view it was just an accident, but they won't believe you. A ferral? No, they'll treat you like the beast you are."

The past started to flow back to her, slowly at first. "You knew...?" she asked, the words morphing from a question to a statement as she spoke them. The memories began to accelerate, rush into her; instructions whispered at the height of her slickdust euphoria, commands that had seeped into every crevice of her brain.

"You did this..." Sylvaine sputtered out. "You told me to...somehow."

"Approach this rationally, please, Sylvaine." Lazarus said, putting his hands together on the table. "How do you think that sounds? Famed philanthropist and businessman Lazarus Roache made me do it, he talked in my mind, he hypnotized me. Do you really think that story will do anything for you with the police, or the court for that matter? If you can afford a good lawyer, perhaps they'll toss you into an asylum. But I honestly doubt you'll even get even that."

"I never thought she'd end up like this," Ewald said, talking to an invisible interviewer. "But she said some odd things, whispered nasty threats against her professor. And, you know how Ferrals are." Then he giggled, as if it were all a massive joke.

It all seemed impossible. That every word Lazarus had said, every promise, every genial wink, was a mere act, crafted artifice. Yet, as she searched her mind, no other explanation presented itself. Her promised future was then a mere carrot at the end of a stick, her ætheric talents not some miracle out of a fantasy pulp but calculated bait. It was all nothing more than the pranks she had suffered as a child, when for brief moments she thought she had been accepted by her classmates, only to suffer the lashes of their renewed mockery. Only now a dead man had been added to the gag.

"You bastard," she muttered, and started to stumble towards Roache.

"Sit!" he commanded sternly.

Her butt hit the granite floor. Ewald burst out laughing.

"Just like a dog," he said. She felt like one.

A smirk rose on Roache's face. "Now, now, the situation's not as bad as it seems, Sylvaine, because the police won't find you. You'll be here, working for me, working for this."

He lifted out a vial of slickdust from his pocket. For a second, she forgot everything that had happened that evening, forgot the betrayal, forgot the lies, her hunger for slickdust roaring ahead of her fear and anger.

"You were using..." She tried to stand up, but her limbs wouldn't move. "Did you even have a supply problem?"

This induced a chuckle. "Come now, I am the supplier. Slickdust is Lazacorp's greatest accomplishment. Made primarily from sangleum and minute amounts of my own blood. Powerful ætherial booster, I found." He swirled the vial. "It has some nasty side-effects in high doses, mutations and the like, which you have managed to avoid, but luckily, its main effect seems quite potent even with your beast-blood. Stand!"

Her body jerked up like it was held by puppet strings.

"Stay."

She tried to run, but her body obeyed Roche's instructions over the screams of her mind.

"How?" she panted out.

"Namter could explain the mechanics in technical detail, but I'm afraid he's off playing tag with some bald fool. Point is, it provides me complete control. Don't feel too bad; I have dozens at my beck and call, all hard at work. I've mentioned my project before, and I think it's worth reiterating what a perfect fit you are for it."

The hatred in Sylvaine's heart burned and burned. Lazarus had never cared for her, had never meant any of his kindness. She was just a tool to him. No, tools were treated with mere indifference; she was just a pack animal, a source of twisted amusement as well as brute labor.

She squirmed and tried to move her legs, but Lazarus words felt like heavy chains. "Why me?" she spat out.

"Designs, mostly," said Lazarus.

Gath nodded. "The æther modulation technology is... deeply impressive. And useful."

Roache nodded thoughtfully. "If you had just accepted my offer in the first place this all would have been much easier. None of this theatre would have been required, these plans, but then again, you are young and bullheaded. I do not blame you too much."

"You..." she tried to think of the words to express her anger, her hatred, but could only growl nonsense sounds, struggling against the invisible bonds in her mind.

"At least my task was made simpler by the fact that you are a ferral," continued Roache. "I mean, if I had to recruit a famous professor or even nab just even a normal, run-of-the-mill student, the police would be asking questions. No one will miss a ferral."

She could smell her own loathing. She could taste it.

Gath turned his head towards the open room. "We should get to work. We've wasted enough time already."

"Oh, come now," said Ewald. "Let's have a little more fun. I want to see the ferral do some tricks."

Gath scowled. "There's no need to keep mocking her, just throw on the locks already. I'm not comfortable with the girl walking around. She's an untested experiment as far as I'm concerned."

"Oh, you're of little faith. It won't hurt to let her know how things stand." Roache smiled. "Come Sylvaine, sit. Roll over. Stand. Stay still."

One by one she followed his instructions, as her rage grew to take up every corner of her mind. There was no room left for anything else, even self-pity. She just hated.

Ewald walked over and stood in front of her. Then he poked her forehead and giggled.

"Can't do a thing!"

"Come on, Ewald," said Gath. "You've seen this show before with the mutants."

"Yes, but this is far more interesting."

He poked her faced, pressing the skin of her cheeks and giggling like a child. "Say, Roache, you ever fucked this thing?"

Her hatred was now mixed with embarrassment and a growing sense of disgust as Ewald looked her body up and down.

"Now, now, I've kept our relationship focused on business," Roache said. "Though I suspected she may have had an interest."

"Been in heat, then?" Ewald suggested. Roache just laughed.

Her hatred devoured these new emotions, growing larger. She could feel herself shaking against invisible shackles.

"But you never tried? No curiosity?" said Ewald. "I'm sure you've forced it before. I know I would with your power."

"Come now, Ewald. I do have standards. She's a beast!"

There it was. Twenty years of mockery, of disgust, distilled into those words. Memories soaked with hatred and humiliation tried to force their way into Sylvaine's mind, but they were drowned out by the roars of rage, or something deeper, simpler

168

than rage. There were no longer coherent thoughts flowing through her mind, but emotions and instincts of the most primal sort. The howls of her chained fury.

Ewald stuck his face right into hers. "I suppose so! I'd imagine you'd get fleas." He giggled without restraint. She could smell the mockery on his breath, imagine the taste of his blood, his neck flesh beneath her teeth.

"Can't be any worse than fucking a dog!" Ewald continued. "Be going from bitch to bitch, if you could even tell the difference!"

Sylvaine roared. She could see nothing but red, but she could smell, she could hear. She slashed toward Ewald. Warm blood met her claws.

"Stop! Heel!" shouted Lazarus.

But she didn't.

"It's her damn beast-blood acting up!" Gath shouted. "She's going berserk!"

The words' meanings, even the idea that words had meaning, seemed to Sylvaine a distant, alien notion. There was only blood and the smell of Ewald's fear.

She heard Gath cock a pistol. "Don't shoot," Lazarus yelled. "We can't attract the police."

"Fuck that," Gath snarled, arm waving for a clear shot.

Ewald swung at her, but she ducked, even before her conscious mind recognized the fist. Then she lunged at the man, claws cutting straight through, the two of them flying back into the dark room behind him. The man coughed blood as he landed, and then, nothing.

Dead. It wasn't a thought but an instinct.

She could smell oil alongside the blood. She started to sense the room around her. It was a small industrial workshop. Huddled figures chained to pipes held wrenches and soldering irons in the near darkness. Her vision was still blurry and crimson, but she could make out the shock of their expression. There was one face she could see clear in the light. It was as if time froze as she saw it, familiar yet grotesquely foreign to her. The man's visage was twisted and burned, his hand callused and bloody, a single grotesque horn grew out of the side of his head. Yet she could recognize his youth-filled eyes, now turned yellow, and his olive skin now stained with bright red strands, poxed further with metallic-colored boils.

"Sylvaine?" Javad asked.

A gunshot rang through the room, ricocheting off the floor beside her. She turned to see a figure blocking the doorway, pistol drawn. Fear screamed for her to hide.

Sylvaine scampered towards the machines on wall, dashing on all fours. She jumped and climbed their tubing, scaling the mechanical mass as fast as if she was running across the floor.

"Where are you, beastbitch?" came Gath's voice as he walked in, aiming at shadows. Sylvaine skulked on the ceiling, hanging from the tangle of pipes. Gath stepped into the pool of Ewald's blood, grunted and scuffed it off his shoe.

From outside came the sound of glass bursting. Gath turned back a moment. "Coward!" he shouted, and Sylvaine took her chance, dropping onto her prey, smashing his body into the floor. The pistol went off as he fell, blasting open a pipe. Steam flooded the room. She went to bite his neck, but he elbowed her jaw. She jumped back into the steam, and he got up, aiming his pistol.

"Don't fucking run from me."

He shot blindly into the steam. A bullet grazed the fur of Sylvaine's back. She leapt behind a machine some muzzled part of her still recognized as an ætherial frequency modulator.

Gath jerked around, pistol forward, blinded by the fog. Sylvaine, however, could hear his every movement and smell his fear.

Two more shots ricocheted around the room. "I'll blow your fucking head off," Gath shouted.

Each gunshot sent her scrambling to a new hiding place, the primal fear of the sound greater than any conscious avoidance of death. The steam condensed on her fur, and blood mixed with sweat. She skulked around the machine, trying to find an angle of attack. Then, suddenly, through the steam she saw two sets of red arms grab Gath's legs.

"Skinsick fucks!" he yelled, and aimed his pistol down. Sylvaine leapt into him, claws and teeth tearing into his stomach and shoulder. He was dead before he hit the ground.

Lazarus. The name rang through Sylvaine's head. She scampered out of that room of shadow and steam. The window was broken open, and beyond it a fire escape. She crawled outside, ignoring the glass as it cut her. Through the dim light of the night she could see a man jumping into a red autocar.

Lazarus.

Sylvaine brachiated down the metal scaffold, leaping floors at time. Her movements shook the structure as she flung herself at near terminal velocity. The autocar's engines sputtered to life while the street flew towards her. As she landed on the sidewalk with a clang, the 'car sped off. Sylvaine gave chase, running on all fours in a mad frenzy. She could feel the metal carapace of the city street under her hands and feet, her claws occasionally cutting sparks.

Lazarus.

The autocar zoomed ahead, careening around pedestrians and skidding by the nighttime traffic. Sylvaine ran as fast as she could manage, pushing herself beyond sweat, beyond pain, but as fast as she ran, as deep as she panted, she could not keep up. Every metre she leapt, the 'car gained another three, until finally it took a distant turn and flew out of sight.

Lazarus...

Sylvaine slowed. The crimson in her vision faded. Her rage faltered and her mind began to focus, with instinct congealing into coherent thoughts. She stopped and looked down at herself. Her dress was torn to shreds, long strands of indigo stained crimson, ragged fur hanging out of its holes. Her claws were covered in blood and viscera, wet and cold. She closed her mouth. She still tasted Gath's shoulder.

A scream grabbed her attention. A woman dashed into her apartment and slammed the door, lock shutting with a deafening click. All around her people stared in horror and disgust. A child ran as she caught his gaze, an old man held up his cane as a weapon of last resort. They were terrified. Terrified of the animal dressed in fur and blood that stood before them.

In the distance, she could hear the sirens of the Icarian police. Sylvaine started to run again. She ran away from the police. She ran from the blood. She ran from whatever life she had built in Icaria. She didn't know where she was running to, or what she would do when she got there, but like a hunted beast, she ran.

Chapter 16

Marcel slept poorly. The past few nights had been miserable, twisting around in bed, his sweat staining the sheets. The dream had returned. He had been free of it for months straight now, but whether it was his time with Verus or the tussle in Fareau's room, something had called the Demiurged-damned dream back.

The Huile Underway blanketed him in its damp, suffocating darkness. Footsteps and the occasional mechanical groan were the only sounds that cut through his gas mask as he skulked. He knew he would pass through sewer pipes, abandoned underrail tunnels, and then into the bowels of the Lazacorp refineries itself. The journey played itself like a cinegraph show, one he might know the ending to but could not halt, only shout in the empty theatre. The difference was in this show he felt everything: the gas mask's grip on his face, the weight of his airtight uniform, the icy stabs of fear, and eventually, the pain.

If only this show were just a fantasy like the propaganda action cinegraphs of his Phenian childhood. Monochrome images of Resurgence heroes fighting Principate madmen in autoarmor of such ludicrous size that they could only exist in some engineer's wet dream. Yet Marcel's subconscious was not kind enough to mutate the day's thoughts into an average nightmare. This dream was taken straight from memory, with only a few artistic liberties.

It was that night in Huile, the night of their victory, the night of red death. It was a chaotic jumble, but that chaos was accurate. They snuck through tunnels leading left, right, up, down, every which way; endless mazes of pipes and steam. His gas mask was fogged, always fogged. He could see nothing past the few feet of his tiny cone of vision. He kept his gaze on his squad mates, the Huile Sewer Rats. As long as they were in his sight he wasn't lost. *Just follow them, just follow them, just follow them,* he repeated the mantra to himself.

In their gas masks they looked demonic, like black skulls attached to torsos of tubes and leather. He wondered which of these demons was Alba. She had given him the option of turning down the task, had given them each that choice. It was her one concession for agreeing to lead the attack. This was beyond their duty, she had told General Durand flatly, and it was an open secret that the only reason their squad had been tapped for Lazarus Roache's desperate mission was that they were one of the few squads to survive the Battle of Huile Field unscratched, the only surviving squad with any recon training, for that matter. They could sit this one out with honor, Alba had told them, but none of them took that excuse, save, of course, for the injured Lambert, who would have been of no use anyhow.

As for the rest, they had agreed to follow Lazarus' plan, to descend through the Underway into the guts of the refinery, each for their own reasons. Some for duty, or for patriotism, for machismo, or for each other. Marcel did it for Alba. He did it to impress her and to protect her, to prove to her that he was the hero he had joined the army to be.

Thousands of Principate soldiers slept only a couple dozen metres above the squad, in their makeshift camp in the Lazacorp refinery of Blackwood Row. Marcel thought he could hear them through the floors, piping and asphalt. He could hear their snores, their whispered talk, their death screams. No, not the screams. That hadn't happened yet.

"Hold up." It was Henri. Henri was dead. No, he was going to die. Marcel tried to tell him to watch his back when he set the bombs, but his mouth wouldn't open.

Henri took out a map. It was the blueprints to Lazacorp, a gift from Lazarus Roache himself. They had been told how Lazarus had fled the Principate camp to join the righteous side of the Resurgence, the evening after their horrific defeat. The tycoon had explained to them how, before he had fled, he had convinced the brutish General Agrippus to keep her camp inside the Lazacorp refineries. His plan, the only hope now for the UCCR cause after the disastrous Battle of Huile Field, relied on them releasing pent up sangleum gas on the Principate army above.

It has seemed such a simple foolproof plan until they had actually gotten below.

Henri and Alba checked the map, while Danel and Rada scouted out front, and Desct and Marcel watched the back.

"You managing to uphold your composure, or are you shitting your uniform?" Desct's voice was muffled through the gas mask.

"Holding," Marcel managed to get out.

"Good. These trousers are a bitch to wash."

Alba waved them over. They snuck past a pile of rusting mining equipment, and down a thin hall, which opened up into the extractor room.

The extractor was massive, climbing up from the depths of the earth, towering above to pierce the surface. Around its trunk, open sloughs released rivers of red liquid to the machines that swarmed the edge the extractor. Heat billowed from these rivers, an acrid scent that pierced even the gas masks. Marcel sucked back the urge to vomit. *Sangleum.* The natural, unrefined æther was highly reactive, and when converted to a gaseous form, highly toxic. Even the fumes were enough to induce illness, and its touch bred mutations, if not outright death. Marcel couldn't imagine what it was going to be like for the soldiers above when they woke to red smoke.

But the Principate had started it. They'd forced their rule onto Huile after assassinating its elected mayor. Lazarus had told the Resurgence soldiers how the Imperator's bootlickers were stockpiling sangleum gas themselves to use on the Resurgence forces, and were even planning to use the remainder against the innocent citizens of Huile as punishment for resisting. Gas warfare did not seem on its surface the most heroic path to victory, but that was the naivety of pulp adventures, the hollow denunciations of pacifists who lived far and safe from the battlefield. Whatever Marcel might personally feel about the methods was immaterial. To allow his reservations to hold him back from his duty would be the most detestable form of cowardice.

Danel and Rada skulked around the exterior of the extractor, turning valves and blocking up pipes. Marcel and Henri took out clockbombs from their satchels, setting each charge at calculated points. He'd helped with the calculations earlier that evening. Looking at the Lazacorp schema, they'd pinpointed which pipes to cordon off so that, when their explosions went off, most of the resulting gas would flow up to the surface. Most, of course, was not all. Hence the gas masks.

The bombs were heavy to lug. Marcel crept slowly through the maze of machinery. It took a century to strap each bomb to the proper pipework, millennia to turn each twitching clockwork timer. Marcel knew they had ten minutes to flee; just enough time, if luck held.

The squad appeared suddenly, like phantoms, six guards in imperial blue armed with shotguns and bayonets, their soft footsteps hidden by the sounds of the great extractor. Marcel nearly walked into the first soldier, jumping back behind a glowing vat to avoid the blades and bullets. It took only seconds for the vast room to be filled with the gunshots and screams. Marcel ran, firing blindly behind him. He could hear, in the brief gaps of the cacophony, the sounds of dozens of boots beating against concrete. Principate soldiers started to trickle in, firing and shouting in confusion.

Marcel saw Henri set the last of his clockbombs. Out of the darkness a bayonet appeared, glistening briefly in the red light of the sangleum before plunging into Henri's back. Gunshots rang out from somewhere in the chaos, and the hand that held the bayonet fell to the ground. The blood of Imperial and Resurgence soldiers mixed in pools. At the far end of the room, he could see one of his masked brothers, Desct it must have been, run down a hallway, firing backwards. Marcel tried to sprint after him, but the flow of Principate soldiers had diverted itself in the pursuit of Desct, cutting off that path.

There had to be another way out. Marcel needed to find Alba. He turned around a vat of bubbling red and found a lone imperial. He aimed his rifle at the soldier, who turned at the sound.

Marcel froze. The soldier was young, barely in his twenties, if even that, his hair a light blond. His soft round face reminded Marcel of Kalem, a university friend. If those two had been in the same room Marcel wondered if he'd even be able to tell the difference.

Marcel had never taken a life. Not during the siege, not during the recon forays, not during the battle. He had once wondered, idly, if it would be like losing his virginity, to kill in the name of liberty.

Now his enemy stood before him. The boot and blade of the Principate, oppression made flesh. Marcel tried to pull the trigger, but found he couldn't. Not when looking the man face to face.

The imperial could.

Marcel felt the burn of metal rip into his right leg. He fell to the ground. Pain. It ripped through his body in a flash, and his vision nearly went black. He squinted through his agony-fogged mask to see the imperial jerking his rifle down towards Marcel, aiming another shot.

Then a bang. The soldier's forehead exploded from behind. A black-skulled figure came out from the darkness, pistol in hand. It spoke with Alba's muffled voice.

"Get up, Talwar."

She gave him her arm and pulled him up, the movement as painful as the initial shot. He hobbled with her, away from the chaos of the extractor room.

"Leave me," Marcel said. "I'm going to slow you down." No, that was a manifestation, an invention of later wishful thoughts. He remembered that in truth he said nothing as he held onto her arm. He merely moaned and screamed, nails deep into her coat, a desperate clutch for life.

A Principate soldier jumped out in front of them. As he aimed his rifle, the world started to shake.

All three of them fell to the ground. The imperial had almost lifted himself up when the red gas started to seep in. Marcel could see the realization grow on the man's face, the solution to the puzzle of the saboteurs' gas masks. It was quickly replaced by agony. He screamed death, blood pouring from his eyes. The soldier scratched at his face, skin melting away, falling to the ground in ribbons. Bulges grew under his flesh, twisting his features, and he started to vomit up chunks of his lungs. Marcel was horrified but couldn't look away; his eyes were affixed to the disintegrating corpse in front of him.

"Run!" Alba yelled, and she started to drag Marcel. He hobbled with her, pain shuddering through his leg with every step. They turned left. Left. Right. Left. Up some stairs. Right. Left. Through a rusted door. Left. Right. Right. Left. Alba had the maze memorized. The gas chased them; with every hobbled step, it gained a metre.

A single pink wisp floated beyond the gas cloud and struck Marcel's open wound. The pain was worse than anything he had imagined. He screamed, tears running from his eyes, and fell to the ground. The world twisted around him as his flesh burned. No, not burned, rotted, a month's worth of post-mortem decay in seconds. He felt himself being dragged. The red smoke covered him, engulfed him, all was pain. Faces, he saw faces in the smoke. Henri screaming in front of him, bayonet bursting through his chest, Kalem clutching at the hole in his face, the Principate soldier crying, flesh flowing with the tears. Beyond all that, Marcel saw a skinless figure in the mist. It was gargantuan, blood pouring like rivers down its sides, its eyes of shadow. The horrific figure grew and grew, until the world was nothing but its flesh, all the while staring down to Marcel, through Marcel, piercing him with his gaze. Marcel screamed, and his screams harmonized with the thousands of screams around him, as the skinless figure fell upon him.

Thud. Marcel's metal leg hit the floor, jolting him awake.

He glanced out, blinking in the dark, sweat dripping from his forehead. His office stared back at him, lit only by the small lamp on his desk and the white of moonlight peeking in from outside.

It took Marcel more than a moment to lift himself from his chair. His back ached, the chair a poor substitute for a bed. He accidentally kicked the pulp sitting on the floor, *The Ghul-Hunters of Tor*, an old pre-Calamity edition. Right, he'd been reading before he dozed. The book was no masterpiece, but he'd paid ninety frascs for it, so he picked up the novella and flicked the light switch, a single bulb buzzing to brightness.

He tossed the book on the desk and stumbled through the screen door behind his chair to the nook he used as a bedroom and kitchen. His leg still burned, and he braced himself on the wall, moaning softly. With a shaking hand, he took a vial of æther-oil from under the sink, and pulled up his pants leg to refill his prosthetic's fuel-capsule. Watching the liquid trickle in helped remind him that the leg was gone, the pain phantom.

When he was feeling a tad more himself, he put a pan of water to boil for coffee. It was very late, or very early, whichever, but he had no intention of going back to sleep now.

Marcel could remember that he had been working when he dozed. Well, "working," hence the pulp. Truth was, there wasn't much to do beside wait for a case, a mystery, a *something* to wander into his office, and since the Fareau case, no one had come knocking.

He took off his sweat soaked shirt and put on a slightly cleaner one. Maybe it was the workless days that sent him into that place, back through the Battle Under Huile. It wasn't much of a battle, though it was a victory. Saved the city, he'd been told, and it he knew it true. It was the greatest thing he had ever done, it was what made him a hero, yet even the thought of it brought on bouts of nausea and splitting agony.

Outside the streets were empty. Huile was a sleepy city by his standards, but it was a free one. He watched the simple nothing pass on by as he sipped his coffee. It was important he didn't forget what he had won; it was vital that he remembered what the sacrifices had been for. It had initially surprised Marcel that the exact methods of their victory had been paved over in the post-war celebrations; he had expected criticism by civilians who didn't understand the necessity of decisive action. Instead, all talk was of courage and spirit, on heroism, no words wasted on clockbombs and sangleum gas. Part of Marcel wanted to bring it up, to defend himself from the attacks that never came, but that was just egoism and foolishness. The UCCR survived on the spirits of its citizenry, public hand wringing over unpleasant specifics did nothing to defend the freedoms that brave soldiers had died to preserve. War meant death, war meant doing thing you didn't want to, acts that would be horrifying anywhere else; in the end, it was for the best, and in the end, a free, just, and prosperous Huile made all his petty traumas meaningless. He knew this, Desct knew this, Alba... Alba had her own opinions.

Perhaps it was the Gileon Fareau case that had been bothering him. Everything had gone well, impressively well, near perfect; Lambert had said so himself. Marcel couldn't quite pin down why, then, it had felt so disappointing in the end. Perhaps it was that his suspicions of Verus went nowhere. Or it was the simple anticlimax, with Gall shipped out of town towards Ordone, where justice would be duly and dryly meted out. Marcel signed a few witness statements and received an envelope of frascs plus a pat-on-the-back as payment from Lambert. Then back to his apartment.

Yet, how was it supposed to end? With some dramatic confrontation, with justice meted out instantly? Summary execution was the style of waste barbarians and Principate tyrants. A sensible world worked slowly and methodically. Things were as they should be, he told himself.

Alba had been right about one thing, though; the real world wasn't a pulp. Sometimes you just had to grind your teeth and do your job, whether it was painful or utterly monotonous.

He poured himself another cup and sat down back at his desk. He picked up the pulp and started to read. Tomorrow, perhaps, work would come knocking. Perhaps he'd be called on for something great, or at least, something to keep him busy.

Until then, he'd sip and read.

Chapter 17

The hours of the night went by in a blurry haze, fear fueling Sylvaine's every step. She could barely remember how she had made it to the bottom of the mountain, dashing around winding back roads, sprinting through sleeping mountainside suburbs, leaping over meltwater rivulets, and scrambling down rocky, scrap-strewn scarps. She ran past late-running agri-factories, sprinting from bush to rock to forgotten junk-pile in a panic. The factories' lights had once comforted her from the distance of her apartment, but now each dusty window bursting with industrial glow seemed to her like searching spotlights.

Late night turned to early morning, and Sylvaine found herself still sprinting, clothes torn, fur matted, through landscapes of rusting machinery, the skeletons of old abandoned industrial towns scavenged hollow. She gave only a single glance back at the distant ætherlamp blur of Icaria. The city that had once been a grand sanctuary on a hill now loomed over her, judging her, its lights a thousand eyes ready to search out the animal who had mauled its citizens.

Eventually her fear dissolved into dazed despair, and she could barely force herself to shuffle forward along the cracked ground, crumbling concrete, and waste-hardened shrubs. She swore softly as a razorbush took off a digit-length of her dress-sleeve, as well as a small amount of skin and fur. She glanced up at the sky: still black, but framed on the horizon by a soft glow. It would be sunrise soon. How soon? She hadn't a clue, but she was near deliriously weary. Her mouth was dry, and she caught her nose searching vainly for the smell of meat.

She let herself collapse and crawled slowly into a ditch that led off from some ruins of an indeterminable function. There she found a large rusting pipe to drag herself into.

She curled up, hands clutching her knees. The face of Gearswit stared even through her closed eyelids. As much as she tried, she found she could not remember how he had looked before, in lectures and in private meetings, but could only see his body curled in a puddle of blood and agony. She clenched her eyes shut and tried not to think, tried not to feel.

Sylvaine had almost made it to some delirious slumber when she noticed a deep humming. It took her a moment to realize it was the voice of a man. She heard footsteps and smelled musk. It was a familiar odor, but in her half-sleep she couldn't place it.

Her breathing slowed, and she squeezed herself into a smaller ball. She tried to remember the scent. It wasn't from any student she could recall. Was the man a cop? They'd have to be searching pretty far, which seemed unlikely, but then luck had clearly already abandoned her. Perhaps her nose had misplaced the odor and it *was* a stranger, some violent raider or greedy slaver. No, she was too close to the city for that. Truth was she could not think of a single person she'd want to find her.

The man interrupted his humming with occasional bursts of hymn-like song, somberly cheerful. She couldn't understand the words, but recognized them as Oradea, the tongue human preachers would mutter in when they went about on their nonsense rituals during Abolinia and other holidays.

She peeked out through a crack and recognized the strange bald man who had accosted her twice. She shrunk back. Wasn't it enough to have her life collapse completely? Now she had to hide in a pipe from some maniac who had most likely been chased out of Icaria. Or worse still, came the chilling thought, had been stalking her.

After a moment, she peeked out again to see that the man had paused at a clearing just above the ditch. He surveyed the ground, and then started to gather dried brush into a pile. With some flint he lit a fire and then sat on an old cinderblock. He still wore the same silver-tinted plate of a mask over his left eye, still held that strange blue-gray bracelet, but in his hand he now held a piece of her torn indigo dress.

The man reached into his bag and pulled out raw meat. Dustsnake, Sylvaine was embarrassed her nose could recognize it, and more embarrassed about how much she ached for it. But why had the man stopped at this ditch? She hoped against all reasonable hope that he didn't know she was—

"Do not think me a threat, Sylvaine."

Her breathing froze completely.

The man took the meat and skewered it, continuing to hum. "If you were to run now, I would not chase, and if you choose to stay and say nothing, I will leave in my time."

He cooked the meat over the fire, turning the skewer slowing in his fingers.

"I did not introduce myself, I realize, back in Icaria," he said. "My name is Kayip. I am sorry for how I acted. I have spent too long in the Wastes. I did not know how to reach you, to warn you. I must have seemed a madman. You are not the first to think that of me. Had I the time, had I been able to speak with you on sensible terms, had I known how to present myself...if I knew now..."

His voice drifted off for a moment. Daylight started to hint at the edges of the horizon, and somewhere a skragger cawed.

"I know what sort of man Roache is," the man said. "I have dealt with him before. I know what horrible things he did to you. All I can say is that I am sorry I was not able to stop him."

He paused, staring into the fire. His face seemed long worn; it hung baggy and scarred. Yet there still seemed some energy to his gaze, some determination. Not ferocity, just a weary resolution.

"It is no excuse," the man continued. "It was my failure. And now an innocent man is dead and more still are forever hurt, yourself included. Were I younger, perhaps I would have said that I know how you feel. Or perhaps I would have said nothing, for I was not one to talk when action would suffice. But the world is bigger than I knew when I was young. The Demiurge made people in all shapes and minds, and I cannot claim to understand the truth of all of them. Instead I will say that I have made mistakes, and that I no longer judge others who make them as well."

He took out a small pouch and sprinkled salt on the snake meat.

"Let me tell you a story. It is from *The Chronicles of the Ascended*. I know engineers are not known for their piety, but perhaps you can find some wisdom in it. The story starts in ancient times, before the Calamity, before the birth of the Principate and the Resurgence, before the regental Republic that preceded them, and even before that first Imperium that gave mankind the gift of æther and the revelations of the Demiurge.

"In this time men lived among beasts, and there were neither Malva nor Salvi, nor Mutants nor Kortonians. Perhaps there were Ferrals then, but if so, they lived no worse than the men, who huddled in tribes, with walls of wood and nothing more than bows and slings to keep the monsters of the night at bay.

"In one of these tribes lived two brothers, Istmol and Ephram. They ruled their village together, and it was a rich village, on the banks of the river Delur, guarded by four walls, so that troglyns and trolls could not harm their family.

"One day, the brothers decided that they should go hunting. They were the greatest bowmen in their village and wished to see who could bring down the largest boar. But there was another man, Fauvius, who lived in the forest. He was a wicked man, a sorcerer, one who spoke to demons, and danced with troglyns and satyrs. This man envied the village, and when the brothers were gone, took fire to it, killing the men and woman alike, until there was nothing left but ash.

"When the two brothers returned, they fell to the ground with grief and lamented their woes for three days and three nights. After this, they spoke with one another. They knew it was their fault, for they were great warriors, yet they had left their village unguarded. Istmol said they should go to the mountains to start again and build a new village. Ephram did not agree. He said they must fight the sorcerer, must make him bleed a drop for every drop of blood he spilled of their family. And so the two brothers traveled along their own paths. Istmol went to the mountains. Ephram went to hunt Fauvius. And true to his word he killed the sorcerer. By this the land was rid of that man's evil."

The wind blew softly from the Wastes, and the meat crackled and sizzled.

"I always thought of myself as Ephram," the man continued, "that I could not see an evil so great, one that had wronged me, and permit it to live. I know the sins of Roache, and I know whatever ill you have to say of the monster it is the truth. You are innocent. But you are also clever and strong—I can see that. If you wish, you could be like Istmol. I believe you could survive it. But I do believe it would be better if Ephram did not go it alone."

He sat there motionless for a few minutes. Then he took a piece of meat and started to chew. Slowly, very slowly at first, Sylvaine crawled out of her hiding spot. The man didn't react, he did not turn to her or get up. She stood and started to walk out of the ditch, tripping once. She was conscious of how she looked, filthy, covered in dirt and blood, not all of it her own. When she got close, the man looked at her with a small smile. With a languidness to match her own caution, he took up a skewer of meat and offered it.

"You look hungry," Kayip said. "And there is much I would like to discuss."

"...And I saw a figure, gilded by sunlight,
Standing on a hill of empty memories,
He stared down at me, ignoring the blight,
Of a land forgotten amongst miseries,
What could be taken from such a man? I wondered there,
Or what could be given?
I cannot tell you, my friends, for as the sun finally left us,
The figure walked off into the night..."

—*"Poems of the Wastes" Collected by Bengard Stranik*

Chapter 18

The Phoenix swayed languidly in the evening drafts, which snuck in through the large open doors of City Hall. Men and women of every flake of Huile's upper crust drank, mingled, and laughed. Debutantes from nearby cities flirted with mustached politicians who made promises both lofty and empty while caravan-lords told lewd jokes, garnering mixed receptions.

Marcel leaned on one of the marble pillars of the multistoried atrium, tulip glass still full, and watched the swaying Banner of the Phoenix. He had been there, two years ago, when they first hoisted the undying firebird up onto those white walls. It was a testament to a new era of peace; the phoenix's howling cry a promise of justice and prosperity for the people of Huile. The banner itself was stunning, strands of radiant reds sewn together by the most elaborate machinery, the eternal bird of flames and freedom woven in a detail that was not lifelike, but truer than life. It was beautiful. It was wondrous.

It was also generic. One of hundreds of the exact same make he had seen come out of factories back in Phenia. Just as rote and routine as this party, utterly indistinguishable.

Marcel sipped his drink. It was an off-brown liquor, speckled with colored chocolate to look like metal shavings. An *Icarian Rusty*, supposedly an import from the City of Engineers, or so Lazarus had claimed. It tasted much like it looked, and Marcel spat the mouthful back into the cup

This was supposed to be a celebration of Lazarus Roache's homecoming, but Marcel hadn't found a moment yet to speak with the man. As soon as Lazarus had finished his speeches, apparently a vital part of the return-party process, he was swarmed by old-friends, well-wishers, and brown-nosers. As of now the man was hosting a conversation between himself, a visiting dignitary from the city of Nortas, and Mayor Durand, spurring both intense nodding and bouts of laughter from the onlookers.

Marcel had walked into this party with a focused purpose. Lazarus was finally back, which meant there was finally someone whose ears Marcel could trust with his misgivings over the Gall case. If there were anyone who might know if Marcel's suspicions about Verus had some merit, it would be the man who had worked with the foreman for most of a decade.

Yet watching the crowd now, Marcel couldn't help but feel foolish. Why should Roache give the idea any more heed than Lambert had? It was all speculation, gut feelings, no proof. If there was any truth to his misgivings, Marcel hadn't managed to scrape it up. Most likely he was chasing a figment: Gall was a brute, Gileon a dead idiot, and Marcel was wasting his time trying to connect dots that didn't exist.

He found that his gaze was searching around the room. It took him a moment to realize what his subconscious was looking for: Desct's grin. Marcel had been to dozens of parties such as this, and every time he had felt at the periphery, at odds with the pomp and schmoozing, he had found that grin. The one other person who would poke fun at the whole endeavor, who could share snide asides in some back corner. The one other person who had actually understood what suffering had been spent to create a city where such frivolities could be thrown so freely. They hadn't always talked much, especially as the years passed, but Desct had always been good for a joke, or at least a smile.

And now even that was gone.

"Ah, Marcel!" The familiar voice cut through the din, as Lambert appeared out of the crowd, a young woman in one arm, a thin mustached man led by the other. Marcel didn't bother to figure out if the woman was new, and Lambert didn't bother to introduce her, instead turning to the man.

"This is Mr. Wojik, a fellow Justice Minister. Please, this is Mr. Talwar, one of my fellow soldiers in the Huile Sewer Rats. Unsightly name, I know, but then, aesthetics hold little clout on the battlefield."

The man took Marcel's hand. "A pleasure."

"Mr. Wojik recently presided over a fascinating case, what did you call it?" Lambert began. Marcel tried to think of a polite-ish way to show that he wasn't interested, but his friend was already in the grip of his own words. "Yes, yes the *Vidish Lumber Defection Case*. You see, we had some smugglers on hire in Videk, transporting wood they had raided from Principate lumber camps. It was all under normal contracts, of course, transport over the Atsols and all that..."

Marcel nodded along and Lambert spoke with his fingers.

"But then they sold half their cargo to uh..." Lambert paused.

"Adaldorf," Mr. Wojik said.

"Yes, Adaldorf! Whose mayor had recently signed a treaty of friendship with the Imperial Governor up in Videk. No surprises there, that city's political whims flick like the leaves in a storm, a sad state of affairs, truly."

"Right," Marcel said, not listening.

"This was an obvious breach of contract, you see, practically selling the smuggled goods back to the Principate. But, of course, the smugglers, scoundrels to the last, claimed that because

Adaldorf had been neutral when their original contract was signed..."

Marcel maintained his blank nodding, allowing the words to fade into shapeless noise until he noticed the woman start to laugh, with Mr. Wojik brushing off what must have been a compliment.

"...13,000 frascs and the ringleader will be facing a two-year sentence if he ever shows his face in Resurgence territory again!" Lambert finished.

"Impressive," Marcel said. Then, noticing the stare of Lambert, he realized the onus of the conversation had fallen on himself.

"So," Marcel began, facing Wojik, "where are you stationed?"

"Ordone," the man said.

"Really?" Marcel said, a sudden burst of excitement now flowing back through him. "How's the Corvin Gall case going?"

"Corvin...?" the man asked, eyebrows tilted.

Lambert laughed. "My dear apologies, Marcel. A mix-up, I don't believe I mentioned, that case was shifted last-minute to Quorgon. It's a whole hubbub you see, just nonsense, bureaucrat stuff. I won't bore you with the details."

Marcel deflated. He opened his mouth to ask another question when Lambert's head turned.

"Oh! I didn't know Gaius Couture was here. Have you met him, Mr. Wojik? He just wrote a most wonderful book on the Second Schism. Excuse us, Marcel."

And the trio was gone, as quick as they had come, disappearing into a ring that surrounded a bald, elderly man kept upright by two metal limbs. Marcel wondered if he should force himself to join them, but knew this, like everything else here, was pointless, empty flattery and vacant nods. Marcel put down his drink. Why had he even bothered to come at all?

These parties could be as vapid as Alba had declared. They were beneath them, or so she had insisted, but then, everything seemed to be beneath her in those weeks after the battle.

"You're just going to waste yourself here," she had said. Back then, the festive mood was constant under the glow of victory, as opposed to the occasional soirees of peacetime. Marcel had lost consciousness clinging to Alba as they ran from the depths of Lazacorp, surrounded by death and gas, but awoke to balloons, music, parades, and champagne. It was difficult in those first weeks to play the role of hero, to put on a stoic face with the news of his dead squad mates, to pretend that his lost leg was a mere warrior's scar.

Alba had made the process even more arduous, giving no time to the crowds, avoiding all speeches and social events. She had dragged him from some mid-afternoon festivity, just a few days after the Phoenix had first made its appearance within City Hall, to take a walk outside the walls of Huile, where the wreckage of their first disastrous battle still marked Huile Field.

He had followed her with some difficulty, lugging his new metal leg more than walking on it, until she stopped and pointed outward towards the rotting ruinscape.

"This is war," she had said. "Remember that, Marcel. Not the parades, not the accolades, or songs, or stories to print in pulps, or whatever. This."

Marcel rubbed his arms in the early chill, glancing quickly at the crumbled structures and abandoned tanks, at the craters and sunken trenches. The only things intact on the field were several silent tread-drillers used intermittently to clear the wreckage. Some skraggers still flew about, searching for forgotten graves.

"I've seen it," Marcel said. "Is that why you wanted to walk out here? Just to take in the...view?"

She shook her head. "Don't know who's listening in there."

"Come on now, don't be ridiculous. We just fought to free this city."

"Yes," she said. "*We* fought to free this city. *We*," and she gestured now to the entire ruined landscape, "suffered to free it.

Not them, Marcel, not the bureaucrats and commanders and damn sangleum salesmen. It's an easy thing to celebrate for them."

"I mean, that's not..." Marcel pulled up his coat, and leaned back on the old towering wall, balancing his weight on the stiff prosthetic. "That's not fair. Plenty of people suffered, plenty of people risked their lives and livelihood, not just us. Like that Lazarus guy. If he had been caught sneaking out of the Principate camp—"

"Then I'm sure he would have made a nice excuse for himself," Alba said.

Marcel just shook his head. The woman was being plain unreasonable.

"Well, if you've decided to forget what the Confederacy stands for, let me remind you that whatever you might think of Lazarus, or Durand, or any of them, we have gifted to this city freedom. The freedom to think what they want, to do what they want, to say whatever in Inferno they want." He kicked dust over a scrap of imperial blue fabric that fluttered beneath him. "Except for Principate propaganda and other such idiocy."

"You've always thought laws were stone," Alba said, stepping onto the remains of a cracked concrete foundation, which crumbled slightly from the weight. "Well, they're not even that, I can tell you. You believe in these ideas, justice, freedom. Inferno, I'd like to as well. But out here, Mar, people will use anything they can on you, any weakness. Don't let your ideals be a weakness."

Marcel stretched out his cogleg. "Demiurge, Alba, I don't even know what you want. We won."

Alba turned back, and stared up and down Huile's wall. The cracks in it had been filled with mortar in places, the rest held in by unmanned scaffolds. The iron spires of Blackwood Row's refineries peaked over.

"They cleared out all the bodies there." She pointed. "All the imperials. While you were still screaming in an unconscious stupor, I went out to see. Haven't heard if they ever found Henri's body, or Rada's, or if they would even be able to identify them if they did."

Marcel shook his head and tried not to think. The faces melting into mush, the screams echoing down the hallways. There was a reason he didn't add in those details when speaking at official events, they were grim, nauseating, agonizing. If only Alba would stop trying to force them back into his mind, maybe one day they might even fade away, like a bad dream.

"I told them it was a terrible idea, Roache's plan," she said. "I argued. I did my duty in the end, but I argued first. If we weren't the only intact squad maybe I could have shifted the job but..." she shook her head. "Any victory that required that, it's not one I'm keen to celebrate."

Marcel felt his own scowl. "It almost sounds like you feel bad for the imperials. You heard Lazarus, they'd have done the same. They were even planning on releasing the gas on their own citizens as punishment."

Alba shrugged and crossed her arms. "So Roache claimed." She glanced out again and sighed. "Maybe I do pity them a little. A leg is one thing, but you haven't seen what that gas does to a whole body. I don't mourn them, though. I hate the Principate more than you do, Mar, I can promise you that, but not for some ideals, not for freedom or history. They were the enemy, the fuckers in those uniforms against the fuckers in our own. This, this whole thing," she gestured towards just about everywhere, "this wasn't fought for some debate you would find in a philosophy book. They had the red stuff in the ground and we wanted it back. So, we took it."

"I can see why you wanted to talk alone." Marcel pushed himself off, and started to walk, stumble, back the way they came. "Henri, Rada, Danel, what would they think hearing all this?"

"I don't know," she said simply. "And you don't either. We will never know." She paused a moment. "I was hoping you would say no, Mar, that you would stay back in the end, that's why I gave you the chance."

"The chance to be a coward," Marcel said, turning back. "I love you, Alba, but you can't protect me. I'm a soldier."

"You weren't meant to be a soldier," Alba said. "You had the ambition and the bravery, Mar, but, Inferno, you were a student. You never even shot anyone."

"I did my duty!" Marcel said, louder than he meant to. "Since when was that not what soldiers did? I fought and I suffered and we won."

She stared at him with those two sapphire eyes, giving him a look he couldn't cleanly read. "We survived," she said. "I'm happy we did, but what happened wasn't something to celebrate. We survived, and others didn't, and now it's past."

"We're heroes, Alba," Marcel said, gaze at the ground. "Danel... Henri... Rada... they're martyrs. These aren't pleasant jobs, but they are the ones we took."

They both held their silence as the frost-tinged wind swept across the ruins. The gust whistled as it flew; it was easy to imagine voices in that sounds, thousands of soft whispers.

"I'm leaving," Alba said finally.

"Yeah," Marcel said, starting to stagger off. "Then let's get going, it's getting cold."

"Huile."

Marcel turned around.

"I'm leaving Huile," Alba said, "Our tour is done, we don't need this mudlion's shit pit, and trust me it doesn't want us. Might act like it does, but it'll get bored soon enough."

"We just...after all..." Marcel had to fight to keep himself from sputtering on his words. "We just freed Huile. It's a new beginning. We can make something of this town, but you just want to abandon it? Inferno, Alba, we have to stay."

She walked up to him, stepping over the rusting shards of a half-buried motorcycle. "Why? For what? Your service is up. There's nothing keeping you here. You don't even have a job."

"Lambert offered me a position in the Office of Justice." Marcel struggled to keep his balance, forcing his cogleg down with his hands when it didn't respond right. "To work establishing real Resurgence law."

"So, what, you're going to be a pencil-pusher?"

He tried to laugh the idea off even though he had considered it. "I'm just saying I have offers is all. Huile needs help getting back on its feet."

Alba shook her head. Her gaze, which had been hard as stone during battle, and surprisingly soft on moon-lit midnights, was now knife-sharp. "Huile doesn't need us, Inferno, it's already just using us as party decorations, as talking pieces." She sneered. "You're more than that; you could have a real future. *We* could have a future, if you wanted one. Could make a life beyond this city and its miseries. We wouldn't need to follow the orders of self-serving, desk-sitting bastards in two-piece suits, but could travel our own path. Don't let this battle be your damn crowning achievement, Marcel. You can do more than this town will ever allow. You're just going to waste yourself—"

Marcel slammed his undrunk Icarian Rusty onto the table, and rubbed his head. He had proved her wrong a hundred times over, each successful case clear proof that Huile had needed him. Yet still, he could never get the memories to fade, never get her words, her pitying, sneering gaze from his mind.

The crowd continued its talking and laughter. Yes, Alba was right about the parties. It was their cyclical inanities that were driving Marcel back to unpleasant memories. Solve a case, wait in his office, visit the next shindig. Over the past two years, Marcel had gone from searching for work to merely waiting around for it to fall into his lap. Well, he didn't need to wait, hadn't needed to twiddle his thumbs, sitting around until Roache's return. This lingering ennui he felt, it was a wakeup, a reminder that *he* had made himself the man he was. His dissatisfaction was a reflection of an unnecessary passivity.

The solution was clear enough, and he was glad that Lazarus' brief sojourn abroad had made it obvious. Marcel would waste no more time, wait no more, take his boots to the pavement and search out his suspicions himself. He had never needed Lambert or Roache's *permission* to do so; he worked for himself. To allow himself to forget that would just be proving Alba right.

With a new determination, Marcel buttoned his coat and made for the door. He would return to Roache on his own terms, when he had the case he wanted to make. He would come to his own conclusions on Gall and Verus, then he—

"Marcel!" Lazarus' voice rung through the air. Marcel turned to see the man's eyes affixed in his direction, a wide smile on his face as he waved him over. Marcel paused his step, and then sheepishly unfixed his coat buttons and walked over, past a dozen other people, a few he recognized from previous parties, others new, who circled around Roache.

"This, my friends," Lazarus said, "is the true hero of the hour, and not for the first time." He raised his glass and the rest in crowd followed his lead, looking at the private investigator as a strange, previously unnoticed, wonder.

"Two weeks from now, on the twenty-fifth of Noth," Roache said, "Lazacorp will be opening its water treatment plant. I think it is a given that you shall all be invited to the opening party. Soon fresh water will be flowing through this city, and it is all thanks to this man right here who rooted out the damnable snake who had been tormenting our work, a scoundrel who had even murdered a fellow employee. Gone now, thank the Demiurge, to his proper justice."

A polite round of applause followed. Marcel couldn't help but give a small blush.

"Thank you," he mumbled.

Lazarus' head tilted for a quick moment, then he turned to the men and women around him. "Apologies my friends, but I remembered I have to quickly attend to some business. Marcel, would you mind speaking with me privately? I could use some advice."

Marcel nodded, "Sure, though I think I'll be heading out in a moment."

"That's all the time it will take," Lazarus said.

Roache led Marcel, a tad befuddled, from the crowd. They moved together through the party, dodging dozens of interested guests who vied for Lazarus' attention with questions, small talk, and unprompted compliments. The man grinned and disengaged in a courteous and strategic manner until he and Marcel were suddenly up on the second floor, out on a balcony overlooking the city. Well, overlooking as much of the city as could be seen from two stories up, but it did give Marcel a nice view down the city-spanning Viexus Boulevard.

He took in the dimly glowing streetlight and above them the shimmering stars that in his childhood had always been driven from the sky by the constant light of Phenia. Their presence was one of the small benefits to a life at the edges of civilization.

"You look uneasy," Lazarus said.

"Well... The Gall case has been bugging me," Marcel admitted.

"Always sniffing," Lazarus mused, then, catching Marcel's gaze, "A joke, Marcel. What concerns you?"

Marcel tapped his fingers on the baluster. He had just planned to build on his suspicions first... but since he was here already there was no point in delaying. "Verus was dogging me at every turn during my investigation."

"Verus is a rough man," Lazarus said. "Trust me, I have much experience working with him. He can be at times... well a griffon's asshole."

Lazarus began to laugh, and Marcel couldn't help but join in.

"Well put," Marcel said, "but he was worse than usual, dragging his feet on everything."

"I was away." Lazarus shrugged. "Verus doesn't like his authority questioned, even when he's wrong, it's one of his less flattering characteristics."

Marcel glanced at Roache. "It really got him going when I mentioned the missing schematics. Was there a reason you didn't tell him about their recovery?" He half expected Lazarus to fold his arms in frustration, or at least get a tad red in the face. Instead the man laughed again.

"You think he was intolerable then? Imagine if I had rubbed his nose in it that you had found the schematics, which he was supposed to be watching over. The man would have been apoplectic." Lazarus's face straightened. "I suspected Gall, and there was no way I could tell Verus about your discovery without those suspicions getting back to the engineer. I doubt you would have caught him if he were so on guard."

It made some sense, Marcel had to admit. "If Verus is causing you so much trouble, why do you even keep him around?"

"I could give you legal reasons, contracts and the like, but that is only surface-level." Lazarus gestured backwards towards the party. "Is each person in that building a noble spirit, Marcel? Is each one likeable and pleasant? I have dealt with more of them than you, and I can respond with an emphatic *no*. But understand, Marcel, that it is only because of them that this city functions. Whether through their labor, or patronage, or political connections, it is because of them this city can remain free and functional. Verus can be a troglyn's shit-and-a-half, but he keeps the pumps running and æthericity flowing. Valor and justice can only ever be half of the equation; we must keep the lights on, and, despite his mannerisms, there is no man with better skill for that than our foreman."

The city glowed soft beneath them, and Marcel could still see the smoke of Blackwood Row floating in the moonlight. "He was very insistent that he get the schematics," Marcel said. "Even after Gall was implicated, he demanded them."

Lazarus sighed. "Useless pieces of paper. He thought he could still glean something from the scribbles of a criminal. Listen, Marcel," Lazarus gently grasped his shoulder, "if you're worried about these schematics, well, perhaps I can soothe your nerves. Those documents are still with Lambert. I can show them to you if you wish. I have no need for useless notes, nor need for Verus to be wasting our time with them. I have new engineers on staff, competent ones, straight and on the level. So even if Verus was some conspiratorial whatever, he has no access to anything. All right, Marcel?"

Marcel nodded. "That is good to hear, I just think—"

"Trust me, I know my company, I know what goes on in Blackwood Row. Things are safe." His eyes caught Marcel, and held not frustration, but a sympathetic glint. "You're used to being the hero, Marcel. Do you still feel one?"

"I mean..." Marcel stammered, unsure how to answer.

"You should," Lazarus said, grabbing his hand. "But not for the reasons *they* tell you to. Not just for your achievements, not just for saving the city, not just for cleaning the streets of Principate traitors. You're a hero for your sacrifices, Marcel, don't think I haven't noticed."

Lazarus's grasp was firm, but his gaze was gentle.

"I've seen your apartment," he continued. "You could be making the salary of Lambert, you could be walking on two legs of muscle and bone, but you gave those up for this city. And because of that, Huile is safe."

There was a warmth to Lazarus' words. When he talked about Marcel's past the memories no longer felt painful, nor claustrophobic or infected with doubt.

"You're used to being the hero, but not all victories end with parades, not all triumphs are as grand as they were in wartime," Lazarus said, letting go of his grip. "It's hard to know when you need to take a break from heroism."

"I'm just trying to do my job," Marcel said. But perhaps the man was right. Perhaps it was his own insistence that something *had* to be wrong that had been bothering him.

"And you have done your job. Many times over." Lazarus turned again to the city. "You're one of the few willing to do what's needed, to make the necessary sacrifices. That's why I knew Huile would be safe under your eyes, that it will continue to be safe. So give yourself credit, Marcel. You did your duty and then some. All is finally as it should be."

Marcel took in the words. He wished he could have heard them from Alba, but he supposed the source didn't matter. Lazarus was right. The man caught his smile, which Marcel had tried to hide, and slapped him on the shoulder.

"Listen," Lazarus said, "I have to keep some of the fancy suits entertained. But take this pressure off yourself Marcel, enjoy your successes without all these unnecessary worries. You've done the right thing. I trust you always will." The man winked as he left.

Marcel leaned on the balustrade. He sighed and nodded to no one, before turning to look over the city. His city. The real city.

Huile was beautiful in its own way. The dim lampposts flickered dancing shadows and the occasional dots of Huilian houses still awake matched, in a loose pattern, the stars above. Here was something worth fighting for, worth suffering for. His vigilance had paid off; his long days of nothing were meaningless compared to the few moments when he had rescued the city. Perhaps for one night at least he would allow himself to accept that, to take the pride he knew he deserved.

He stretched and caught a glimpse of something. A figure on a roof, lit only by the slight glow of midnight. It was a tiled roof, with no terraces or clear stairway entrances. Strange enough for one to be wandering about on such a rooftop, but at such an hour? He couldn't make the figure out, but thought for a second he noticed a glow off its eyes.

Had he drunk more than he realized? He rubbed his eyes and turned to see if there was another to corroborate his vision, but by then the figure was gone.

Marcel shook his head and walked back into the party.

Chapter 19

"Well, Roache was definitely present," Sylvaine said as she crawled through the window back into the old garret. "I mean, it's his party, so no surprises there."

"And the man?" Kayip asked, glancing through a hole in a curtain which had seemingly gestated several generations of moths.

Sylvaine glanced again at the photo Kayip had given her. Compared to the rest of his grim collection, this one was fairly tame, showing a young, sharp-chinned man in uniform sitting in a parade autocar beside Lazarus Roache. Roache looked as he always looked, though paler in the black-and-white photograph. The darker-skinned man resembled, fairly exactly, the figure she had seen chatting with Lazarus outside.

"It seems to be this Talwar guy," she said. "Is your friend reliable? I have a hard time trusting his faith in this private investigator."

Kayip took the photo of Marcel and examined it under blinding handtorch light. The moonlight seemed plenty bright to Sylvaine; it was easy to forget that humans' sight was far more limited.

"He knows this man well," Kayip said, "I trust his judgment."

"I'm just saying this Marcel seems pretty friendly with Roache."

"So were you at one point," Kayip said. He caught Sylvaine's scowl before she realized she was making one. "I am sorry," the monk said quickly. "I didn't mean..." He glanced at the photo again, then after a moment shook his head. "You are not alone. I have fallen for Roache's words. So have many others. And, regardless, Mr. Talwar is the only one who has the full set of schematics the mutants stole."

There was little argument with that. Sylvaine had never visited Huile, hadn't even heard of this backwater Wastes-edge city until Kayip mentioned it, but the monk apparently knew the city quite well. The rewards of his last trip had been schematics of Lazacorp's recent project, some of which had made their way to Gearswit, and then to her. Those vital notes had been, unfortunately, left in Roache's apartment. Neither she nor the monk had thrown blame onto each other; if he had been able to sneak a meeting with Gearswit, or if she had had the wit to understand the meaning of the schematics, then perhaps they wouldn't currently be hiding out in an abandoned attic in Huile.

Kayip now returned to his customary silence as he crossed his legs and closed his eye in thought. This, she had gathered from their few weeks spent traveling together, was his usual state. The monk was polite, even oddly gentle at times, but he seemed either unused to company such as hers, or, more likely, company of any sort.

The journey from Icaria to Huile had been a strange one. Sylvaine had only traveled once before in her life and that had been up from her parents' home in Taliers to Icaria itself. That trip hadn't been in luxury—no Phenian æroship for the daughter of a middle-class clerk—but it had been safe. She had managed to book train tickets up through most of Bastillia, and then bought her way into, if not entirely comfortable, at least relatively safe caravans, whose paths hugged the more civilized eastern edge of the Border States, near the foot of the Skyknife Mountains. She hadn't seen much of the Border States properly outside of the occasional motor-inn, and she hadn't time to stay long in any one city.

Kayip, however, did not move through the networks of the most reputable Border State cities. Instead his path skirted west through the more waste-touched lands. Here the men and women were rougher, their styles scavenged, the food strange tasting, and the environment stranger still. The deeper they got—and Kayip assured her they had not gone truly deep—the more altered the animals and plant-life. Trees grew twisted, some oozing red sap that smelled like sangleum, others were armed with leaves like barbed wire or flaunted nuts that resembled rusting bolts. Taur herds were a common sight, and farmers bred spikefowl, complaining to any who would listen about the constant pestilence of needlecats or opportunistic strixes. Kayip would nod and ask for directions to the nearest fuel-up station where men would pour poorly filtered æther-oil from leaking jugs down a funnel into Kayip's autotruck. Of course, this was only after Kayip negotiated the ludicrous prices the men offered. It had felt odd to see such value placed on fuel that in Icaria was burned routinely, but if the men determined that Kayip played the pauper too heavily, they were quick to display their holster and demand payment *now*.

Luckily the monk had been skilled with his words and had only had to display force once when an ill-dressed, half-mutated hulk of a man asked if Sylvaine ("that beastwoman thing" were his exact words) was for sale, and, ignoring Kayip's answer, started listing prices. As the situation grew heated Kayip unfurled his blade, that long slender azure sword which morphed by ancient and arcane mechanisms was unparalleled even by modern engineering, and used it to cut through three stacked cinderblocks the man had just seconds before used as seating. This seemed enough to terrify the man's mouth shut.

It was also the first sign, besides from his pious musing, that Kayip was in fact the hieromonk he claimed to be. Sylvaine knew well that the devotees of the Demiurge wielded their own form of æthermantics, a poorly-understood, superstition-infected branch of æther manipulation kept in the dark by centuries of rigid rituals and inquisitorial censorship, but still. Kayip displayed no such supernatural abilities, and the few times the topic had been raised, he had given her only a solemn silence.

She didn't push it. Priest or not, Sylvaine didn't much care, and she felt in no position to judge someone for the presence or lack of æthermantics. For the terror of the Wastes had not been Sylvaine's main haunting. A silent fear had stalked her along her trip down, one that she had not been willing to put into words with the monk. He must have known, he had seen her groan and moan, heard complaints of the headaches, the sudden nausea. The slickdust withdrawal had not been nearly as severe as it had been in Icaria; Roache's injection had served some of its ostensible purpose, and now her head felt near clear most days. Yet in Icaria she had been confident her symptoms were just a temporary malady, to be cured by hidden pinch of the narcotic.

She had been separated permanently from the man's poison; it should have felt like a lifting of a burden. Yet, without it, would her Knack last? The injection had changed something inside her, but how much or for how long, she wasn't sure. Even Roache was vague about the details, perhaps out of deceit, but perhaps out of genuine ignorance. No one had even awaked the Knack in a ferral; the effect could be permanent or utterly ephemeral.

If she only understood the drug's mechanism, but there was no clear analogue in any engineering text she had read. Unstable æther did supposedly have influence on the mechanical workings of the body, but it was also, well, *unstable*, chaotic, erratic, utterly uncontrollable, producing nothing more than random mutations. It would remove some of the humiliation if Sylvaine could just reduce her experiences to formulas on a page. It sickened her knowing that Roache's lies flowed through her veins, yet more than anything else, she was more horrified by the idea that she might lose her Knack forever.

Kayip snorted softly and re-crossed his legs in a new permutation. Deep in thought, evidently. The monk wasn't particularly entertaining company nor a man with much concern for creature comfort, but after the insanity with Roache, after her life in Icaria, her career as an engineer, her *everything* had collapsed, there was some solace to be found in the monk.

It was not an intimate solace, admittedly. Kayip was private with his thoughts and as flat with his emotions as the mask he wore over his left eye. He had talked little about himself during their travels, divulging nothing of any depth about his past. Their few conversations had tended to be focused on the here and now of survival, occasionally broken up by the monk's unrequested sermons, which were often esoteric and yet somehow still utterly jejune.

The few exceptions were the handful of nights when, the campfire fading, Kayip had decided to explain to Sylvaine the magnitude of Roache's crimes. The monk had collected a long list of vices and atrocities, told with a dour slowness, as if each word took a great effort. Though Sylvaine was usually suspicious of church-folks' accusations, Kayip's details fit exactly with what she had already seen firsthand, and she didn't doubt a word.

Sylvaine took a moment to look again through the photos the monk had shown her. Mutants, men and women, in states of utter anguish, bodies bent, bruises oozing, corpses lying flat on the floor, all in blurred monochrome. It was grimmer even than what had lain hidden in Roache's penthouse. Sylvaine was not the only one to have good reasons to want the sangleum tycoon dead, but she still held her own anger tight to her chest.

"Very well," Kayip said, Sylvaine jumping slightly from the sudden noise. "I have a plan."

The Sightless City

———∞———

The sign on the side of the blotched wooden door was clear enough: *"Marcel Talwar, Private Investigator."* Earlier that afternoon Kayip had led Sylvaine through the Underway up to the sewer entrance near the front door of the three-story apartment building before leaving her on her own with awkward words of encouragement. She did not feel much encouraged. Sure, it made sense that out of the two of them Roache was more likely to have warned Marcel about the monk, but that still didn't make her chances all that great.

She held her bag close and fidgeted with the ætherglove hidden in her coat pocket. If Marcel wasn't as trustworthy as Kayip's friend thought he was, then it was good to have some tool of self-defense. Admittedly, if she got caught close up then she wouldn't have the time to slip the glove on, but then her claws... No, no, that was worse. She wasn't going to let herself descend into beasthood, not again.

Sylvaine closed her eyes, breathed in, and raised her hand to knock, before noticing a small hanging chain. She pulled that instead, and a bell clanged from behind the misty glass.

"It's open."

She walked into a small office. It was lightly furnished and poorly decorated, with a few photos and a large bookshelf. Sylvaine would have thought a long-time friend of Roache's would have been set up nicely, but by the look of the open screen door behind the desk, it appeared that Marcel both slept and worked in a unit that was half the size of the apartment Roache had given her. Marcel didn't seem to live in squalor exactly, but the cramped spartan office was a far cry from luxury.

"You have a good time inspecting my door?" the man asked. The tone was joking, but Sylvaine wanted to curse. The office had looked a blur through the glass from her side; she didn't realize how obvious it had been from the other side that someone was standing outside, nervous. She wondered who he had expected would come through the door. Based on the décor, and the excessive numbers of pulps she had read as a kid, the man had been probably waiting for some *'dame with legs to kill for'*.

"Wanted to, uh, make sure I was at the right place," Sylvaine said, trying to laugh.

"Only private eye in Huile," Marcel offered. He wore an old beat-up coat and faint stubble on his chin. His right leg was resting on the table, pants scrunched up a bit, so she could see the glimmer of a cogleg. By the look of it, the mechanical limb was of military design, functional and heavy, factory-made, with no artistry or vision.

"I take it you're new in town," he said. She tried to keep the shock from her face. How did he know? The answer hit her a moment after. *Ferral,* right. It was doubtful that a single woman looking remotely like her lived within the city limits.

"Yes," she said, "I was coming in because you knew a colleague of mine." She focused to make sure she would pronounce the name right. "A Mr. Heitor Desct."

"You knew Desct?" This got Marcel to finally pull his leg down and sit up straight. He stared at her. "I don't think he ever mentioned you."

"He talked about everyone he worked with?" she asked, perhaps too defensively. It was obvious why he would have mentioned her.

"Well, no," Marcel admitted.

"He's a friend of a friend," she said. "We never met directly." This seemed to satisfy Marcel somewhat. "Desct and I were in collaboration on a story. I write for *The Times of Icaria.*"

"Icaria?" Marcel asked, suspicious of the one detail of her story that was actually true.

"Yes," she said quickly. "We were making good progress until I stopped receiving letters."

Marcel slumped. "Yeah. Well no mystery there. You probably heard about the wastelung."

"Sure," Sylvaine said, which she realized quickly was probably not the most tactful response. "Well," she continued, "part of our investigation involved Lazacorp. There were diagrams Desct had mentioned in his letter, ones he thought would be vital to our investigations."

"Diagrams?" Marcel asked.

"Schematics," Sylvaine explained, "of a central building in Blackwood Row, and its machinery. I was hoping you might know a way to get a copy."

Marcel shook his head. "Not sure that's possible. I mean, that's more in the range of corporative espionage, breaking into private business offices, not exactly legal private investigation."

"Well," she said, "maybe there's a copy floating around somewhere." Like the one Kayip had said he'd left on this man's desk.

Marcel stared at her, eyes sharp. "Seems unlikely. Who did you say you worked for?"

"*The Times of Icaria.*"

The man grunted in response. It was clear enough he didn't believe her, thought her suspicious enough that he was willing to lie about the very existence of the schematics he owned. Sylvaine silently gritted her teeth. Talking anyone into anything was far from her expertise. She had only been able to convince people she was an engineer thanks to Roache's damned drug. Why did Kayip think she stood a chance at this?

She turned her gaze out the window, trying to hide her anxiety, and nearly yelped. A policeman was walking outside. Kayip had warned her that Roache had eyes even within the police force. If they were following her here then perhaps they had been found out, though by what mistake she wasn't sure.

She squinted closer and realized that her fearful imagination had gotten the better of her. This "policeman" was simply a man in a blue coat with some strange, most likely waste-scavenged, cap. Her immediate relief was then overcome by the realization she had been staring panicked out the window for several seconds. Marcel was already past wary of her, and odd behavior like this certainty wouldn't alleviate his suspicions. Gear's-grits! She hadn't even gotten to show him the photographs, and she was already blowing her cover. She quickly shifted her gaze around the room, looking for some excuse to change the tenor of the conversation...

"Oh!" Sylvaine said, in earnest. She reached down and grabbed a book from the shelf. "You have *The Bladedancer of Unha'Khul?*" On the browning cover was a fading image of a man, dressed in flowing linens, thrusting upwards a long, curved sword that shined in some unpainted sunlight.

"You know it?" Marcel's tone changed instantly. He walked over and bent down to the shelf, eagerly perusing his own collection. "Yeah, I have the whole cycle, *Swordsman of Unha'Khul*, *Prince*, uh, well, except for *Exile.*"

"*Exile of Unha'Khul* was the weakest anyhow," Sylvaine said, putting the book back and glancing over what she was now realizing was a small library of old pulps. "I didn't even know they were still in print, I only read it because of my uncle's old copies."

"There's a press down in Phenia," Marcel said, "trying to save as many pre-Calamity pulps as they can, I think. Hard to get many more out here."

"Well, I'm glad you at least brought *The Æroships at Dawn*," she said, pointing to the elaborate copper-carved image pressed into leather binding.

"Actually, that one was a gift," Marcel said. "Could never get into it. Got too technical on the inner workings of the ships, felt almost like I was reading some engineering manual."

"I think that was the point," Sylvaine said, realizing suddenly why she had such a love for the series.

Marcel nodded. "So, what were you researching with Desct?"

"Yes," Sylvaine said, "right." She paused and pulled the binder from her bag, placing it on the man's desk. The man was now as receptive as she might ever get him, but she was still dreading the task at hand. There was no way to reveal what she needed to delicately, so she hoped shock would work.

"It might help if you take a look at these," she said. "I was sent them by Desct."

Marcel shrugged and opened the binder. He picked up a photo from it, and his eyes narrowed. He turned it slowly, as if that would change it somehow, then put it down, and picked up another. Then another.

Sylvaine glanced at the remaining photos. They were still as disturbing as when Kayip had first shown them to her out in the Wastes.

In one stood a young one-armed mutant man, working on a large piece of machinery, his other arm a poorly bandaged stump, his body covered in welts. In another photograph, eight mutants slept shoulder-to-shoulder in a shanty the size of a dining room table, made out of shards of sheet metal and some tattered cloth. There was one photo displaying a barely clothed mutant, his horned head leaning on a woodblock pillow, some sort of dark liquid dripping from his mouth. Then, there was one of a bulbous mutant being helped to walk by two others, his belly twisted out and tumorous, thin oozing stalks running up his chest and the side of his head. He was covered in sores, and had legs that were entirely fused together, dragging behind him like a malfunctioning prosthetic.

"Where is this?" Marcel asked, staring at a photograph of sickly woman with a scab-cracked arm, at work pushing a load of barrels through a crowded refinery floor.

"Blackwood Row," Sylvaine said.

"No," Marcel said. "No, I've been around Lazacorp, it's nothing like this."

"You've been all around?" Sylvaine asked. "They let you explore freely?"

"Well no, but..." Marcel started, and then stopped. He looked up at her. "I know Mr. Roache. He wouldn't allow anything like this."

Naivety dripped from his words. She wanted to laugh at him, or rather, she wanted to want to laugh at him. But there was something desperate in his words, a hidden panic. If someone had told her, as she flew high in Icaria, that Roache, the source of all her success, the man who built her into the women she knew she was, was a liar, a monster, would she have believed them? Inferno, Kayip had tried as much. She couldn't hate Marcel for this, even if she wanted to.

"Perhaps..." Sylvaine spoke slowly. "It's happening without his knowledge. There was a man Desct mentioned," she struggled to remember the names Kayip had drilled into her, "a foreman named Verus? Yeah, I think he was the focus of Desct's investigation."

"Oh," Marcel said, the hesitation in his voice disappearing entirely. "Still, I'm not sure how he could possibly hide all of this."

Sylvaine tapped the notepaper underneath the pile of photos. "Well, it might be time to do a little reading."

Chapter 20

Marcel leaned against the wall of the alleyway, waiting for Sylvaine. The sun was starting to set, and the nearby streetlamp flickered into life. He glanced around for the ferral and double-checked the street signs. *Sutgate Way*, just a few blocks from the edge of town. It was the right place, the right time. The woman had claimed she was going to take him to meet another of her associates. He was starting to wish he asked more about who-in-Inferno this "associate" was, and why the man couldn't come up to meet him in the office, but at the time all his thoughts had been on the photographs and the notes the woman had given him. Even now he could barely believe their contents. Marcel inched to the side and used the dim ætheric light to reread the notes again, hoping silently he could find some error, some proof of fabrication.

...Fourteen hour shifts the norm, beaten if they collapse and are taken away. Others that disappear: those caught speaking up, those who resist, those who are too heavily mutated. The latter seems an inevitable outcome given enough time. Interview subjects claim to have been injected with some unknown material, seems a greater cause of mutations than even the leaking machinery, though those are far from safe...

He riffled through the pages.

...food barely edible and in small quantities. Bathroom facilities nonexistent. Stench of body and feces fills every corner of sleeping camps, sanitary rules enforced by mutants themselves, but insufficient due to conditions. Disease rampant....

Some were written in full, others simple scribbles on crumpled paper.

...They seemed to have formed their own pseudo-government. Lazacorp guards avoid entering camps. Some injured, ill, or injection-sick hidden there. Lazacorp keeps tabs at mealtimes, those too sick to appear to work given no food, whole community on perpetual edge of starvation. Mealtimes apparently when they induce the "injections"...

Marcel kept squinting at the handwriting, trying to convince himself that it wasn't Desct's hand. But he knew the scribbles well, the distinct slanted dots over his i's, the ways the words squished together when the man got excited or nervous.

...most seem sure dead, just dumped somewhere. Less sure about others that disappear, those overly-mutated. Warmonk claims they are taken to the Wastes, but why? Interview with Lazacorp guard necessary, impossible. Unsure who to trust in City Hall...

Interspersed with these notes were other documents. Legalese with strict "silence clauses," underlined in pen, often attached to strange payments forms written to Huile families. Records of purse-snatchers and vandals given reduce sentences in order to participate in *"Labor Retraining,"* a government program Marcel had not heard of. One crumbled paper was a form from City Hall denying a request for formal investigations into the disappearance of a man named Alfred Nurzhen.

A sound of clattering metal and he nearly jumped only to see a raccoon scamper from an open trashcan, old sores glittering off its back. Marcel rubbed his head. Desct had clearly written these notes for his personal use; they were vague on some subjects, seemed meant more as reminders than complete descriptions. Who was this warmonk? What were the injections that he mentioned? The one thing that was evident was the scale of suffering. How had Verus kept these conditions secret, and why hadn't Desct ever mentioned his investigations to Marcel?

He glanced down again at the nauseating revelations in his hands. He half expected them to be blank paper, the images of agony just a waking fever dream, some mishmash of old memories brought on by... something. But in truth, he didn't have the imagination to create those photographs.

Another creak. He squinted down the darkened alleyway. A sewer grate was pushed up, and a hand appeared. Then a whole body. Sylvaine walked a few steps forward then gestured. He glanced around and slunk towards her.

"You're traveling through the sewer?" he asked.

"Well, the Huile Underway in general," she said, pulling down a scarf she had around her mouth and nose.

"So, mostly sewer."

She grimaced in answer. "How did you think we were going to check on the veracity of the notes? Just walk up to the gates of Blackwood Row, knock, and ask to poke around?"

The woman had a point. Though when she had claimed earlier that she had a way in to see the mutants, Marcel hadn't quite realized what he was agreeing to. He stepped over and glanced down into dark of the Underway.

"Forgive me for being a little wary," Marcel said.

"You're forgiven," she replied, glancing around the street. "But we should get going."

"Who is this associate?" Marcel asked.

"Another investigator, of a type anyhow," she said. "Listen, it was his idea to rope you into this. At this point, I've dragged myself through enough sewers not to give a damn one way or another. I don't have time to debate, you can come with me, or not, but if you back out, we'll need the notes back."

Marcel clenched his jaw and tried to not show his unease.

"I was told you had been a soldier," she said, "that you had plenty of experience in Underway scouting, but if it's too much..."

"I can handle myself," he said quickly. It wasn't like he was sneaking under a Principate camp; this was nothing worse than the sorts of exercises he did for training under Alba's watch. Before he could think any more on the subject, he slid himself down into the opening.

"We weren't called the Huile Sewer Rats for nothing," Marcel called back as he stepped carefully to avoid splashing in stagnant filth. Sylvaine crawled down beside him and closed the grate.

"Glad you have a good attitude." She wrapped her scarf tightly around her nose. "Come on, let's move."

She stepped quickly and carefully down the piping and through a rusting opening. The stagnant air sat heavy as a wall, and as Marcel pushed through it, Sylvaine's handtorch cut deep into the shadows. They crept slowly deeper into the labyrinthine mess, Marcel keeping his breathing slow, trying not to let old nightmares sneak from the back of his mind.

The city above had certainly changed in the last two and a half years. Huile had grown, developed, evolved. It had gone from a slapdash town recovering from war to a prosperous, modest-sized modern UCCR metropolis, but none of that was evident in the Underway. The tunnels were as Marcel remembered, cramped, wet, ceilings of leaking pipes and walls of abandoned machinery. Drops of something drizzled onto Marcel's head from time to time, and he struggled to avoid imagining the droplets' source. They passed by landmarks he had last seen through the lenses of a gas mask half a decade ago. As horrific as the memories were, he started to wish he still had that mask; the smell of stagnant rot was everywhere.

"Are we meeting your associate in Blackwood Row?" he asked as they turned by the crumpled remains of some forgotten bunker and down a path that cut through a boarded-up, rust-decorated factory basement.

"No," Sylvaine said, voice muffled. "He'll lead you there. Knows the way better, and, gear's-grits, I'm not staying down here any longer than I have to."

A strange place for a rendezvous. He was glad he had brought his pistol with him; the situation was more than a little suspicious, as was the woman. Yet the photographs, the notes, he couldn't ignore them, couldn't head back home knowing there was some chance that they reflected a hidden reality. Still, he listened for every echo, every strange noise and splash of water.

"And this associate, where is he from?" Marcel asked. "How'd he get caught up in this?"

"Ask him yourself," Sylvaine answered as a large man stepped out from behind a mass of pipes. The man was tanned, his clothes covered in a layer of waste-worn rags. He smiled as they approached and put out his hand, an azure bracelet dangling from his wrist.

"Hello Marcel," he said. "It is a pleasure to finally meet you."

Marcel took the man's hand and shook it. It was hard to see in the dark, but he could make out a plain metal mask covering the stranger's left eye. The mask seemed familiar, somehow, though he was quite sure he had never before met the man. Something from a pulp, maybe? He couldn't recall.

"My name is Kayip," the man said.

"Nice to meet you, Kayip," Marcel responded, glancing down a hallway. "So how exactly do you know the way to..."

Kayip. He remembered the small snippet of Roache's conversation, forgotten amidst the hubbub of the Gall case. In those early days after Desct's funeral he had had his eye out for the man, the tall Torish maniac, but he had never showed. Just another empty lead, easily forgotten.

Until, like an idiot, Marcel wandered into his ambush.

"Shit!" was the only thing Marcel could think to say, as he jumped back and reached down to his holster. Sylvaine responded with a similar explicative, shoving her hand into her coat pocket. Marcel pulled out his Frasco six-shooter and spun to aim at the man, but with sudden movement, Kayip's large fingers had encircled Marcel's wrist, aiming the gun away into empty space.

Marcel grunted and thrust out his other fist, which was caught just as easily. He found himself grappled. His kicking and struggling did nothing to loosen Kayip's grip as the muscular man held him tight and close.

"You cog-loose maniac!' Sylvaine said. Marcel could see she was lifting some overwrought glove at him. "You want to send bullets ricocheting in here?"

"We are friends, Mr. Talwar!" Kayip said. The man overpowered him completely. After slowing his breath some, Marcel realized that Kayip was making no effort to harm him. He simply held Marcel firmly in place. Then, with a swift, and only slight painful pull, the large man disarmed Marcel.

"I understand your fear," Kayip said. "No doubt Lazarus Roache has told you about me."

Marcel was held only by one arm now. Gunless, he considered his options. He could try to break free, take them on hand to hand, two against one, him versus a giant and a ferral. He could also try to sprout wings and fly away. It would likely have the same success rate.

So instead, he simply nodded.

"Roache likely said horrible things about me," Kayip said. "Perhaps he even believed them to be true, but they are not."

The man let go of Marcel, who rubbed his wrists.

"You take him as muscle?" Marcel asked Sylvaine.

She shook her head and glanced at the man. "He took me. And if we're throwing things on the table, I should admit I never worked for *The Times of Icaria.*"

"So where are you from then?" Marcel asked.

"Icaria!" She paused and lowered her voice. "I worked as an engineer."

"An engi—?"

"Yes," she said quickly.

"I was the one in contact with Desct," Kayip said. "But I did not think it wise to see you myself considering..." He gestured to the gun in his hand. Then, with slow care, he handed Marcel his pistol back.

"Kayip, what in Inferno?" Sylvaine asked.

"We are friends here," Kayip said. Marcel took the pistol grip, and, sheepishly, uncocked it. Kayip raised his arms.

"I am unarmed, Mr. Talwar. I was told that I could trust you, and I do. If you wish to leave you have it within your power."

Marcel patted the large man down, to double-check his words. Sylvaine shook her head as she watched him, and he felt almost embarrassed by her stare. The man was as weaponless as he said, the only metal on him, besides his mask and his bracelet, was an odd necklace. Marcel pulled it out slowly, studying the blue-tinted metal. It was a small circle, fractured at several points around the edge, with strange symbols, church-writing if he had to guess by the form, encircling the hole in the center. A Cracked-Disc, the symbol of the Church of the Ascended, most likely an imitation, considering the rarity of the genuine artifacts.

"A simple reminder of the Demiurge," the man said. "I know the Resurgence is not renowned for its general piety, but I should hope my sentiment does not worry you."

"No, no," Marcel said, returning the periapt. "We had a church healer back at my medical school; he used a real one." Though even in his brief medical work Marcel had never been convinced the chaplain was doing any more than occasionally elongating the last breaths of dying men. "You're a priest?"

"Of a sort," the man replied.

Marcel stepped back, and Kayip made no move. If the two wanted to kill him, they had had the chance and then some. Marcel had been, perhaps, foolish to trust them this far, yet they hadn't betrayed that trust in any dangerous ways.

"So you knew Desct?" Marcel asked the sort-of priest.

The man nodded, "We worked together before. I'd like to see his work completed."

"He didn't mention you in his notes," Marcel said.

"He did mention a warmonk, no?" Kayip gestured to himself.

That was true. Even Lazarus had mentioned that the man considered himself some sort of battle priest or something.

"The war part?" Marcel asked

"A life ago."

"Listen," Sylvaine said, "I've been holding back the urge to vomit down here for long enough. Do you want to see the mutants, or just shove your head back into sand? I'm fine either way, just please decide soon."

"And if I leave?" Marcel said.

"Then you leave," Kayip replied. "We could use your assistance, Mr. Talwar, but you have no obligation to assist. I would ask that if you leave us now that you do not mention our work to others, but even that we cannot enforce."

"Right," Marcel said, pausing to think. The possibility of running back to his apartment had its appeal, but then what? If Verus were behind these abuses, he'd be walking away from definite proof. As much as he wanted to trust in Lambert's skill, if the accusations were true, he needed to make sure the foreman had no outs for denial.

Marcel sighed, "Well, then lead the way, I guess."

They left Sylvaine behind and continued down a twisting path of abandoned substructures, dry pipeways, and dug out tunnels in the direction of Blackwood Row. Marcel kept his hand near his holster and his eye on the monk. The latter task turned out to be difficult, as Kayip was not the easiest man to keep pace with. Marcel had to jog to keep up. It would be easy to slip away if need be; the monk made no effort to keep him, and the only risk was the convolutions of the Underway itself. Marcel could remember some of these pathways, but the monk took a few different turns than he expected and never needed to pause to gain his bearings.

He did stop once, suddenly, arm out, finger to his lips. He flicked off his handtorch and Marcel did the same. The darkness was complete, the only sounds distant echo of gurgling water and an occasional mechanical groan, the only sensation the constant, still, cold.

After a few minutes of black, Kayip clicked the light back on, and they continued.

The two took a right at a smashed boiler, went down a set of concrete stairs next to rows of hissing pistons, walked through an abandoned underrail station, turned left at the collapsed basement of what once must have been some sort of factory, and followed a river of sewage.

"Okay," Marcel said. "Audric Avenue is above the abandoned sangleum pumps, which are there." He shined his handtorch down a thin hallway, half flooded with brown water that glistened in reflection. "So if we turn here," he illuminated a dark underrail track, "we should sneak right under the walls."

Kayip shook his head. "Chokeshrooms."

"Shit, really? Must have grown in the last couple years."

"There is a smashed wall a few metres this way."

Kayip spoke soft and walked softer. Marcel couldn't imagine what the man was expecting to find down here. Even Huile teenagers rarely haunted the Underway much since City Hall imposed harsh penalties on "dangerous urban exploration." Still, the muffled shadows did seem to impress some vague, sleeping threat, though perhaps that was simply Marcel's repressed memories growling. It was far too easy to imagine glints off old pipes as Principate bayonets, to hear any echo as footsteps, to imagine every gust bringing with it that red gas.

"So, exactly what sort of monk were you?" Marcel asked, eager to distract himself from the creeping thoughts. "Populo Auditas? Or one of those Church-first people, what's-it-called? Don't tell me you were some Orthodox Imperator ass-kisser?"

"We were... independent," Kayip said, leading Marcel around a sinkhole of muck. "We maintained a monastery deeper in the Wastes, but also performed priestly rites as well when the opportunity arose. Which admittedly was rare in those lands. I suppose we traced our lineage to what you call Church-first, the Genitor Primus..."

"Right, right." Marcel waved his hand torch as he walked, scaring cat-sized scraprats from their nests.

"...but we were more practical minded, and less concerned with politics. We believed that the truest form of meditation demanded the blade."

"So you were one of those—" He stopped himself from saying 'lunatics', "—uh warriors, out in the Wastes, fighting troglyns and ætheric aberrations?"

Kayip flashed his light up to a doorway above a rusted-away staircase. Marcel put his torch away and climbed up a few metres of disconnected pipes before pulling himself through the opening. He lent a hand to Kayip, but the man waved him back before simply leaping, grabbing the bottom of the passageway, and pulling himself up in one movement.

"Demons," Kayip said. "That is the...proper term for those things, those 'aberrations'. Though that is all I will speak of them. It is unwise to invoke ill presences in places such as this."

"Right."

They continued on. It had been years since he had talked to a true believer; fundamentalism wasn't in vogue in Resurgence lands. It was strange to hear someone still use the old, superstitious terms. They conjured up childhood sermons, full of Infernofire and damned souls forever tormented by the manifestations of their sins. Marcel had found the stories silly as he grew into his adolescent faithlessness, but as a kid they had brought more than their share of night-terrors, augmented by the displays of his priest. It was too easy to imagine those horrors resting in some hidden corner down here.

"So," Marcel asked, "are you a miracle caster? My priest used to shoot balls of orange light from his fingers during sermons."

Kayip paused mid-walk, and Marcel noticed his hand twitch up to his face, but stop, as if an instinct had been shot down.

"No."

"Really? I thought it was common among warmonks." He had read in a history textbook that such ætheric skills were important in maintaining military power and prestige in the old orders of the Imperial Church. Or maybe that was from a pulp.

The pathway ended suddenly at a puddle-strewn crossroads. The straight path was cut off by large iron bars, buried deep into the walls of what must have at one time been a large underrail station, possibly Huile's pre-war central station.

"That's new," Marcel said.

Kayip nodded and gestured towards the right. "I know a detour a ways down."

Marcel shined his light leftwards, where the pathway curved into dark. "I think this heads the same way as—"

Kayip grabbed him as he started to walk. Silently the man took a few steps forward, leaned down, and blew. Gleaming beneath the dust and the grime was the red shine of sangleum. Marcel felt a faint pulsing pain in his leg; he was surprised he hadn't smelled the oil.

"A leak?" he asked.

"That implies it is unintentional," Kayip said. "We take the detour."

He led them through a series of tunnels, some concrete or tiled, some dug from the earth, to a small room, where, removing brick by brick, he made a small opening in the wall. After they crawled through, he replaced the bricks with the same care.

"You afraid someone will notice?" Marcel asked.

"It is wiser if we do not speak from here on. I would not care to be caught off guard by whatever may lurk in these shadows."

"You don't need to worry." Marcel replied, half for the monk's sake, half to remind himself. "Ever since we cleared out the imperials, the Huile Underway has been as safe as the streets above."

He almost tripped over the first corpse.

Marcel froze, then his handtorch discovered a second body in front of him, then a third, then a pile. For a moment he saw them in Principate blue, a squad of dead soldiers. A second, more sober, glance shook away the illusion. They wore mere rags, and though they were human in shape, they were stranger in features. Some had horns, others had red skin or lizard-like claws, some had brass-colored chitin or fused limbs, and a few had twisting boney growths or scars that weaved and twisted like indecipherable runes.

Mutants.

They sat in different states of decomposition. The one closest to Marcel could almost be mistaken for sleeping, some further down were barely more than skeletons, stripped down by hungry scraprats.

Marcel swore under his breath. Kayip whispered something in a strange language. Before Marcel could form his thoughts, he heard footsteps echo down the hall.

The two jumped behind a rusting drilling machine, eyeing the dark. Kayip rubbed his bracelet and whispered more of his strange words. Marcel felt something, an odd fluttering sensation in his torso, as if a light gust had flown through him, *through* him, that instead of blocking that force, his body had swayed like wheat in the wind. Kayip's bracelet started to change. It unfurled and widened, bits opening up along invisible fault lines as the metal stretched out into a long, silver-blue sword in the man's grasp.

The blade was unadorned but beautiful. Marcel had read about such artifacts, ancient Ascended artifacts of protean functions and near indestructible make, but mostly in pulps. He had never seen anything like it in person. Marcel was also instantly furious, somewhat at Kayip for lying about being unarmed, but more at himself for believing the monk.

There was no time to stew in the anger, as the footsteps had gotten closer, and he could make out two men talking.

"Oh, bleeding bloatbeast's arsehole, this one is heavy," came a scratchy voice. "Didn't know we were feeding them enough to get them this big."

"The weight's all in the horns," said a second voice, deep.

Something heavy was being dragged, bumping against the floor and sloshing through muck.

"I don't see why we don't just burn the skinsick bastards in the incinerator," said the first voice.

"Waste of sangleum," the second grunted.

The two figures finally lurched into view, walking towards a great corpse pile in a distant corner. The first had a scraggy beard, and the other was completely bald. Both were heavily tattooed and wore Lazacorp uniforms. With a coordinated swing they added a body to the pile: a short man with a cleft lip and a hole in his forehead.

"Wish they just pumped him fully," came the scratchy voice beneath the scraggy beard. "Then he would be transport's problem."

"Heard from Gax that he died after some tiny, routine injection," said the bald man, shaking his head.

"Eh, Gax probably just botched it," the scraggy man stretched, glancing over the hallway of corpses with no discernable concern. He paused, his eyes widening suddenly, gaze not far from Marcel and Kayip's hiding place. Marcel held his breath, Kayip angled his blade.

"I know where I saw this taurshit before." He turned back and kicked the corpse. "He was that Steinmann guy, that lazy-arsed mailman. Stiffland-be-fucked, he complained endlessly. 'Innocent,

innocent, I didn't do it.' What in Inferno did he think this was? Why would that matter?"

The bald man started to walk back the way they came. "Surprised he made it this long."

Scraggy beard followed, rolling his head. "Eh. Just wished he starved away bit more first, my neck is killing me." The voices echoed down from the hallway. "Need to get myself on transport duty. Be a relief to be back out in the Wastes."

"Eh, don't worry, won't be a need for this soon. We'll be out of this pisshole for good."

After a long silence, Kayip folded his blade back around his wrist, and they started to move again. He said nothing, and Marcel could not manage to get words to mouth himself. It was the bodies, the abstractions of the photographs congealed into cold flesh. It was Kayip's blade, proof that the situation now stood widely outside Marcel's grasp. It was the Lazacorp guards, callously tossing a corpse with the familiarity of a newsboy chucking the daily paper.

And the corpse they tossed. Marcel tried to convince himself it was a coincidence, but as he walked by it he recognized the face, even past the horns, the mutated skin. Steinmann, a petty mail-thief with Principate leanings, supposed to be in a jail cell somewhere. It was Marcel who had found the evidence, Marcel who had followed the trail, which started when Lazarus Roache told him...

Marcel stumbled, his cogleg giving way. He caught himself on the wall, nauseous, pain burning up from a shin he no longer had.

"Are you all right?" Kayip whispered.

Roache.

There was always stuff on the ground level that those above didn't see. Soldiers looting when the eye of their general was focused on the battlefield, mayors unaware of the grift of the common clerk, poor conditions hidden in the workshop. And Roache was very much high up. Was it possible he didn't see, didn't know? That for years he had never become aware of what was happening in his refineries? That no one had spoken to him, that he never toured unexpectedly, that he never asked? That he never signed the documents ordering it?

Yet Roache had pointed him in Steinmann's direction. Had lavished such exuberant praise when Marcel finally found the missing mail under the man's floorboard...In a Lazacorp owned apartment...*Demiurge*, he had never made the connection! The pitiful man had acted so surprised when Marcel found his half-written letter admitting...no, Steinmann was never the one acting.

How many cases had Roache brought to Marcel? He struggled to count them. Dozens, at least, if he was including those incidental suspicions dropped in conversations, hints that near invariably lead to an arrest. Were any of those faked? Marcel stomach turned at the notion that the real question was if any of those cases *weren't* faked. That if he started to inspect those rotting, red faces he would find familiar grimaces.

Marcel vomited. The bile burned up from his through his throat and splattered on the ground. He coughed and spat, before glancing up at Kayip.

"You both knew it wasn't just Verus," Marcel said.

The monk nodded back. "I thought it best to ease into the truth."

Then Roache had betrayed Huile. Betrayed the UCCR. Betrayed Marcel. Perhaps even what the man had played off as a patriotic defection had just been another of his games. The savior of Huile, just a rat seeking a new ship, willing to use brave soldiers as his escape raft. It disgusted Marcel to think that even his friends' sacrifices might be tainted by Roache's scheming. There was no dagger large enough for such a stab in the back.

The monk opened his mouth with concern in his voice, but Marcel shook his head and forced his leg forward.

"Let's go," he said. He wasn't going to shrink away from the truth now.

As they continued on, further signs of Lazacorp security started to appear. Chain-link fences covered dry sewerways, old basement hallways were completely barricaded by scrap and stone. Three times they had to stop when their torches came over glints of tripwire attached to jury-rigged shotguns.

Stranger still was the voice that echoed like a spirit, increasing in volume with each step. As they got further into the heart of Blackwood Row's Underway, the voice became clearer, its source dictaphones bolted to the ceiling, the tone distinctly Lazarus Roache's.

"Return to your workstation. Return to Blackwood Row. Return to your workstation. Return to Blackwood Row."

It felt mocking in its monotone, its bland complicity, its indifference. That the truth was all just kilometres away, yet the man had been grinning out his lies to Marcel for years over wine and expensive cheeses.

Finally, Kayip tapped Marcel's shoulder and pointed to a rusting ladder. They climbed up out a sewer grating and into the night-chilled air above.

Chapter 21

Marcel wasn't quite sure where in Blackwood Row they had popped up. It was clear enough, though, that they were beyond the façade, beyond the clean streets, the fine offices, and the well-maintained show units. This deep, everything was covered in red-black soot, from the skeletal iron refineries to the dense towers of shanty-structures that sat between them. Detritus lined the street, rusting mechanical junk left by the wayside, often sunk into pools of fecal-smelling liquids. Sharp spotlights shined some of the structures into blinding contrast, but the streets, for the most part, wallowed in shadows. Now and then the torches of guards would appear, moving in languid patterns, stopping occasionally as they shouted at some scampering mutant.

Kayip led Marcel around the edges of the streets, through pathways of tightly-packed metal, into and out of mutant shanty towers built of scrap metal and cloth, looking more like decaying scaffolds than true buildings. In these hovels twisted figures scurried and sat. Some cooked pitiful meals in rusty buckets over weak embers, others slept shoulder to shoulder in minuscule tents. Many stared at the two men, some gazes curious, others fearful, but not a one of them made a sound. Marcel fought the urge to stop and thank them for their silence. If a single mutant had wanted them dead, all they would have needed to do was shout.

Once or twice on their several block journey they almost ran into the guards, but despite the occasional shouted threat, the guards seemed more focused on their spiritless conversations than the mutants they were supposedly keeping in line.

They turned into a nondescript alley beside a large brick structure. A putrid smelling pile in the alley's corner several metres away was proof enough that Lazarus had skimped on toilet facilities for his workers. Marcel made a note to report that too, as a footnote to the torture, murder, and slavery.

Kayip walked up to an iron door and knocked seven times, pausing after the third and fifth. The door creaked open to reveal a man's face—or rather, a face that was vaguely man-like. The eyes were more similar to those of a snake's, and a tiny, curved horn grew from a scab-marked bump on the mutant's red-tinted forehead. He glanced at Marcel, eyes wide.

"A friend," Kayip said.

The mutant nodded and squeaked, "I should... I mean, I need to ask... I don't..."

"It is all right, this is the man I said I would bring."

The mutant sucked in his panic and nodded, gesturing them inside.

It was a struggle squeezing through the cramped hallways of the building. Machinery took up most of the space, and what few square metres remained were occupied by tiny rag tents. They had to step over several sleeping mutants whose twisted forms were accentuated by bulging ribs and deep scars. Only one in every three light bulbs could even so much as flicker, and steam that flowed from some hidden heart of the facility damped the remainder of the light. As Marcel twisted round tight corners he took more than a few nicks and bruises from dark pipes that blended with the shadows. The mutant, however, had no trouble slithering through the gaps. Even Kayip, despite his prodigious girth, seemed to manage his way.

They descended several flights of stairs into the depths of the building, stopping at a large storage tank built into the wall. Their silent guard knocked the same code as Kayip. The tank groaned, and a side panel opened, the mutant slipping in. From within Marcel could hear snippets of murmuring and conversation.

"...as we wait, more and more die or are sent away. Is that what you want us to become? A gang of corpses and bloated sacks of nothing?" A woman's voice.

"And how do you think your fucking hammers and makeshift truncheons will fair against motorguns and Roache's slickdust commands?" A male voice, hoarse, but strangely familiar.

Marcel made to follow the mutant who, panicked, gestured at him to stop.

"Uh," their guide said.

"Their project within the monolith is almost done," the woman continued, "They have engineers working on it every hour of the day. Then they'll do what they always do when one of their damned construction projects finishes. Pump up half of us till we're sagging bags of flesh and send us out to our deaths. Are we going to allow that? It's better to die fighting anyhow than live another day with that man's voice in our heads and his poison in our veins."

Marcel snuck his head around to glance in. It was clear this machine was just a façade. Inside was a dark circular room; the roof was a series of pipes and the ground looked as if it had been dug out by hand. He could smell how cramped it was in there. A dozen mutants sat on crates or chairs made of scrap-metal and tape. A mutant woman turned towards the opening.

"Excuse..." their guide tried again.

"What is it?" the speaker snapped.

"It's uh, the monk, and the man he brought, the other, I mean..."

Marcel could see her pull out a hammer from her rope of a belt. "What are they doing?"

"Sedate your shit, Celina," came the male voice. "I gave the orders to bring back our eremite friend."

Kayip lifted himself up and offered Marcel a hand into that cramped space. As he entered he heard the male mutant gasp, then break into sudden laughter, pointing. "You magnificent purveyor of orthodoxy and decapitation, I honestly didn't think you'd convince him!"

"Well I did convince you, no?" the monk said.

"Marcel!" the mutant said, smiling. The voice was definitely familiar, but Marcel had conversed with only a couple of the workers here and could not connect that voice to any of them. He squinted in the dark, trying to make out the mutant's features.

"Who in Inferno is this?" asked the mutant apparently called Celina.

"Marcel Talwar," the mutant said, "fought with me in the Battle Under Huile."

"I'm sorry, I don't..." Marcel began. The mutant walked into the light. His face was all red, a single horn jutting from the side of his head. But his familiar black hair, slightly curled, his smile, a tad higher on the right side, his one unmutated eye, still with the twin glints of the academic and the prankster. It couldn't be him, and yet it was, as undeniable as impossible.

"Desct?" Marcel asked.

"Marcel, you magnificent shithead," Heitor Desct said. "A sight for weary fucking eyes that's for certain."

"Desct?" Marcel had to ask again. He couldn't believe it. The man had died, had been cremated and buried and mourned. "I was at your funeral."

Desct walked over through the crowd, which had started to murmur. He grabbed Marcel's face with a leathery hand, as if to make sure it was real.

"I hope they imported the finest libations for me, the decadent bastards."

"Desct...Demiurge, Desct...it's you, it's...but I...." Marcel felt himself descending into blubbering idiothood, but he couldn't help it. That Desct lived was a shock greater than any bullet wound, a burst of sudden joy, tempered by a sense of the world being upside down.

"What happened to you?" Marcel asked, touching, softly, the man's horn.

"The same damned misfortune that befell us all." Desct shook his head. "Arrested. Mutated. Forced to work."

"But the mutants are from the Wastes. They..."

Desct's shot his eyes to Kayip. "You didn't explain?"

Kayip shrugged. "I thought it better he see. He is, what you would say, a skeptic."

"Lazacorp's line is nonsense," Desct said. "I'll give you the long and short of it. Roache's goons waylaid me while I was trying to interview workers on the sly. They injected me with this slickdust shit, some sort of sangleum-infused poison. And well..."

He pointed to his horn.

"...it led to this. Now take my story and multiply it a thousand times. Other snoopers, Roache's political foes, old Principate sympathizers, petty convicts, anyone Lazacorp wanted gone. Kidnapped, mutated and enslaved."

Celina snorted.

"And then there were those enslaved first," said Desct.

"Captured by raiders and sold," said Celina. "I was a scrap trader. Brought to this miserable town in the back of a sangleumtruck. Better to be a waste-slave than poisoned like this. Better dead than serve this rot of a town."

"Either way," said Desct, "they work us hard, feed us only enough to live, and sometimes not even that. Anyone who speaks up, makes a run for it, or annoys a guard gets a bullet in their head."

"Demiurge, Desct, I had no idea," Marcel said.

Desct shrugged. "Few people outside Lazacorp do, and fewer still care. Of those there are none I'd trust to do something at this point."

"Has no one escaped?"

"A few of us tried," said a mutant in the back. "But Roache's drugs..."

"The slickdust shit," Desct said. "What he uses as a mutating agent. Injected directly into our veins. Dominates our psyche. Whatever taurshit escapes Roache's mouth, we follow like marionettes. You can feel your own fucking blood pulling your limbs, you become helpless."

"That's...impossible," Marcel said, "I mean, I think it is. I've...never heard of any engineering that can affect the mind."

"My order fought demon-worshipers," Kayip interjected, "some who claimed to have powers over the minds of others."

Marcel scratched the back of his head. "The situation is insane enough, Kayip. We don't need to be dragging in demons or ghosts or whatever. It's not demon magic; that's superstition, I'm sure it's just..." Marcel paused and thought, but realized he hadn't a clue on how such a drug would work.

"I can claim no elucidation on its workings," Desct said. "All I know is that it does work, can make you move, can make you work, can make you kill, even. The only thing the drug can't seem to do is compel you to tell the truth, thank the Demiurge. For that they resort to humble torture."

"Are you done, Desct?" said Celina, arms crossed, "Or will we waste all night on this? You are distracting us from the issue at hand. We've spent far too long in numbing passivity."

"As long as those dictaphones are live and Roache's voice is being pumped through, we have no chance of victory," Desct said with the calm of a statement rehearsed and restated a thousand times. "We need to smash the ætheric generators in the monolith, cut the power and blackout Blackwood Row before we make our move."

"Your move?" Marcel asked.

"Rise up," one of the mutants said.

"Burn this shithole to the ground," Celina concurred.

"A riot, Desct? People could die," Marcel said.

"Yes," laughed Celina bitterness infecting every tone, "that is the point."

"I can report Lazacorp's abuses to Lambert," Marcel said. "He can put a stop to this."

Celina's laughter turned to pure cackle. "Tell me, Mr. War Hero, Mr. Brute-who-spilled-blood-for-Lazacorp's-profits, how do you think the whole of Blackwood Row could exist on slave labor without the support of the entire city?"

"They can't all...I mean, maybe a few." Marcel turned to Desct. Desct avoided his gaze and shook his head. "I don't know, Marcel. I don't know how I was discovered, who we can trust."

"No one," Celina said simply. "And we aren't just going to wait to die. Revolt!"

This got more than just murmurs, even a cheer or two, followed by a quick *shh*.

"When we have the *proper* moment," Desct said.

"Which is *now*," the woman hissed. "You drag your legs so hard they're leaving marks on the cement. They'll do a purge when they finish their next project, as they did last year and the years before. And we haven't a clue when they'll finish."

"Noth twenty-fifth," cut in Marcel.

They glanced at him.

"Roache announced the completion of the water treatment plant," Marcel said. "If that's what you mean. The twenty-fifth of Noth is when he announced they'd be complete."

"Then we have a week," Desct said, starting to walk in as dignified a manner as was possible in the cramped space. "Let us not waste our opportunity by preemptively engaging in some taurshit confrontation before the conditions are optimal. This will not be the first attempted uprising, but it must be the final one."

The mutants nodded along. Celina thrust out her hand. "The man just admitted to talking friendly with Roache. You promised us the schematics, the schematics we helped you steal, Desct, and instead your monk has brought in a collaborator. We can't trust anything he says. He could report this all back to Lazacorp as soon as he leaves." She stared Marcel down, yellowed eyes striking. "*If* we let him go, which at this point seems like suicidal madness."

Desct stamped his foot. "You know me, friends, I've been fighting for liberation since before I was enslaved to our shared terror and drudgery. I know who on the outside is credible, who can be turned to our cause, and I am, if anything, fucking conservative on this account. Marcel can be trusted completely, one of the few we can depend upon as an ally. If you wish to lay a finger on him, you must first thrust a dagger through my back."

"I'm sure she didn't mean it like that," one of the mutants, an old, or perhaps just deeply mutated and scarred, man, said. "But you did promise us the schematics."

"Schematics?" Marcel whispered.

"I had Kayip send them to you for safekeeping," Desct explained. Marcel glanced at the monk, who simply nodded. "Notes on their recent endeavor with the water treatment plant. It's something peculiar, the machines here are near entirely mutant-built, sweat and blood pouring over every taur-fucking metre of iron. Yet only a handful of who those bastards facetiously believe are the most 'loyal' of our brother and sisters have been sent to work on this enterprise. Most of the labor is done by actual Lazacorp employees, but what our chosen few have seen, well, it is *not* a water treatment plant, at least, not only. Why else would it take so long to finish, why else would they keep it hidden in the same walled complex they keep their generators and other essential organs?"

"What is it?" Marcel asked.

Desct shrugged. "That's why I sent the notes to you. You'd get them to an expert out of town, figure out what's up, and bring the prying eye needed to root out this rotting abscess. Perhaps I should have been explicit, but I held to subtlety and implication, lest the wrong gaze fall upon them. I didn't need anyone else implicated, another friend pumped full of slickdust."

Show To An Engineer! Desct's words, no doubt, written in Kayip's scribble. Marcel felt the fool he was. Desct had tried to thread the needle, throw him a clue that was not incriminating, yet still gave Marcel a path to the truth. If he had found an engineer, maybe the irregularities there would have led him back to Desct. Instead, he had misread the clue completely.

"Cowardice," Celina spat. "Why should he not have to risk his life, when hundreds of us do?"

"It was a miscalculation," Desct admitted. "But all is in order now. Marcel has the schematics, and he can bring them here. Then we shall find the arteries to Lazacorp's heart and rip them to fucking shreds!" He raised his arms with flair, and glanced towards Marcel.

"Of course!" Marcel said. "Next time you see me, you'll have the guide to your salvation." He shot his eye quickly to Desct, who caught his meaning, the uncertainty he couldn't afford to speak of here. The man's smile faded for a moment, but he quickly recovered his confident airs.

"Soon, my brothers and sisters, soon!" Desct said. "And we won't wait a minute longer than we need; we will take our freedom and again taste liberty." The crowd seemed enchanted by a sudden air of hope. Celina scowled, but nodded. Desct beckoned. "The sun is rising. We have a new ally, and he will be back, I promise. Until then, patience, keep your heads low, and prepare for our future assault. Lazacorp will bleed, I promise you that."

Desct led Marcel out of the room, and as soon as they were all free, embraced his old friend. His skin was rough, and he smelled a hint rancid, but Marcel eagerly returned his embrace.

"Desct..." Marcel began, unsure of what to say now that he had the space to talk freely.

A groan and a scuffle, and the mutant who had guided them dropped to the floor, falling halfway onto the two for support, nearly knocking them down with him.

"Sorry! Sorry!" the mutant squeaked.

Marcel gathered his balance, while Desct helped up the prone mutant.

"Gil, it's alright," Desct said. "Go check upstairs, see if Edwige has seen any guards meandering about early. Then make sure our assembly disperses before morning, and that Celina doesn't attempt a riot before I get back."

The mutant nodded and dashed off.

"I recently worked a case with a Gileon," Marcel said, realization dawning on him.

"Gileon Fareau." Desct nodded. "Yeah, I am aware. Well that's him."

"He wasn't murdered?"

Desct shook his head. "Apparently he started to get indignant when he recognized one of the workers as some old buddy out from in the Wastes. So Roache ghosted him away and added him to the workforce. Not very popular, being ex-Lazacorp, but he makes himself useful."

"Then Gall..." Marcel had been set up, had put an innocent man behind bars. Or maybe sent to a worse fate. No, almost certainly sent to a worse fate. Part of him wanted to go through the list of past cases with Desct, hear if any other names rang a bell, but a larger part of him feared what that might uncover.

A grunt, and Kayip lifted himself down from the storage tank's opening. "We can't spend much more time here," he said.

Desct nodded. "We're lucky the guards spend not a pittance of thought on us during the night, but when work starts right before dawn, they will be out in fucking force."

Desct—it was still strange for Marcel to think of him as alive—led them up a winding path through the growth of dense slums. Cramped walls were constructed out of sheet metal and rough, often soiled, fabrics. Scaffolding poles held up cracked floors of wooden planks. The mutants, who had ignored them before, smiled at Desct's passing, glancing up from their meager meals or just from the floor. Some pressed their fist to their chest in some manner of salute.

"Forgive our anfractuous dwelling. We keep our quarters labyrinthine shitholes for a reason," Desct said. "We've... well, those who came before me, managed to win a modicum of privacy through the density and filth. As long as we work and make no clear sign of resistance, the guards rarely care to cut through here, and it adds some good hiding spots when the need arises. It isn't pleasant, but it's how we survive."

He led them on a circuitous route that went up and down makeshift ladders, over resting mutants, down narrow, nonsensical pathways through what looked like solid piles of junk.

"Demiurge, Desct," Marcel asked, "how did it get so bad?"

"Blackwood Row has always been this way. For me, it was the monk who opened my eyes to the perfidy and repugnance of Lazacorp. So I suppose it's him I need to thank for how I am now."

Kayip's face sank.

"A joke!" Desct said as he led them down a stairwell made of fused tin cans. "In truth it started with my Gazette. Had a man working for me, old fellow, Alfred Nuzhen. He had lived in Huile before the fucking war. Strode in one day, demanded a job, was a damn sharp writer, so I hired him. Was instantly critical of the Resurgence government, from day one. Our discussions descended into shit-shouting matches, more than once, over some of the articles he wanted me to print. Would always end with him saying, 'I thought the U-double-CR stood for a Free Press.' Smug sentiment, but you know what? He was correct. So I printed them in the editorial section every few weeks. Got some friction from City

Hall, there were still fears of Principate sympathizers, turncoats, apostates, and all that. Who knows, maybe he was one, maybe he'd had some family killed in the battle, a tight-lipped man, but I defended him well enough, even had Lambert sit me down for one of his tea parties, trying to talk me around to the idea of letting him go.

"Eventually he had this large piece on the war, real deep accusations, especially about Lazacorp. He more than questioned their loyalty; he damn near insinuated that they had offed the old mayor, that *they* started the war. This was almost too much, we debated for hours, but I eventually let it go to print. Wasn't sure if anyone read it at the time.

"I waited for his next article. Never came. A month later I heard he had passed. *Wastelung*, they said. So I went to his wife to give my condolences. I'd met her before, an affable woman, but she seemed almost fearful of me when I visited. Everything she said fit the official story, but her mannerisms, her speech, it was fucking suspicious to say the least.

"Then I got a letter, addressed to Nuzhen. The appropriate thing would have been to pass it on to his wife, but, well, I don't have a proper excuse for it, I opened it. It was from a man, whom I eventually discovered was Kayip, but at the time, it was just some stranger, offering evidence to support Nuzhen's theory. I met with him out in the Wastes, and eventually I found myself leading him through the Underway to disprove his assertions. Instead I found the truth. I should have told you then Marcel, but I'll admit it, I was frightened to do so, for among the gaunt mutated faces was Nuzhen's own. The idea that I might condemn another of my friends... or perhaps I just took on the duty for baser reasons, believing myself the sole hero, the savior.

"Kayip pushed for action, I attempted a more cautious route. I began to assemble the evidence necessary to bring Lazacorp down, either through City Hall, or from a nearby Resurgence-aligned city, or even Phenia itself if it came to that. I took pictures, made sketches, and conducted interviews while Kayip left to follow Roache up to Icaria.

"That's when they caught me. I'm not sure how. Likely they'd been watching for a while, but one night a pair of cops were at my door."

He paused for a moment. "They stuck it into my veins, that slickdust stuff, they pumped me until I screamed, and then kept going. Do you remember, Marcel, when they cut off your leg?"

Marcel shook his head. "It's a blur to be honest, I just remember the pain, then waking up."

Desct pushed aside a scrap-made wall and gestured them on. "Better that way. I was beside you, so was Alba. There was some debate among the medics whether to try to save the leg. I thought that lunacy looking at the wound, it was mere red mush, but one of them insisted it might be possible to treat. Maybe."

He pulled down a ladder hidden behind a cloth wall, and they descended two floors of residential scaffolding.

"The real concern was the fucking sangleum poison, it welled up in that wound and the easiest way to cut off the flow to your bloodstream was to just sever the damned limb. The surreal thing was that you were the one advocating for that path the most. I didn't think you were conscious, you didn't respond to anything, but you kept shouting, 'Cut it off, cut it off!'"

Marcel was suddenly aware of the heft of his leg.

"I felt the same way when they pumped me with slickdust, I shouted for them to cut it off." Desct continued. "Except I was yelling about my whole body. Isn't that true insanity? I wanted them to cut my *body* off. It makes not a single kilogram of sense, but I never wanted anything more in my life."

"Demiurge, Desct."

"Not sure why I'm wasting our time discussing old wounds," Desct said. "Maybe there wasn't anyone I could tell that to before— all the mutants here have already felt it a thousand times over.

"Still, I had known many of the workers here before I was captured, Nuzhen especially, who was a respectable fire stoker until the guards took their rifle butts to his head and disappeared the man. I suppose those connections helped earn me a degree of respect. I never stopped fighting, though now I guess I'm fighting for myself as well."

Marcel shook his head. "I'm sorry, Desct. If I had figured it out..."

"Mistakes were made on every side," Desct said.

Kayip nodded. "I attempted to take down the man himself in Icaria. He is slippery. After we cut the power to Blackwood Row, while the mutants free themselves, I will find the man."

"Then let me take the evidence to City Hall," Marcel insisted, "to Phenia. You have the notes, we just need to publish them."

"No," Kayip said, with a quiet tone that still held the force of a shout. "I have tried such methods before."

Desct shook his head, "Unfortunately, I have to agree with the warmonk. We don't know who is trustworthy or who would overhear. Even if we went as far as Phenia...well, to be frank, I am unsure I would be able to keep the peace here. Celina pushes every day for quick action, and though I have more authority, I'm close to losing it."

They stopped by a back alley. There, Kayip unwound his strange azure blade from his bracelet and cut the fasteners of a sewer grate.

"So it all relies on the schematics," Marcel muttered. "If sabotage is to work."

"We have manpower, but it's those words that damn us. Set off a recording and they'll lull us to peace. For any uprising to succeed, we need to take down the æthericity grid, silence them." Desct stared at Marcel with a stoic countenance, but Marcel could see the hints of fear hiding in the lines around his mouth. There was no excuse in hiding the truth any longer.

"I gave the schematics back to Roache," Marcel admitted.

Kayip muttered some words in his indecipherable tongue, clutching at something within the layer of his rags. Desct thought a moment. "Well, shit," he said. "Troll-fucking griffon-ass shit. That puts us in a damnable fucking bind, doesn't it?"

"But I can get them back," Marcel said. "They're still in City Hall; I can retrieve them," he grabbed his friend's shoulder. "I can make this right."

He said his words with a confidence he didn't know he had. For so long he had been taking odd jobs in Huile, feeling hollow as the city grew around him, wondering deep down if he had been meant to stay. Now, it was clear why he was here. Whatever mistakes he had made, whatever betrayals he had suffered, he would now make it right. He was what Huile needed now, and he knew he could save the city.

Desct smiled, a more melancholy smirk than those he had ever shared on their old treks through the Border States. He looked Marcel up and down, and patted his friend on the shoulder.

"Yes," he said. "Yes, I know you will."

"Then we must go to prepare," Kayip said, lifting the heavy sewer grate. He led Marcel down. Marcel moved slowly, hesitant to leave Desct now that he had found him, but aware of the pointlessness of delay. Desct stood above until Marcel had descended deep into the shadows of the Underway, then with a final wave dashed off, the glimmer of pre-sunlight starting to color the buildings above.

Chapter 22

Sylvaine's papers lay before her on the basement floor in an organized sprawl. Her notes, written on yellowing waste-paper, held the sum of her memories, her theories, her re-creations, and her best guesses. She had been struggling to remember, since the night she had taken up with the hieromonk, the exact details of the schematics she had once scratched her head over. The schematics that Desct had helped to pilfer, that Gearswit had ignored, that she had failed to make sense of, those damned schematics that sketched out the exact anatomy of the very heart of Lazacorp.

It was not just the mutants' plight that pushed her to her task. If it were, she would have long ago given up. Her memory was too engulfed in haze, and Kayip provided no help, having kept only a few poor imitations scribbled out in his hand, resembling a child's doodle more than anything technical. Marcel, despite his intransigence, supposedly had a copy of those notes in full, and all the mutants needed was mere patience. No doubt the mutants would hold onto their prize dearly, necessary as it was for the practical goal of blowing Blackwood Row to smithereens. It was an admirable aim, one that Sylvaine supported, but at no point in the mutants' plans did they seek to answer the question: what in Inferno was it that they were going to blow up?

Lazarus Roache had wanted her, had wanted her negative-density generator, or at least something technologically adjacent to it. For that he had been willing to poison her, to wrap her mind around his finger, and slaughter her professor. It was a simple deduction that her research must have deep, vital relevance to... something.

It wasn't so much the idea that her inventions might be used for some atrocity that bothered Sylvaine. The job of an engineer was to create, not to wring their gloves in worry over how those creations would be used. Nor was it the fear of Roache's words exactly that pushed her; rather it was the fear of what his words had *unleashed* in her. There was something inside Sylvaine that was more powerful than the ætheric bindings of slickdust, something primal, something horrific and beastly. She had escaped Roache's apartment only by losing touch with everything civilized and sentient, by descending into what she had been always told she really was. She had been in that moment just a savage ferral, a wild animal that belonged in a cage.

No, Sylvaine would take Lazacorp apart the right way, methodically, piece by piece, in full control. Like an engineer.

She closed her eyes and started to cycle through the backlogs of her mind, trying to remember each moment of her work with Gath. The man had been subtly pushing her towards an end, to develop some technological breakthrough they could use. She could only recall the broad outlines of his advice, her time working now obscured behind the haze of her weeks of euphoria and her hours of horror.

Water Treatment Plant: useful, boring, mundane. Mechanisms: varied. Purpose: to input polluted water and output potable water.

Negative-Density Generator: expensive, complicated, cutting-edge. Mechanism: manipulation of æther-wave frequency to force matter into a state of density below zero, providing æromantic buoyancy. Purpose: to induce flight.

Not much overlap.

Sylvaine put down her notes and leaned back. She had written over or drawn dozens of pages and wasn't any closer to a workable conclusion. Her only hypothesis so far, *"Lazacorp wants to make Huile fly,"* had been dismissed for being impractical.

Unfortunately there wasn't all that much else to do while she waited for Kayip and Marcel's return. Their lodging, as it was, consisted of an abandoned cellar the monk had discovered on a previous journey, decorated with two burlap cots, a pile of old scrap, a kitchen pot, a miniature stove, and a puddle.

It was strange. The warmonk could be surprisingly sensitive at times. As they had traveled, Kayip listened with patience as Sylvaine talked at length of her experiences with Roache, though she had been reserved with the precise details. He nodded and spoke softly, and at times he reminded her of an oddly youthful grandfather. He treated her like she was normal yet did not try to pretend like she had gone through life in a normal way. It was a subtle sort of empathy that somehow cut through his awkwardness, a kindness that she was unused to, but appreciated all the same.

All of this was in contrast to the fierce violence the man was able to summon when threatened or enraged. Screaming, with blade out, fully prepared to kill. She had watched him go from grandfather to barbarian and back, in a span of under a minute. The man had two personalities it seemed, but unfortunately, if his choice of hideout was evidence, neither personality cared much about basic comfort.

Sylvaine stared again at the notes in the light of her handtorch, which sat in the middle of the room like a miniature lamp. There was no point smashing her head against the problem again, not when the real schematics would be coming by soon, assuming Kayip was right about this Talwar guy.

She reached into her bag and pulled out a misshapen ball of wrought iron. Then, slowly, she took out her glove and, finger by finger, put it on.

Her heart raced as she lifted her hand. She had been hesitant to attempt æthermantics much since they had left Icaria. She had tried, a few times, out in the Wastes, on old bits of rusting machinery or junk like the ball in front of her. It was more difficult than she remembered, more erratic.

Sylvaine narrowed her eyes and focused inwards. A spark! She pulled it out of her, and the ball started to morph, slowly at first, as she threw her will into it. The ball transformed into a cube, then a cone, then a rough gear. The process was labored, her focus slipping off in strange directions, the shapes never quite in perfect symmetry. The power felt strange to her, not an extension of her limbs, of her mind, but a rough and foreign tool that she could barely wield.

What if it wasn't part of her anymore, she wondered suddenly. What if it never was hers in the first place?

The metal mass exploded. She shrieked and covered her mouth with her free hand, the fur at the edge of her leg singed by the metal, now starting to cool into solidity. She cursed and checked herself for burns. Nothing some cool water and a bandage couldn't fix. She glanced back at the focus of her work, now just a shapeless blob of nothing on the floor. Anger struck her, followed by waves of frustration, despondency, fear, and despair. The one emotion she didn't feel was surprise. This was exactly how her experiments in the Wastes had gone.

It was said that engineers were judged by their crafts. What a craft then, what an invention: the world's first immobile paperweight. This hunk of shapeless metal would be an embarrassment to any engineer, she mused, if she still even was an engineer. If she ever had been an engineer.

Sometime later the sound of footsteps awoke Sylvaine from a confused sleep that she hadn't realized she'd fallen into. Dim morning light filtered in through a slit of a filthy, twice-boarded window that pressed up against the ceiling.

She stretched and listened. Yes, there were definitely footsteps, two sets, echoing through the Underway paths just outside the rust-worn doorway. She grabbed her glove and a small shotgun that Kayip had bought from a wasteland trader, though she wasn't keen on the idea of using either. Not that she could likely talk her way out of trouble if it were some strange scavengers wandering about, or worse, the police. Even if they had no notion of her past in Icaria, out here in this nowhere city her presence as a ferral would be enough to rouse suspicion.

She tiptoed up to the door and placed her ear by it. The footsteps stopped, half a metre away. Then a whisper: "Sylvaine. It is I."

Kayip's voice. The relief was instant; she could feel her fur unbristle. Wasting no more time, she undid the several rows of locks and opened the door.

The large man entered, followed by Marcel who staggered sweat-covered and bleary eyed.

"Did it go well?" Sylvaine asked, setting down her shotgun. "I mean, did you, uh..."

Kayip nodded, Marcel looked around, and then sat, slumped, on one of the cots.

"The schematics?" Sylvaine asked. The private investigator rubbed his forehead.

"I gave them back to Roache."

"You gave them back..." Sylvaine stuttered. "Just now?"

"What?" The man shook his head. "No, when I first got them. I didn't know...I mean..." He lay deeper in the cot. "Demiurge, I'm tired."

Sylvaine followed his lead, leaning back on the wall, shaking her head. "Mucked cogs, we're screwed," she mumbled. All this travel, hiding in sewerways, and now what? Roache had a whole city on his side, what idiocy had made her think she could actually do anything to stop him?

"We can still get them," Marcel said. "Gall's notes are kept in City Hall."

Sylvaine glanced at the monk.

"I believe him," Kayip said. "If Roache wishes to keep those notes out of the hands of his foreman, that is where he might keep them."

"It *is* where," Marcel said.

"So we just ask for them?" Sylvaine said. "Or are we talking about breaking and entering? Robbery wasn't exactly in the Academy's curriculum."

Marcel forced himself to sit upright with a groan. "I know how to sneak into these places. We go from below at night."

"I am familiar with the Underway beneath City Hall," Kayip said. "Whatever paths I once used have most surely been blocked, but I imagine I can find some route where your engineering could cut us in."

"And when we're up there?" Sylvaine asked. "Do we know where these documents are?"

"I have little idea," Kayip admitted.

"Let me have a go at it," Marcel said. "You have paper?"

Sylvaine grabbed a notebook from the mess on the floor and gave it to Marcel. The man sketched out a very rough floor plan.

"Most likely they will be kept in the main records room here," Marcel said tapping the pen.

Kayip kneeled down to the map. "How well guarded would you say the building is?"

Marcel laughed. "Barely. I mean, who would they be watching for? There might be a skeleton crew near the front, a policeman or two for emergencies. I've gone there plenty of times late at night.

It's a ghost house; sometimes I have to bang at the door for several minutes, or find a vocaphone to call in, just to wake them up. I've picked locks, so I should be able to break us in without too much trouble."

Sylvaine raised her glove.

"Oh," Marcel said. "Right. I suppose that works."

Kayip scratched at the side of his mask. "I would not be so foolhardy in this. There may be more than we expect. If need be, I can take on several men in these close quarters."

"What?" Marcel said. "No, no, these are U-double-CR cops and officials, good men. We're not... going to fight them, kill them. Demiurge, Kayip, I know we've seen some horrible things, but let's be reasonable. You should stay below, it'll only make things worse with more people."

"Are you sure?" Kayip asked.

"Trust me," Marcel said. "I know—" He yawned. "What I'm doing and—" He yawned a second time, louder. "Sorry, it's been a long night."

Kayip nodded. "It will soon be another." He stood up. "Perhaps it is best we rest until then."

...the dust storms abated sometime around noon. A few of the townsfolk still lived. Many had been heavily infected by the Sin emanating from the sangleum, which by the hour tore itself from the earth. That which days before had been valued as gold, and fought over as bitterly, now gushed out like water, a deluge of Sin. Some of its victims wore mere marks of red skin, others were twisted beyond recognition, limbs elongated, sores open and oozing a strange black substance, bones twisted out of their flesh, resembling in a strange manner the shape of pipework.

A number of the Order suggested mercy killings; it was surely the will of the Demiurge that these pitiful figures be put down. Santi Vitan would hear none of it. These were still the children of the Demiurge, if they had been spared the "horror" so far, (and that was his simple word then, for the name Calamity had not yet come about), then it was the Demiurge's will that they should be protected.

The debate did not long continue. From the horizon, between the towering ruins of what had once been one of the most beautiful cities of all of Vastium, we could see movement. Shimmering forms coagulating themselves out from the oozing sangleum, molding flesh and steel into strange mockeries of the human body. Demons. Not one or two, not in numbers suited for exorcisms, but a host of them, an army.

Many panicked at the sight, other spoke foul words despite their oaths. A few with more composure grabbed their Cracked-Discs, whispering out their prayers, but others staggered backwards, mouthing out nonsense.

Santi Vitan gripped his sword and commanded order among the ranks. His demeanor was calm, but I could see the pain in his eyes. It came not from the sight of the foul manifestations of

Inferno, those congealed masses of Sin. No, for he could see, and I as well, that the demons were not alone. Encircling them were men and women, not crying, not fleeing, but bowing, worshiping the foul avatars that had brought ruin upon us all...

—"The Life of Vitan: First Santi of the Calamity, As Told By a Confidant" By Levat Aman. Veracity debated. Listed as "profane literature" by The Hierocratic Synod.

Chapter 23

A bulbous bag of crimson flesh in the rough shape of a man lay on the floor. Namter walked around the mutant, if it could even be still called that, as it moaned and oozed. He inspected the tag stitched onto its arm, the scrawled numbers displaying results of a blood test. His pen clicked, and three checks hit their marks on his clipboard.

"Is all in order?" asked Brother Avitus, staring down at another mutant, once a woman, who whimpered softly. Namter nodded.

Two more mutants lay in the garage, apparently part of a gang of five food thieves. The fifth had not survived his injections. This bout of disobedience was not of great concern to Namter; the mutants were a shiftless lot, and their tendency to rebel against their proper place was to be expected. The loss of five more would do little damage to Lazacorp's labor force, and their bodies would serve a purpose still.

Namter signed the export form and handed it over to the second of the two Lazacorp guards, who stood beside their autotruck.

"Send these over to Narida Heights," he ordered. The men silently assented and started to load the seeping mutants into the back of their truck, which resembled, to ease the minds of Huile nitwits, a small sangleum tanker.

Brother Avitus walked over. "Narida Heights?" He spoke softly, having the sagacity not to display his misgivings to those outside the Brotherhood. "We are sending them still to that slickdust farm?"

"It is Roache's order," Namter said simply, watching the guards work. They wrapped the mutants in chains, hoisted them up, and then inserted into them, with force, the orogastric tubes necessary to keep the bodies fed through their trip out into the Wastes.

"But we are so close to Reification," Avitus whispered. "To waste Tribute on feeding raider brutes' slickdust habits, seems, well, I do not wish to be impertinent, Watcher."

"You may speak freely with me," Namter assured him, "but it is not our place to question such things. The blessed time is soon approaching, but until then, the balance must be retained."

"Is the Awakener aware we are, even at this hour, still sending caravans to Narida Heights?" Avitus asked.

Namter answered with another nod. It was technically the truth; Verus *was* aware. He didn't like it, but then again, Verus liked little Roache did these days. Namter glanced out the soot-covered window. Through the haze and buildings, he could just barely make out, in the distance, the large featureless block where their final Enterprise in Blackwood Row stood, nearing completion.

"Do not worry, Brother, The Flayed Prince will soon have the blood he requires."

The autotruck revved. As the large garage door started to clunk upward, a broad-chested man ducked under from the street outside and stepped toward them.

"Brother Namter," Dutrix Crat said, conveniently forgetting his superior's proper title. Namter bit his lip.

"Brother Crat," he said simply. Namter wouldn't lower himself to some base trading of insults, though the man, like many of the other Brothers had, since Roache's return, spoken to Namter with only heart-aching coldness. It had been irritating enough playing the middleman to Roache and Verus's feud, but now it seemed that Verus was poisoning his reputation among the Unblind Brotherhood.

"You are needed," Crat said. He glanced over towards Avitus, who kept his gaze, and did not move from Namter's side.

"For...?" Namter began.

Crat shrugged. "Roache's command, I don't know the reason."

"So you're taking orders from him?" Namter said, an unusual state for one whose ear had always bent in Verus's direction.

A shake of Crat's head. "Roache desires it, but the Awakener ordered it, perhaps to curtail the latter's pitiful caterwauling."

"Ah," Namter said simply. So the two men were face to face. Regardless of orders, that was a situation where he was needed.

"Rejected! Those arse-for-a-head, taur-taint-lickers rejected it!"

Namter could hear Verus's voice from a floor below. He let his shoulders fall and rubbed his forehead in a rare moment when eyes were not on him. Things had been going smoothly on most accounts since he resolved the tumult up in Icaria. *That* had been a mess that took some cleaning, dozens of people to bribe, several bodies to bury, and one imported El'Helmaudi rug that needed to be hand-washed three times over to get the damned bloodstains off.

It was a small mercy that the ferral girl had run off without speaking to anyone, no doubt her words would have been discounted, but it was one less nuisance to deal with. More disconcerting had been the disappearance of the monk, but then, his previous attempt to make connections here in Huile had ended in the quick removal of his only possible ally. Within the walls of Blackwood Row, they were quite safe from any mad attempts at assassination. Namter would have preferred the man dead, but perhaps it was divine will that the monk live to see his repeated failures bear fruit.

On the Wastes-side of things, raiders back in Stinktown still raised issues of slickdust pay, as always, and Clan Vapulus had been marauding the occasional caravan, but these were eternal bugbears, ones which would soon be made irrelevant. What mattered was that the Enterprise was on schedule, and with any sense, the Reification should be completed without any real issue.

Of course there was still one quite real, quite senseless issue. One issue with two names, *Roache* and *Verus*. Namter gathered his strength and strode up towards the shouting.

As expected Verus stood, legs planted, teeth gritted, in Lazarus Roache's office. Lazarus, for his part, sat behind his desk, a look of focused indifference upon his face. He altered the facade slightly when Namter entered.

"Ah, good timing. Namter, please put a pot on, we have a guest," Roache said.

Verus didn't even spare the butler a look but instead sneered on.

"You haven't answered my question, Roache," he snarled, finger pointed like a knife at Lazarus's chest.

"Come now, it's impossible to start a civilized conversation without a cup of tea," Roache replied, as Namter heated up the kettle in the tea nook.

Lazarus Roache's office in Blackwood Row was considerably larger than the one he used in Huile proper, and more ornately decorated. There was no need, up here, for even the small layer of false modesty the man put on display for the Huilian spittle-lips. For Namter, however, the expensive pre-Calamity paintings had long faded into an indistinct background, as had the statuettes looted from Vastium manors and the custom-made gold-leafed lamps. What Namter found his gaze stopping at, even after these many years, were the older decorations: the framed contracts of early Lazacorp endeavors, the variety of cheap knickknacks from youthful years of frivolous travels, and the faded photograph of a young blond-haired child, sitting stiffly in the living room of a gray-toned manor. Namter remembered dusting these objects even as a boy, training under his father at the Roache estate. How odd they seemed here, junk from a left-behind life. Part of him wondered if these memorabilia spoke to some hidden sentimentality in his master, but he knew the far more likely truth. They stood as reminders of what Roache had surpassed, the refuse of a pathetic life scrounging for every frasc and aurem, when endless knuckle-wearing work couldn't even keep the lights on. These were the treetops one looked down upon from the summit of a mountain, to see how far one had climbed, to laugh and mock on how miniscule they now looked.

The brat in that photograph was long dead and completely unmourned.

"Roache, stop wasting our time," Verus said as Namter started to pour. "We own this town—why in all troglyn-fucking madness was my application for a new engineer denied?"

Lazarus Roache leaned back, taking a cup from his butler's hand and sipping. "Come, Namter, why don't you explain?"

Namter would have liked to curse, but it wasn't as if he had a choice in the matter. "Apologies, Awakener," he said, "but the mutant engineers we took back from Icaria are making strong progress. An additional engineer, of unknown skill, would only delay the Reification."

"Unknown..." Verus said. "Is my word not enough? No, you're making more taurshit excuses to keep me out. This is a partnership. You damn well know I don't like that, but I keep up my end."

"Your end has been delaying the Enterprise for months," Roache said, putting his cup down and folding his hands. "I do not need to remind you our contract is almost up. Seven years does fly by, and we cannot afford to be behind schedule."

"Schedule...contract..." Verus spat the words. "You speak of our holy task as if it were some business dealings."

"Don't blame me for efficient thinking," Roache leaned back, "unless you want to explain our failure to produce proper output."

"Proper output?" Verus smashed his palm into his good eye and shook his head. "It rots my brain, Roache, hearing you complain to me of delays. You're the one shoving in that griffon-fucking module last minute. That wasn't part of our plan."

"Namter, please elucidate to our guest as to why we needed to modify the water-infusion plant."

He knew what Lazarus was doing, clear enough. Lazarus didn't care that Namter never truly understood the technical details. The tycoon knew full well that Namter never had a voice in the decision to remove Gall, that he had no real opinions on the matter. But Roache kept pushing him on as his mouthpiece, in order to present a united front.

The role of the Watcher was to watch, to shepherd silently the one who held his true Master's gift. It didn't matter how much he actually liked Lazarus, nor did it matter that he more often sympathized with the Awakener. Duty was duty; individual will could only be tolerated in the service of divine will.

Namter closed his eyes. "The Enterprise...though simple in one sense, is quite delicate in another. The slickdust infusion must be regulated perfectly, with a gradual but consistent buildup. All will fall to ash if the Huile residents say, observe that their tap water is suddenly crimson or notice an odd taste. Were it only as easy as injecting the mutants here, to simply lock their chains tight and pump them until they are proper Tribute...but to prepare an entire city, without them noticing, demands immense precision. It is a difficult task, which has required significant breakthroughs in our æther-modulation and infusion technology. We can't afford any further disruption or uncertainty." He opened his eyes to find what he expected, complete contempt written on Verus's face. Utter dismissal by the man who had trained him in sacred rituals, who had once revealed to him the truths of the world. Namter did his best to hide the hurt.

"It would have been fine," Verus said. "Gall had almost figured it out, would have, if you didn't obstruct every damn thing. All was fine until you fucked me over a log."

"Oh, no need for such harsh words." Lazarus gestured for Namter to pour him another glass. Verus had, unsurprisingly, not touched his first. As Roache sipped he pulled out a box of cookies from a drawer and dipped one in his crimson drink.

"Fancy a snack?" Roache asked, lifting up the box. "Brought them from Icaria. Funny things, molded in the shape of little gears. I'm sure they're just for tourists, but they're surprisingly delicious."

Verus stared. "Are you mocking me, Roache?"

"Come now," Lazarus said. "I'm an ambitious man, I have no reason to waste my time with such trivial tasks."

"Go fuck yourself," Verus responded over crossed arms.

"I don't wish to speak out of line," Namter cut in, "but I think it is proper to remind you both that we are all on the same side here. We work for the same task, the same Master. Is it wise to argue so bitterly over details of execution?"

Verus turned his piercing squint in Namter's direction. "Did the 'details of execution' require the murder of my own engineer?"

"Now, now," Roache said.

"I never liked that dog of yours, that mog-lizard, shit-licking Talwar," Verus said, thrusting out his arms. "Unnecessary show, if you ask me, but at least the idiots he got arrested were people we actually wanted gone. What twisted thought wormed its way into your head for you to send him against me?"

"It was the simplest way to resolve things," Roache said. "That engineer wasn't even competent enough to keeps his notes from being stolen. Inferno knows where those ended up. Could have that mad monk gallivanting the Wastes with a copy of them. No, best to finish up things here quickly, and if that meant going behind your stubborn back, Verus, I won't apologize."

Verus gave one last glance to Namter. His gaze spoke clearly of the man's suspicions, all founded in shameful fact. Of course Namter had been the one to forge Gileon's letters—did he have a choice? It was necessary. As were the varieties of letters he had had to forge in the past, often for the eyes of the same fool, a task that Verus had made no criticism of at the time.

"We are almost finished," Namter said. "It doesn't matter what we think of each other, we have done our duty."

Verus spat on the three-times washed El'Helmaudi rug beneath them and pushed it in with his boot.

"You two would still be some Wastes-wandering morons without a pot to piss in if it weren't for me," Verus said. "Some wrinkled old heir to a company you couldn't keep above water and his hired brownnoser. I entertained the idea that one of you had potential," he waved dismissively at Namter, "but I'll admit, I never thought of either of you as much more than a pair of grasping idiots who had access to drills and auto-diggers." The words cut deeper into Namter's heart than perhaps Verus realized. "I made you what you are, and now you think you're somehow better than me? More competent? Makes me laugh." Though he certainly did not.

The Awakener turned to leave, pulling the door open with a slam. "Fine then, do it your way. You, Watcher, keep your watch, Roache, just get the fucking plant running." He walked out into the hallway, muttering. "Remember that it's not me that you need to impress."

Chapter 24

Sylvaine felt the large metal panel through her glove. She breathed in, letting the darkness that surrounded her dissipate, and filtered out from her mind the distractions of the distant drips, the scraprat squeaks, the gurgling pipes, and the nervous breaths of Marcel and Kayip. The smell of the place could not be so easily ignored, even through the scarf she had wrapped over her nose, but it was not so overwhelming as to prevent her from feeling out the form of the metal with a subtle touch of æthericity.

"Yeah," she said, "definitely hollow. Some machinery behind it as well, though can't make out much more than that."

"You think this is City Hall?" Marcel asked, staring at a Huile map they had brought, trying to do the math.

Kayip swung his cone of handtorch light down the corridor in the opposite direction. "Yes. Yes, I do remember. I ran down this way, cut through a weak part of the wall. They must have patched it up."

"You had to escape City Hall?" Marcel looked up from his map.

Kayip nodded, staring downward. "This has not been my first attempt to reveal Roache's crimes." Sylvaine wondered if Marcel noticed how guilt-weary Kayip looked, deep lines pressing in on his forehead, or if the monk's face was too hidden by the dark.

"And they didn't believe you?" Marcel asked.

"No," Kayip said, "I made some progress with the old mayor of Huile. Then I woke up to discover he was no longer the mayor, and I was a criminal. Such are Roache's politics, or perhaps just politics."

"Hmm." Marcel seemed to think on this. Then he shook his head and checked a pocket watch. "It should be late enough. I mean if there are any really ambitious bureaucrats working long hours... No, I don't think we need to worry about *that*." He glanced up at Sylvaine. "So can you...blow a hole in the wall? Or something?"

"That would be both wasteful and a pretty big giveaway. An engineer can be considerably more precise," Sylvaine said as she breathed, focused, and silently hoped she wasn't about to accidentally blow a large hole in the wall. She traced out an elongated circle in her mind, a simple cleavage of the bonds of metal. Then with a spark and a push, a roughly human-sized oval of the wall fell forward.

"See—" she started. Steam blasted out, buffeting her, from some suddenly sliced-open pipe. "Damn it!"

"Quiet!" Marcel said.

Sylvaine jumped into the basement and turned to the cleaved machine whose dismembered limb had been gripping the hewn wall.

"I got this." She tore out a chuck of metal from the wall with one burst of æthericity and then reformed it into the cut piping with another. She patted the metal to double check her jury-rigged repairs were secure, then wiped the hot condensation off her forehead and arms.

"Good as new?" Marcel asked as he walked through.

She nodded, though she was, at best, only 70% percent sure she had fixed the machine instead of just temporarily clogging it. Still, at least it hadn't exploded.

"Are you certain you do not wish me to join you?" Kayip asked from the far side of the wall.

Marcel propped the metal oval up. "I can handle this, Kayip. Don't worry."

"Let's go," Sylvaine whispered.

Marcel led her up the stairs at the far end of the basement. She focused herself for the subtle task of lock-cutting but found the door completely unlocked. This led into some back hallway, rows of wooden doors and brass nameplates, the floor of cracked marble with heavy use of grout. The filigreed æther-lamps were out, but Sylvaine waved for Marcel to turn off his handtorch. Instead she turned on her own, custom-made, and set it to a low glow.

"Is that even on?" Marcel asked. "Still can't see a thing."

"Then tell me where to go and follow my lead."

They skulked around the corners, Sylvaine having to describe the names over the doors to her night-blind partner. She kept her ears attuned to any noises and stopped only once.

"Footsteps. Some coughing," she said.

"Where?"

"Other side of the building. By the echo sounds like a large room."

"The atrium?"

She nodded.

"Do you think it's the atrium?" he asked again. She started to nod, realized her mistake and then just said, "Probably."

Though they moved slow, and Marcel mixed up his memory of the place a couple times, they finally made it to main records room, which was indeed locked. Sylvaine grasped the knob and focused. A quick morph, a turn, and the door swung open.

Fortunately, the room lacked windows, and even more fortunately it didn't contain any lingering bureaucrats, so Marcel was able to turn on his handtorch. It was a medium-sized space, taking up the length of several personal offices, lined with rows of metal files cabinets, each unsurprisingly locked.

"Let's start with..." Marcel's light wandered. "Here."

He pointed at a seemingly random cabinet, without explaining his reason. Sylvaine lifted her glove to the lock, focused, felt for the bolt, and disconnected it. She pulled it open, and Marcel looked through the files.

Five minutes later he shook his head. "Not this one."

Sylvaine pushed it back, focused, and reconnected the lock. No one would notice the change, unless they disassembled it entirely and inspected the mechanism with an unusually keen eye.

Marcel pointed to another cabinet, and as she worked he jogged to the back of the room. He came back with a binder and checked the numbers on the cabinet.

"My mistake," he said, "no, it should be this one."

She kept back a curse, re-fused the cabinet, and opened the one to its right. Marcel checked its contents and came up empty handed. The man pointed down the row, and they repeated this process.

Nothing.

Then again. The precision was exhausting.

After the seventh time she shook her head. "I can't," she panted. "I just need a minute."

"Is it difficult?" Marcel whispered.

"It's tiring," she said. In truth, she was quite certain that if she pushed herself further, she'd end up with a smoldering melted knot of metal as opposed to an unlocked cabinet.

Marcel leaned back and thumbed through the binder. "It's not under G, for Gall, nor F for Fareau. Not L, Lazacorp. I would think it'd be categorized as old evidence, or if not that, confiscated material." He checked through the book, squinted at a far cabinet.

Sylvaine closed her eyes and massaged the side of her forehead. The work had hazed up her mind, and she fought back the thought that the simplest way to clear the haze would be slickdust. She heard Marcel whisper something.

"What?" she asked.

"Hmm? I didn't say anything." He flipped through some pages.

More whispers.

"Turn off your light, someone's out there," Sylvaine said, waving the man back. They ran back, choosing to hide behind twin sets of file cabinets. Light leaked in from the bottom of the door, and Sylvaine could make out the sound of two male voices.

"Sorry again for getting you up. Just foolishness on my part," said the first, soft and weary.

The second voice laughed. "Part of my job, sir. In here?"

"Hopefully."

There was a jingling of keys, just outside the door. Then the handle turned.

"Huh, wasn't locked," came the second voice.

A rotund man entered. "Ah well," he said, speaking with the soft voice. "Someone is lax at their work."

The second man, in a police uniform, waved his a handtorch about and shook his head. "That's Alson's job, locking up. I can assure you I'll be on his ass for this."

The first man laughed. "Ah well, set the light, will you? It must be in here somewhere."

Sylvaine glanced at Marcel. The man held the binder but did not go for his pistol. So he was set on talking his way out. Could he explain her presence if it came to that? Or would he not even try, leave the ferral to fend to herself? The thought sat bitter in her mind.

The bulbs hummed and came alive, setting the room ablaze in white. Sylvaine blinked out the light-blindness.

"Now where would I have left them...?" The fatter man started to walk down. Were their shadows noticeable? Sylvaine held her breath. If it came to it, she would fight and run. She could let Marcel explain *that*.

"Stupid of me, I must have left my keys here after the meeting," the man continued.

"Meeting?" the policeman asked.

"Yes," said the bureaucrat, walking forward. "The Opuday financial one. Terribly dull. And guess who is always thrust the notes to file away."

They were close. A spark could slam the cabinet against them, and then hopefully she could make it to the door before the gunshots started. She sucked in and focused, as the footsteps approached.

"But it's Finday," said the policeman.

The soft-voiced man stopped, a few metres down. "Is it? No...yes, yes you're right. Then I...No I wouldn't have come down here today...Ah, Simone's office. Yes, that'd be the place I left."

He turned and walked back toward the door. The policeman shut off the light.

"Apologies," the bureaucrat said, "clearly my mind is taking a walk tonight."

"Don't think of it," the policeman laughed. "No harm done."

The door shut. Sylvaine and Marcel released their breath simultaneously.

"Well, good news," Marcel said, putting down the binder. "I have a new theory."

Sylvaine followed Marcel's instructions and in turn led Marcel down a few darkened hallways and a set of stairs until they reached a door with the nameplate: *Minister of Justice Lambert Henra*.

"If Roache is desperate to keep the notes from Verus," he said as she worked the door, "well, he wouldn't have it shoved in some public space where one might easily slip it away while claiming to search for some records or other nonsense."

The inside of the room was overly decorated, cabinets pushed out of the way into corners to make room for paintings, Phenian-style stained-glass floor-lamps, and even a small bronze statuette of a soldier, bayonet raised. She moved back to inspect to one of the metal cabinets, but Marcel tapped her shoulder and pointed to the giant oak desk.

"Try his personal notes. In here."

She stared at the desk. On its side, near the arm of a leather chair, was indeed a drawer. She pulled on it—locked. She sensed some metal inside, maybe a pen? Not enough to work with.

"It's a wooden lock," she said.

Marcel nodded. Then, when he noticed she wasn't trying to open it: "Is that a problem?"

"Wood resonates mostly with natural æthers, even crafted wood-products have largely unworkable frequencies, and interact poorly with mechanical æthers," Sylvaine explained. The man stared blank. "I can't do anything to wood," she simplified.

"Oh." Marcel turned his stare to the drawer. "Well, then."

He pulled on it a few times and then paced around. Finally, he sighed and pulled out a flickknife from his belt and started to cut at it. Sylvaine stood by the door, listening in, occasionally shushing Marcel as he grunted.

It took a good long while, splinters of wood piling on the floor to mark the minutes, a soft drizzle on the shuttered window slowly growing into full rainfall, but finally Marcel whispered, "Done." Sylvaine walked over, and Marcel pulled out the drawer, with some difficulty. Inside, lit by Marcel's handtorch, was a beige folder, thick with documents.

"That's—" Marcel began. A sudden snap, somewhere under the desk interrupted him. Then, a quarter of a second later, a bell at the upper corner of the room started hammering. Then warning bells rang down the hallways, dozens of them, a horrible symphony in honor of their mistake.

"He trip-wired it," Marcel said.

"Run!" Sylvaine said.

They dashed down the hallway, lights now flickering to a blindingly bright from some unseen switch. They turned down a bend, the stairs to the basement to their left, when Marcel threw out his arm.

He opened the folder and started leafing through it in a frenzy. "This. And this one. Any others that are important? Take them, and them only. Quickly." He thrust several pages from into Sylvaine's hands, diagrams, schematics, and pages of notes.

"What?" she stammered out but dutifully grabbed the most vital of the papers. Why didn't he just run, they had more than a head start?

"I have to...I just have to try. I've got a plan here, trust me," he said, eyes still ripping through the pages, until he grabbed a last handful and thrust them to Sylvaine. "Go. Go!"

She could hear footsteps. Not far off now.

"I don't understand," she said.

"I'll meet you. I just have to...I won't tell them about you or any of it. If I fail, they won't know. Just go!"

Arms full of papers and plans, head swimming in panic, she went.

Chapter 25

Marcel straightened his coat as he listened for Sylvaine's footsteps to dissipate, which they did, moments before the policemen reached the end of the hallway. Good, he had done his duty, to her, to the mutants, to Desct. If this went to shit, they still had their notes, had their chance at revolution. But revolt meant violence, death, bodies on the streets of Blackwood Row. No doubt Roache had corrupted some of City Hall, but there were many in the government who had fought to free Huile. These were soldiers of a just cause; if the veil was flung off of Lazacorp's brutality, if the light of truth shone down upon Roache's hypocrisy, no doubt these soldiers would burn with the same indignation that Marcel had, display the same horror-tinged resolve for justice. Blood might not be as inevitable as Desct or Kayip assumed. If there was any chance to peacefully defuse this clockbomb before it was set, to purify Huile from the top down, Marcel had to take it.

He spent his last seconds neatening his collar and trying to calm his breathing. It would be difficult to present an air of professional ease when caught breaking into a municipal office, but Marcel would try his darndest.

Two policemen turned the corner, one older, with short-cut graying hair, holding a rifle, the other younger, freckled, his pistol out in his shaking hand. They stopped as they saw Marcel.

"Working late, gentlemen?" Marcel smiled as best as he could manage. "It's fortunate I found you. There's something urgent I need to discuss with Lambert."

The younger policeman glanced at the older, who glanced down at the thick file in Marcel's hand. He took a few cautious steps forward, then jammed the butt of his rifle into Marcel's stomach.

Pain rushed through Marcel as Gall's papers spilled over the floor. He doubled over, knees knocking onto the ground, groaning as the policeman tossed aside his rifle and began to cuff Marcel's hands behind his back.

"Call Mr. Henra," the older policeman commanded his partner.

Marcel sucked in his lost breath, and held back an urge to vomit, before muttering out a weak, "Thanks."

The policeman turned to him, then shook his head and chuckled.

The pair kept Marcel locked to a chair in the cramped, brick-lined interrogation room for the better part of an hour. He tried to initiate conversation, but the night guards ignored him. They weren't outright contemptuous, instead wary, unsure of what to make of the private investigator. At times Marcel thought of insulting them, or otherwise egging them to conversation, something to break the monotonous silence, but decided against risking another rifle thrust to the gut. The only sound to distract his thoughts was the patter of rain on the shuttered window, which grew alongside his anxieties.

Finally, the younger policeman opened the door to let in a very tired-looking Lambert, coat misbuttoned, a steaming cup of tea in his hand.

"Normally you call first," Lambert said.

Marcel forced a weak laugh. "I'll admit, I was trying for some independent research."

Lambert nodded and sipped. "Glad to hear 'independent.' Seemed unlike you to be stealing government documents on Verus's behalf."

"Is that what you thought?" Marcel turned his head, smirking. "Yes, I could see how it could be confusing, with all the effusive praise I've thrown upon that man."

Lambert laughed. "No, no. I was just puzzling out all possible theories, even the outlandish ones. You must admit, Marcel, this is...aberrant behavior for you. I don't recall ever giving you a warrant to break into *my* office."

Despite the loose humor, Marcel could sense something behind Lambert's words. Fear? Anger? Disappointment? The man was holding his cards close.

The Justice Minister skimmed the loosely reorganized pile of Gall's notes. "If you're still concerned about the Gall case, Marcel, I can assure you these are all mere technical documents. I did go through them. Just architectural plans and mechanical schematics, nothing interesting, unless you have recently taken up a study of filtration engineering."

"But you kept them locked, specifically in your office, trip-wired."

Lambert watched Marcel's stare and then tilted his head, acquiescing the point. "A favor to Lazarus Roache. We did expect some possibility of robbery, though we had predicted, if it did come, that it would come from Verus's men, not from you."

He lifted up his tea and took a long sip.

"Politics, Marcel. I know you have no handle on politics, and I've done my best to keep you out of them. I have never asked for thanks, but I will admit it is a gratitude-worthy job. From your own, admittedly helpful, corner, you don't see even a tenth of what happens in this city, but there has been considerable conflict between the two partners of Lazacorp. Quite disruptive, particularly in the last half year. Now, one of those partners is a law-abiding citizen who has donated much to the Resurgence cause and saved this city from utter ruin, the other is, well, Verus. The details of why Roache can't just rid himself of his foreman are, truthfully, beyond me, but occasionally we do a little here to safeguard the man's enterprises, many of which benefit our own city."

"But there must be a line, Lambert, right?" Marcel said. "The Confederacy serves its citizens, not Lazacorp. Don't you ever worry that that line has become too eroded?"

Lambert paused a moment. "Funny for you, of all people, to make such an accusation, Marcel." He pulled his chair forward. "Now I don't wish to be impolite to a good friend, but I must remind you that I am sitting in the interrogator's chair, and you the suspect's. So I ask, if not for Verus, then why?"

Marcel leaned in. "Do you know what goes on in Blackwood Row?"

"Marcel," Lambert spoke with more than some frustration, "I know everything that goes on in this city. It is part of my job description."

"I saw pictures," Marcel whispered. "Of the mutant workers in Blackwood Row, I saw deprivations and—"

"You saw Desct's photographs," Lambert cut in. Marcel sucked in a gasp. He steadied himself against the table and nodded.

Lambert smiled and even let out a soft laugh. "Ah. I see, I see. Well, perhaps this misunderstanding was in part my own fault. Yes, I spoke to Desct several times before his death. He had become...somewhat delirious in his sickened state. Bought some photographs, forgeries, from some wasteland traveler, and in his illness had taken them to be real, kept going on about it. I even showed him the truth in person, but well, the man was too far gone. I was planning on getting him institutionalized down in Phenia, but then the source of his illness, and madness I suspect, made itself known, and he passed rather quickly. I'm sorry I never mentioned this to you, Marcel, but I thought it would have been distressing."

So many lies. How many did Lambert truly believe? Marcel's heart ran a sprint, and for the first time since being handcuffed he felt truly trapped. It seemed impossible that Lambert was in on Lazacorp's corruption. The man had lost the same friends Marcel had to keep this city free. Could he have sent away another, for *Roache's* sake? But it was clear enough the Justice Minister was not fully ignorant. He had to know he was speaking some taurshit.

Marcel sucked in his breath. He had gone this far already; Lambert was still his only hope.

"Have you seen the refineries?" Marcel asked. "In person? Without Roache's permission."

Lambert kept quiet a moment as he studied Marcel, who could feel the cold of sweat drops slipping down his neck.

"That seems less like the jurisdiction of a Justice Minister," Lambert said slowly, "and more the bailiwick of a private investigator."

"I think..." Marcel began, "that considering the evidence, an official investigation—"

"Have you broken into Blackwood Row?" Lambert cut in suddenly.

"They're being tortured!" Marcel said, with a sudden force that surprised even himself. "And they're not just foreign waste-mutants, they're being mutated here, captured human slaves and stolen prisoners, some of them are even Huile citizens."

"I see," the Minister of Justice said, face falling. "I see."

"Lambert," Marcel said, trying to keep the desperation from his voice, "we have to do something."

The man sighed, fist clenching and unclenching. He gathered himself, put on a small, somber smile and asked: "Marcel, why did we attack Huile?"

"To free it," Marcel said, without hesitation. "To punish the Principate coup, and to let the city know liberty."

"True, true. But there any many cities that suffer under the iron chains of tyranny, in one form or another. We can't well go liberating them all. We haven't the armies for it," Lambert said. "So why Huile, specifically?"

Marcel sighed. "Because of the sangleum."

"Because of Lazacorp refineries, yes," Lambert said. "You may not remember this, or even have been aware, but when General Agrippus's army came down from her northern campaign to reinforce Huile, well, many people thought this might be the precursor to the big attack. That the forces of the Principate would rush down from Anklav, and it would be a new Severing War. Chaos like our great-grandparents knew it, blood on the streets of Phenia, perhaps even a second Calamity, who could say? Well, that nightmare never came to pass, in no small part due to the heroic actions of men like yourself and Lazarus Roache. So, perhaps there have been the occasional mistakes, let's say, necessary shortcuts, expedited labor recruitment drives, maybe some sacrifices in the exact letter of safety regulations in the name of efficiency. Huile runs off Lazacorp sangleum, and the excess—and my dear friend, there is much excess—is used to facilitate alliances with many other Border States to keep what happened during the Battle for Huile from ever happening again. Our bulwark against Imperial encroachment relies on Lazacorp. You must understand that."

Lambert knew. He had always known. Desct had warned him, Kayip had warned him, but Marcel had been sure the man was innocent, that if only his friend had known the truth, he'd rise up to stop it. He wanted to ask how many of the men and women Marcel had helped arrest had disappeared beyond those walls, had been forced into that disposable, tortured mass of slave labor. Instead Marcel just nodded.

"You look tired," Lambert said. "Would you like some tea?" He pushed his cup forward, across the table.

Marcel glanced down at the reddish water, smelled a familiar acrid scent.

"What blend is this?" he asked, a further horror growing.

"It's good stuff, invigorating," Lambert said.

Marcel shook his head slowly, and the man shrugged.

"But you do understand, don't you, Marcel?" Lambert continued. "You can't go talking about this with other people who wouldn't. A soldier's duty never ends, and it seems our duty to the Resurgence requires us to...overlook some things. For Huile's sake."

There was no place left for truth in this building, perhaps in this whole city. Marcel forced his smile. "Of course, Lambert. I get it now. You don't need to be worried."

Lambert smiled back and tapped the table. The older guard came around and stood beside Marcel as Lambert leaned to pat Marcel's hand. "You were never a great liar, my friend. Don't worry, I'll work this all out."

He stood up.

"And Marcel," Lambert continued, "I am so very sorry."

Marcel felt a sudden burst of pain in the back of his head, and the world descended into blackness.

Chapter 26

Sylvaine searched and scrambled through the winding subterranean hallways and sewerways. The rainwater from the surface was making its way down with ferocity, gushing in rivers through cracks and broken pipes. Pathways they had taken a mere hour or two before were now impassable torrents or rising swamps of excrement and oil. They had planned to meet Kayip at an older underrail station that stood beneath the wall to Blackwood Row. He had shown her the path, had explained it to her and even drawn up a map, but that was for a dry Underway.

Perhaps it would have been easier with two sets of eyes, even if one were near blind in the dark. Sylvaine had waited for Marcel, had listened in the basement, but when it was clear that the man's plan involved being knocked half unconscious by a rifle butt and dragged away, she had crossed into the Underway and sealed up the hole.

He had seemed so confident; he knew the city better than she did. He had friends in City Hall, he had bragged about it. The more she tried to convince herself that she did the right thing leaving the man to his own initiative, the less confident she felt.

There was no going back now; instead she closed her eyes, pulled down the scarf from around her nose, and sniffed. The air was putrid, though a softer, wetter putrid than before. It was still overwhelming, and she spent half a minute gagging before she could force herself to try to sniff again. Though she had initially tried to ignore Kayip's smell, she had spent enough time traveling in cramped conditions through hot wasteland afternoons with the warmonk to be very familiar with the idiosyncrasies of his odor. Now she tuned her nose for it, though it was like listening for a whisper in the middle of a concert. Though in this particular fetid concert the lead musician was a man slapping a cat against a violin and the harmonium player had passed out on his keyboard. Despite this cacophony of odors, she was able to make out a hint of Kayip, somewhere in the distance.

She followed this, sometimes down dead ends or up to tiny pipes that functioned as vents. After half an hour or so the scent started to get stronger. She closed her eyes and trusted her miserable nose. The scent grew and grew and Sylvaine leapt over small streams and followed winding passageways through old basements in pursuit, all the while holding Gall's papers tight to her chest. Then suddenly the smell was overwhelming.

"Sylvaine!" Kayip whispered.

She opened her eyes, the man a mere metre from her.

"Are you alright?" he asked.

"Yes. Fine," she said, wrapping her nose again in blissfully suffocating fabrics.

"Where is Marcel?" the man asked. They were standing near old tracks, in a dilapidated station, the words *Audric Central* on a faded sign, the stairway covered in rotting boards that gave way at its bottom to a shallow river.

Sylvaine shook her head. "He stayed back. I think he wants to reason with his friend."

"The notes," Kayip pointed.

Sylvaine handed them over. The man searched through the documents. "These are not all..." he said. "But perhaps these will do. At least the man sold his life for something valuable."

"Sold his life?" Sylvaine said.

"I warned Marcel." Kayip sat on a century-old rusting bench. "I told the man the truth. But I believe he will stay silent. He has the will of a martyr, for better or for worse. Yes, I think we may continue without him."

"So you think they're just going to kill him?" Sylvaine said. "Are we just going to sit here then? We might still have time."

Kayip shrugged. "Perhaps, but it is too much to risk. This was all we could have expected Marcel to assist with. It is a tragedy, but if we must lose him...then yes, now would be the sensible time."

"We can't just leave him!" Sylvaine kept herself from screaming, almost taken aback at her own anger.

"Many have already died because of Roache." Kayip's gaze fell to the ground. "I cannot sacrifice their justice to save a man eager to doom himself."

"He did this out of a sense of his own justice," Sylvaine said, surprised with the vehemence with which she was defending Marcel. "I'm not sure I even like the man—he's cocky and more than a bit of an idiot, but he was willing to risk his life, sell his life for a bunch of people he didn't even know." She grabbed at and massaged the hair of her forehead. "Fuck, I should have stayed, should have talked the idiot out of it, grabbed him, something."

"You cannot let yourself swim in the guilt of all you have left behind. It is too much. You will drown," Kayip said.

Was this all that Marcel's life was to Kayip, a playing piece, a strategic trade in the battle for justice? She thought she knew the monk, at least a little. He had always treated her like she mattered, but did any life matter as much as his revenge? Sylvaine couldn't speak; she just stared at the man. This was not what she thought she had agreed to. Her vengeance was a reason to keep living—it had never been a reason to die. This wasn't a game to her.

But then, it wasn't a game to him either; she could hear it in his voice, in his slow, tired breaths. Marcel's fate weighed on him, even as he accepted it as necessary, perhaps he had already decided that he would soon follow.

"Marcel wasn't the first, was he?" Sylvaine said.

Kayip shook his head. "I could have given up after any number of my failures. Perhaps I deserve to drown, the Demiurge has that final judgment. I only know that we are risking far more than just one man. We must do the wise thing, even if it hurts, even if it cuts us down to nothing."

"What if it were me?" Sylvaine said. "What if you had no need for an engineer? Would you have left me there? Up in that municipal hall or sunstroked outside Icaria?"

Kayip stared up at her but said nothing. She could read the lines on his face; despite his words he did not display callousness. Instead it was pain, layer upon layer of pain, so many that it would be easy to fit another fold without making any visible difference.

She walked up to him and grabbed the diagrams out of his hand. "What can you do with these?" she asked. "Do any of the mutants have technical training? Do they know how to follow æthericity lines, to cut off power, where to block something up to blackout the whole system?" She crossed her arms. "We have to try. You can either help me, or we go our own ways."

...*Rex Sharpeye pushed his hands deep into the billowing sanctuary of his long and well-worn trenchcoat, which billowed in the dark rainy wind of the city's midnight. The woman said she'd be here, no amount of beating by rain-gutter brutes could knock that memory out of his head, and he had taken a beating. Then again, he had given it back twice as hard. Yet still, if she said she would be here, then why wasn't she? Had his own lover betrayed him? Rex knew this was a very real and very dangerous possibility. Dames, you could never trust dames.*

Trusting his own masterful, honed instincts, Rex retreated deep into the gloomy deep shadows of the dark shadowy alley. The shadows would protect him he knew, but maybe not protect him enough. He slid his fingers over the steel coolness of his pistol that he held in his pocket. The weapon had got him through many a night like this one. Maybe it would get him through this one as well.

As he hid, three men approached the very spot he had been standing in moments before. He recognized them as the brutish henchmen of Madame Treetar.

"He's not here," said one in a voice that reminded Rex of a dullard he had known in his youth.

"He must have ran off," said a second with a voice like a drunken bear.

"Then we must run ourselves," said the last, an El'Helmaudi man by the look of him, wearing a scarred face and strange hat. "Lest he try to beat us back to our Mistress's hideout."

With that the three ran off. Rex snuck out after them, and as his foot hit the cracked pavement of the long, untended road, whose cracked cobblestones matched his own cracked heart at the betrayal he had now realized had taken place under the auspices of the woman he thought he had loved, the roar of an æroship roared.

Rex Sharpeye watched as a great bulbous ship of metal floated above the roofs of the city and then floated away. Other men in such a situation would have cursed or bewailed their fate or cried unmanly tears. Rex was not such a man. Justice had been corrupted in the city of Annocance, but that just meant there was more work for him. He smiled as he loaded his pistol. There was work to be done...

—*"Rex Sharpeye, Private Investigator. Book 5: The Murder at Goldford Hills" By Klaus Askoy. A Pre-Calamity pulp. Received lukewarm reviews upon first publication.*

Chapter 27

It sounded like rain. Strange, as Marcel could see the sun clearly through the window. His head pounded, and he wasn't sure why, though perhaps that answer could also explain the strange noises that echoed softly from some far-off corner of nothing.

Where was he? Marcel couldn't quite remember. Everything was a bit fuzzy. He heard the sound of an autocar driving by, some men talking outside. He focused through his headache, and the world became clearer.

He was in his apartment. Of course it still seemed strange to him, as it was brand new. Lambert had told him it used to be some Principate official's place, some high-up who fled after the battle. Marcel would have thought that those high on the Imperial command would requisition nicer housing, but the cheap rent suited him, as he was technically unemployed.

The room itself was unfurnished, aside from his new bed in the backroom and his desk, which he assumed would be useful at some point. He also had some photographs in a box, but he'd get to those in due time.

Instead he tried to distract himself with the pulp in his hand. *Rex Sharpeye, Private Investigator*. He wasn't sure which one it was exactly, *The Mystery of Stempston Street* or maybe *The Hallowed Fens*; he had brought a couple up all the way to Phenia. It was hard to read the words. They kept wiggling. Why did his head pound?

His metal leg, still store-fresh shining, moved sluggishly, and as he tried to stand up, he kicked over a glass on the floor.

Malson's Waste-Brewed Whiskey. He hadn't drunk more than a few sips of alcohol since his university days. Except for that night before Alb—

Ah. So Alba was leaving today. That explained the alcohol and therefore the headache, as well as the strange tugs, as if the world was shifting slightly around him.

Well, so it was. If she wanted to leave, she could leave. She had done her duty. It was within in her rights to abandon all common decency, abandon the city, abandon him. He couldn't stop her, wouldn't try. Anymore at least. If she had anything to say—

As if on cue, knocks on the door. He had been reveling in the idea that she would come crawling to him seconds before but now dreaded the conversation.

"Who is it?" he shouted.

"Me," came the voice of Desct.

Marcel sat up. "The door's open."

Alba opened the door. Marcel leaned back on his chair in an aggressively casual slouch and tossed down the pulp.

She strode into the room wearing a sleeveless shirt, her old military pants, and a taur leather jacket that gave her the look of a wasteland wanderer, which was her intended career path. Desct slunk in behind her.

Alba didn't say anything. She didn't apologize or beg or even toss out some final insult. It was unlike her to be so stone-faced. Marcel also didn't say anything. He knew he had nothing to apologize for. If anything, he had a few choice words for the woman, some biting remarks crafted bespoke for just such an occasion. But he couldn't open his mouth, couldn't risk his tongue ignoring his brain's commands, his desperation overriding his pride. Were his lips to move, he might find himself begging, pleading. He couldn't let that happen, so he clenched his teeth tight.

Finally, Desct said something.

"I thought it was, I don't know, fucking proper that you two should have your send-off, regardless of whatever complications of Demiurge-damned..." he petered off and shook his head. "I'll leave you to it, I guess."

Desct left, and the two continued to not talk for some time. She was a tough one, maybe that's what attracted him to her, but then, she couldn't let herself be beat. She'd rather push them both into misery than admit she was wrongheaded. He didn't even want an apology, really, didn't want to hear anything. The silence was fine, if she only stayed. They could both just pretend then, pretend it was like the way it was before. Just for a little bit, even.

But her eyes were clear enough. Not angry, as he half-expected, not a cutting gaze, but a firm one all the same. If it spoke of anything it was not insult, not mocking rage, but a hint of pity. It would have been better if she were angry.

Finally, Marcel sighed. "So you're leaving."

"You know the plan, Marcel." Alba had her hands in her pockets. "But I am still looking for hires. You have experience with a rifle."

"Eh, I never fired the damn thing in combat anyway."

They both chuckled.

"I could ask Lambert for work for you," Marcel said, frustrated that his heart was naïve enough to pulse with hope.

"I've seen where taking orders leads me," she said. "Tired of spilling blood for other people."

"Better to spill blood for yourself?" Marcel said. "Better to line your own pockets than to help build something like this?" He gestured to the window, where the city sat in a strange vague haze.

Alba shrugged, not nearly as bothered by Marcel's accusation as he would have wished. "Better to make my own decision on that front." She followed Marcel's arm to the window, staring not at the city, but past it. "I'll see what's out there for a free woman, see what the wide world can offer."

"And what will you end up with when it's all said and done?" Marcel asked. "Just some aurem."

"A life," she said simply, before turning back to Marcel. "When it's time for the skraggers to dine, it'll all be the same either way. It's the life before that counts. Don't look only at the end, Mar. If you want to wait around here to make sure it'll all be okay, well, you're in for a disappointment. It's never all okay, it's never happily ever after. It's just more life, just more mess, a different mess maybe, if you're lucky.

"Then I can, *we* can, clean the mess."

She shook her head. "Nothing you're going to do here, Marcel, will change what we did. Nothing will clear the bodies from our memories. You want to wash off the Lazacorp gas. You want to clean away the blood."

"There's nothing to wash," Marcel said, trying not to shout. "We did what we needed to do to secure a future for Huile."

"I'm not blaming you either. I'm just saying." She walked over to his desk. "You want things to be okay. I want things to be okay. They won't be. So move on. I just worry that you'll trap yourself here, sitting around, waiting for people to tell you how great it was that we killed thousands of men in their sleep, how heroic. It was suffering. For them and for us. Necessary suffering? Maybe. I can't judge that, can't change it. But I can, *we* can, move on."

Marcel held his breath, trying not to explode at the woman he once loved, the woman who took the last moments of their time together to torment him, to try to chip away at wounds that had not yet fully healed.

"And Desct?" Marcel said. "He seems satisfied to stay here."

"He's working for himself, found his own path," Alba said. "Not sure how it'll work out, but at least he's keeping an eye on the bastards running this place, as opposed to doing their paperwork."

"I'm not taking Lambert's job," Marcel said. Even if he wanted to, Alba had poisoned that idea, made it sound less like a hero's just reward and more like a stray dog's table scraps. That's what she seemed to think of him now, even after all he had done.

"So what?" She raised her eyebrow slightly. "You'll just try to skim by on a military pension?"

"No, I'll..." That had been part of the plan, but Alba could make anything sound pathetic. He glanced down to the floor to avoid her gaze. The pulp stared back, a man in a wind-battered trenchcoat, lit by stylized moonlight, a clope in one hand, a pistol in the other.

"I'm going to become a private investigator," Marcel said.

Alba raised her eyebrow all the way. "Private investigator."

"Yeah." Marcel stretched back. "Work for myself, won't be beholden to City Hall or Lazacorp or no one. I'll clear up the cases that slip through the cracks, help the average Huile citizen, the sort of folk the UCCR stands for."

She kept her eyebrow raised.

"I'll turn this into my office." He gestured. "Don't need a living room anyway. And I got Lambert on board." Of course, Marcel's friend hadn't even heard of the plan, but that could be smoothed out with ease. "You can leave this city. I'll keep watch on Huile. I'll finish what we started, on my own terms."

He waited for the inevitable insults. That he was being a child, playing at some troglyn-headed excuse for game, hiding away in his pitiful little hole. He waited for Alba to walk over, to notice the pulp on the floor, to pick it up and burst into mocking laughter.

Instead her eyebrows relented, her gaze softened, and she just shook her head. "Okay. Okay then, if that's what you want, Mar."

The hum of an autocar engine rumbled steadily louder. Marcel tried to smirk, but his head hurt too much. It was so cold in the apartment.

"I need to get going," Alba said. "I'm glad I saw you. Just...take care of yourself, Talwar."

It really did sound like rain, and Marcel's vision was fuzzy again. He tried to shout out, "I'll handle myself fine!" but suddenly he couldn't get his lips to move. Strangely enough everything else felt like it was already moving, like the world was shaking around him. There were voices, two of them, neither of which were Alba's nor Desct's.

He blinked heavy lids that seemed determined to stay closed and finally, with great effort, was able to open them. He could make out occasional colors, but it was most often darkness. His head hurt worse than ever. He could breathe but only with difficulty. His mouth tasted like old laundry. He tried to move his hands, but they were stuck together somehow.

"Turn left here," came one of the voices, older, gruff, slightly familiar.

"Hmm?" came another voice, lighter. "But isn't the drop off point—"

"Damn it, Hughes, you think I don't know where we're going?"

"Okay! Okay! Apologies, sir."

The world shifted, and Marcel found his face pushed against leather. He pulled himself up and felt cold glass. He blinked. It *was* raining.

"We're going back to the place we took Gall," said the older voice. "You know, that automotor factory."

"Sir?" said the second voice. "I wasn't on the Gall case."

"No? Oh, right that was Alson. Mix you two up sometimes."

Marcel heard a click and smelled tobacco smoke. He tried to mumble something but realized his mouth was stuffed with a gag.

"Alson, sir?" said Hughes. "We look nothing alike."

Memories started to flow back in ice-chilled trickles. City Hall. Gall's notes.

Lambert.

After all they had been through, the man was willing to throw a friend under the proverbial autobus that Roache drove. Marcel groaned, though that was more from the pounding in his head.

"Yeah, because you know," the older man said, "you're both into that...backroom stuff. Tyrissian bathhouses and all that. I don't know, I've never been religious."

"Sir, I have no idea what you're talking about."

"Eh, never mind. Turn right here."

The 'car screeched and made a sharp turn, flinging Marcel back in the other direction. Then it slowed to a stop.

"Yeah, well, Lambert don't want this guy saying anything to Verus, and don't want to let Mr. Roache know there was a breach in his confidential whatever. *Politics*, that's how it is. So we're doing this old style," the older man said, getting out of the car.

Hughes opened the door and dragged Marcel out. Marcel tried to struggle, but his body felt as if it were filled with iron ball bearings, and when he attempted to head-butt the man, it felt like tapping his forehead against stone. Hughes didn't even notice.

"Old style?" the young cop asked, dragging Marcel. The lights were dim in the alleyway, and Marcel could see the walls of Blackwood Row above them. He was being pulled into an old factory, a grave of rusting industry, decorated with piles of dead machinery, deep-cut holes in the floor, and crumbling walls that were, in many places, patched with pieces of sheet metal.

"What do you think it means, Hughes? Just because you're too young to have worked war days don't mean you don't have to get your hands dirty sometime. Put him here. Noise won't travel far."

Marcel tried to think of a meaning of "old style" that didn't involve a bullet, but the young cop pulled out his pistol and there wasn't much ambiguity about that.

Hughes stared at the weapon in his hand. "Demiurge, I've never had to kill a man before."

The older cop leaned on a conveyer belt. "But didn't you...Right, Alson." He puffed out a cloud into the dim. "It ain't hard, just pull the trigger. Oh, but place him a bit closer that a-way. There's an old sinkhole there. You can just kick the body down."

Marcel tried to pull all his rage together in a desperate squirm—his anger at Lambert for choosing comfort over justice, at Roache for betraying Huile, for using Marcel as his weapon. The last of his fury fell upon himself, for being such a damn fool. Despite his efforts, Marcel couldn't do much, bound as he was, and he couldn't even raise his anger above his own self-pity. Alba had been right. She had been so damn right. He tried to imagine her face, smiling in the moonlight. He wanted his last image to be of beauty and bliss, but he could only manage to picture her shaking her head as she turned to leave.

Hughes took some bullets and tried to load them into the revolver. Marcel could hear the clink-clink as the young cop dropped them.

"You know he was a war hero?" the old cop said.

"Him?" the young cop replied, scrambling to pick up the bullets.

"Yeah. You never heard of Marcel Talwar?"

Marcel could hear the man's coat rustle as he shook his head.

"Eh, you greenhorns have no head for history. I remember. We spent a week digging mass graves for the soldiers he killed. Not himself, of course, with gas. Disgusting, heads turned to mush, was worse than shoveling taurshit."

Now the only image Marcel could imagine was the bleeding, melting face of Principate soldiers. The price necessary to save Huile, only for Roache to rot the city from the inside. The faces glared at him from memory, agony written clear even as flesh turned to liquid. He tried to vomit, but it didn't escape the rag.

"We had to add a few bodies of course. Old style. Principate bureaucrats and the like. I had to shoot Mr. Legros. Not a bad man, actually, ran a good bakery. I used to get cheese tarts there, but then he went and married a Principate officer. Dumb. Best to be apolitical, but now I'm just rambling. Hughes, you going to shoot the bastard or what?"

"Do you have to keep using my name?" said Hughes.

"Who's gonna hear? This bastard? Yeah, I'm sure he'll bitch you out to the Lords of Inferno."

The pistol shook in the cop's hand. Marcel could not help but wonder if the young man knew what he had signed up for when he joined the force. Did he know he'd be murdering for cash, or did that only come up later?

Hughes muttered some curse and pushed the pistol deeper into Marcel's neck. "Any last words?" he asked

Marcel tried to reason with him, tried to reach whatever inkling of humanity was clearly left in the man. Of course with his mouth bound, all that came out was: "Mmmmhrpgmmllm."

"Right," said the cop as he pulled back the hammer. Panic shimmered through Marcel's body—it felt like a static buzz. He heard a strange sound and then:

A click.

It took Marcel an entirety of a second to realize that he wasn't dead.

"Inferno was that?" said Hughes. He fiddled with the pistol. Marcel bent over, wanting to vomit, tears wetting his gag.

"Demiurge, Hughes, you couldn't shoot spikefowl with a shotgun."

"It's not my fault," muttered Hughes, "something went wild with this, looked like a photo-camera flash or something. Now the chamber's fused tight."

"Here," said the old cop, "if you can't handle it."

Another click of a hammer.

Then a sudden shout. Not one of frustration or fear, but a battle cry.

Kayip.

Marcel kicked himself back, away onto the floor. He watched the old cop turn, as Kayip ran from behind a wall of junk, sword already swinging. The cop tried to fire, but he was far too slow. His scream was cut short as Kayip sliced his torso in two.

The pistol bounced on the floor. Hughes shrieked and then jumped toward it, grabbing the gun as it bounced. A spark flew from the dark. The pistol exploded into molten metal, burning the man's hands. He screamed ear-splitting pain, his fingers now more molten metal than burning flesh. Kayip turned and silenced the man with a slash.

Then, for a moment, silence.

Kayip shook the blood off his blade, and with a word it reformed and spun around his wrist into his simple bracelet.

Sylvaine walked out, hand shaking. "Shit," she said.

Marcel could echo her sentiment. Kayip helped him up, removed his gag, and unlocked his cuffs. Marcel shook with nausea. He felt the twin emotions of utter euphoria at his sudden deliverance and guilt-twisting disgust at the bodies on the floor.

Kayip pulled out his Cracked-Disc, whispering some strange prayer, before turning to Marcel. "For the dead. It is never a holy act, nor a pleasant act, even if it was a necessary one."

Marcel just nodded, keeping his gaze from Hughes's expression. "Thank you," he said.

Sylvaine shook her head as she walked over. "Yeah. Well, we're lucky we found you."

"There are only a few good places for them hide a body in this city," Kayip said.

"You knew they would try to kill me," Marcel said.

"It was possible they might mutate you instead," Kayip said. "But I had to guess, and death is, I think, worse than mutation."

Marcel nodded. "Well...thanks."

Sylvaine glanced around at the police corpses staining the concrete floor.

"We should probably go," she said.

Chapter 28

Marcel followed Sylvaine down to their rendezvous spot in an abandoned underrail station. Kayip had stayed behind, to remove the bodies.

"I do not think we can hide your escape," he had said, "but perhaps disposing their corpses might buy us a few hours."

As they had descended into dark of the Underway, Kayip promised that he would join them after he'd "prepared some things." Marcel knew he should have asked the monk what he meant to "prepare" for exactly. Kayip was not exactly an easy man to read, but in that moment Marcel had just been eager to leave. Now he rested on a sleeping mat while Sylvaine spread Gall's papers out over a tarp and examined her prize in exacting focus by the light of her handtorch.

Marcel's head still hurt but less so now. He had led Sylvaine through the checklist of symptoms of brain injury he had memorized at university. There was no evidence of severe damage, though the exact list of symptoms was blurry to Marcel, and he was faintly sure memory loss was on there somewhere. Still, he had survived the night, and though the world had turned upside down, though who he had thought were his friends had betrayed him and

Huile, though innocent workers were being tortured and enslaved, and though Marcel no longer even had a safe place to call home, at least that was one thing to be thankful for.

Also it had stopped raining. So two things.

Kayip took his time. More than an hour passed, at least by Marcel's vague reckoning. Sylvaine had been not much for conversation, enraptured by the notes. As Marcel's worries about his head lessened, anxieties about his surroundings increased, the odd noises, the shifting shadows, the stuffy air, the smell of ambiguous rot and oil.

"Found anything interesting?" Marcel asked, if for no other reason than to break the silence.

Sylvaine didn't respond. Marcel asked again. And then after a few minutes, a third time.

"Hmm?" she said. "Oh, uh maybe? I'm not sure."

Marcel walked over and squatted. Lines and scribbled words covered the pages, diagrams that looked more like abstract art than any machinery Marcel could visualize. One or two pages exhibited some resemblance of a shared reality, cylinders and lines that might have represented some sort of piping. Maybe.

"We got a good map of the central compound here." Sylvaine pointed. "If the mutants can get someone inside here, they could easily shut down the whole grid, but Kayip said security is tight, so I'm not sure there's any easy way to make that happen. Unfortunately, the sketch here is pretty vague, so I don't know if there are any pipes wide enough to sneak a man through or sections of flooring that might be dug through. Maybe further details were in those notes somewhere, but I don't have them."

"Sorry," Marcel mumbled.

She shrugged. "It might not even have been written down. These diagrams aren't even from Gall's work, just general building plans." She pointed to another stack of sheets. "This is his work. Are you interested in water treatment?"

"Not particularly," Marcel said.

"Well then these won't be particularly fascinating. What is useful is to see this ætherwire setup here." She pointed toward a bunch of lines. "Sever that with, say, a hand-drill, or if you're short on time, explosives, and that could shut down all power to the neighborhood."

Marcel slapped Sylvaine on the back. "Damn good work!"

The engineer flinched, then stared back at Marcel and gave a confused nod. "Thanks, I guess."

"I just mean, well, you figured all that out in just an hour," Marcel said. "Impressive."

Sylvaine laughed. "Oh? That's just from a cursory glance. Is it not obvious?"

Marcel slunk back. He had never taken even a theoretical engineering class at University and was feeling an illiterate fool staring at the esoteric mess in front of him.

"So why is it so important, then?" Marcel said. "Why would Verus and Roache be fighting over these notes?" And why was Desct so convinced it was something more?

Sylvaine scratched her chin and moved a few pages around. "Not sure. But they are unusual."

"How so?"

She tapped her finger on a mess of pipes and boxes jutting off the side of the big cylinder and then toward another page that might as well have been a sketch of a spider's web for all Marcel could make of it.

"This seems to be the focus of his work," she said. "As far as I can tell, it's used to infuse something into the water."

"What, to sterilize it?" Marcel asked.

"Maybe? Seems unneeded since they do extensive filtering already elsewhere," she said. "It's just an...absurd design. For one, this section is connected to a sangleum pipeline and seemingly not for power but as part of the infusion process. Here seems to be the contact point, where it adds some sort of powder to the water, and this here would allow it to vary the doses."

The smell of Lambert's tea rose up in Marcels mind.

"Slickdust?" he asked.

Sylvaine blinked. Then, with a quiet franticness, she looked over the papers and her notes, "No, no. I mean...possibly?" She stared down at the diagram. "If that were the case..."

If Lazacorp was infusing slickdust into the water, then whatever Roache was planning was not limited to merely making money off slave labor and cheap fuel. Could the man be planning to poison the entire city, to make them thralls to his words? After what Marcel had seen, even that no longer seemed impossible.

"No," Sylvaine said finally. "I mean, it could be something akin to slickdust, but this would produce exceptionally high æther-frequency."

"Too much sangleum?" Marcel asked. He wasn't sure if that was better or worse. No, on a second thought that definitely sounded worse.

"More highly *activated* sangleum," she said, tapping her pen. "Æther reacts with certain frequencies. I'm sure Kayip would claim it has something to do with spirits or the Demiurge or whatever, but it's all math in the end. I don't know the exact chemical makeup of slickdust, but if it used fully-activated sangleum, I would have noticed. This machine seems to be fairly rough in its construction, it just charges its injected sangleum to a theoretical maximized frequency ceiling."

"So..." Marcel began, trying, and failing, to understand. He stared at the notes intently, hoping that it would somehow reform into sensible, readable phrases. When it didn't, he decided to go for the simple, and most important, question: "What would happen if you drank that slick...whatever-infused water?"

"Well..." Sylvaine started, "when we worked with highly activated sangleum in Icaria, we had to wear full body personal projective equipment to avoid contamination...so I would say...something bad. Something quite bad."

Marcel sat himself down on the rusting bench, trying to ignore the sudden aching pain in his cogleg.

"Is it functional?" he asked.

"Hmm?" Sylvaine looked up. "Oh, no. At least it wasn't when these notes were written up. I mean, the water filtration part is set up, but there are several issues here that would need an engineer to work out. For one, there's this module here, which I can't make heads or tails of."

The woman went back to her work, seemingly more concerned with the theoretical engineering questions than the possibility of impending doom.

"Well," Marcel said, "I guess it's all the same, as long as we can blast it all to Inferno."

"You speak far too loud for a man on the run," came Kayip's voice, half a metre behind Marcel. He jumped a little, as did Sylvaine.

The silent-footed monk let out half a smile. Marcel got up, and Kayip handed him a key.

"You must move soon," he said. "I left, a good time ago, a motorbike hidden in a collapsed basement under Huile Field. I have supplies for several days. You could travel many kiloms, I think, before City Hall realized you had escaped."

"Travel?" Marcel asked.

The monk opened his bag. "Water. Dried rations. An extra pistol, if you need it. I even have some old, forged identification papers, if you wish to go by the name of Saht Isim."

"Are you suggesting I run?" Marcel said. "I can't leave, not now. We have what we need to support Desct."

Kayip nodded. "Yes. You have helped greatly with that. But now City Hall will look for you." He placed his large hand on Marcel's shoulder, single eye staring with an intense yet still softened force. "You have done your duty to your friend and your city. It is best now if you leave."

Marcel left the man's grasp and started to pace. He had been tricked into helping to doom Huile; he had to save it. The idea of fleeing was out of the question. "I can hide with the mutants," Marcel said.

"If they believe you are still in the city, they will call Lazacorp," Kayip said. "We can ill afford the attention."

"Then...we'll fake my death," Marcel said.

"How?" Sylvaine asked, leaning back amidst her meadow of notes.

"With..." Marcel snapped, trying to think, but no plausible method arose. "We just need someone who could verify that I died..." He paused, then: "Verus."

"Verus?" Kayip spat the name as if it were a piece of grub-rotten taur steak.

"Yes," Marcel said. "He's at odds with City Hall, with Roache—he's the only one who, in their eyes, could have saved me."

"To what?" Sylvaine said. "Shoot you himself?"

"Probably," Marcel said, "all the better, I mean, if he says that. But I think I can bargain well enough for my life." Marcel grabbed up a handful of notes, Sylvaine shouting out a "Be careful with those!"

"I can bring him these notes or a copy of them or we keep the copy for ourselves, it doesn't matter. Convince him to take me in, tell City Hall he's taken me out." Kayip's face had started locked in shock but seemed to morph now into at least some form of consideration, which was a step up.

"Verus hates me, but he hates Roache more. All I have to do is convince him I'm better to him as a bludgeon against the man than as a corpse."

"You'd be gambling your life," the monk observed coolly.

"You'd be throwing it away," Sylvaine muttered, less coolly.

"But then we'd have someone on the inside, someone with an ear to what's happening in Lazacorp," Marcel said. "My presence alone could distract them, get the attention off the mutants."

"We just saved you!" Sylvaine said, standing up. "You cog-loose maniac."

"And this is how I'll pay it back," Marcel replied.

"I wasn't asking you to..." Sylvaine pressed her hands into her face and groaned.

"And if he decides you are better dead?" Kayip asked.

"Then I'll take what I know about the mutants to the grave," Marcel said simply.

Kayip scratched at his mask, forehead wrinkled with thought. Sylvaine shook her head and turned to stare at the man's subtle, shadow-obscured expression. The look of growing horror on her face told Marcel that he had won.

Several hours later, as the sunlight started to stream over Blackwood Row's walls, Marcel found himself climbing out from the Underway into a grime-covered alley beneath vomiting smokestacks. He waited there, holding tight the notes in his hand. The morning light cut through the black clouds, and Marcel tried to suck in his fear as he glanced at the sky. He had never been very religious, never believed that the sun was a divine gift of the Demiurge, yet even still he found himself taking heart in the coming of day.

Then he noticed the voice he had been listening for, heard the footsteps, and discerned the hulking shadow of the one man who he knew would take him to Verus. Marcel did not give himself time to think, but dashed out into the street, right in front of the surprised visage of Dutrix Crat.

Marcel thrust up the folder. "I need to talk to Verus!"

Chapter 29

It was the second time in twenty-four hours that Marcel found himself in chains. Dutrix Crat had taken him into custody with more bewilderment than anything else, leading him forward with an odd gingerness, as if he were unsure that Marcel was indeed his prisoner, or instead was some strange envoy, or just very confused. As they walked, the man read through the folder, eyebrows raised.

Another guard, some slightly befuddled tattooed man, kept a gun pointed in Marcel's vague direction. He muttered occasional insults as they led Marcel into the basement of a nearby building but glanced several times in the direction of Crat, as if to make sure his taunts hadn't gone too far. The whole affair wasn't exactly pleasant, but it was preferable to his last imprisonment. At least this time they hadn't bashed him on the head first, and their threats to kill him were contingent on his attempting to escape, which he had no plans, nor real hope, of doing.

Still, as they walked under the slave-fueled bustle of the refineries above, through long and dimly lit corridors, Marcel couldn't help but start to question his strategic instincts that led to his life being held at the whim of a man who unambiguously hated him. Kayip's support for the plan had given him some hope. The monk had apparently dealt with Verus on previous visits and gave Marcel some advice on how to work the foreman. Marcel silently mouthed Kayip's words behind closed lips: *Display anger at the betrayal, show disdain for the entire human race including yourself, seek answers, and pretend to eat up whatever taurshit he tells you.*

Sylvaine had offered considerably less advice, and her suggestion to "try not to die" came only after cursing out the "ungrateful, foolish, suicide-eager" Marcel for a good half-hour. Only with great effort had Kayip been able to convince her to make a copy of Gall's notes and begrudgingly let go of the originals.

Marcel's escorts led him up a stairwell into a small foyer. It was plain and undecorated, unlike the warmly lit and luxuriously furnished rooms Roache had once toured Marcel through.

Crat approached and traded whispers with a strange man who stood behind a desk. This man wore what appeared to be a leather jacket, with a hood hanging unused in the back. Marcel got a glimpse of a necklace swinging low, at its end a red glass orb. The sphere did not seem wholly solid but instead some sort of hollow container, where an indeterminate liquid sloshed, though it had no clear lid or stopper. The man's face was covered in tattoos, not unusual for Lazacorp guards, but the designs were strange, not the usual skulls, thorns, gearworks, monsters, or naked women but instead odd, sharp letters, in a script Marcel didn't recognize. On his shaved forehead there appeared to be an abstracted tattoo of an eye.

Kayip *had* warned Marcel he might meet some "odd-looking ruffians" in Verus's entourage. He had also claimed some of them might be demon-worshiping magicians, but Marcel had decided to take the monk's more outlandish accusations with the skepticism they deserved.

The odd-looking ruffian muttered into a vocaphone speaker at the edge of the desk, and after a few moments, nodded and pulled a lever to bring down a clanking lift from up above.

Verus's office sat on the top floor. It was a large, sparse space, dimly lit by irregularly placed floor lamps that were not up to their task. The foreman had windows, large ones in fact, but they were completely shuttered, letting in only the barest hint of sunlight. The room was filled with unadorned cabinets and cracked vitrines, intermixed with old mining and industrial tools long since taken by rust. Its walls held faded paintings of strange angular figures and red-brushed landscapes, which Marcel could not quite make out the details of. The room reminded him, oddly, of a temple or cathedral, admittedly one decorated by a half-mad recluse.

Verus sat behind a heavy, plain desk, dressed in his usual torn-up and stained black leather. He pushed himself up, staring as Crat and his crony led Marcel into the room.

"Funny. Talwar. Funny," Verus said. "I've had a funny day. Been maintaining a pleasant silence with that taur's arse Roache when he, well, his traitorous lickspittle, calls me up to warn me that his viscous lap-hound, his priggish little knife-blade that he had shoved so gently in my back, that you, Mr. Talwar, had gone rogue, had betrayed 'us.'" Verus used air quotes on the 'us'. "I didn't know there was an 'us,' but apparently in times of panic, we're best of friends."

Marcel opened his mouth, but Verus didn't give him time to speak.

"So I get told to put my men on alert, that, in the unlikely event you were idiot enough not to skip town, you might try to stir up trouble, as if that wasn't your basic fucking instinct. So imagine me, Talwar, sitting here, wondering how Roache had possibly managed to screw the wastehound so damned well on this, when, just fifteen minutes later, I get another call that you have come knocking straight over to me."

Marcel stared down at his feet. "Roache betrayed me," he said. "Used me as a weapon to find dirt he planted, to perform political

303

hits." Marcel tried to sound genuine and realized it took no effort. The pain in his voice was not put on.

Verus snorted. "Worked that out for yourself? Did some investigating?" The last word was thick with mockery.

"I was an idiot, believed it all, needed to believe it," Marcel said. Verus stared at him, his one eye piercing and prodding. "I went along until I dug just a little deeper. Was all it took, really. The truth was never far from the surface. I was just too blind to know where to dig."

Verus crossed his arms. "To be frank, I thought you would have been wheeled into it. Paid off or drugged up like the rest of them. Guess it wasn't all an act then. You were genuinely the nuisance you seemed. I took you as a fool, Talwar, but I didn't know you were that much of a fool."

Marcel winced. It was surprisingly easy to act the part, since the man's words did sting true.

Crat opened his mouth to speak, but Verus raised his finger.

"Or," he said, smiling, "you're still the paid hound, and Roache has you by the collar."

"What?" Marcel said.

Verus waved around his desk, an unusually genuine smile cracking across on his face, an unnerving look. "Another game from Roache? What did he tell you, that you wouldn't be in danger? That if I saw through your little ploy, your little game to get another pair of ears in this room, that I'd simply send you back? Marcel, why would you ever think that I would miss an opportunity to plant a bullet in your forehead?"

"Roache betrayed me!" Marcel said, nearly shouting. "He lied about my own friend's death. Corrupted City Hall. Inferno, Lambert tried to have me killed."

"And you figured this out all on your own?" Verus raised his eyebrow.

"Ye...Yes!"

The man simply snorted again. "Not worth the risk. Crat, take him to the Underway. Make it quick, before Roache starts to complain."

"Yes, Awakener," Crat said, a strange title, one Marcel didn't have time to muse over.

"Crat!" Marcel shouted. "Show him the notes."

Crat glanced down at the folder in his hands, unsure of what to do.

"Awakener," Crat started, "Talwar came in with some—"

"Don't listen to him!" Verus spat. Then after a moment, "But give those here."

Crat threw the end of the chains to his lackey and walked over to Verus. "He had these on him when he came shouting. Was waving them around."

Verus took the notes and started to leaf through them, genuine surprise in his eye.

"A gift," Marcel explained. "They were yours, properly, anyway."

"Should I?" Crat asked, pointing to Marcel.

Verus didn't look up but waved his hands as he kept reading.

The two guards stood still, sparing only the occasional glance to each other or toward Marcel, who held his breath. His heart beat heavy as Verus slowly inspected his prize.

"Sorry, I wasn't able to sneak all of it away," Marcel said, gesturing to the notes. Verus ignored him, flipping through the pages, one after another.

"How?" Verus said simply.

Marcel shrugged. "I helped steal them in the first place."

"I knew it!" Verus said. "Knew Roache had to be behind that somehow."

"I was told it proved that you were conspiring against Huile." Marcel shook his head. "All lies, just some game Roache was playing. Makes me sick. I'd kill them all if I could."

Verus sucked in his breath, staring at the notes, tapping his finger on the page, his face cut between rage and vindication. Then, a hint of a grin snuck out the side of his face as he released a stuttering half-laugh.

"This is the first time," he finally muttered, "that one of you stifflanders ever made my day better."

"Stiff?" Marcel caught himself asking an unnecessary question.

Verus raised his eye. "Not wastefolk. You, Roache, Lambert, and all the other idiots and scumsuckers out here."

Marcel laughed. "A bunch of shitsacks."

Verus lowered the notes. "Don't think I'm Roache. Don't think you can kiss my arsehole and nod in agreement to my every word, that that'll win you anything."

"Noted," Marcel said, shaking his head. "I just want to get back at the fucker who betrayed me. I thought these notes might help." Or at least prove he wasn't allied with Roache.

Verus closed the folder in one hand and leaned on his desk. "Fine. Maybe you're not with Roache. Maybe you are just a raging taur, trying to thrash at the man who tied you to the ground and fucked you. Doesn't change anything. You came to me. You're scared, Talwar. Knew you'd be hunted in Huile, can't handle running to the Wastes. You want to hide in my den like some beaten wastehound pup."

Marcel shook his head. *Betrayal, anger, disdain,* that's what Kayip had said. "I don't care what you do to me, doesn't matter anymore. As long as these notes make sure you fuck them over. The whole crop of them are nothing more than mog-lizard shits given waistcoats. This city deserves to burn."

Verus actually laughed; it was a frightening sound. "That it? Don't want me to transport you down to some Resurgence town? Don't want to be offered some stiffland office, covered in the desecrated corpse-meat of a decadent past? Don't care if I have my men shoot you, toss you in the sewer?"

Marcel shrugged. "Pointless now. It was all lies. What would the UCCR offer me now? Just fancier lies."

"You've spoken more sense in the last couple seconds, Talwar, than in the past couple years." Verus waved a finger. "But what we're doing here, it's not for some petty revenge. Oh, they'll get their due in time, the lot of them, but they also have their role to play, for now. Unlike all you rats, we," and Verus pointed to his quiet, tattooed guards as well, "work for a greater good. The *only* good."

Marcel looked up, a mask of genuine interest covering his disgusted curiosity. The foreman clearly had strange pretensions, though to what exactly, Marcel couldn't guess.

Verus crossed his arms. "But it doesn't matter if you work for Roache or not. I don't need you. Crat, you can take him—"

"And that greater good," Marcel said, trying to think of any excuse to keep the conversation going as Crat turned and grabbed him, "it involves poisoning all of Huile?"

Verus froze a moment, then gestured for the man to let go. "Not poisoning, exactly. No, quite the opposite, but it may seem...unpleasant. We're simply preparing people for their proper service. Some serve in life, many more through death, even your damned Confederacy knows that. But yes, we're turning Huile into an abattoir of sorts." He stopped and at scratched at his eyepatch. "You knew that, and still you came in to help me."

"Like I said," Marcel spoke with a manufactured calm. "They're all worms. If you poison them, slaughter them, why should I care—it is better than they deserve."

"And how did you discover I would do that?"

This, Marcel had not prepared an answer for. "I..." he started. "Well, from the notes."

"You can read these?" This seemed the most surprising development for Verus.

"What did you think I went to university for?" Marcel said, hoping Roache hadn't spoken to Verus on that subject.

"It's not something I considered worth my attention," Verus admitted.

"Engineering," Marcel explained. "Well, the practical sort, just mechanics really. Didn't have the Knack. Was near a genius at it but didn't see the point of being some corner-store gadgeteer." Marcel pointed toward the notes. "You're infusing something, something with sangleum, into the water, but you're having some issues."

Verus nodded. "I guess that's the long and short of it, at least of what's in here. There were some...modifications Roache's arse-licking workers made to what was supposed to be a *collaborative enterprise.*"

"Let me have a look at it," said Marcel. "Just give me a few of your mutants as assistants. Let me see what I can find."

Verus squinted down at Marcel, his gaze attempting to drill past the façade that Marcel held together with all his will.

The vocaphone rang suddenly, breaking the exhausting examination. Verus picked up the end.

"Eh?" he said. "Right." A pause. "Idiot." Another. "So damned impatient, it was his own problem. Well, tell Roache the truegods have smiled on him. Found the taur arse's body in the Underway. Moron tripped one of the mutant traps, brains splattered across the floor. Eh? Yeah, the two cops as well. Rat food." Verus rolled his single eye as he listened. "Lambert can get better police next time, I don't care. Listen, I have things in order, as always. So stop bothering me and keep proper watch on the gilded griffon-shit, Watcher. That is your duty."

Marcel released a long-held breath as he listened to Verus, who nodded along to some mumbling echo on the other side of the earpiece. What in Inferno the man meant by "truegods," he wasn't sure, maybe Kayip's accusations had some twisted basis, but it seemed his execution had been delayed. His confidence started to return. He might not have a talent for manipulating machinery or a strong sword-arm, but he could talk his way out from the brink of death.

This brief self-assurance faded as Verus started to mutter some words into the vocaphone in a strange tongue. It was no language Marcel had heard, something deep and unsettling, its tone unlike any human speech. It did not even resemble animal grunts. The words reminded him of the chants of priests and the grinding of metal but also something more, something deeper, like the sounds of a rolling storm. They struck him suddenly and overwhelmed him. Each syllable was alien, and yet, he had the strangest sense that if he just listened closer he could understand their meaning, but every instinct screamed for him to close his ears. His heart pounded, he was terrified, though he didn't understand why. A panic grew in him greater than the real and exact fear of death he had just been hiding from, a strange terror that eclipsed Verus's threats or even Marcel's own fear of failing Desct, of failing Huile. It was a deep, overwhelming horror at the implacable sounds coming from Verus's mouth, as if their secret meaning held implications worse even than his own annihilation.

Then, Verus slammed the vocaphone receiver down, and the fear was instantly gone. Marcel struggled to recover, to breathe, and his existential terror was replaced by the more standard fear for his survival.

Verus chuckled, watching him. "You really are pitiful. Think you have even a shit-shard's sense of what's going on." He walked over, the guards stepping back as Verus lifted the man up, patting down his coat, his grin a hair's length from his prisoner's face. "Very well, Talwar, you want to work? We'll put you to work."

Chapter 30

Engineering was the art of planning, of melding intricate thought with brilliant inspiration and putting the result to paper, then putting that paper to metal. The material of the machine, even the æther that gave it life, was secondary to the true medium of engineering: the well-organized mind. Even the greatest skill with the ætherglove was useless, if one could only plan out the haphazard and chaotic.

Sylvaine didn't know what to call Marcel's "art." "Private investigating" as she understood it (which was mostly from pulps, admittedly) was supposedly an art of careful consideration, but Marcel seemed to lack that completely. Perhaps the man practiced "advanced stupidity," the art of the charismatic and suicidal. Worse still, Kayip had supported the man's plan, given him advice over the rationally-derived insults Sylvaine had thrown. The Church might have revered the martyrs, but Sylvaine thought that was no reason for Kayip to be exporting martyrdom.

Fine, Marcel's life was his own. If he wanted to throw it away, who was she to stop him? He had the need to be at the center of everything, it seemed, and if that meant getting himself killed, why should it matter to her? It would have been better if she had never bothered to try to save the man in the first place. Then Sylvaine might have had the time to nap. She damn well needed one.

These were the thoughts Sylvaine used to distract herself as she frantically scrawled out a copy of Gall's notes, eyelids dripping, head fuming. It felt easier to fill her mind with anger than with fear.

After Marcel left, and Sylvaine stared into the dripping, echoing dark, she asked Kayip. "He'll be okay, right?"

"Certainly possible." The man nodded, lifting up his bag. "Yes, I think he may live. There is a chance."

Sylvaine rubbed her eyes and forehead hair into her palm. The monk cared not for physical comfort or, apparently, emotional comfort.

"Let's just get moving," she said.

It didn't matter if she was concerned about the fate of the idiot; they simply didn't have time to waste worrying. The notes were to be delivered to Desct sometime before sunrise, and Kayip's rusting watch ticked forward relentlessly.

The monk led her deeper through Huile's Underway, past the underrail station into a subterranean Infernoscape of booby traps and corpses. Kayip had warned her of what she might see, but the sight of the rotting bodies still unsettled her.

As they walked, Sylvaine put her glove to any metal outcropping she could find, feeling for anything dangerous. She sensed a jury-rigged shotgun and raised her hand to disarm it with ætheric ease, when Kayip grabbed her shoulder.

"It is best we just avoid them," he said. "Lazacorp men may notice the change."

The paths the man led her down were convoluted, but they made steady progress. Sylvaine still found herself surprised by the monk's agility, his proficiency in the arts of leaping and scrambling. Their travel progressed quickly; it was almost relaxing in its own way. The smell of the place was still horrendous, but, walking among the piping and the old forgotten machinery, it reminded her a tad of Icaria, of crowded workshop basements. She felt calmed, until she started to hear a voice. It was soft, distant, a scratchy recording, but one that was familiar.

"Return to your workstation," it said in a tone, which, despite its almost bored banality, had a force that cut into her ears. *"Return to Blackwood Row. Return to your workstation. Return to Blackwood Row."*

Her breathing picked up. She felt her veins run fast, hot, burning. It was Roache's voice. Roache's commands.

"Sylvaine," Kayip whispered.

Sweated oozed from her, her vision turned to fuzz, the smells of rot danced between overwhelming and nonexistent. The words dug past her ears, digging into her mind. Their force wasn't as overwhelming as they had been a month ago, but the repetition cut into her with each word. *Return...return...return...*

Kayip moved to touch her. She turned, stifled a scream, or perhaps a growl, and ran.

"Sylvaine!" the man hissed and dashed after her.

She stumbled up staircases and down flooded hallways, leaping over collapsed machinery and pushing through holes in the walls. The world blurred around her, and she could feel Lazarus's presence, commanding her, mocking her. She heard the shouts of Kayip in some far-off world, heard the snap of a tripwire, heard the blast, felt the warmth of shotgun pellets flying mere centimetres from her skin, calibrated for slower prey.

Walls of wire blocked her, but with a shout and a spark, they melted into nothing, steaming air to be pushed aside in her flight. Or her pursuit. She wasn't sure; she couldn't tell if she was running away from Roache or to rip out his throat.

Then suddenly, she was there. The voice was not some distant echo but the aural secretion of a dictaphone hanging on the ceiling above. She did not wait to think. With a spark she flung it from the wall, onto the ground, where it smoldered in a melted pile.

The voice was gone. Roache had been slain. Her breathing slowed. The world came into focus. For a brief, beautiful second she had won.

Then she heard it again. Distant, quiet echoes. "*Return to your workstation...*" And then another voice, the same recording but from a different angle, "*Return to Blackwood Row...*"

She pushed her ears in on themselves and sucked in to stave off the panic. *It's not him. It's just a recording. I'm not on slickdust. I don't have to listen to his voice.* Yet the commands kept droning, her blood kept boiling. Sylvaine's breath quickened, she was panting, close to hyperventilating; her mind dimmed, her instincts roared.

No! She couldn't let herself lose control, let herself scream and run, or to go berserk in a wild rage. To lose her mind in a bestial fervor was no better than losing her will to Roache. Rationality must be her escape, to flee *into* her mind, not away from it.

Of course there'd be multiple dictaphones, she reasoned, fail-safes, a wall to keep the mutants in. It was just a system of machines, designed for a logical, if vile, purpose. A psychological barrier instead of a physical one, but nothing more.

Sylvaine started to walk forward, wandering directionless, her eyes open but ears as shut as she could manage, humming to herself to distract her attention from the needling pressure of Roache's voice.

She tried to think through Lazacorp's planning, calculate the exact measurements one would make in order to make an ideal wall of sound, the methods needed to estimate the range of the echo, the amount of insulated wiring required for such a project. These were pointless thoughts, purposeless math, but it kept her mind busy as she moved. She couldn't manage anything more.

———— ⌒⌒⌒ ————

By the time Kayip caught up with Sylvaine, she had wandered far past the echoes, to a distant corner basement, where she sat, slumped. The man came and sat beside her.

"I'm sorry," she said.

Kayip put his hand on hers. "It is my folly," he said. "I did not think of their effect. It is my fault."

Sylvaine pulled in her knees. She was drenched in sweat, her fur matted to her arms. "I can't go back through it. Maybe it's not as strong for me as the mutants...but I can't try to cross that barrier again." She paused. How could she explain her fear? It wasn't just Roache; it was something inside of her. Something primitive and animalistic, something more powerful than the voice. To be a machine to another person's will was horrifying but temporary. To become a beast would prove true every word of loathing and disgust that had ever been lobbed at her.

"It's too much," she said finally. "I'll help how I can from Huile, but you'll have to make the trip to Blackwood Row on your own."

Kayip stared down the darkened corridors. "You must have lost yourself in that maze," he said. "We have already crossed over."

She closed her eyes and breathed in. Yes, she could smell the air from above, dimly. Somehow it smelled even more wretched than down here.

Despite Sylvaine's panic, the two still made it into the bowels of Blackwood Row before sunrise. Kayip searched out a timid mutant there, whom he called Gileon. This guide led them through the dark streets and dense shanties, down in the basement of some half-abandoned pumping facility, where they were able to make the tail end of a meeting hidden inside an extraneous water tank.

The Sightless City

The mutants inside greeted Sylvaine and Kayip with hushed cheers, their initial nervous bewilderment at the intruders turning to complete exhilaration at the sight of the schematics, even second-hand copies as they were. The mutants all smelled, to a person, terrible, but their warm welcome and soft exuberance seemed to deafen the odors, in some sort of reverse synesthesia. The only exceptions to these friendly greetings were the cold welcomes of a woman in the back named Celina, as well as the equally terse grunts of several other mutants that seemed to huddle around her. They scoffed at Sylvaine's appearance, questioned the veracity of her notes (to no success), and seemed keen on insulting Desct whenever possible.

Desct, on the other hand, was the most outgoing of the bunch, and whenever Sylvaine's voice faltered, whether due to nerves or just exhaustion, he would step in. He congratulated the engineer, praised her swift hands and clear eyes, he argued for the need of careful sabotage, and uplifted his audience's spirits with promises of imminent liberation.

"So we wait even longer then?" Celina snapped.

"A few days. After all the indignities we have suffered, do we not have the damned fortitude to make proper preparations for our emancipation?" Desct barked back. Most of the group nodded, even those who had seemed wary of Sylvaine's presence were won over by Desct's determined confidence.

He explained his plan simply: they would use clockbombs, set at exact points that Sylvaine would calculate, to force a blackout of Blackwood Row, and during this temporary silence of Roache's booming voice, attack. Celina questioned the specifics, and though Desct admitted some details needed to be hashed out later, he did not have to argue long before it was clear the general mood favored his plan. Before daylight could sneak over the walls of Blackwood Row, this plan was ratified in a quick vote. It was near unanimous, and though Celina and her gang muttered some vague misgivings, they simply abstained, offering no real opposition.

———— ∞ ————

Desct led Sylvaine and Kayip out as the rest of the mutant council swiftly ran back to their hovels or early morning workstations. The monk planned to retreat into the Underway, to return at the next nightfall for further planning. As for Sylvaine...

"I can't make it back," she said.

The mutant leader nodded. "We can find habitation for you, if you don't mind a little squeeze and perhaps a whiff of foul odor."

Sylvaine did mind, but since there was no alternative to the poor conditions that were the height of the Blackwood Row hospitality, she agreed without voicing any explicit complaints. Kayip bent down to her as they approached the opening of the Underway.

"You will be well?" he asked.

She nodded, with the modicum of confidence she could rally. The monk raised his arm, haltingly, and then slowly embraced her. She was shocked still a moment, but then put her arm around him. It felt strange...but comforting. Despite the unusual circumstances in which they had met, and the beyond unusual circumstances they now found themselves in, Kayip had become something like a friend. Sylvaine wasn't sure she had ever had a real friend.

"You *will* be well," the monk agreed. As he released her and started to descend, he nodded to Desct. "And I *will* return, with food and any other supplies I can manage."

"Good idea," Desct replied, then, turning to Sylvaine: "You don't wish to share the shit nourishment we must suffer."

Kayip disappeared beneath the street, and Desct led Sylvaine, alone, into the mass of shantytowns that covered the space between two large refinery structures.

"This was once some sort of courtyard, I think, when the refineries were first opened," he explained. "They had sufficient lodging for the population of mutants years ago, but from what I can gather, their shit-cursed operations expanded, and it was cheaper just to throw us to the trash heap and let us build our own fucking quarters ourselves."

The structures were webs of welded pipes and iron poles, upon which were placed dirty cloth and cheap wood. Some buildings were old machines: tread-driller arms reused as support pillars, decayed hulls of transport-trucks converted into cramped huts, melted scrap from a thousand origins used to fill in corners. The macrostructure was large, rust and filth covered, but more than anything else, it was *dense*. Travel through its winding paths seemed more plodding than even the worst of the Underway, requiring even more climbing, crawling, and sneaking through hidden passageways, some between walls of rags, others behind non-load-bearing "walls." Sylvaine tried to imagine what architectural plans for such a structure would be but concluded that it would be madness to try to sketch it out.

Still, the dwellings didn't lack in their human elements—or rather, their mutant elements—Sylvaine mused. Dozens, no hundreds; a whole village's worth of mutants slept in its every nook, cranny, and makeshift bed. Some looked up to watch them pass. Some saluted with a fist to their chest, but most were deep in sleep, worn out bodies huddling for whatever rest they could manage.

Desct deposited the engineer at a building, if it could be called that, somewhere in the middle. The structure looked like it might have once been part of a wide metal smokestack, removed and renovated with pieces of scrap, before having been dug down into the concrete.

"Here's your sanctum," Desct said.

Inside, the only path was a haphazard stairway down into what appeared to be a long-abandoned basement. The walls of the upper section of the structure were covered in layers of burlap, old towels, and even Lazacorp uniforms. The space was dim, lit by a couple of handtorches either tied to or dug into the walls.

As they descended, Sylvaine noticed forms on the floor, their mutations far beyond the worst of what she'd seen above. Bulbous and twisted bodies, open sores and strange growths of gear-like keratin. Some had doublings of their faces, lifeless mimics on the side of their heads or growing on their open chests, expressions of frozen agony. Others had limbs that bent in strange angles or fused back into their bodies. Only two mutants were exempt from these extreme deformities: one, a man, who rested in a small cot at the far end, the other a one-armed woman, who walked between the sprawled bodies, helping the sickly figures drink from a stained bowl.

"This is the closest we ever managed to a medical station," Desct explained. Then, catching her expression: "Nothing contagious, of course, certainly not to you. Poisoning by slickdust injections. Lazacorp normally drags them away when they get to this point. We don't know to where, but somehow I doubt it's a refuge for them to live a long, healthy life."

The woman walked over and saluted Desct, who smiled and explained Sylvaine's presence.

"I don't want to be a burden," Sylvaine said. "I could stay above."

Desct shook his head. "They expel Roache's damned commands at such a high volume that it smothers the entire camp. Their workaround, I suppose. The slickdust poisoned are especially susceptible. This is the only space we've managed to soundproof sufficiently. At least, the only space Lazacorp hasn't found."

It wasn't much of a space, and Sylvaine started to wonder if perhaps she could try and brave the Under...no. If it were the just the booby traps, just the smell of rot and death, but to have Roache in her head again, to lose herself again...If the only way out of Lazacorp was to blow it up, well then she would stay down here making clockbombs.

Desct slapped her on the shoulder and bid his goodbyes, with some vague words of hope. As he left, the woman mutant, who introduced herself as Ysabel, led Sylvaine to a cot at the far end. She pushed away some boxes to create a modest enclave of free space and gave Sylvaine a bowl filled with water.

"It's...as fresh as we can manage," the woman said.

Sylvaine tried not to show her disgust as she sipped, muttering thanks. Placing down the bowl and dropping her bag, she rolled herself up in her cot. The fabric was coarse and foul smelling, but considering what surrounded her, that seemed a beyond petty complaint. How strange it was that just two months ago she had been one of the greatest young engineers in all of Icaria. Floating above everyone, an untouchable prodigy with pretensions of genius, until she had crashed down like the city itself. No, not quite; Icaria had actually been airborne at one time, but Sylvaine's ascension had been a lie from the beginning. A deceit of Roache's construction. For better or for worse—no, assuredly for worse—this place, this buried attempt at a hospital amidst a refinery's forgotten landfill, *this* was the truth. Sylvaine had lost nearly everything, but she had a purpose—to destroy all that Roache had built. A project and the means to complete it; in the end that's all an engineer needed, right?

Sylvaine sighed and closed her eyes. She tossed her jacket over her head, trying to find a nap in the closest place to Inferno she had ever stepped foot.

Chapter 31

"That's the monolith, right?"

Sylvaine almost jumped. Ysabel was right behind her. The mutant stepped back and put her lone hand to her mouth.

"Sorry, sorry!" she said. "I didn't mean to frighten you."

"No, no, it's all right," Sylvaine said, turning back to her notes, on which she had made almost no progress on despite an hour's worth of intense staring. The mutants were confident about their plans, but for Sylvaine it wasn't enough. There was something odd about the machine, a baffling design whose purpose must have been the source of Roache's interest in her. It was clear enough that the device was infusing some sort of sangleum product into the water, but that didn't explain the function of this strange outcropping on the side of the complex. Sylvaine was all aboard with destroying Lazacorp's creation, but she needed to know what, exactly, she was destroying, what Lazarus had wrecked her life to try and finish. Even Gall had seemed unsure of the purpose of this section of the machine, as many of his notes focused exactly on that odd module, but he had made pitiful progress. The notes just weren't giving her enough. Or perhaps *she* just wasn't enough.

Sylvaine closed her eyes and rubbed her face. Maybe it was just the lack of sleep; her "nap" had barely even been that. At least her æthermantics were still working, if only somewhat. She flicked, with her free hand, the cubes of scrap she had formed in her morning practice and tried to ignore the one metal puddle she had fused to the floor during a momentary loss of focus.

"Wait," Sylvaine said suddenly, "what's a monolith?"

"Oh, right," Ysabel said, "that's what we call the central complex here."

Sylvaine nodded, mentally slotting that information into the "useless" category.

"I forget that you've not been here long," said the woman.

Sylvaine laughed and gestured to her fur. "I think I would look a bit out of place."

The woman laughed. "True, you look far too good."

Sylvaine wasn't sure if that was a compliment or just proof of how miserable conditions here had become. She tapped her pen on the empty page of her notebook and then sat back, resting her eyes on the not-so-comfortable sights around her.

One of the nearby mutants groaned, half bulbous with tumorous growths. Ysabel walked over and removed the rag from his forehead, replacing it with a slightly fresher one, before assisting him to drink.

"You need help?" Sylvaine asked.

The woman shook her head. "I can manage fine."

"Yeah, we're the lucky ones," shouted the male mutant, who was now rising from his cot. Sylvaine was surprised at how well he had managed to sleep. He had been out cold when she arrived and did not so much as snore while Sylvaine tossed and turned to the groans of the sick. Even more of a surprise was the man's right leg, which Sylvaine now noticed was simply a pipe attached to a stub by a net of leather bands, likely slit from some scavenged jacket.

"We're too damaged to work," he said, "but strong enough to care for the really fucked up." The man hobbled over, turning his head to stare at Sylvaine. "Who in Inferno are you?"

"Sylvaine," Sylvaine said. "The engineer."

"Oh, fuck me." He leaned on the wall. "Desct said we'd get an engineer. A real engineer, Guild-trained and everything. Idiot I was to believe him. Celina's right."

"She's real, Gualter," Ysabel said. "I saw her working this morning." She pointed at the metal cubes that laid beside Sylvaine. The man stared, eyes heavy with suspicion. Sylvaine sighed. She raised her gloved hand and lifted up a block, changing its shape in midair. The man's eyes widened, and then he looked away suddenly, as if unwilling to view something that might harm his precious ignorance.

"Well, since you're finally up, Gualter," Ysabel said, "can you wash Horst?"

The man grunted and started to wet a rag.

"You two work early," Sylvaine said.

"*I* do," the woman replied, "but it's not exactly early. It's almost noon."

"Really?" Sylvaine had no sense from the windowless room but reached into her bag and checked her watch. Indeed, it was 11:37. Whatever Marcel's fate was, it must have been decided by now. Sylvaine tried not to dwell on the thought, struggling to hope that maybe he had actually pulled off his deceit. Still, theories on the many dooms the man might have walked into ate at her. Or maybe that was actually hunger.

She pulled some salted taur jerky out of her bag, a tasteless breakfast provided by the cuisine-ignorant Kayip, though at least his cooking had never made her sick.

"I didn't see you eat," Sylvaine said, mouth full, noticing the man and woman's stares.

Ysabel shook her head. "Takes time for our friends to sneak up some from meal tents. Even feeding just us two is difficult. Many need to offer a small scrap, gifts from many dozens of meals, since no worker can afford to sacrifice more than a bite. And then someone has to sneak it down here. The guards don't like the idea of us keeping the sick alive and away from them, so that's not a simple task. Each one of us," and she gestured to her patients, "makes it more and more likely that someone will get caught sneaking away food. And then..." She didn't elaborate on the consequences, just sunk her shoulders.

"I'm sorry," Sylvaine said. "Here," she offered.

The man eyed the jerky, but the woman shook her head. "We've managed so far. You need to be strong and focused if you're going to help take down the monolith. We can make it a few more days until our freedom, but for the first time, we really have hope. Thank you for that."

Sylvaine felt herself blush, the first time in weeks from something other than shame.

"It's an excuse to wait," Gualter said, sitting on his cot and scowling. "So Desct can keep us quiet and placid with his lies. Bet that's why Lazacorp haven't offed him yet. We used to resist, you know that, 'engineer?' There was a time when we fought back, in any way we could. Under Desct we just nod our heads and do whatever Verus, or Roache's voice, tells us." He pointed to his leg. "I didn't come in like this. I earned it."

"Accomplishing what?" Ysabel spat back. "Now we've given ourselves some breathing room. The guards rarely ever come by. We set ourselves up now for one clean shot."

"We wait like taur-cattle, like animals." Gualter was now staring directly at Sylvaine.

"Aren't you supposed to be working?" Ysabel said. The man grunted and started to wipe down the half-conscious mutant beneath him.

The door above suddenly flew open. The three froze for a half-second, until their eyes adjusted and it was clear the man above was a mutant, not a guard. A familiar mutant in fact, Gileon.

Gileon skittered down the stairwell and approached Sylvaine, shaking slightly.

"Marcel..." he stuttered. "Needs you."

"Marcel?" Sylvaine asked. "Is he okay?"

The mutant nodded. "Hired by Verus, to work at the monolith..." He pulled up a makeshift tin-can water bottle from his belt and drank. "Needs help...Uh...Pretending to be an engineer. Think that's what he said."

"Pretending to..." The man had survived but only by plopping himself in a more idiotic pit. "How exactly am I supposed to get to him? I don't exactly blend into the scenery."

The mutant wiped off a thin layer of sweat as he continued to nod. "Marcel has a plan."

The inside of the monolith (no, the *Lazacorp facility*, damn, now Sylvaine was even thinking it) was different than how she had envisioned from the schematics. This wasn't because the schematics were particularly inaccurate to the reality, though there were a number of metal walkways that it didn't display, but more because of Sylvaine's new vantage point. That is, from the inside of a crate, covered in burlap sheets and few metal tools, staring out from a small hole cut in its side, which was also her only source of air.

Sylvaine had quickly grown to hate Marcel's "plans."

Still, this particular plan did seem to work. After the sun had set, she had been pushed and dragged on a dolly through Blackwood Row without raising any eyebrows or alarms, then left for a few hours at the loading bay of the monolith. It was a thoroughly unpleasant wait, and more than once she panicked at the sound of footsteps, almost making a mad run for it. But she forced herself still, and when someone did push against her crate again, it was with mutant hands. The mutant pushed her up into the tenebrous structure, where finally the lid was ripped off to reveal Marcel's face, alongside several mutants.

"You feeling okay?" he asked, as he helped her up.

"Drag me here in a Demiurge-damned box and you want to make small talk?" Sylvaine grumbled. Despite her tone and the dull pain in her back thanks to a poorly placed wrench, she was happy to see Marcel alive in one piece. But she wouldn't let herself show it.

"Sorry, sorry," he muttered. "I thought you might want to get a look at the machinery up close."

"And...?" she demanded

He scratched his chin. "And I may have bet my life on pretending to be an engineer."

Sylvaine sighed and pushed a welding iron off her back. "Let's get to it."

In truth, she was a bit excited. It was exhilarating to be back among machinery, even machinery built with ill intent, and the faux water treatment plant was an impressively massive structure. Though the lights were dim, she could see that the machine was several floors high, a towering cylinder of black metal. Great pipes skewered it in several directions, some feeding in water, others meant to hold raw sangleum. Every square metre was covered by walkways that led to different sections of the hulk, where hundreds of thermometers, flow-meters, æther-meters, and other meters displayed the inner workings of the half-functioning machine.

Marcel led her slowly as they circled up, speaking in whispers.

"We have to be quiet. We're not supposed to be here, I mean you, obviously, but technically Verus is sneaking me in."

They passed by several mutants, a few who watched them, a few acting busy, most keeping watch. The mutants' belts were full of hammers, screwdrivers, drills, and other tools, and though some stared at random sets of piping and idly prodded with their tools, none were actually working on the machine.

"His men are focused watching the outside to make sure Roache doesn't notice," Marcel said, "but they could walk in at any moment, so the key is speed. And calm. If you hide and I can act the part..."

Sylvaine touched her glove against the machineworks. It was clear enough the bulk of it was a variation of a general sangleum filtration unit and re-oscillator, common equipment for transforming raw mutagenic sangleum into usable æther-oil, though not usually attached to pipes leading to water treatment facilities.

"There's a module," Marcel explained in frantic whispers. "Verus is interested in it, seems like he had hired Gall to investigate it specifically. Now, I know we need to plan the sabotage, but in the meanwhile, I promised Verus that I would figure out—"

"Take me there," Sylvaine said.

"Yes, great!" Marcel nodded. He led her up a flight of stairs, to where mutant assistants had already hoisted up her crate. There, in the back corner, an odd cylinder jutted out. Marcel stared at it with a sort of wariness. Sylvaine grabbed a screwdriver from one of the mutants and got to work.

"Thank you," Marcel said, "for bailing me out again. I just need some information. Technical terms, something, just anything that I could report back so that Verus actually thinks..."

Sylvaine had already removed the outer casing of the module to stare inside at the series of pumps, cogs, gaskets, and gearworks. She nodded to whatever Marcel was saying and let the man's nervous drivel fade into the background as she placed her gloved hand into the beautiful intricacies of the machine.

Chapter 32

"...Just be careful with your æthermantics. We can't leave any evidence of you here for Verus, or any evidence of me for Roache, for that matter," Marcel said. "You got all that, Sylvaine?"

The woman, head deep in the machine, grunted, and waved him off. Marcel nodded and watched Sylvaine work. She poked and prodded, unscrewed bits and held her glove up to the machine. Marcel started to pace back and forth on the walkway. After a few minutes he glanced over again, and then, satisfied in his uselessness for her task, he stepped out toward the guardrail.

The room was dimly lit, only a few hanging industrial bulbs at half-power. Vaguely-formed shadows flickered around every corner, all innocuous and all liable to make him jump. A mutant leaned on the far railing, a young man named Sabyn who had been on monolith duty before. He had told Marcel that he was once a third generation taur-herder. Marcel hadn't even been aware that there were that many generations of taur-herders. The man now smiled at him.

"Don't worry, I'll keep my eye out," he said.

Marcel nodded, hands in his pockets, flicking the end of his belt with his thumb. "You're managing to keep calm," he observed.

The mutant raised a shoulder and an eyebrow. "Every day there is a chance that guards might catch me doing something I'm not permitted or just come across me while they're in a bad mood. At least today I don't have to break my back while watching for them."

It made enough sense, and Marcel joined the mutant, staring down. He could see a few of the man's comrades running back and forth, taking fake notes from the hundreds of dials on the goliath machine. All on Marcel's orders, of course, to keep the act up in case a guard did come walking.

Marcel gripped the railing and let his breath out. He had done well by his own reckoning. He had stolen Verus's trust, or at least something vaguely analogous of his trust. The foreman had thrust Marcel into the back corner of a mutant camp, the place least likely for Roache's men to find him, and where Verus believed (with some prompting) that Marcel would be the least able to get into trouble. The lodging was unpleasant, doubly so since Crat had chained his leg to a pipe during the daytime, but it had given Marcel direct access to the mutant resistance, and honestly, the company wasn't bad. The news of the schematic heist had spread fast, and though being chained in a foul-smelling subbasement wasn't much akin to the parades of the past, the hushed cheers, the awed whispers, and the wide-eyed stares felt all the grander.

Marcel had done his part, more than was expected of him; now it was up to Sylvaine. That seemed to be the nerve-racking part—he had done all he could. Now he just had to wait.

Sabyn jabbed him with his elbow and pointed down. A mutant was waving up. Marcel listened and could make out footsteps below, the hot glare of torchlight cutting into one of the side doors of the complex. He nodded and moved swiftly but silently back toward Sylvaine.

A mutant beat him to it, whispering to the engineer. She grumbled, and slunk back to hide in the crate, while Marcel took her place.

A minute later Crat stepped up the walkway. He moved with soft steps. Marcel wouldn't have heard him if it weren't for him cursing out a nearby mutant.

Marcel turned, wrench in hand. "Yes?"

"Work?" the man asked, as if it were a complete question.

"Ongoing," Marcel said, turning back to the inside of the machine. His answer did not satisfy the man, who grabbed his shoulder and pulled him back.

"It better be," Crat said. "If you're trying to deceive us to extend your life, trust me, it is not worth it. There are slow ways to die."

Marcel kept the man's gaze. He reached into the machine and pulled out a piece of something. "Do you know what this is?" Marcel said, lifting a small box decorated with a variety of wires. "Or this?" He pointed inwards at some sort of pipe-thing. "No? Then let me do my job."

The man let go but continued to watch Marcel. "What have you discovered?"

"I believe I was hired by Verus, not you," Marcel retorted.

"Hired?" The man snorted. "Do I have to remind you of your position, Talwar?"

"Here you go!" came the shout of Sabyn, who handed Marcel a screwdriver. Marcel inspected the tool, grateful for a second to think. "I asked for a slotted head, not a cross slot." He shoved it back into the mutant's hand and kicked him in the shins. "Go on, do your job right!"

Marcel thought he heard Crat chuckle as Sabyn ran off, but the man's face was grimly stolid when he glanced back to him.

"As you can see, Crat, I'm busy here, but if you want to waste my time chatting about stuff I'm just going to tell Verus tomorrow anyhow, well, I can include our useless interlude in my report to him, so he'll know what help you've been."

Crat sneered and shook his head. "All right then, work. But be damn quick about this. We can't be sneaking you in here night after night."

With that, he left. Marcel stood beside the open module, until a mutant gave him the thumbs up. He wiped nervous sweat from his forehead and stepped back as Sylvaine returned and took up her spot.

Sabyn walked by, thrust another screwdriver into his hand, and gave him a quick kick to the shin.

"Hey!" Marcel said. "I was just trying to play my role."

Sabyn shrugged. "I was just playing mine."

The excuse didn't make sense, but Marcel didn't press it. After all the horrors, atrocities, and just plain shit the mutants went through, they had earned a shin kick or two.

Sylvaine was more than eager to get back to work. Her brief separation from the machine had only increased her excitement to plumb its depths. She knew she should be more afraid—they were one mistake away from attracting an armed guard—or horrified, at either the machine or Lazacorp in general, but in truth she was exhilarated. She had been too long left with only abstract diagrams and shards of shapeless scrap. Now she felt around the many complicated organs of the module, each one its own fascinating mystery.

Someone said something behind her, but the tone lacked urgency, so she ignored it. She was working through several competing theories on the function of the module, each heavily supported by some parts of the machine and completely disproven by others. Individual pieces made sense, but as a whole, the module was senseless.

She had a moment of near-eureka when she noticed that several components of the machine, recent additions by the look of them, matched many of her æther-frequency modulation designs, but she quickly deflated when she realized that several of the additional æther-circuits, if powered, would only serve to disrupt the delicate task of æther modulation, making the purpose of the machine again incomprehensible.

Sylvaine dug deeper, removed some piping, and inspected a strange canister. It was glass on one end, revealing half-a-litre of empty nothing. Sylvaine unscrewed the canister and tried to make sense of its purpose. It was an irregular design, a small needle spiking from one end into empty space. She shook her head. Perhaps she was going about this wrong.

She stepped out and pressed her glove to the edge of the machine, closing her eyes and focusing in. With each micropulse of æther, she could feel out the gargantuan complex, sense its layers of pipework. So much of it was a beautiful interwoven masterwork, but the module seemed like chaos, a screaming child clanging spoons in the middle of a grand symphony.

"Find anything?"

She jumped back and turned to see Marcel glancing over at her.

"I didn't know you were still here!" she said.

He stepped back. "Sorry, I didn't mean to interrupt you. I was just asking again if you found anything."

She shook her head. "No, just, I don't know, maybe?"

"Just something I can tell Verus, it doesn't have to be important," Marcel said, a hint of anxiety in his voice. "Well, it might help if it *sounded* important."

She went back to the open module. "It's a strange one, I can tell you. There are components here that don't make a millilitre of sense. Some seem to fit with the injection hypothesis, but other parts seem like they would be better suited to an ætheric neutralizer or some sort of industrial filter, but some of those aren't even installed correctly."

"Okay," Marcel said, eyes upward, his fingers tapping together as he tried to memorize her words. "Strange mess. Injection hypothesis. Pieces of filters and ætheric fertilizer. Wait, no, did you say neutralizer?"

"You don't fertilize æther," Sylvaine said. "I'm not sure what's going on. Maybe they made a mistake, but some sections seem almost genius in their design...And then..." She pulled out the canister. "There's things like this."

"Hey, be careful," Marcel said. "Remember, we can't leave a clear mark. Don't go damaging things."

"It's okay, Marcel, I got it," she said, turning the canister in her hand. "It's an odd design, wouldn't be able to handle the corrosive effects of sangleum, seems overly complicated for water. Maybe it would hold some sort of catalyst."

Sylvaine twisted the lid opened and sniffed inside. She expected the smell of sangleum perhaps, or some industrial strength coolant or other chemical. Instead, a horrible odor hit her, metallic yet biological, knocking her back with shock. She shuddered violently and dropped the canister in a blind panic. It bounced on the walkway, with an arc heading straight past the railway. Marcel lunged, grabbing it right in mid trajectory, above the clanking abyss. He gripped it tight, inspected it, then showed it to her, uncracked.

"Demiurge, Sylvaine," he muttered.

"Sorry, sorry," she said, panting, leaning on the side of the machine.

"Something toxic?" Marcel asked.

She shook her head. "It...I think there was *blood* contained in that. A while ago perhaps, cleaned since then, but still the hint of it remains. I just..." her voice faded. Blood was not that shocking, but it was not often that she could tell the source. Lazarus Roache. The scent of his blood ripped into her, as if the man himself were here, trying to cut into her brain with his words.

Marcel grabbed her shoulder and handed back the canister, which she quickly implanted back into the machine.

"That's not the only oddity," she said, when she had calmed herself well enough. "Parts of this machine seem familiar, very familiar. Things I worked on."

"Some...machine you fixed in Icaria?" Marcel asked.

She shook her head. "My school project. A negative-density generator."

"A negative—"

"For æroships," Sylvaine cut in. "Helps them float."

Marcel furrowed his brows. "So they're trying to make the machine...float?"

"No," Sylvaine said, retreating to the open cavity of the machine. "That would be...very dumb."

The engineer went back to her work. She examined interwoven piping, compared ætherflow readings with quick pulses, disentangled æther-circuits from their wiring, inspected them, then re-entangled them. Minutes passed. Maybe hours. She wasn't tracking. At times she noticed Marcel's nervous pacing, his occasional glances over. Progress went slow. The more she understood the workings, the less the machine made sense; some parts weren't even hooked up to a power source, and a few of the pipes led only back to themselves. It was no surprise to her that Gall had completely failed to make heads or tails of this module. It was excessively strange, as if the point of the machine was simply to confuse her.

"Ah!" Sylvaine said suddenly. Marcel rushed over.

"What is it?" he asked.

She shooed him away with a free hand. "Shh. Breaking focus, you're...just shh!"

Sylvaine frantically glanced through the machine, inspecting with her ætherglove each individual component, making quick mental notes of which hooked up to one another, which she could make sense of, and which were placed in nonsensical places.

It took well over twenty minutes, but finally Sylvaine pulled her head out, leaned on the wall, and let out a long breath.

"What is it?" Marcel asked again.

Sylvaine started to chuckle and then shake with quiet laughter. "Nonsense..." she said. "Of course it is nonsense..."

Chapter 33

"Our initial hypothesis about the injection of some sort of sangleum substance are correct," Sylvaine said.

Marcel sat in the back of the crowded storage tank in the midst of a dozen mutants, and Kayip, watching Sylvaine explain her findings from the previous night. His legs were still heavy with the iron cuffs that Crat had latched onto them, but Sylvaine had at least undone the lock, so he could stretch them as far as the cramped space would allow.

The mutants whispered among themselves. They were nervous as day meetings, even those held in early mornings, were rare and required considerable effort. Other mutants needed to cover extra shifts, meals were missed, excuses had to be crafted, the chance that they'd all be discovered was significantly greater, but the time of their revolution was approaching. Risks had to be taken. Desct listened to the chatter, scratching the end of his chin, and then nodded solemnly to Sylvaine.

"So they're planning to commit the violations they brought upon us to the whole damn town?" Desct asked.

Marcel rubbed his eyes and forced himself to stay awake. Despite the dire situation, the localized apocalypse Sylvaine was outlining, the simple truth was that he had had little sleep in the last couple days.

"Sorta," Sylvaine said. "Slickdust is comparatively mild, a low dose of sangleum, and more importantly, a dose that is at a weak frequency. Not the case with what the machine could pump into the water. It'd be high frequency, heavily activated."

The mutants' confused looks spoke for themselves.

Sylvaine shook her head. "Listen, in simple terms, higher frequency equals more mutations. Slickdust only really mutates when injected in high quantities over a long period of time. The stuff this machine makes..."

"Will mutate its victims damn more expeditiously?" Desct offered.

"If it doesn't just straight up kill them." Sylvaine nodded. "With this infused into the water, it would take less than a week to turn all of Huile into..." she shook her head, "those poor men and women who you hide in your infirmary. Bags of flesh barely able to move."

Marcel held down nausea. What purpose could such cruelty serve? The mutants murmured with an intense focus on that exact question, with wild theories tossed about. Some suggested it was revenge for some unknown slight, others hypothesized that it was all part of some mad experiment, and there was even talk of a rumor that the mutated corpses would be grinded up to make slickdust. The arguments circled round and round each other, with no progress and not a hint of resolution.

"What does this matter?' Celina interrupted. "We're here to discuss the clockbomb plans, the revolution, not to get the technical readouts on some new Lazacorp product. We don't have the time to waste on dissecting their schemes. It doesn't matter. Let them poison this shitpit. It deserves no better."

This spurred intense shouting. '*What!*'s, '*How dare you*'s, and '*let the engineer speak*'s were flung around, echoing off the wall.

One older mutant stood. "City Hall may be corrupt, but I still have family in Huile. Many of us do."

A few tried to defend Celina. "If they don't care about our lives, why should we waste a moment caring about theirs?"

Desct stood suddenly and silenced the crowd.

"Continue Sylvaine," he ordered.

"Right," the engineer said, looking through her notes. "Well, this module is somewhat strange within the overall structure, at odds with, really, the machine's general purpose." She pointed to a sketch and the technical gibberish she had written. "The module is filled with many distinct subunits, whose purpose I won't get into, because they don't exist. They're superfluous. Fake. It's why Gall's notes were so damn confusing. He was being misled by the very machine he was trying to study."

The mutants murmured again, unsure of what to make of this.

"Roache is putting one over on Verus," Marcel said.

"Why?" asked one of the mutants. Marcel could only offer a shrug. That Verus and Roache hated each other was as evident as the earth, but what divergent goals they could be fighting over, Marcel still couldn't deduce. He glanced over to Kayip, who was intently staring forward at nothing in particular, fist over his mouth.

"I don't know the reason for the deceit," Sylvaine said. "All I know is the only half-functional piece of the module is this." She pointed to a bunch of scribbling, what Marcel could only assume was a detailed schematic. "It's an æther-modulator," she explained. "I worked on something similar for my own project. I had assumed it was my whole invention Roache cared about, but it was really just this technology, one that is far from efficient in this implementation. What this unit does is that it changes the frequency of the sangleum, lowering it significantly. It accomplishes this by comparing the frequency of its purposeful sangleum effluent to some other material, I think, in this case, blood." She paused. "Roache's blood, if I had to put frascs on it. This would allow it to exhibit the same mind-altering effect slickdust has, specifically attuned to a certain individual, i.e. Roache."

"So, then they *are* pumping slickdust into the water," Marcel said.

"Yes, effectively."

More whispered discussion. Several independent debates broke out before Desct silenced them all again. "So there is some malign rationality to their shit-stained brutality. Why didn't you begin with this revelation?" he asked.

Sylvaine rubbed her arm as she stared down at her notes. "Well...because...it's backward. If they just wanted to inject slickdust into the water, there are far easier solutions, ones that don't require this initial hyper-activation, don't need this re-adjustment and these fake structures. It's clearly *meant* to pump this first product, but it is changed at the last minute to instead inject slickdust."

"Could this first product be like slickdust?" Marcel asked. "A mind-controlling drug but for someone else, maybe?"

Sylvaine picked up a piece of paper and pointed to her equations, which added little to Marcel's understanding. "No, no, the frequency is hitting a ceiling. I mean, it *could* function like that, but only if the person in question had sangleum for blood. And sangleum for organs. And sangleum for skin, for everything. If that person was literally a pool of raw æther, then yes, sure, it would have a similar effect, but I doubt a puddle of oil is going to be doing much mind-controlling." She sat down, clearly exhausted by the questioning.

Well, that was one dead end. The way Verus had spoken of his plans had made them seem less like some grand manipulation, and more like blatant mass murder. For what reason, Marcel could only deduce insanity on the foreman's part, though that didn't strike him as a satisfying conclusion. Roache's alterations at least had a logical goal, control, though being a complete thrall to Lazarus Roache didn't strike Marcel as that much better than being dead.

Kayip tapped his boots. The echoing thuds grabbed the mutants' attention, and the monk turned to Marcel. "This is good," he said. "Marcel, you are to tell Verus of this. Of Sylvaine's discoveries."

"What?" Marcel said.

"What?" Celina repeated, with more venom. "You are going to give these secrets to our enemy? See! See what these outsiders are—"

Kayip slammed his boot down. "These are two machines. Do you not see? They are at odds and at separate purposes. One machine to inject this mutagenic poison, one to inject the lesser poison of slickdust."

"Which we don't understand the reasons for," Desct cut in.

"The reasons do not matter," Kayip said. "What matters is that Verus and Roache are opposed in goal. The removal of Gall, this hidden module, it is all part of their feud, and we now know that Roache has made a move against his foreman. Do you understand?"

Marcel nodded. *A wedge between the two.*

Celina snorted. "We have wasted enough time on this. While you played engineer, we have been gathering what we can for the clockbombs." With this, two of the woman's allies brought forward bags of metal bits and baubles. Sylvaine walked over and started to inspect them. "We never agreed to fight for Huile," the woman said. "We take down the æthericity lines and attack Lazacorp. That was what we voted for."

"We didn't know—" Desct began.

"We can do both," Sylvaine cut in. "Easier in fact, to do both. Get the sangleum flowing first, and with half the explosives, we could produce enough energy to demolish the structure, the æthericity lines, and most of the building."

"It'll turn this shit-stained monolith into an open pit to Inferno," Desct reiterated.

The engineer nodded, and the murmuring now took on an excited tone. Even Celina made no complaint, her bitter sneer falling back a bit to reveal a hint of excitement.

After this, the meeting descended into the dots of the details. They discussed how many arms they could muster from old tools, what were the best methods to strike, the best time, the best place, and of course, how they were going to sneak in the clockbombs. This, it seemed, would be Marcel's job. He nodded and promised success, trying to hide his apprehension. He had pushed Verus's trust as far as he could manage, and he was doubtful he could sneak in so many explosives past guards without raising more than a few eyebrows. Lax as security might had been, Marcel suspected it might spark suspicion to be caught installing clockbombs in the machine he was supposed to be studying.

Desct brought the meeting to a close; they had taken as much time as they could afford. In ones and twos, they snuck out. Marcel was led by Gileon and several other mutants through underground passageways back to the corner of the crowded sleeping quarters that Verus had tossed him to. Sylvaine followed long enough to re-lock his chains to the same pipework, and then snuck away without a word.

The upcoming sabotage weighed on Marcel more than he could show, as did his weariness. He lay down and tried to temporarily toss the thoughts off. He could figure out something, he told himself. He had gotten this far—he wouldn't fail now. He just needed sleep and something would come to him.

Something did come to Marcel, just a few hours later. Specifically the sounds of thumping footsteps, shouts and threats, then two Lazacorp guards, led by Crat, who shoved a gag into Marcel mouth and dragged him away without a word.

The Sightless City

To Gearswit!

This is my third application to your shit-suckling Academy, and I will not waste any more time on paperwork and other stiffland idiocy. I have written and rewritten my designs out three times, I know you have read them! I am an engineer, you are an engineer, that should be enough, but the fact that I cannot even speak with you direct and have to resort to scribbling down my complaints...

Enough blather, I will be direct. I do not care about you or your Guild's feelings toward wastefolk. This is about craft, and my craft is far beyond the pitiful efforts of any of your current students. As I have shown in my designs (which you have never returned!), there is untapped potential in applying engineering principles directly to the human body. This is obvious enough from those market-sold coglimbs hobbled together by all sorts of brain-dead engineers, guild or waste-trained. Yet these devices are always extensions, externalized hunks of metal, crafts lacking any imagination. I have read (in books published by your taurshit of a guild) that the human body is infused with mechanical æther, and I have seen the human body called a "machine" in those same books. This is not poetry! Not a metaphor! It is truth! Flesh, bones, organs, blood, mere names for machine-parts of a difference sort. So why then is not æther used directly upon them?

Cowardice! The same reason my applications have been rejected twice! I have shown clear that injections of sangleum products can have effects beyond mutation, that there exists the potential for influencing behavior by use of ætheric engineering on those such injected. Imagine what could be achieved were I not stuck in the Wastes, forced to scrap and scavenge, were I to continue my experiments in the workshops of Icaria. Imagine a future where we might control the minds of men in the same manner that we control machines! What foolishness causes you to spurn such power? Your superiors have made their mewling excuses in my previous rejections: "violations of established engineering theory," "excessive costs," "complete moral infeasibility." Bah, nonsense words, fancy ways of writing nothing. You are young, you have clear eyes, Gearswit. Cut through their stupidity. Get me into your Academy. I can promise powers a man would sell his soul for.

Miga Veneficus

—Letter addressed to then-Associate Professor Meir Gearswit. Discarded without response.

Chapter 34

"Ugh," Marcel said, which seemed to be the only proper, and for that matter only possible, response to having a knee jammed in one's stomach. He would have buckled over, were his knees not already on the floor and his arms held aloft. Dutrix Crat, who held Marcel's right arm, now slowly removed his kneecap from his victim's stomach.

Marcel squinted in the dim of Verus's office, only a single wisp of sunlight able to sneak through the blinds. The foreman himself leaned on the front of his desk, tearing open envelopes with a knife too long for its role as a sensible letter opener. He glanced through the contents of his mail, and then tossed each letter aside. Verus all but ignored the beating, acknowledging it only by the occasional muttered-out command for the next punch, kick, or stomp.

Every centimetre of Marcel ached, aside from his metal leg, which merely creaked a bit as he wobbled in the brief moment before Crat thrust his elbow into Marcel's back. Still, the pain was tolerable, but the dread was not. Verus had not offered any explanation for Marcel's abduction, nor his abuse, and had not given Marcel space to ask.

What had gone wrong? Had Crat uncovered Marcel's deceit? Had one of the mutants betrayed the cause? Had Verus never bought Marcel's story in the first place, but had just been stringing him along, using him as bait for the mutants? Marcel wanted to shout to Desct, loud enough, somehow, louder than the dictaphones' drone, that the mutants had to act now, that they had to strike before Verus did... whatever he was going to do.

The foreman paused to study his prisoner, as the other tattooed guard stomped down on Marcel's quite real leg. Verus drew small circles in the air with his knife, before landing it gently above the bridge of Marcel's nose. It appeared double in Marcel's vision, and he could feel the blade pushing against his skin ever so slightly.

"What are you up to?" Verus asked.

"Nothing!" Marcel said, eyes crossed. "Just doing what you told me, I mean, trying to figure out on your behalf... I'm just trying to survive."

"Lower back," Verus whispered, his blade retreating. Marcel felt a knee slam into him at the requested spot, and he groaned.

"What does Roache know?" Verus insisted.

Roache? "I told you everything," Marcel said, trying not to let his relief show. If Verus was still asking about Roache then perhaps he still didn't understand Marcel's true loyalty.

Verus waved the knife back and forth. Marcel couldn't help but follow its movements with his eyes.

"You spent plenty of hours chitchatting with the man over the years," Verus said. "What did he tell you? About me?"

"That..." Marcel focused his memory, to add the spice of some vague truths. "You were brutish. A fool. A pain in his arse."

"And the troll called the mountain rocky," Verus mused. "Did he tell you about our work here?"

"Only what he told everyone," Marcel said.

Verus pulled out a small canister from his pocket with sudden haste, shoving it towards Marcel's face. An acrid smell assaulted his senses. It reminded Marcel of Roache's tea, and he recoiled instantly.

"Hmm," Verus said, closing it. "So the idiot never got you on his leash."

"Leash?" Marcel said, understanding, but remembering that he shouldn't.

"Always thought his words were enough, even without the gift." Verus shook his head, then he waved to his men. "Continue."

The next minute was filled with pummeling; rapid, hard, a barrage that left Marcel coughing, near the point of vomiting, with the taste of blood in the back of his throat. Then suddenly Verus lunged forward, grabbing Marcel by the scruff of his neck, and shoved the knife right up to the edge of his throat. Marcel sucked in, feeling the sharpness of the blade.

"Tell me everything," he said. "Speak! Speak!"

"I did," Marcel said, words suffocated, each syllable pricking. "I told you."

"He can't save you."

Marcel held his breath, each movement stinging against the knife blade.

Verus pulled back some, and then started to speak. He spoke in that strange tongue, that language that didn't seem to be a language. Dark words that grabbed Marcel by his very veins, striking deeper than his ears. He almost forgot the knife, the fear of the man overwhelming the threat of the mere blade.

"Speak!" Verus said again, suddenly. Marcel felt his gut twist, his false leg burn. The world seemed to fall away, collapsing into darkness under the echo of the words. Terror shook him from his very blood, which rushed through his veins in a mad torrent, his heart beating against his ribcage, threatening to break through. Even Verus seemed to disappear, only the chanting syllables remained.

Marcel struggled to free himself, to thrust his hands against his ears, to grab the blade and cut out his eardrums. He had promised to take the mutants' secrets to the grave, he had prepared for the beatings, the brutality, for any pain Verus could inflict upon him, but these words spoke to something past pain. It was not mere agony, but a fear that overwhelmed his pitiful body. He knew, though he did not know how he knew, that even the end of his mortality was not enough to escape the horrid sounds, which seemed to echo beyond the bounds of reality. Verus's mouth was now an abstraction, the words an unending void described sideways. Marcel clutched in at himself, retreated back into a desperate solipsism, to be somewhere, anywhere away from *this*. He hid from the overwhelming vibrations, curled up to be crushed by the weight of some terror he could not even categorize, seeking refuge in some sliver of himself not yet drowned out, crawling desperately to some corner of memory where he was safe.

Then there was black.

An empty nothing without thought.

At some point a boot slammed into Marcel's side. He blinked, eyes wet. The world was a fuzz. No... that was the carpet. The boot hit again. He groaned under the familiar pain, more relieved than anything. The monstrous words had left him, replaced now by:

"Get up, Talwar."

Marcel pushed himself up from the floor. Verus stood over him, the two guards standing back. How long had he been out? It felt like days, at least hours, but the daylight that snuck through the blinds hadn't changed its tone.

A fresh panic jumped through him. What had he said? What had he revealed in that confused fever dream?

He heard something behind him. It took him a second to realize that Crat was failing to choke back a laugh.

"Pathetic Talwar, pathetic." Verus shook his head. "Who is Alba, anyways?"

"I think that was the um, soldier, who led Roache's whole attack," offered the second of the guards.

Verus snapped his finger. "Ahh, the swine-headed mercenary bitch. Crying for her?" He scratched at his eye. "You know, I break a lot of people, Talwar, some give up secrets, some beg for mercy. This is a first, laying down and crying for their old captain."

"What?" Marcel began.

Crat couldn't hold his laughter in. Verus ignored him.

"A waste," Verus said. "Just, 'Alba... Alba... help me...'" Took me half a dozen kicks to even knock you out of it."

So he hadn't said anything. Marcel hung his head. It seemed Alba had saved him again, in a manner of speaking.

Verus grabbed his hair suddenly, knife blade back.

"It is no surprise. Roach hires cowards," Verus muttered into his face. "Men he can use. Men who talk easy when their life is on the line." The foreman studied Marcel. "Perhaps you are unusual. A pitiful wretch, but maybe one who knows it."

He turned the knife slightly, pressing it against the bottom of Marcel's chin. His eye locked onto Marcel's, an unblinking stare, a stare that did not even permit the theoretical possibility of blinking. "I could cut you to pieces, Talwar. Not in the obvious way, I could open you, inspect your every flaw, outline them with my blade, cut them away, bit by bit. I could slice your skin from your flesh, Talwar, I could make you wet and hairless, as before you were born. I could give you the pain you deserve. Do you want that, Talwar? Do you wish it?"

Marcel could only shake his head slightly.

Verus glanced up at his men and sighed. "No, it's not the moment, is it? Maybe if we were earlier, but now... I don't have the time."

The foreman released Marcel, who slumped over. He felt water drip from his face and realized he had been weeping. Verus tossed the knife on the table and sat there, opening up a file.

"Ok, Mr. Talwar," he said, in a casual tone. "Why don't you tell me what you found on my machine?"

Marcel was unable to speak for a full minute. Finally he asked: "What?"

"The...filtration unit. You spent all day on it, you must have found something, or else what am I keeping you around for?"

"Roache...?" Marcel couldn't help but ask, unable to let the interrogation pass without question.

Verus shrugged. "You don't seem to be the man's rat. Didn't seem so yesterday either, but it couldn't hurt to check."

Marcel steadied himself, almost falling. Part of him wanted to laugh. "So you just beat me then for no reason?"

"You walk with too much confidence, Talwar. It's not my policy to let men work for me unbroken. Come on, let's see what you discovered."

So the man had taken his revenge then. All an act to release his rage. Or was it even that? Marcel tried to force his mind back into focus. Was this just the way Verus did things? He glanced back at his guards; neither seemed offended in the least by this waste of time. Maybe this was just Verus's equivalent of a morning meeting?

"Talwar?" Verus said.

Marcel shook these thoughts away and tried to remember what Sylvaine had told him, what Kayip had advised him to say.

"Well, um," he said. "I mean, I did discover some oddities."

Ysabel held the spiraling torsion spring up in the dim light. "It's like the scrap we'd find in the dusthomes," she said.

"Yeah?" Sylvaine said, glancing up from her work. Several clockbombs sat beside her, completed aside from the concentrated canisters of sangleum that would be their explosive cores. It seemed wise to keep the mutagenic explosive material away from the sick and wounded.

Ysabel nodded and handed the spring to Sylvaine who fused it with a quick æther-spark onto the current, half-made, clockbomb beneath her. Ysabel's eyes were wide as she watched Sylvaine work her engineering. The engineer, for her part, put on a show of confidence, which had grown over the past hour from faux bravado to genuine ease. She had never constructed high ordinance before, but the process wasn't all that different from any other project Sylvaine had taken up in Icaria. Put the pieces in place, focus one's æthermantics and hope it doesn't all explode.

"Me and my brother would go out when we were kids," Ysabel explained. "Find what we could in the dusthomes, then walk back with great bags of the stuff."

"Dusthomes?" Sylvaine asked, while also pointing towards an æther-igniter in the pile of scavenged and stolen machine parks.

"Oh right," Ysabel said, picking up the small metal cylinder. "You know, the giant houses out in the Wastes. I guess they must have been mansions or something a century ago. Hard to see why anyone would need that much space. Now just dust lives there."

"You would go as kids?" Sylvaine asked, eyes down on her project. The small talk was strange, but pleasant. Since leaving Icaria she had had little light conversation. Kayip's closest equivalent had been his long, meandering sermons from *The Chronicles of the Ascended.*

"Yeah, my brother took me along since I was six. Father had to tend to the taur herd, or would be gone, chasing away raiders."

"It wasn't dangerous going off by yourself?" Sylvaine asked

"Oh no!" Ysabel shook her head. "I mean, we found a few troglyns and some wastehounds, but I shot them good."

Sylvaine paused her work to look at the woman. "You shot them? I thought you were six."

"Of course," Ysabel said, with perfect earnestness. "You can't let a six-year-old wander off on her own without a rifle."

Sylvaine just laughed and went back to work. "I guess city-life is different after all."

"I've never been to a stiffland city." Ysabel sorted the pieces around her. "Except for this one, I guess."

"Not the best first impression," Sylvaine said.

"No, I suppose not."

"You girls almost done with the bombs?" Gualter shouted, as he sloppily wiped off the oozing sores from one of the groaning mutants on the floor. Sylvaine shot him a glare, and he muttered something vaguely offensive and turned away.

"Ignore him," said Ysabel. "He's just irked to be stuck on medical duty. He's too taken by Celina's talk, of being 'the weapon to rip to pieces the men of Lazacorp, the tool to take this place apart, screw by screw.'"

"Well he's a tool, sure, just not the useful kind," Sylvaine said.

Ysabel stifled her laughter into her hand, and Sylvaine couldn't help smiling.

Above them the door burst open, the midday light blinding. Sylvaine froze, but relaxed some when the door closed and she could make out the horned form of a mutant. She tensed back up as man dashed with a frantic panic down the stairs. He dumped a few tin cans, each full of food, before scurrying over to Ysabel and Sylvaine, Gualter following.

"Guards," he whispered.

"Where?" Ysabel asked, all mirth gone from her features.

"Up in the camp. Saw them as I was moving back. They're cutting through in a rage."

Chapter 35

Marcel surprised himself with his ability to remember the technical details of Sylvaine's findings, even when he still couldn't even begin to understand them. Whenever he stumbled on a word, (æther... *neutralizer*, he was pretty sure) Marcel would fabricate a quick anecdote about his discovery process, stealing details from Sylvaine's work. The stories annoyed Verus some, but they bought the time for Marcel to remember exactly what he was pretty sure Sylvaine had roughly said.

There was silence after he finished. A good minute of silence. Then a good five minutes. Verus leaned back, eye closed, finger to his forehead. Marcel waited in an equal silence. He thought he had told his story well, acted the role, but Verus's unwillingness to pass judgment made him wonder, then fear. He could feel his heart pound and fought against the urge to push Verus to speak. To say something, anything.

Verus just stood there, still, mouth curled. The two guards were equally frozen. By the look on Crat's face, Marcel judged breaking the foreman's quiet would be close to suicidal. So he waited with him, trying not to show his panic.

"So he's altering the oathblood then," Verus said suddenly.

"Well, I don't—" Marcel responded.

"I wasn't asking," Verus said. He opened his eye and gestured toward his men. "You're dismissed. We need to talk technical details."

The two men left quickly and without question. Verus tossed Marcel a key. Marcel held it for a second, unsure if this was a test or...

"Come on, get on with it. I'm not afraid of you, Talwar."

Marcel nodded and undid his locks, as Verus kicked forward a chair

"Sit," he ordered. Then glancing Marcel up and down: "You need the rest, you look like shit."

Marcel took the chair, feeling every ache as he sat. "I wonder why that is."

"You looked like shit before this morning, Talwar. Griffon's arse, we're all shit in the end, its barely even an insult. Though some are more shit more than others."

"You talking about Roache?"

Verus nodded, smiling. Then his face fell and with a sudden burst of speed, he picked up his knife and slammed it into the table. Marcel yelped despite himself.

The foreman ruffled his hair back and caught his breath. "To think you, of all people, Talwar, figured it out, was able to peel back Roache's lie. And you don't even understand it."

Marcel started to speak, but Verus cut him off. "You don't need to understand. At least not all of it." He paused, staring at the wall. "Foreman... A stiffland job title, like something you'd see in the wanted pages of that damn Gazette. It was Roache's idea, a joke, or something more. We are supposed to be partners, equal, and even that disgusts me. It's his duty to handle the business side of things, to deal with the political nonsense, and the gift."

"The gift?" Marcel asked.

"Shut up," Verus said with a bored tone. "I handle the wastefolk, the day-to-day operations, the skinsick, and most importantly, matters of spiritual enlightenment."

"Spiri—" Marcel started, before catching himself.

Verus turned his eye to Marcel. "You're not blind Talwar. You can see something larger is happening here, even if you don't have the clarity of vision to make it all out. We're putting an end to the lies. The lies of the Principate, the lies of your Confederacy, all the insipidity of the false Demiurge and his mawkish church."

Marcel nodded, not knowing what else to do. It was clear enough that the man was insane, that could be the only explanation, but he seemed to have had disturbing success proselytizing his madness.

"The Calamity was supposed to be mankind's wake-up call," Verus continued, "but even the end of the world can't knock people from their slumber. Not just the stifflanders, even most wastefolk refuse the truth buried beneath their feet. Talwar... the things I could teach you if I had the time. You are ignorant and arrogant, but you are full of rage, and that is the first step. We are so close... so damned close. But Lazarus Roache..."

Verus pressed his palm onto the heel of his knife, pushing it deeper into his desk, until it suddenly smashed through the surface, wood cracking, splinters flying. He stared at his pointless destruction, then at Marcel, his lips flat but twitching. Finally, with a sigh, he slumped onto his desk, head grasped between his boney hands.

"Do you know how long we've been running this refinery?" Verus asked.

"Uh, a few years before the war, I was told," Marcel said.

"Seven years in total, just about," Verus illustrated this fact with his fingers. "And I found this place for Roache. Found the man a sea of sangleum sitting under a tiny piss-puddle of a town, held together only because it still had some walls standing and other ruins didn't. No one knew about it then, no Principate or

353

Resurgence idiots bickered over Huile, this was just some shit town, just like the rest of them. Still is a shit town, but now it has money. Roache took the credit, of course, not that I cared. It's all just material, the befouled rot that we toss back and forth to prove that we've been successful, that we're big men somehow. But me and Roache, we had a deal, Marcel, not some coarse contract on paper, not some spoken promise worth the skin of a rat, a real contract, a *true* one."

"I don't understand," Marcel said, which was an honest truth.

"I told you, you don't need to." Verus opened up a side drawer of his desk and pulled out a bottle. Marcel squinted to see if it was water, or sangleum, or...

Verus uncorked it and sucked a gulp down. It was whiskey. "You drink, Talwar?"

Before Marcel could answer, Verus shoved a mug in his hands, and poured him a cup. It smelled strong.

"This may surprise you, Talwar, but I have a reputation to maintain, can't let them" and he pointed out the door, "see that I'm a man just like the rest of them. This ain't a holy drink, it's as profane as it gets." He took a swig. "But damnation if it doesn't help."

Marcel took up the mug and sipped. It burned, but actually wasn't terrible.

Verus sat down, his feet hanging off the desk, and toasted roughly. "To those who have been stung on the foot by fucking Lazarus Roache."

Ecstasy. The pain was ecstasy, spiritual fulfillment beyond any lies the priests of the false one could promise. It was excruciating pain, not the tearing of skin from flesh, or flesh from bones, but of spirit from spirit. All the sins of mankind, all the collective guilt of uncountable millennia pulled from his very soul, ripping his very being apart. It was the glorious destruction of the self, and

Hieronymus Lealtad Namter embraced his end if it should come. Let him not be a petty butler, let him not be an aging man with all humanities' perversions, let him not even be a Brother of the Unblind. Let him be pure, he wailed to the pain, or let him be destroyed.

In this agony there was no place or time. There was only the divine punishment. Visions passed through him at a storm's pace, of a world beyond the world, of spirals of azure marble, of crystalline castles greater in size than cities, of titanic beings of bountiful mirth and sorrowful beauty, of machines that made mockery of all the achievements of men. He grasped for these, aching to see more, desperate to finally cut through the filth and the lies, to see the majesty of the forgotten truths. Yet the splendor overwhelmed him, burning his vision and cutting at his body, all veins and blood and raw skin.

He faltered, screaming, and was flung back like a leaf in a storm, through a maelstrom of agony, through a second world, one of his putrid ego made manifest. His abominable humanity polluted his glimpses of perfection, rotting away the divinity. This was a world of rust and ash, of fetid citadels crumbling, of cities of skin and pus. He wailed to himself as he was flung through the nightmare, this horror that he knew *he* had brought in. He tore at himself, desperate to remove this pollution of his spirit, which blinded him from the incandescent truth. He screamed for it to be scrubbed from him from him violently, with all the pain he deserved—no, to be unmade completely, to be separated forever from all that which chained him to his pitiful existence.

Then it was gone, and Namter fell back into the world. His memories, his failures, his individuality, his whole pathetic being jammed back together. He shouted out and thrust his bleeding hand forward, grasping at the bowl of boiling Oathblood that sat in the center of the room.

"Calm, Brother, calm," demanded Avitus, who held his left arm. Remius held his right, and after a moment, Namter was able to collect himself, as odious and unfortunate a task as that was.

"Apologies, Watcher," said Remius. "You had thrust your whole arm in, you were writhing, we thought it was too much."

Namter weakly nodded his agreement, his body still shaking.

"Did you see?" whispered Avitus.

Namter felt the warm of tears on his face. "A little, my Brother, a glorious glimpse."

The two led Namter to a chair in the back, and Avitus tended to the self-inflicted gash in his hand. His vision came into focus. The room was spacious and mostly empty, kept windowless and black except for the light of candles. There were no light bulbs nor handtorches, no machinery birthed out of the pitiful engineering of man. Namter's Brothers stood around a central bowl of Oathblood, which roiled over onto itself. The Brothers studied their Watcher intently, as he sat, recovering from the rite.

There were fewer of them than he wished. Despite his own efforts, the schism between himself and Verus had not yet healed. The Awakener still distrusted him, and many of the other Brothers refused any service that Namter led. They could not even perform the holy rituals in their usual space, the basement beneath Verus's office. That itself had never been the ideal location, but it was at least was completely bare. The current room still held a few boxes of excess Lazacorp uniforms shoved in a back corner.

Namter preferred the days when they'd practice their faith out in the Wastes, when they could let their screams echo across the sky. Here in Blackwood Row it was necessary to keep hidden the ecstatic screams of the Unblind. Their rites were unusual even by the lax standards of the raider-folk who Roache often hired as Lazacorp guards. The hypocrisy stung Namter. Raiders were eager to waste the blood of their slaves in gladiatorial fights, but when a follower of the Truegods harvested slaves as Tribute for a greater cause, suddenly these same raiders would develop a concern for

356

human life. Namter shook away the thought. Such anger was of ill worth.

He felt strong enough to stand, finally, and he pushed back any feelings of disappointment or reservation. It was not his duty to feel such things. The task of the Brotherhood was near completion, and he would lead it to its final culmination

"My Brothers," he said, "the time of Reification is fast approaching. The long recalcitrance of humanity shall be punished, and the rot we see infecting every town, city, farm, or any other habitation where mankind has left their mark shall soon be cleansed..."

"So when I tell Roache that I found a good engineer, he said I'd need to go to that cesspit of a City Hall and get the proper forms to register him before I could even bring him in the city." Verus gestured violently as he told this story, just one of many he had already ranted out. "Dozens of forms, hours of works, nonsense back and forths with Gyurka and Lambert and Marceau and all those stiffland shitsuckers just to get one man past these walls."

"Really?" said Marcel, forcing incredulity.

"Roache brought in hundreds, thousands of mercenaries, workers, even his own engineers from time to time, and not a word went to City Hall. But when it was me?" Verus drank, "I knew then he was plotting something. But the man is always plotting *something*. I thought I could keep myself higher than his machinations. Use his money, use his gift. That *he* was given such a gift.... It's not for me to question. Still, I thought I could keep above this bickering."

"You know," Marcel said, "he sent me on a lot of seemingly pointless jobs, investigating Lazacorp workers."

Verus raised his eyebrow and snorted.

"Yeah, and whenever I came to him," Marcel continued. "His questions would always lead back to you. 'Were they talking with

Verus? Did I see Verus? Was Verus doing anything suspicious? You know."

"Like who?" Verus asked.

"Oh, uh," Marcel searched his memory for plausible names, as Roache rarely introduced his staff. "Setius, Garson, and uh, Martus." That last one had been a real case.

"Ah, Martus," Verus nodded. "I suspected you had been meddling with him."

"Roache would complain," Marcel continued, "to me and Lambert, and others, about you. About your manners, your clothing, accent, even your smell. I didn't take part, of course, but Roache seemed to have a new joke about you each week."

Verus drank some more. "My father taught me many things, Talwar, taught me the secrets of the world, taught me the wisdom of the whip, also taught me this," he pointed to the bottle, "which may have been accidental. But he always told me that you can trust no man. But if you must trust someone, never trust a stifflander."

"Wise words," Marcel nodded. He had finished his mug of whisky under Verus's gaze and was now on the second. It was an oddly relaxed conversation, considering the man and the situation. He moved side to side to feel his bruises, to remind himself of the danger, and not let his attention become lax.

Verus got up and pulled down one of the blinders of the window, glaring at the sunlight streaming in. "We own this town, Talwar, you know. Lazacorp built it, and then rebuilt it after its mayor got uppity. But it was never supposed to be more than kindling. And now Roache wishes to burn me with our own kindling?"

"Kindling?" Marcel asked. "I thought it was abattoir."

"I'll mix my metaphors as I damn want, Talwar," Verus snapped back with a sneer.

Marcel muttered out an apology. Verus leaned on the wall. "He's made this impossible from day one. Insisted that his voice was enough to keep these mutants in line."

"And you think?" Marcel asked.

Verus smiled. "Mutants are like any other. Men foolishly seek to avoid pain. Give them the pain they deserve, and they won't bother you none."

The foreman sat back down, chuckling to himself. "These red fucks used to be trying all sort of trouble, coming up with escape plans, ambushing guards. All because Roache trusted himself too much. The one bright spot in this whole pond of shit is that Roache has been distracted long enough from the day to day, what with his Icaria traveling and his City Hall arse-kissing. Got them all to my own devices, used my own methods." He smacked his backhand against front. "Not a peep from them."

"Showed them who's boss," Marcel said.

"And when you worked, did they give you any trouble?" Verus jabbed his finger.

Marcel shook his head. "Did as I said without complaint."

"Tools, Marcel, they're just tools. With a little discipline you can remind any man, mutated or not, of that truth. They serve their purpose and are disposed of, as it is with us."

Marcel nodded along, trying not to think on the reality behind that statement.

Sylvaine tuned her ears for the sound of the guards. It wasn't hard, as there was no subtlety to their movement. It was all shouting and kicking and the occasional gunshot. She kept her finger out, tracing their exact location, while Ysabel and Gualter led her through the maze of structures in the pointed direction.

"What are they doing here?" Ysabel said, "Ever since we've kept peaceful, they haven't tried a raid."

"Desct's nonsense for what it is," Gualter muttered. "We lie on our backs, and they step on our legs anyhow."

"Ssh!" Sylvaine said.

They snuck through an empty scrapshack and down into a path of torn-up piping. The camp was near silent, aside from the shouts of the guards, and the occasional footsteps of a few mutants. One stumbled past, pausing only to point, frantically and silently, in the direction that he came from, before running off. They circled round past, climbing over a rusting autotruck frame, where another mutant hid. Sylvaine was able to make out the voices now, two men.

"Damned shitwork here, this place smells like a taur's arsehole," came first voice.

"Figures you'd know," said the second.

"Ahh eat my—hey!" A loud shout. Then a gunshot.

"Damn bastard scurried off." The first again.

"Be careful you don't spark something. Lost a whole camp-load of the fuckers to a fire last year." The second.

"Eh, I wouldn't mind torching this whole place."

"Keep your focus. Never know when one might come swinging a hammer from some shitpile."

Sylvaine whispered out what she heard to Ysabel and Gualter, who listened intently, drivel as the conversation was. She focused her ears to guards' footsteps and gestured to move back. The men were getting closer.

"Why don't we have Neers on this?" The first voice.

"Because he pushed it on you." The second. "There's one. Hey! Come down here." Another gunshot. A scream.

"Nice!"

"Nah, was aiming for the legs."

Some more footsteps, and a series of curses. Sylvaine could also make out a faint groaning, pained.

"He won't make it long. Damn it." The second voice. "Won't be good for talking."

"Eh, it'll scare them well enough, half the point."

"Calm for so long, now making trouble."

Sylvaine felt her hair bristle and could see a similar fear in her companions' eyes as she spoke. What trouble had the guards found? Had Marcel messed up?

The footsteps picked up, followed by cracking, grunting, and the sound of crashing structures. The men seemed to find it easier to smash their way through than working out the mutants' own pathways.

The three moved back in response, having to scramble as quietly as they could manage. Sylvaine noticed that they were retreating towards the medical structure.

"It's in their direct path," Ysabel whispered.

"I'll move the sick," Gualter said.

"We haven't the hours for that," Ysabel said. "Not even the minutes."

"Did they find the one who tried to escape?" said the first voice, close now.

"Doubt it made it out of the Underway," said the second. "Maybe didn't even try, just scrapped that dictaphone speaker and fled back. Either way, we'll find out."

Dictaphone speaker. Sylvaine staggered, struggling to keep her hand from shaking. In the Underway... Roache's voice... It had been *her.*

They could see the men now, fully uniformed, rifles in their arms, the bayonets shining. They moved forward, kicking down the plywood and metal that stood in their way

"Sneak back, as silently as you can manage," Ysabel said. Sylvaine turned to ask a question, but the woman was already off, running through the camp. She dashed forward in a clear line to the guards. Sylvaine moved to follow her, but Gualter grabbed her arm tight.

"Let me go," she hissed, "They're going to—" She saw his face. He was crying silent tears.

Ysabel ran, clanging against metal and smacking her feet loudly against the concrete. The distraction worked instantly, the guards shouted and ran toward the woman, who fell prone onto the ground. The men didn't grab at her first, but instead kicked her, boot against stomach and back, as she moaned, and curled up into a ball. They battered her as they latched her arm onto the second man's belt.

Sylvaine looked away. She could stop this. She could pull out of the man's grip, she could ambush the men, turning their weapons to slag. Gualter stared at her, tears dripping down his stone-still face. He didn't have to speak. If she helped, more would come, guards in their twos and tens and hundreds. They would tear this place up, make examples, find the sick and take them away, cut the hands off of the revolution before it could even begin.

She closed her eyes, shuddering with her own grief, trying to maintain her silence as she listened to the men drag Ysabel away.

Chapter 36

"I don't enjoy this, you know," Verus said. He gestured a circle at the desk on which he sat, then spun his pointer finger up and around at his whole office, expanding the motion until he was just flailing his wrist, before shaking his head and drinking.

Under the man's gaze Marcel had actually finished off two full glasses. He sipped now on his third. He wished he had kept up the habit, since it was getting difficult to think with a sharp focus.

"But you keep doing it," Marcel offered finally.

"You do what you do," Verus said, "because you have to do it. Like that chair you're sitting on."

"Yeah?" Marcel repositioned himself on the stiff wooden thing.

"Well, it's made for you to sit on it. If it didn't work, if you just fell off or it crumbled into splitters... then what's the point? Would be a shit chair."

"It already is kind of a shit chair," Marcel observed.

"Don't get smart with me, Talwar," Verus pointed finger and bottle at Marcel. "It doesn't suit you."

"Sorry."

"Point is, we're all shit unless we do what we were made to do."
Verus started to pace around his office, patting paper stacks
together and softly kicking file cabinets. "I didn't think I'd be doing
this for seven damn years, but here we are. Didn't think I'd be
wasting my days managing damn lazy mutants and snobbing it
with a bunch of stifflander fops."

"And Roache," Marcel turned his chair to follow Verus's
journey, "was his purpose to get in your way?"

Verus stopped dead and turned, finger thrusting. "That's the
thing, that's the thing. He knows what he's supposed to do. I didn't
want to be partners with him any more than he with me, quite a bit
less in fact, but I played my role. Now he... now he's trying to take
it all for himself. Trying to steal our enterprise away. No, not our
enterprise, if it was only that petty..." The man slouched on the wall
and muttered to himself.

"I can remove the... Roache's addition," Marcel said, "But—"

"You *will* remove it!" Verus commanded. "Don't forget your
job is to work for me."

"Sure, sure, Verus," Marcel said, "but I'll need help, a good
number of mutants. I'm not an ætheric engineer. I need manpower
and tools."

The man shrugged. "We can get you one of Roache's
engineers."

"You're just going to tell him?" Marcel said, his stomach
turning.

Verus snorted. "I won't just tell him, I'll scream it at him,
shove his nose in it, force him to help dismantle his own treachery.
Make him fulfill his promises."

Marcel laughed, half put on, but half genuine. "And he'll take
it? Roache *never* does as he promised. Think about it, he's already
undercut you, he's gotten in with City Hall. Do you think he'd do
all that, and then fold once you call him out?"

"You don't even know what we're planning here, Talwar, not
really," Verus said.

"I know Roache," Marcel said, an idea starting to form in the back of his mind. "Know what a worm he is. He has been building the trap all around you, Verus. I saw how he built one around me. He's not giving in."

"I'll force him," Verus said, an uncharacteristic lack of force in his own tone.

"When he has all of Huile behind him? And whose name is on the Lazacorp guards' paychecks? I don't know how long he's been planning this betrayal, but it's clearly not recent. He's made his mind up long ago if I have any guess, been poisoning your reputation for years, consolidating his forces."

Verus eye flicked back and forth, as he stroked the side of his bottle.

"He has you, or he thinks he has you," Marcel said, smiling. "But you know. You know, and you have the jump on him." Marcel scooted his chair towards the foreman. He wondered how far he was stretching his luck, if he could just stretch it a little further.

"We're partners..." Verus muttered, the words empty.

"Partners takes two. He betrayed you," Marcel said. "And he'll betray you again."

"...We must not allow ourselves to fall to ego. Our task here is only a pitiful service, the barest we wretches can give to the true Masters of humanity. But through our service, our pain, we raise humanity up from our own filth, and each eye made Unblind is another servant of the divine." Namter paused, letting his words sit a moment. "Now we shall welcome into our ranks a new Brother," he said, gesturing to a thin young man, who stepped through the door, chest bare, led in by Brother Travert. "He comes from a raider gang of the Wastes, a life of hedonism and ego. This we will strip from him. Let him seek the truth beyond this world of filth. So may we all."

"So may we all," came the combined voice of the Brotherhood.

"Let him seek a purpose beyond the lies of civilization. So may we all."

"So may we all."

"Let him seeks righteous punishment, to feel the pain of millennia, to be torn down so he may serve his proper Masters. So may we all."

"So may we all."

The young man moved with a slight hesitation. His face was still swollen and red from his first markings: twin eyes on his cheeks, surrounded by Truewords that even Namter had not been gifted the knowledge to read. Namter noticed that the man was shaking. With fear? With anticipation? With some emotion he himself could not know? Then Brother Remius took his blade and spoke the sacred words. The other Brothers chanted along, led by Namter.

The blade slashed, a movement faster than could be seen, and the young man screamed, as he had assuredly never screamed before. Skin flapping off blood-gushing flesh, his hand was thrust into the bowl by the attending Brothers. His screams now moved beyond the human, to pitches above the range of the mortal, splitting sounds that cut through the threads of reality. The Brothers held him, and Remius locked his hand in chains, so the man's writhing would not wretch him from the grasp of the Oathblood.

Namter could only smile, bliss-filled on behalf of the young man. If he survived his first brush with the Truth beyond all truth, then he would be a true Brother of the Unblind. Namter could remember his first experiences with the Brotherhood, eight year ago. Then, he had been nothing more than a servant for some sangleum tycoon without sangleum, the prodigal son without the riches needed for his lifestyle, or even for Namter's paycheck. He had been sent out on rumors that an iterant, self-proclaimed waste-prophet held strange knowledge of sangleum wells, could dowse for them with methods unknown to any other.

Such was the least of Verus's skills, the smallest of his gifts. Greater still was the knowledge of the truth beyond this world, of the beings who had formed it, who, by right, should rule it. Namter had learned such in the first of his lessons, when Verus had personally beat him, taken stick to back, boot to stomach, and then, blade to throat, asking if Namter wished the prophet to cut his ego away, to carve out his very soul, slice down so there was nothing left. 'Yes!' Namter had shouted, 'Yes!'

The boy screamed and jutted back, his wrists clanging against his chain. Namter wondered what visions the boy saw, what bliss came riding with the agony. The rest of the Brotherhood stood watching, but Brother Valere crept from the doorway to Namter's shoulder.

"Watcher," he whispered. "Roache has sent a courier. He says it's important."

Namter nodded, hiding his consternation, and gestured to Brother Avitus to continue. If Roache had sent for him during the middle of his rites it must be vital. He stepped out of the room, and then ran down the hallway, up the stairs to where a Lazacorp guard stood, leaning against the open door to the street.

"Yes?" Namter said. The guard glanced down at Namter's hand, still bandaged and red. "Roache's message?"

The guard nodded and took a piece of paper from his pocket. He stared at it, mouth moving as he read, which seemed like a recently developed skill for the man.

"Mr. Roache says, well he says it an emergency." He squinted. "The, uh, for the water fil... the water plant, for the party, for the water-plant the cake topper is bad."

"What?" Namter said, grabbing the note. It was as inane as the man said, Roache's complaint scribbled that the custom cake-topper, ordered to mount the three-tier cake that would serve as desert for Roache's upcoming gala, was of insufficient quality, blotchy in color and ambiguous in form. *"It is imperative,"* the note stated, *"that the decorations fit the theme of our grand opening and maintain the prestige of the Lazacorp brand. The current topper fulfills neither of these and is unacceptable. I assume you understand the gravity of the situation and will...*"

Namter crumpled the letter, holding his fist to his face a moment, as he filtered out his frustration. "There is a bakery on Montuere Street, *The Admar Twins' Finest*. Take one-hundred-and-fifty frascs and demand that they send their designs to my desk before beginning. Go, now."

Namter waved away the guard, then leaned his back on the wall. *Truegods...*They were only days away from finally harvesting this town as Tribute, yet Roache still deemed it necessary to interrupt Namter's duties in order to maintain the minute details of every aspect of their soon-to-be utterly irrelevant public image. No doubt the man was anxious about the end of his role. Once they were finished extracting Tribute from Huile, Lazarus would no longer be required to act the playboy, a job the man enjoyed far too much by Namter's reckoning. Such a life had always been the Roache's dream, and he wished to squeeze every last minute of it.

Soon it would be over; Namter just needed patience. Soon his duty would be complete, and the world would be placed on its proper path. All these irrelevant nuisances, these passing humiliations, the endless games his master played, all would fade to memory. The time of Reification was near at hand.

Calming himself well enough, he turned to find Brother Valere walking up the stairs.

"Watcher," he whispered, "our new Brother did not succeed in his initiation. The Brothers are taking it as an ill omen."

Namter closed his eyes and let out a sigh.

"Well, remove the corpse. I'll address them."

Verus held the bottle between his legs as he sat, somewhat slouched, eye focused forward.

"I can…" Marcel began, as Verus thrust his finger up and continued to think. He had been like this for the past ten minutes. His gaze moved slowly around the room, and then finally landed on Marcel. Verus stared at him with something in his eye, not quite suspicion, not quite anger, some sort of puzzlement, mixed between frustration and bemusement. Or perhaps Marcel was merely reading that into the man, his countenance was a strange one. Then, slowly, a smile started to crawl over Verus's face.

"It's a gift," he said.

Marcel nodded along, not sure his meaning.

"A gift. My own gift, subtler and sublime. You see? The contract is broken, with no fault on me." He stood up suddenly. "I always knew the man was scum. I've been waiting long for the moment I could leave him behind, but duty, Marcel, duty demanded I stay. Now I get to wipe the scum clean away. It's a gift, a gift for my service."

Marcel stood as well. "Let me dismantle his machinery. Let me sneak in what I need and I can have it done before the twenty-fifth, have it ready by his opening day."

"You will, Marcel," Verus nodded, "while I throttle the man. I will wrap my fist around his neck and force him to watch as his treachery falls to pieces." There was a feverish glint of glee in his eye. "After all these years it will be the last thing he sees."

Verus stepped over and grabbed Marcel's bruised shoulder with such force that Marcel's vision turned to black for a second, and he swore. The foreman just grinned.

"In another time you'd have been a brother, Talwar," he said. "Maybe there will still be such a time, but now." His smile was the widest Marcel had ever seen on the man's face, stretching his wrinkled, dust-worn skin. "Now, we squash a Roache."

For the Eyes of Colonel Goss,

Maintain your forces in Holtag, reinforcements are not necessary. Victory has been achieved in Huile, the UCCR assault has crashed and been routed. Though defensive actions have never been my ideal, our foe was easily baited and destroyed. Send word back to Kaimark that our campaign shall continue onwards, any retreat now will only bring conspicuous shame upon the Imperator. No doubt those cravat-collectors have prayed that the star of Agrippus would burn out here at the edge of Bastillia. Let them sit in their cowardice and spite, our victories have merely begun.

Continue surveillance on Colonel Lechslov. The more I gather in this rats' nest, the more convinced I am that he has played a role in the coup here. I find it preposterous that provincials would rise up on their own accord, without some promise of military aid, overt or covert. This town is a prize I have no interest in, and I do not think its sangleum fields, gravid as they are, are worth the blood we have spilled in order to protect them.

On that note, send orders to the East Vidish Extraction Co. I have too long suffered the presence of this perfidious Mr. Roache. He is convinced that his hand in the whole coup imbroglio assures his own continued control of the refineries here. That is a misconception I had great pleasure in correcting. I informed the man that we shall transfer control to imperial oversight within a fortnight. Do work to make my words truthful.

This Roache is nothing more than a sycophant with pretensions, and if a certain prisoner's testimony is correct, completely unworthy of trust. He even attempted to earn my favor by recommending the use of sangleum gas as a weapon against our enemy. *A cowardly and shameful tactic, more befitting Resurgence terrorists than the honorable soldiery of the Imperator. The blond brute even runs his excuse for a refinery with mutant slave labor. It is barbaric. We will soon euthanize the pitiful mutants who remain and turn this slum of waste-scavenged machinery into something worthy of the Principate.*

Glory to the Imperator,
General Agrippus

—Final order sent by General Belona Agrippus.

Chapter 37

The location of the meeting had been switched, under Desct's insistence, to the subbasement of a subbasement of an abandoned show apartment. As they waited for the final stragglers to arrive, Desct explained to Sylvaine that the apartment above had once been the focus of a tour for him and other Resurgence noteworthies. At the time it was hailed as proof of Lazacorp's commitment to his mutant workers' safety and comfort. The structure had never been filled, dozens of empty rooms left for storage, the sewage and water lines never even connected.

It was a worse hideout, uncomfortably close to the Lazacorp guards' apartment complex, but the space was needed, for the revolution had spread beyond the mutant's council. Three dozen more were in attendance, plans needed to be arranged and fast.

Or so went Desct's logic. Sylvaine could only nod along, without words. The man commended her work with the clockbombs, a pile of which sat in the middle of the room, and she gave the requisite thanks, but she could manage nothing more.

All she could think about was Ysabel. Sylvaine had not asked Gualter, or any of the other mutants, what would happen to her. Ysabel's expression had said it well enough. A quick flicker of realization that she was not going to leave Blackwood Row alive. Ysabel hadn't hesitated, but had run forward, to throw her life down and clean up the mess Sylvaine had unthinkingly created.

When the meeting proper started, Sylvaine slunk to the back of the crowd. Marcel took up the center of the room and everyone else's attention. He explained, through some long-winded narrative whose details Sylvaine could not bring her attention to, how he had set the two Lazacorp partners against each other. The tinder had apparently been dense, and he had only needed a simple spark, or so he claimed. It was good news, theoretically, and maybe even impressive, but then again the man was a UCCR soldier. After a century of rebellions, Sylvaine half-heartedly mused, maybe fomenting civil wars was just in his blood.

"It will be the damn-near ideal diversion," Desct exclaimed, listening to Marcel's tale, "the two will wrap rope around each other's throats, and we shall provide the final noose."

Sylvaine leaned back on a rotting, old crate. How strange it was that she should care for a person she had barely known. She would not have called Ysabel a true friend, though perhaps in time she could have been. They had talked a few hours about childhood misadventures, out-of-date gossip, and other inanities. It was a light conversation about nothing significant. It was one of the few such conversations Sylvaine could remember.

She noticed that the crowd had gone silent a moment. All eyes had turned onto Celina, who sat arms crossed. The mutant woman allowed the nervous tension to hang a moment, then another moment, before finally nodding.

"I've said since the beginning we need to act," she said. "As far as I'm concerned you all finally caught up. Get the two fighting, blow up the monolith, as long as we can smash some Lazacorp skulls."

With this assent the crowd exploded back into discussion, relief clear in every word. Now the revolution was real, the enemy divided, themselves united. Sylvaine tried to gather some hope from this, from the fact that she was helping bring about their freedom. But not for Ysabel. No victory could help her now.

Discussions cycled through one another, on organization, timing, angles of attack, armaments. Marcel offered to fight. Desct shot his offer down.

"When the smoke dissipates," Desct said, "Huile will no doubt have questions about what in fucking Inferno has occurred. We'll need a liaison to get to them early, convince them our enemy is Lazacorp, not Huile. City Hall will be recalcitrant, too many have their fingers embedded in Lazacorp's pie, but I have hope for the citizenry. You're a war hero, Talwar, and more vitally, not a mutant. We need you to talk, not die for the cause."

Marcel assented to his role after a very short debate, his outward bravado undercut, in Sylvaine's eye, by the fact that his stiff posture and fear-tinged words had instantly relaxed once he realized he would not be in the line of duty. She didn't judge the man much for his muffled hesitancy; it was good sense not to want to throw oneself in front of bullets and bayonets.

The man's sense or cowardice did not take up too much of Sylvaine's thoughts, she was instead caught up in her own fear. The mutants cared for their kind, and no doubt Ysabel's capture had not gone unnoticed. Nor, no doubt, had the death of the other mutant shot in the chaos. She dreaded the questions that would arise. Why had the dictaphone been destroyed? At whose feet should the blame be laid? The answers were clear enough, and Sylvaine wouldn't lie. They would see her as the failure she was.

Desct coughed for attention.

"My brothers and sisters," he said. "Before we march to our glory, it is imperative we remember those we have lost. Three more have perished since our last meeting, three more souls to be avenged. Tricius Mal, a venerable member of our council, and personal friend, passed away this morning from a longstanding chest infection. He will be missed. Yury, a recent addition to our community, was killed by gunshot during a cowardly Lazacorp raid. And finally Ysabel Delag," Sylvaine lowered her head, "captured in the same raid. A minute of silence, please."

The room fell to quiet, only the distant drips of water echoing. Sylvaine waited for the questioning, waited for the accusations, waited and wondered why she had the power to doom the woman, but not save her.

The questions didn't come. As soon as the minute was over, the mutants were back to discussing practicalities of the coming battle.

"We still have a cache of hammers, wrenches, even some makeshift spears down in the sewers near the western wall," one mutant offered.

"Make sure to avoid the wider streets," Desct ordered, "alleyways work to our advantage."

A shared minute was all Ysabel got. Her death was simply accepted. None thought to blame the engineer. This, it seemed, was just something that happened, another body tossed aside.

And so Sylvaine sat, alone.

"We have reached the decisive moment," Desct said, standing in the middle of the group. "Here stands the culmination of years of planning, we shall reap fruits grown from countless deaths, untold torment. But we have made it. Three mornings from now the sun shall shine on a freed Mutanthood." He strolled in a circle, taking time to look every person in the eye, even Sylvaine. "That is if, and only if, we come together as one. We must fight with the ferocity of the chained and the cunning of the revolutionary. We must fight with love in our hearts for our brothers and sisters who have suffered and with fury unyielding for those who have induced that suffering. Though our aims are freedom, we cannot forget our pain, nor forgive our adversaries. I can promise you that Roache and Verus will not be allowed to live, that I will not rest my hand until both have been ripped to tiny fucking scraps."

He gestured to a mutant at a far corner who waved down a cramped hallway. Three more mutants walked in, led by the first, their bodies thin, their ears scabbed.

"Despite claims that we have been sitting idle under the boot of Lazarus Roache," Desct said, a quick glance towards Celina, "our preparations have in fact spanned years, predating my own tenure. There are those among us who have already made their sacrifices, have taken blade to eardrum in order to deafen that horrid voice, so that they may strike unimpeded against the very head of this monster called Lazacorp." The three figures sat, looking towards Desct. Their expression were flat and grim, the faces of those who had long been willing to die for their cause, with little concern for their life after. "They will be our sword against Roache. And our dear ally, Kayip shall lead their assault."

Kayip nodded. "You have been kind to allow me here, to stand with you. I have known the sins of Verus and Roache for many years. It is my own sin that I have not been able to put a stop to them, that I have not been able to prevent the horrors that have befallen you. I seek to atone for this sin through blood, be it mine or theirs. I shall join your fight, I shall execute the twin demons, and will gladly die by your side if it should come to that..."

Sylvaine sat and watched as Kayip continued his speech, as the monk thrust his arms up and promised blood, as the closest thing she had to a friend she had offered again and again to throw his life away.

The meeting cleared without incident. Sylvaine and Kayip led Marcel back to his quarters, where the man fell asleep almost instantly. She walked with Kayip down through the winding shanties of the mutant camp, to the entrance to the Underway.

They passed down into a collapsed basement, and Kayip turned to give his farewell for the night. Before the monk could speak, Sylvaine found her lips moving.

"It was my fault," she said. "With Ysabel."

The man looked at her, but did not respond.

"The dictaphone," she explained, "the guards came because of me."

"I know," Kayip said. His tone wasn't angry, nor gentle, nor confused. It was a plain statement of fact.

She stared up at him. "They should know. I think."

"Desct does," Kayip said. "He was worried that some mutants were attempting their own escape, that they would draw attention. When I told him what happened his nerves were soothed."

"Soothed?" Sylvaine said. "A woman was dragged away to her death, a man was shot! People died."

"Yes," Kayip said. "And many more have died before. And more will die tomorrow."

Sylvaine pulled her arm to her chest. "That's not exactly comforting."

Kayip thought on this, and then sat on an outcropping of pipes. "Comfort does not change it. But I will say this. You did not pull the trigger, nor did you tell her to sacrifice away her life. If I had not taken you through the Underway, you would not have damaged the dictaphone. If Roache had not abused you so, you would have never come here."

"I still lost control." Sylvaine said. "I went wild like an anima..." she choked back the word and hung her head. "I... lost control and people died. Again."

"I will not tell you not to feel guilt," Kayip said, "but you must not let yourself be crushed by it." The monk went silent for a moment and scratched at the side of his mask. "I have made mistakes, Sylvaine, and in my haste to remedy my deeds I have made... further mistakes." He shook his head. "Redemption is the domain only of the Demiurge, one must bear the burden of their past. For some this burden is light, for others, the respite comes only when they reunite with their creator."

"And is that why you're so keen on tossing your own life away?" Sylvaine said, with sudden rage in her voice, "Why you'd gladly die fighting? Nothing we can do can bring Ysabel back, can bring anyone back. Why do you need to die too?"

"Sylvaine... I..." The engineer was even taken aback by her own anger, and Kayip seemed doubly so. "I need to fight. I am one of the few here trained in the arts of combat, one of the few immune to Roache's words. And I have business with that man."

"So if we succeed, then what?" Sylvaine was barely able to keep from shouting, her hair stood on end. "If you die fighting, what am I to do when the smoke clears?"

"I admit I haven't planned beyond the fight..." Kayip started.

"You need me, you need me for the clockbombs."

"Sylvaine!" Kayip said, a hint of anger in his own voice. "This is larger than us."

"I just... I don't have anything. Nothing. Just revenge, but then what? You're the only one left, Kayip." Sylvaine slumped back on the wall. "I know I haven't suffered the worst here, I know that this whole... whatever, is more important. But this was never my fight. I'm just some ferral playing engineer."

"Sylvaine..." Kayip said, grabbing her shoulder.

"This isn't my fight. So don't I deserve something? Not money, not success, just... someone left."

The large man kneeled down, his one eye soft in its gaze. "We will strike quickly, an ambush," he said. "Roache's voice is too much a risk, but we will be sudden, and careful. Then I will return. You are right, this isn't our fight, I will not waste time in the streets, one strike and I will return to you, safe. Is that all right, Sylvaine?"

She nodded slowly, only now realizing that she had been crying. "Thank you."

Chapter 38

Marcel pushed back the tubing, trying to orient himself inside the guts of the machine. He forced himself not to rush, to think clearly. They were almost finished, tonight would be the night of revolution, the night when Lazacorp was purged, the mutants freed, when Huile would finally shed its past and become the city he always knew it was meant to be. But that was all incumbent on placing the clockbombs correctly, and the pressure of the coming uprising felt more crushing than the overwhelming clunking mass of the machine that surrounded him.

He searched between bent pipes, dripping canisters, and inert gearwork for the proper location to place the hunk of metal. Sylvaine had explained the spot in utterly bewildering detail, drawing out the technical schematics and pointing exactly, but as it turned out the darkened inside of the machine bore little clear resemblance to that scribble on notebook paper. He was sweating, but unable to lift his arms to wipe his forehead, struggling as he was to keep ahold of the weight of the clockbomb. He was unsure if its prodigious heft was due to the extra faux casing Sylvaine had installed as a disguise, or some weight he was giving to it himself.

He coughed and blinked in the dark. He wasn't wearing a gas mask, and had no rifle slung over his back, but he couldn't shake the odious familiarity. Last time he snuck explosives into Lazacorp he had lost his leg and his friends. He slowed his breathing and placed his shirt over his nose to keep out the dust. This time would be different, he promised himself.

"You okay in there?" Sylvaine asked from outside, her voice echoing in the machine.

"Yes," Marcel whispered back sharply, "don't be so loud!"

"We're good out here. You don't have to be exact, just get it close to the high-pressure centrifugal piping unit."

"The...?" Marcel asked back.

"The... twisty pipe thing. Looks like a giant spring."

"Got it," Marcel said, staring at a tube that was maybe at least vaguely twisty, vibrating slightly as something whizzed through it. He placed the bomb down gingerly, turning its hidden dial, before pushing himself out of the machine.

Marcel wondered if he had needed to snap at the engineer for her volume. The night before had been tense as they worked together to finalize the ideal spots for sabotage, Sylvaine deep in the guts of the machine, Marcel pretending to look busy. Several times mutants had come running to warn them that Crat was coming to warn Marcel that other Roache-loyal Lazacorp guards were on their patrol. So Sylvaine would hide, and Marcel would wait to nod at Crat's warning and then hide as well. After the footsteps echoed Crat would knock his signal and leave. Then Marcel would crawl out, followed by Sylvaine, and the whole play would reset.

This night had, oddly, been far quieter. Not a single guard had walked by, and the clockbombs had been planted with ease. Everything was going to plan so well that it was making Marcel nervous.

He tried to hide his fears as several mutants assisted Sylvaine in lifting up a large piece of chassis near the bottom of the machine, and then set to work screwing it back into place. The engineer was covered in dust and soot, but wore a smile wider than Marcel had ever seen grace her face.

She looked up and down the machine. "It's a thing of beauty in its own way."

"You having seconds thoughts?" Marcel asked.

Sylvaine chuckled. "No, no, I'm glad to be sending it to Inferno, but..." She shook her head. "Never mind."

He glanced at the titanic machine. "That'll do it?"

"Yeah," Sylvaine replied. "But I know I built a few more clockbombs than this."

Marcel's brief panic must have been visible because Sylvaine quickly blurted out "but I planned to have more than needed. We have enough."

"And you're sure it will take out the whole facility?"

"Listen," Sylvaine sighed, louder than she needed to. "Think of this machine as a heart. We are grafting bombs to its veins: the sangleum pipes. Destroying them will remove the liquid pressure, like we're cutting the wrists of the machine, meaning no sangleum will flow to the generator, so no power. The whole facility will bleed out, as such."

"Sure," Marcel said, "but what if they are able to somehow refuel—"

"Now imagine that this blood is flammable, and that we are also striking a match in its very heart, so that even if they could make a last minute infusion of sangleum blood, it wouldn't matter because the heart would be a smoldering mass of metal."

"Ok, I ge—"

"And! Imagine this 'heart' had more explosive blood flowing through it at any one time than through the rest of the body combined, so when it lit up it would combust with enough force to turn all the other organs into red splats on the wall."

Marcel crossed his arms. "I think you lost track of your metaphor a few times there."

Sylvaine laughed and wiped blackened sweat from her brow. "Point is, I'm an engineer, Marcel, I know how to make things blow up."

"So we're finished, then?" Sabyn asked, as he finished attaching the last piece of chassis. Sylvaine nodded, and the mutant gestured to his comrades below. He grabbed a hammer and swung it a few times, before starting to walk down the stairs.

"We got Nozka coming to help make sure you guys can make it out. Otherwise..."

"Thanks," Marcel said.

"I was hoping for something more on the lines of 'good luck,'" Sabyn said, as he started to jog down. The man was eager, whether for freedom or revenge, Marcel couldn't guess, but he didn't begrudge him either way.

Marcel glanced back at the machine. It groaned in its half-awakened state, as if it knew what was coming. "So... How big an explosion are we talking about here?"

Sylvaine scratched her arm. "Well, given the amount of sangleum it's currently pumping... I can't do exact calculations... but... probably would be best to stay outside a three-block radius to be safe." She pulled out her watch. "Better to do so... soon. Very soon."

As they reached the bottom of the machine, Sylvaine crawled back into her crate, with only a small, perfunctory complaint. Marcel slid the lid over. It was, mercifully, the last time they would have to go through the charade.

He pushed the crate down back hallways of the monolith, stopping every few seconds to allow Sylvaine to listen in for footsteps. Each time she knocked and Marcel shoved on towards the back exit. He was surprised by how quiet the structure was. Even during the previous midnights there had been one or two guards wandering around, whether under Verus's influence or Roache's.

"I think we're clear," Marcel said, as they approached the final bend.

Sylvaine didn't respond.

"I said I think we're clear."

Three quick knocks reverberated from inside of the crate, code for 'shut up.' Marcel stopped, and then leaned down. Sylvaine whispered something. He put his ear to the wood.

"I smell blood," she said.

Marcel stood back up slowly, turning as he made out a sound behind him. A mutant leaned out from another hallway, silently but frantically gesturing at him to come back. Marcel held his breath and started to turn the crate.

"Talwar?"

It was Crat's voice. Marcel halted a moment, but it was too late. The man had heard him, Marcel had no choice. The mutant was already scampering away.

He pushed forward around the bend. Crat was there, before the shut loading bay, standing over a body of a Lazacorp guard. The slumped man's neck was slit, as Crat wiped his knife clean with a rag.

"You finished, Talwar?" the man asked.

"Yes," Marcel said, trying not to stutter as he watched the dead guard's blood pool. He noticed a second corpse lying a few metres behind, long since bled out.

"No thank-you's?" Crat asked, gesturing his blade. "I made your task easier. That one behind me is a Roache loyalist anyhow, so it's easier now than later. Not sure about this one, but best not to take the risk."

"Right," Marcel said. "Well, good, then." He started to push the crate forward again. Crat stopped it with his boot.

"It's all fixed?" he said.

"Yes, I told you." Marcel said.

"Then I'll take you down to Verus," Crat said. "He'll let you explain Roache's treachery to his face."

Marcel tapped the box. "I'll meet you there. I just need to return this."

Crat's boot didn't move. "What's in the box?"

"Oh," Marcel said. He pushed back the top a little bit and reached in. The layer of machine parts and disguised clockbombs that they had previously hid Sylvaine with were now entirely installed in the machine, leaving only a ragged and torn sheet of burlap to blanket the engineer from any prying eyes. Marcel grabbed the only piece of metal he could find, a heavy wrench.

"You know," Marcel continued, waving the spanner around, "just my tools and all that."

"I'll get someone on it. Come on, don't waste time," Crat said.

"It'll only take a minute," Marcel said.

Crat squinted at him, then pointed his knife down. "What's in the crate, Talwar?"

"I told you," Marcel said, but Crat pushed past. He lifted up the top and tossed it aside.

"What in..." the man started.

Marcel swung. He swung the wrench as fast and as hard as he could manage, right into the back of Crat's head. There was a crunch, and the bulky man fell to his side.

Sylvaine scrambled up and looked down, eyes wide.

"Shit," Marcel said, grabbing the unconscious man's hand. "We need to get him out of here, so when he wakes up..."

"Marcel," Sylvaine, said, as he struggled to pull the body, "I don't think he's getting up."

Marcel stopped, and took a moment to feel the man's pulse. A chill ran through him. There wasn't a beat.

"Demiurge," Marcel said. "I killed him."

"Well you did hit him pretty hard. I guess the revolution's starting early."

Sylvaine pulled herself out of the box as Marcel stared at the body. Crat had been a brute who had made his money off slavery and sadism. Marcel knew that many such men would die this night, yet still he had been a man, a living, breathing man, just seconds ago. Now he was a corpse.

Marcel staggered over, leaned on the wall, and vomited out his small dinner.

"You okay, Marcel?" Sylvaine asked.

He nodded, spitting up a wad of bile. Marcel had planted bombs before, had made plans that he knew had led to fatalities, but he never realized how different it felt to kill someone directly. His hand was shaking, and he realized he had never let go of the wrench. Its end was stained red. He dropped it quickly.

"Psst!" came a voice.

The mutant had reappeared. He walked over on a stiff, chitinous leg, and eyed the body before gesturing to follow. Marcel swallowed his sickness as best as he could, as the mutant led them out the door.

Their guide introduced himself as Nozka and ended pleasantries there. They followed his limping form through the backways of the refineries, down hidden alleyways, under silent pumps, and through mutant shanties, a cautious circuitous route.

The streets were deathly silent. As they walked, Marcel could make out mutant forms, hiding behind and glancing from doorways and drilling equipment. On a closer look, Marcel notice that they were each holding hammers, or wrenches, or some variety of long sharp objects scavenged recently or long since hidden away.

"Best route out, down by the sewer entrance near the wall," said Nozka. "Still some guards 'round, smarter to wait them out." He glanced to Marcel. "You set the bombs, right?" There was a slight fear in his voice, as if he didn't have the hope left to believe it.

"Eight minutes," Sylvaine said, flashing her watch.

He led them up a shanty tower built on the fire escape of an old tenement near the wall. It took a few minutes, clambering past other mutants who sat and watched with eagerness, but they were able to find their own spot, near the top.

From that vantage point they had a clear vision of the monolith, several blocks away. The streetlights were dim to near black, which was usual. What was stranger was the lack of torchlights flickering up and down as guards made their usual rounds. One flash did appear around a street corner, two Lazacorp guards strolling around the bend, talking among themselves. A pair of shadows descended upon them from an open doorway. Not mutant forms, but two men in hoods, with quick blades. The guards were dead within seconds.

Verus's coup was underway.

"They're gathering," Sylvaine whispered. She pointed and Marcel followed her finger down the streets, where he could just make out, through the frames of two blocks of buildings, the brickwork of one of the central offices. All seemed usual until, *there,* he made out some quick movement, a man kneeling by the edge of the building, rifle in hand. Then two men, then three, then a dozen, their shadows thrown by the bright lights shining out from the windows of the office. No doubt that was where Crat had wanted to take Marcel. An ambush destined to be ambushed itself.

Nearer still, some of the mutants appeared to be getting antsy. A few had stepped onto the street, looking around, walking in the direction of the office. Marcel grabbed the handrail and some of the mutants around him whispered nervously. The two hooded figures who had been dragging away the guards' corpses now noticed the approaching mutants and shouted something. They waved their blades and the mutants stopped, seemingly unsure of whether to move forward and attack, or run back. One of the two hooded figures dashed into the nearby building, and the standoff continued.

Then, suddenly, a crack of gunfire. Shouts echoed out from around the office complex, the men dashing out to surround the building. Muzzle flashes lit the streets, light flicked on from dozens of other buildings, confused guards running out into the street. The squad of mutants took this moment to move forward, the hooded figure running back in a panic, as more mutants left their hiding places and moved in the direction of the chaos.

It was all a strangely familiar sight in its own way, watching over a battlefield from up high, unable now to make any contribution one way or another. Again, Marcel was in the middle of it all, but completely detached, he could see the violence, but was totally removed from it.

A crackling sound screeched out, and the familiar monotone of Lazarus Roache started to drone out of the dictaphone speakers around them.

"All workers remain calm. Stay inside your quarters. All workers remain calm. Stay inside your quarters."

Instantly, as a single entity, the workers froze, some nearby groaning. Those on the street jerked in stiff motions and slowly started to turn back into the buildings.

Sylvaine bent over violently, stifling a scream, clutching the railing as if it were a life raft. She shook and jabbed her ears into her arms.

Marcel grabbed her arm. "Are you okay?" he asked.

She muttered something that he couldn't catch.

"Sylvaine?"

"Four," she said.

She was holding something in her hand.

"What?" Marcel asked.

"Three."

Marcel leaned in to see.

"Two."

It was her watch.

"One."

Chapter 39

"Promptness," Lazarus Roache leaned back in his chair, "is the key to any functioning business partnership, don't you agree?"

"Yes sir," Namter said as he signed Roache's name to the bottom of an export document, one of hundreds stacked beside him.

Lazarus sipped his tea and studied the empty conference room. As the office building functioned as a neutral ground of sorts, it held none of the ornate and expensive decorations that Roache habitually hung over every wall. Namter's master tapped his spoon on the side of his cup as he thought.

"No, that is too modest a statement," he said. "Promptness is the key to any functional relationship at all, in business, in diplomacy, in married life I would imagine, that grimmest of partnerships. To leave one waiting, why, you might as well piss in their tea. Do you understand my meaning?"

"Of course, sir," Namter said, staring down at the scrawled letters, stunned by the gall on display. Did these raiders really think Lazacorp would pay double for transport? Sure Lazacorp's upcoming demand would be high, but this was unacceptable gouging. He tossed the estimate into a side folder. He would deal with these idiots later.

"It's been seven years, Namter. We are nearing the end of our contract and still Verus insists on burning our time like firewood." He sipped again, finishing the tea. Namter poured him another cup with a free hand, continuing to work with his other. "It's near midnight," Roache said. "What under the sky could Verus need a meeting now for?"

"I can't claim to know, sir," Namter said.

"He's bitter, that's what it is. I've done his job better than he could, so now he needs to keep us up on the eve of our triumph." Lazarus yawned. "I'm going to be baggy-eyed for the party tomorrow."

"I'm sure you will look very well," Namter assured him, as he wrote out some orders for nutrient-gruel to be delivered to Narida Heights. They would be transporting damn near a city's worth of Tribute; it was vital they were fed well enough to survive the journey.

Roache glanced down at his butler's scrawling pen. "Do you need to be doing that right now?"

"My apologies sir, but we are behind on some of the logistics. If I don't get everything in order, we may need to delay the Enterprise even further."

"Your worry will drive you into an early grave Namter. You let your mind swirl like this, well, I can't see how you'll even enjoy the party."

As if Namter had *ever* enjoyed any of Roaches farcical shows. He tapped his pen, then started on another form. "I don't wish to disagree with you sir, but I don't think we can risk letting the Tribute starve and rot while we are still organizing our caravans."

Roache sighed and sipped. "Fine, fine, at least put the pen down when Verus arrives. It makes us look unprofessional."

As if on cue, the door swung open. Namter stood, Roache sat, as the Awakener strolled in. His face wore an unusual calm, and

Namter's heart rose with the sudden hope that maybe this meeting was the stage for the reconciliation he had prayed for. Namter pulled out a seat for Verus, but the man remained standing.

"Took your time," Roache said, arms crossed. "What sort of business requires that I stay up until near-midnight, yet gives you the excuse to come thirty minutes late?"

"I thought a friend might be able to join us," said Verus, smirk wide, eye narrow. "He's still busy, it seems."

"A friend." Roache's gave an impression of a laugh. "I never took you as a man who made friends."

"Exceptions for all things," Verus replied. "And he is a mutual friend. Who you might have mistakenly thought a *late* friend."

"Later than you, it seems," Roache replied. Verus rolled his eye.

"Our Enterprise is complete," said Namter. Verus turned to him with a bitter gaze. "Have you taken the chance to inspect it? Soon we will be entirely prepared for the Reification, Awakener. I know we three have not always been amicable, but all is nearly finished, we've succeeded." His words had no effect on the man. If anything his anger seemed to grow.

"And you, Watcher," Verus said. "If you have indeed kept Watch. Is there anything else you would like to tell me about the Enterprise? About the work your master has done?"

"It's all there," Namter insisted. "It's as we planned. There's no need for past grudges to rule us when we are on the eve of our holy task."

Verus stepped closer. "Fidelity and obedience are essential, Watcher, you know this. Is there not something that you should be telling me?" His breath heated Namter's face, the anger overwhelming and incomprehensible.

"Don't speak to my butler like that!" Roache exclaimed. "Namter, back here." Namter reluctantly retreated back to the side of his master. Verus spat on the hardwood floor.

"Fine," he said. "I suspected as much."

"So did you just come here to get in one last jab?" asked Roache. "Still bitter about the Gall affair and realize you're running out of chances to complain? Fine then, say your piece, but do try to be quick about it."

Verus rested one fist on the table. "You're right, I am interested in engineering, but Gall is old news. Let's talk about Marcel." He leaned in across the table. "I never took the proper interest in that man, but I can see why you used him. Every conversation a new surprise."

Lazarus raised an eyebrow, but said nothing.

"You never told me, Roache," Verus said, face inching forward, "what the man did for his university studies."

"Is that the mystery you're searching for? The man flunked out of a medical program."

Verus halted his leaning. His eye flickered back and forth. "Even now you retreat to lies? What of his studies in engineering?"

"Is that what the man told you?" Roache laughed.

"He did more than tell me. He showed me some interesting findings."

Lazarus Roache stretched back on his chair, studying Verus. The two men did not speak for half a minute. They simply watched each other.

"Namter," Roache finally said, "don't you still have work to do? Filling out those inventory forms and authorizations and all that? I'm sure you can find a quiet room somewhere around here."

"Yes, sir," said Namter. "But I can wait until after the meeting."

"No need to wait," Roache waved him away.

"You heard your master," barked Verus. "Go on. Leave us."

Namter gathered his papers and left without a word.

He headed down the central stairs of the building, past a guard lounging in the hallway, taking a right at the main foyer, into a small empty office. He swept the papers of some insignificant clerk off the desk and got to work.

Once again he had been pushed to the side, in favor of his two masters' unending bickering. Once again the unity he sought was kicked to the ground and spat on.

He pulled out a letter written in near scribbles, a raider's approximation of text. Threats, it seemed, pleas and petitions for more slickdust, insistence that if their needs were not filled, the gang would not only fail to provide transport services, but instead practice their more habitual trade on Lazacorp caravans. This would require a response, maybe even a retaliatory order to one of the other raider gangs to keep things in line. How weary Namter was of raider bluster, how glad he was that he'd soon be done with it.

Namter heard a cough from outside. He glanced through the darkened window. There were no handtorch lights, no walking guards. Was some mutant skulking about past hours? He got up and squinted, the street outside was completely empty. Wait, no, he espied a figure there, a Lazacorp guard, in the dark, huddled against the side of the wall. Then another, a rifle in his hand, a hooded Brother beside him. Namter stared at the odd scene, unable to make sense of what the men were doing.

He turned suddenly at the sound of footsteps.

"Brother Lacius," Namter said with some surprise. "Did you come with the Awakener?"

The Brother wore his hood, his Oathblood orb hanging down and his hand deep in his pocket. As one of Verus's closest followers, it had been a good while since Lacius had last spoke to Namter with a friendly tone, yet still his sneer was shocking in its viciousness.

"Do not dare speak of him, traitor."

"Trai...?" Namter was only able to get out the first syllable before Lacius leapt at him, knife in his hand. He plunged it forward, and Namter jumped back, hand out. The blade slashed, cutting through Namter's glove and into his palm.

"Brother!" he shouted, as he grabbed his assailant's wrist and struggled. The man was younger than him by decades, stronger too. But Lacius was overeager, Namter twisted to the side and let the blade fall with the weight of the man, into the table. Lacius grunted as he tried to tug the knife out.

"Stop, Brother!" Namter shouted again.

Lacius started to scream out Truewords, grasping at his orb. He smashed it together between his two hands and winced as the glass cut his flesh, hesitating a moment with the pain. Namter took the chance, thrusting his already bloody hand into his Brother's, his blood mixing with the Oathblood coated on the embedded shards.

Namter shouted out his own command and the Oathblood responded. Lacius's arm burst into red, skin flying back in ribbons, flesh melting away into a pulsating mass of seething blood. The man screamed as this arm, not *his* anymore, swung back and forth from his shoulder, before plunging, suddenly, into his chest, cutting through skin and bone as it dug towards his heart. His shriek was intense and momentary, a last echo of pain as his body slumped over. The arm dissolved, leaving a caustic mark on the concrete floor.

Namter stumbled, panting, and caught himself on the table, unable to comprehend his brother's madness. He spared one look at the splayed form on the floor. It was a shame to use the power of the Truegods such, but Lacius's insanity gave him no choice. What could have driven him to attack his own Watcher so?

"What happened?" A guard stepped into the room, rifle in his hand. He glanced down at the corpse and retched. "Inferno's pits!" he spat.

Namter steadied himself to speak when a shot went off. The window blew in with a wave of glass and the guard was flung back, head burst open. Namter ducked the window as more gunshots cracked.

An attack! he realized, though the *who* and *why* escaped him. He crawled out to the guard's corpse and grabbed a pistol from his holster, before sneaking over to the main foyer. A single guard stood there with his rifle aimed towards the front door, a bewildered look under his helmet. With a bang the lock on the door was shot off from outside, and men in Lazacorp gear stormed in. They peppered the single guard, who missed his lone shot, before turning toward Namter.

He didn't waste time, tossing out his hand and shouting. Drops of burning blood flew out, summoning up a wall of black fire that blocked off the entrance, and covered the room in a sudden gale of smoke. Men screamed, stumbling back as they were caught in flames that swung at them with needle-nailed hands and amorphous mouths, tearing and biting as much as burning.

A voice droned outside. Roache's. *All workers remain calm...* Someone had set off the alarm, mutants were causing trouble, but that gave no explanation for the attack. Namter didn't have time to make sense of it all, he kept low and tried to make his way to the main stairwell. Bullets flew above him, and he tried to make sense out of the many shouts. They were a mix of screamed orders and panicked pleas, but one stood out:

"Get Roache!" he heard, clear as anything.

The world shook, a great boom reverberated throughout the building, glass shattering and people shouting. Just as suddenly, the lights went out.

Namter blinked, reorienting himself as he crawled forward. He squinted out a far window. Shapes moved through crackling gunfire, but the buildings behind them were black, the moon the only source of constant light. Lazarus's voice had been silenced.

He crept up to the main stairway. Footsteps clanged upwards. Had the assailants found another entrance already? Namter glanced in, back against the wall. The only light was muzzle flashes, but in those brief moments he saw them, mutants, wielding cudgels and blades, and at their head:

The monk.

Accursed blade unfurled, gaze forward, leading the charge, the damnable monk.

Namter slowed his breath and tried to think. *The back stairwell!* He dashed, through a narrow hallway, keeping his head low. The door to the stairwell was locked. He had a key ring in his pocket, but no time to cycle through them. With his hand on the knob he demanded it be open.

The door flung back, hinges smashed, as centuries' worth of rust overtook it. It folded in on itself as hand of metal formed from its edges, pulling it into its center with a violent rage, until it was nothing more than crumpled ball of pained metal.

A scream from above.

"Stop, stop, I command you to stay back!"

Lazarus Roache rushed down the scaffold of stairs, a mutant right on his heels, swinging a sledgehammer.

"Stay, sit!" Roache shouted, but the mutant made no reaction. The pursuer's ears were bandaged, and Namter understood immediately.

"He's deafened himself," Namter shouted, as he raised his pistol and fired. Two missed bullets clanged up the stairwell, before the third hit its mark. The mutant fell to the ground, choking on blood and agonized moans.

"Namter, dearest Namter, you haven't betrayed me?" Lazarus asked, as he grabbed his butler.

"Of course not!"

Lazarus held him with both arms tight. Namter stiffened under the unprecedented display. "Oh, my precious Namter," he said. "My gentle, loyal friend."

Namter felt wetness on the side of his arm. Was Roache crying? He stepped back to see it was blood, a great gash on Lazarus's side, through his coat, undershirt, skin, open flesh oozing.

"The mutant did this?" Namter said. "Or... the monk?"

"The monk?" Roache said. "Yes...I saw him, in the madness. But no, no, it was Verus. He has betrayed us!"

Namter mouthed the name but couldn't speak it. The accusation was impossible, but then, who else could had the power to plunge Blackwood Row into chaos?

"Verus has betrayed us," Roache repeated, "betrayed our cause."

He moaned and limped forward. "Where are we going?" he said.

Namter hadn't a plan until that moment, but as the gunshots echoed down the hallways, and shouts from above, he realized the only option.

"Down the Underway," he said. "There's a garage only three blocks from here. Can you walk?"

As he said this, he noticed that his master's wounds had already healed halfway, the blood moving like grasping tendrils, and interweaving among themselves, skin stitching itself back together like a clasp locker. The Oathblood within Lazarus, his gift. Sometimes even Namter could forget its power.

Without a further word they descended down to the basement of the building. With slow groping Namter was able to find a pair of handtorches in a supply closet. Carefully following the beam of light, they searched out a service tunnel Namter had ordered built some years ago but never visited. He remembered the project having gone faster than he expected, and, as he had suspected, shortcuts had been taken, old Underway passages repurposed in lieu of, but still billed as, completely new structures.

A few dozen metres down the light hit a hole in the unpainted stone. The new passageway was cleanly cut. There was only one blade he knew of which could slice through stone, but there was no time to dwell on that, nor on the horrors above, which he could hear even down there. With a nod he led his master forward.

The route was meandering and foul-smelling, but they made good speed, Namter using the piping as a guideline. Normal sewage for the guard's apartment complexes, fat and silent pipes for the old pumps. He desperately triangulated the direction in his head, and pointed the way of his best guess. Roache shuddered as they waded through muck of indeterminate origin, but he held his tongue well enough.

They came up through some narrow stairwell, Namter hoping his math was correct. No, the situation was beyond him now, he could only pray that through this destruction he still held the favor of the Truegods, that they would lead him on his path.

His piety was rewarded as he turned a corner to see several rows of autotrucks. The garage doors were wide open and beyond them, pandemonium. Mutants and Lazacorp guards fought each other, bayonets stabbing desperately against mobs of red bodies, who fought with a mad frenzy. Madder still was that it appeared several of the guards were brawling amongst themselves, or else shooting indiscriminately. If this was a coup, Namter could see no sense in it. Verus was burning the whole of Blackwood Row to the ground!

He gestured for Lazarus to stay back, then snuck to the key hanger and grabbed several. There were a few autocars parked, all too small, and a large multi-armed tread-driller, which was far too slow and conspicuous. He set his gaze on a large autotruck near the front, which looked like it had the horsepower to trample over some bodies if need be. He stepped close and waved Lazarus over, when a shout cut over the chaos.

"Roache!"

One of the mutants by the gate was pointing, and several more turned, with both fear and rage in their gazes.

"Stand in place!" Lazarus shouted. The nearby mutants froze up en masse, though some immediately started to twitch, desperately trying to break away from the chains of Lazarus's voice.

Namter jumped into the driver seat and pushed opened the passenger door, before twisting the key and spurring the autotruck into life.

"Look at the mutants next to you. Kill them. Now!" Roache shouted and then ran.

The slaves did as they were commanded. Some struggled fruitlessly, their movement slowed, but unyielding. One bludgeoned the woman next to him, another drove her sharpened, rust-shard spear into another slave's stomach, and one unarmed mutant took to strangling his comrade. By the time Lazarus made it to the autotruck all were dead or dying, aside from one woman, who, task completed, dropped her blade in horror. She screeched and clutched at the decrepit old mutant who bled out beneath her, trying to mend the wound she had a moment before opened.

"Drive, drive!" Roache commanded, but Namter didn't need the instruction. He plowed through the dead and dying, crashing into the street. He turned and put his foot to the pedal, swerving between or just driving over the combatants, both mutant and man. Gunshots perforated brick walls, and bodies lay in their dozens, but after a few blocks the intense melee cleared some, and they were able to turn onto one of the main roads.

It was here Namter noticed the smoke, first from his rear mirror, the plume billowing up and blocking the stars behind him. The realization hit him at once: why the power had gone out, what the earth-shaking blast had been. He could imagine Verus turning against Roache, even Verus encouraging such bloodshed, but that... that was their Enterprise, their holy goal, the realization of seven years. To destroy that was not to betray mere men.

Namter drove, Roache panting in the seat next to him, out from the chaos, from the carnage and screams, from the deaths and that smoking pile of rubble that had once stood as a beacon of true, agonizing redemption. He drove away from Blackwood Row.

Chapter 40

The world shook. The monolith burst out in flame. Walls crumbled and the roof fell into a billowing cloud of smoke that burst out in every direction. Thousands of lights blinked out to black, and with them Roache's voice cut off suddenly.

Sylvaine sighed, holding her watch close, as the fire escape she stood on shook from the reverberations. The voice was gone, the horrible clawing words had crackled out into nothing. She was shivering, nauseous, hair drenched in cold sweat, but she was herself again, in control.

The silence of the dictaphones was now filled by jubilant cheers, mutants running out from every structure, thousands of footsteps charging towards the office complex, or else up into guards' apartment buildings. The mutants on the fire escape, who had been watching alongside Sylvaine and Marcel, now rushed down the stairway, with the sole exclusion of Nozka. Some whooped with excitement, jumping steps at a leap, others said nothing, their expressions grim. Within a minute the whole structure was vacated, the mutant silhouettes below illuminated by moonlight. Gunshots rang out, but now their sounds combined with the shouts of the mutants' assault. The muzzle fire revealed glimpses of chaos, panicked visages of Lazacorp guards as they were hit by a wave of red flesh.

"It's like the Battle of Huile Field," Marcel mumbled after a minute.

"What? Sylvaine asked.

"We can see it all from up here. Close, but so distant, like a cinegraph show."

Then a gunshot echoed close and glass shattered few metres above. Marcel leapt back to avoid the falling shards.

"Not that distant," Sylvaine said, as she started to descend the stairs.

The streets had made themselves suddenly bare. Whatever sickly, slave-fueled life this neighborhood had once contained was all gone now. The dark streets and empty husks of buildings reminded Sylvaine of her brief time out in the Wastes.

Of course, this illusion of deathly calm did not trick Sylvaine's ears. The cacophony of the nearby combat was lively enough, and even this far she could smell the blood. Marcel moved with clear agitation as they snuck through the streets, following their mutant guide.

"Perhaps we should stay," Marcel said, glancing back. "It's not fair to the mutants that I'm fleeing right as the fighting begins."

"Now don't you start," Sylvaine snapped. "Gears-grit, as if you were going to be any use. You'll be more helpful in Huile, anyway."

"Right." Marcel nodded. "Of course, I was just... Never mind." Her tone had been harsh, but now wasn't the time to let idiotic fancies grow.

"This way, quickly," Nozka said, leading them down an alleyway. They cut past an empty growth of shanties and through the guts of a silent refinery structure, into an open boulevard.

"Back!" Sylvaine said suddenly, ears perked from the sound of rapid footstep.

As they stepped back several Lazacorp guards dashed out from an adjoining street. Sylvaine hadn't a clue if they were Roache's men or Verus's, or if that distinction even mattered anymore. As the guards turned the corner, out rushed a dozen mutants. One guard turned and fired, killing two of the mutants, but the rest of them charged onward, launching themselves onto the panicked guards, swinging down cudgels and blades. They moved swiftly, grabbing the rifles out of the dying guards' hands. One even took a helmet, which he struggled to fit over his horns. A woman at the back turned and squinted, unsure, in Sylvaine's and Marcel's direction.

"Revolution!" Marcel shouted, fist to chest, with Nozka quickly joining his cry.

The mutants cheered and rushed back towards the fray, newly armed.

After this their travel was almost easygoing. They moved further and further from the center of the fighting, even as it seemed, from the distant sounds, that the battle itself had spread. Finally they reached a large Underway grate, sitting below and stained by an interlocked mess of pipework extruding from several nearby buildings. Sylvaine focused and lifted the heavy grate with a spark from her glove.

"It's a clear path from here," Nozka said, before turning. "Just follow the abandoned pipeline, then take a right at the first underrail station you find."

"You're going back to fight?" Sylvaine asked, looking at the man's stiff leg.

The mutant simply nodded and walked off into the darkness.

The engineer shook her head and leaned her back onto one of the dried sections of piping.

"I'll just be glad to be done with this," she said. "This place is misery incarnate."

"At least we're finally tearing it down," Marcel said.

"Sure," she said, staring down the block, listening for footsteps. Kayip had promised his attack would be quick, that he would strike, and then retreat to meet them here. Yet she could make out no sounds of approaching footsteps, nor smell the man over the wafting sewage and the chaotic odors of battle.

Marcel followed her gaze. "Part of me wishes I could see the look on Roache's face, once he realizes that all his lies, all his brutality, are going up in smoke." He paused, a pain rising up clear, first from a twitch in the side of his mouth, then obvious in his gaze. "It would have been better if we could help somehow," he said. "Just escaping while others..."

"Marcel!" Sylvaine hissed.

"I know," he said. "I just..." Marcel shook his head. "No, we need to be planning for the future."

"Yeah," Sylvaine said, thinking on that empty space, that unplanned void that lived beyond the sunrise, the world where her vengeance was complete, and yet, she was still alone, still without a home or hope. "The future."

Marcel glanced around. "Where is Kayip anyway?"

"Coming," Sylvaine said.

"Sure, but if he's caught up... or worse." He must have caught her expression, because he quickly mumbled, "I'm sure he's fine. Just if he's taking a while, it might be best to go on ahead. He's knows the way," Marcel said.

"He's coming," Sylvaine repeated, softly.

Suddenly she heard footsteps. Her ears perked up, first with excitement, then with fear.

"Well, hopefully he should..." Marcel started.

"Shh!" Sylvaine held up her finger. Marcel glanced hopefully, but she shook her head.

The two snuck backwards, waiting and listening. The footsteps were quick, panicked, far too light to be Kayip's. She listened for the boot smack of a guard, but no, it sounded more like feet on the pavement, feet perhaps covered with thin socks or wrapped rags.

The footsteps slowed as they approached, and Sylvaine relaxed some when she recognized the smell.

Marcel had lifted up a solid chunk of concrete in the meanwhile, clearly aiming for the approaching figure's head.

"Stop!" Sylvaine shouted, running up and grabbing Marcel's arm.

"What?" he said.

"Ahh!" screamed Gileon, who staggered back, panting.

Marcel sheepishly lowered his bludgeon and muttered an apology. The mutant's face was a pale pink, and he stuttered and panted for the greater part of a minute before he was calm enough to speak.

"How's the battle?" Marcel asked.

"I don't know," Gileon said, "I've just been trying to find you."

"Why?" Marcel asked.

"Where's Kayip?" Sylvaine added.

"Yes!" he said. "I mean, he sent me. Sent me with a message." The mutant closed his eyes, supporting himself on the piping, his breathing slowing to a mere race. "He said. Um. Said. Sorry. To Sylvaine. He cannot leave this fight, could, uh, could never have. Was going to continue his, uh, righteous... something, to fight until the battle was won, or, uh he." The mutant paused. "Until he fell. Until he redeemed himself with an honorable death."

"That shithead bastard," Sylvaine swore. "That stubborn, eager to die, piece of...." She couldn't decide what he was a piece of, instead, releasing a sound somewhere between a groan and a scream.

"Where is he?" she asked after gathering herself for a second

"I don't know, he didn't tell me much else," Gileon said. "No one tells me much."

"Well... Probably somewhere near Verus or Desct," Marcel offered.

"Great deduction," Sylvaine said dryly. "So at the very center of it all." She started to walk.

"Wait!" Marcel started to say.

"I'm going," Sylvaine interrupted, and she was. "Whatever you do, that's your choice, Marcel, but I'm finding Kayip." She stormed off down the street, her stiff, furious strides tolerating no argument.

That bastard, that lying, eager to die, manipulative, unbearably noble bastard. Sylvaine knew that in the literally riotous and death-filled circumstances she could little afford such fuming thoughts, but she couldn't escape them. That man had lifted her up, had given her the closest to kind words she had been offered since her life fell apart, and now had the gall to try to throw his life away. She would find him, grab him by the collar, and pull him back, even if it would be the death of her, which some rational voice in the back of her head screamed out it would be.

"Hey," Marcel said, as he ran up behind her.

"Don't try to stop me," she said.

"Here," Marcel thrust something into her hand. It was an arm's-length pole, and at the end of it was a shard of scrap metal, tied on.

"I found it on a... well I found it," Marcel said. "It's not much, but it's marginally better than nothing." The man himself held a large hammer.

Sylvaine took the weapon. "You don't have to come with me."

"We won't leave a friend behind," Marcel said. "Let's stick to the shadows. Grab him and get out of this mess in one piece, alright?"

Sylvaine nodded and even smiled. Maybe the man was a tad quixotic, but she could use the optimism.

Gileon followed a few metres behind, holding a small knife he had gotten from somewhere. She wasn't sure why the mutant was following them, but then again, perhaps he had nowhere else to go. It was not a night to be wandering alone.

They turned down a street. Several guards ran past, half-dressed. One stopped, staring in Sylvaine's direction. He seemed more confused than anything, and after a moment, spent perhaps deciding whether he should shoot, he just ran onward. Gunshots fired down the street a few second later, and Gileon pointed them down a back route through a refinery complex.

Blackwood Row had changed significantly in the brief time they had waited for Kayip. More fires, for one. The city was alight in several places, and by the flames' flickering illumination she could see bodies. Mutants, guards, and some other men as well, wearing wasteland garb or strange robes, lay together in random patterns along the sidewalks. The smell of blood was dense and inescapable.

"Inferno," Marcel said.

A blast went off suddenly, echoing down the street, a sizeable sibling to their own demolition earlier.

"What was that?" Gileon asked.

"Maybe a sangleum depot caught flame?" Sylvaine ventured, as she kept walking. In truth the explosion didn't sound right for that, but she couldn't determine much about it, besides that it had happened somewhere east. There were too many disconcerting noises to focus on any one. Her ears twitched for the sound of Kayip, but she was overwhelmed by the screams, shouts, gunshots, rumbling blasts, autocar engines, footsteps, clanging, and even, in the distance, police sirens. She couldn't seem to find—

"Wait." She held up her glove suddenly, and then pointed. "That way."

Yes, she had heard him, most definitely, possibly. Maybe. She kept her ears tuned as she dashed, Marcel and Gileon barely keeping pace. It was his shout, it had to have been, might have been, maybe wasn't—no there, again, she heard it, deep and fervent, a sundering war cry that split through the chaos, that seemed, even at this distance, to vibrate in her bones.

They scrambled through a now trampled shantytown, guards and mutants fighting it out nearby, scavenged rifles replacing scavenged cudgels in the mutants' hands. The three approached a wide boulevard. It was open with little cover. At its end roiled a massive melee, seemingly the bulk of the fighting from the office, which now appeared to be engulfed in flames a few blocks down. Sylvaine caught a whiff of Kayip's odor, but it was suffocated by the smoke.

Her ears fared no better here, a great grinding roared over the battle, the sounds of metal against metal, and metal against flesh.

"Sounds like some maniac's trying to use a tread-driller," she said.

"What?" Marcel shouted his whisper.

She waved him on, pointing towards an alleyway that opened just behind a line of mutants, who were pushing their way forward, swinging whatever they had. A distillation tower loomed at the alley's far end. With any luck she could find a ladder and a better angle to scout out.

They kept low and moved up close. As she turned the corner a bullet shattered the pavement behind her. She ducked back. Several Lazacorp guards had barricaded the width of the alley, mutant corpses in a pile at its base.

She turned around and started to lead them down back the way they came, when the engine groan of the tread-driller burst into a shriek. The machine drove forward, turning a bend and into sight, barreling through all in its path. The twirling mass of drills drove its desperate push forward, with no care to distinguish between friend and foe.

"Shit!" Marcel yelled as they tried to run.

The tread-driller drove forward, bodies flying from it or crushed underneath its treads. The machine flew up toward them in mere seconds, and behind its cracked and bloodstained windshield, stared a crazed, one-eyed face.

Sylvaine lifted up her glove, without time to think, and with little to act. She grabbed whatever she could find inside her. A spark grew and shot out in an arc, her focus on the rapidly approaching engine. It burst into flames, the treads unraveling, the drills melting, but the machine didn't slow. It plowed down the streets pushing up waves of asphalt as Sylvaine aimed her glove again. Her life started to flash before her eyes, but she didn't make it past primary school before the wall of metal was upon her.

Chapter 41

There was the scent of smoke, the taste of blood in his mouth, an ache throbbing inside his head like a mad prisoner pounding on jail cell walls. Marcel tried to blink, his lids heavy, his vision blurred. Two questions formed slowly in the morass of his mind: where was he, and why did everything hurt?

He leaned on his shoulder. It protested in pain, but it held. He was able to push forward with one leg. His other was limp and heavy, like it was made of metal.

It took Marcel a second to remember that it indeed was. Unfortunately the cogleg refused to move, and as Marcel's vision cleared he could see the issue. A burnt metal shaft stuck out of his artificial shin, æther-oil dripping down its length.

He noticed a wet spot on his left arm and felt around to discover a small gash. It was painful to touch, but he could still move his arm well enough. He pushed himself a few paces, glancing around, suddenly aware of the smoke, the gunshots, the screams. Nearby lay a large smoldering wreck, some sort of large, treaded vehicle, giant drill bits melted into the asphalt. Beyond the smoking aura, shadowed forms ran to and fro, slashing and firing.

As the world was just starting to coalescence, his memories suddenly crashed in on him.

The charging machine. Verus's face behind the windshield. Sylvaine jumping out in front. The explosion.

A figure crawled out of the wreckage, knocking back the smoke around him, snarling. It was Verus, though he looked taller than Marcel remembered, fiercer.

The foreman's one good eye met Marcel's.

"Talwar," he snarled. "You rat! You traitorous, taur-fucking... you lying sack of... you shit-brained..." He sputtered, seemingly unable to summon a proper insult, instead starting one, then another, before shaking his head in a confused rage.

Marcel disattached his broken limb and pushed himself over. He patted the floor around him looking for a dropped rifle, or pistol, or his hammer, or anything.

Nothing.

A sudden movement caught Marcel's gaze. Verus reached up towards his eyepatch, grabbed it in a fist, and tore it off.

Marcel had seen many injuries during his brief military career, amputated limbs, bullet wounds, blade gashes, and even missing eyes. What Verus had resembled none of these. There was no eye behind the patch, nor a glass eye to fill the hole, no healed flesh for where an eye should have been, nor even an open wound.

Verus stared out with an eye socket of nothingness, an empty void where an eye should rightly have been.

The world around him seemed to freeze still as Marcel stared into that abyss. It was massive, too large to fit in the man's head, a hole open to a darkness wide as the night sky. No, much, much larger than the sky. It was a tenebrous, sprawling cavern of a material that was clearly nothing, yet just as it clearly was gas and liquid simultaneously. It was a bright crimson and a dark black and possessed no color, cold and motionless, as it swirled in frantic burning spirals, shuddering and slithering and perfectly still. Verus's eye was a window to elsewhere, the furthest *elsewhere*

Marcel could ever have imagined, an empty world of dread. All that Marcel hated, all that he feared, seemed to lie beyond that eye, not distinctly, but as an infinite potentiality, a haze of unbounded malevolence. Everything was lost in that void, whatever might exist beyond that marble sized hole melted away, was too insignificant to consider. He stared at it for seconds and years, a lifetime of no time at all, an endless instant. Some voice, in some distant and lost world that he had once called his mind cried out for him to *move*, to *run*, to find a gun, to do *something*.

But there was no Marcel left to hear it, just an endless nothing.

"Down!"

A bulk smashed into Marcel's side, and the void snapped away. Marcel blinked, unused to colors and depth.

"Do not look into his eye," Kayip yelled, from on top of him. "It is demoncraft." The monk's face was bruised and bloodied, mask dented slightly. He held Marcel down with one arm and lifted his sword up with another.

"Monk!" Verus screeched. "Are you so eager to throw more bodies on the pyre? More corpses for your crusade? If your honor demands death, I can give it to you."

Kayip did not answer, did not flinch. He instead rose with a scream and charged Verus.

The foreman, though Marcel was now quite sure he was something else entirely, focused his empty "eye" at the monk, who hid behind his sword as he ran, avoiding the gaze.

Verus screamed out horrid words from that strange language, their meanings' alien, but each syllable was damp with hate. A ball of black fire formed around the man's fingertips, growing in an instant. He flung the flame towards Kayip with a shout. The monk slashed and the black fire split around him, staining twin lines of melted asphalt along the sidewalk.

Marcel glanced around the ground again, frantic for a weapon. Flames behind Verus's wreck lit a glint, a rifle's bayonet, several metres away, which Marcel started to crawl towards.

Kayip dodged in zigzags as he charged, balls of black flame streaking by him. A well-aimed shot knocked Kayip to his side, but the monk rolled, and was immediately back on his feet, embers raining off his smoldering jacket sleeve. Verus screeched out some new loathsome sentence and flung his hand out, a whip of shadowy something extending beyond his reach, slashing at the ground in front of Kayip. Each strike burst forth pillars of fire metres up from the cracked asphalt.

Marcel grabbed the rifle, only for his hands to crack through the charcoalized wood. Up close he could see the rifle had been heavily burnt, the back of the barrel melted, the stock smashed. He glanced back to see Verus whipping this way and that, Kayip jumping back and forth with frantic footwork to match. Marcel chucked a hunk of wood. It flew over and hit Verus in the arm.

The man grunted and staggered back, glaring at Marcel. The monk charged forward in the brief reprieve. Verus leapt up with surprising alacrity, onto the hull of the tread-driller, and swung his whip towards Marcel.

The heat was intense, Marcel rolled himself back, and felt the blast of asphalt a few metres in front of him.

"Back, Marcel!" Kayip shouted and he didn't need the encouragement. He crawled in haste; it was obvious enough that he was useless in the monk's fight, and could serve only as an easy target. Even the engineer would be better suited for...

Sylvaine. Demiurge, where was Sylvaine?

He panicked, glancing around for the woman. He dragged himself back, and while frantically searching the street, spied feet poking out from a collapsed sheet-metal hut.

Marcel could hear her breathe as he pulled himself close. He was surprised, but grateful, that the woman was alive. Were all ferrals able to survive a blast like that, he wondered, or was Sylvaine unusually tough? He tried to ignore the battle scream of Kayip and the devilish curses of Verus as he checked the woman's vitals. Unfortunately, a battle between a screaming monk and whatever-in-the-Demiurge's-name Verus was could not be so easily ignored.

With a quick glance he saw that Verus had retreated some, up the burning pile of metal that had been the tread-driller. Kayip danced back and forth with an agility that seemed unnatural for a man his size, dodging Verus's whip and occasional blasts of flames. Every time he managed to get a step in, to come almost within sword range, a black ball of flame would knock him back.

Sylvaine coughed back to life, her eyes blinking open one after the other. She held her head.

"Ohh, that hurts. I feel like I was hit by..." She paused as she noticed the smoldering wreck down the street.

"Well... that," she finished.

"Burn!" Verus screeched. "Burn with your false idol!"

Storms of fire flew from Verus's arms, the air around him shimmered, the void of his eyes seemed to leak out into the world around him. Marcel turned towards Kayip to avoid the foreman's gaze. The monk shook as if grabbed by invisible hands, stumbling and struggling to remain on his feet. He closed his eyes and screamed, charging blindly. Red smoke billowed as Verus's whip flew out to wrap around Kayip's sword. The monk grunted and pulled it toward his chest. Verus spat something in his discordant language, and tore the whip back, flinging the blade across the road.

The whip snapped with a snake-like celerity and struck at the unarmed monk, who jumped to the ground to avoid its bite. Verus muttered hate as a new blackness grew in his grip. On his face grew a smirk of sadism to match it. The black fire formed into great ball that he raised in the direction of Kayip. The monk shielded himself with his arm, waiting for the flame to strike.

It didn't.

Verus's smile shuddered halfway through his guttural incantation. Blood oozed out his mouth, and his look of triumph collapsed into confused pain. His eye moved downwards, and

Marcel's gaze followed, to a bloody shard of metal sticking of his chest.

The black ball dissipated into smoke, Verus's false eye faded to reveal mere scarred flesh. The foreman fell, sliding down the side of the car, hitting the asphalt with a sickly crack.

Standing where Verus had stood was Gileon, looking just about as shocked as everyone else.

"I killed him," he said. It half-sounded like a question.

Sylvaine got up and, noticing Marcel's leg, helped the man to his feet. They shuffled over and caught up with Kayip, who now stood beside Gileon, staring down at the corpse.

"It is done then," the monk said, face of stone.

Below, Verus lay limp and curled, his expression, so often sharp and hard, now loose, sagging and worn, his hand hung over his chest wound, covered in crimson. In all, Verus's corpse looked like any other Marcel had seen.

Marcel lightly patted Gileon on the back, who flinched only a little "Good... Good job. Thank you."

The mutant tried to smile.

"It is done," the monk said again, blinking slowly. "I thought I would be... It should not matter the hand, I suppose..." He bent down to pick up his blade off the ground.

"It is good that you are well," Kayip said quickly to Sylvaine, before turning and walking off.

"Hey. Hey!" Sylvaine yelled, her injuries forgotten in her sudden fury. "Where are you going?"

"Roache was... driving towards the... south gate." Kayip said, steps slow and uneven, voice losing its energy.

"Wait," Sylvaine said, fury replaced by fear.

She dashed, and Marcel limped after her. Kayip was stumbling, keeping himself up with his sword. Sylvaine grabbed the shoulder of the man. Marcel patted his torso and felt the wet sticky sensation of blood. He pulled back and tore off some of the cloth. There was a gash marring the side of the man.

"Demiurge," Marcel said.

"Not him," Kayip muttered. "Bayonet. Roache is still running. My oath is unfinished, Roache is stillllll..." he slurred the L as his bulk fell onto Marcel.

Chapter 42

"Hand me the rag, please."

Sylvaine watched as Marcel took the steaming ball of cloth from Gualter and, with one hand still holding closed the stained red linen around Kayip's wound, dabbed and cleaned the blood which leaked at its base.

The monk did not flinch, leaning back on an empty sangleum barrel. His shirt lay on the floor, revealing his wide, muscular, and deeply scarred torso. Sylvaine mused that this was far from first time the man had been cut, or stabbed, or by the look of it, shot, but she worried all the same.

"Okay, it's finally oozing less," Marcel said. "We're lucky it didn't hit a major artery." He tossed the cloth back into the steaming pot. That had been Sylvaine's one contribution, as medicine was not a subject of much interest to most engineers. The body was far too messy of a machine for her tastes, but at least she had the wherewithal to realize that an æther-bolt-melted ball of scrap served well as a source of heat.

"How's my leg?" Marcel asked back to her.

"Oh. Good, close to done," Sylvaine said quickly, turning back to the still-somewhat smashed prosthetic. It was strange to watch

Marcel sit with only a single leg, but it seemed the man managed. Sylvaine herself had made slow progress on the prosthetic, distracted by Kayip's condition.

"I am fine," the monk said, catching her worried glance.

"You might be fine if this were a real medical institution," Sylvaine snapped in response. Gualter's makeshift infirmary was nothing more than few mattresses dragged to the ground floor of what had recently been one of the guards' apartment complexes.

Mutants around them groaned and twitched. Some injuries were treated well enough by a wet rag and drinking water, but many of the mutants were clearly not long for the world. Gualter and a few others helped as best they could, but with little more than water, cut-up clothes, and a handful of scavenged foodbars there was a limit to their ability.

"I have suffered many worse wounds," Kayip said, grinning, half from pain.

"Well why did you seek this one!" Sylvaine said. "Why did you lie to me?"

His forced smile fell. "It is my fight, Sylvaine. I had to see that they were brought down."

She tossed an iron nut at his shoulder. The monk grunted, and Marcel yelled a "Hey! I'll need that."

"Maybe spare a moment to think about what happens after you get your revenge," she muttered.

"It is not mere revenge," Kayip said, pushing himself up against the barrel. "It is far more important than my life. Roache is still out there. Marcel, am I not yet well enough? We have to catch the man."

"You're well likely to get an infection, the way you are now," Marcel said.

"Roache was heading to the south gate," Kayip said.

"Yes, three hours ago. Where do you think he is now?"

Kayip slumped back. "Then I have failed. Again."

416

Marcel removed the linen, dampened it, and reapplied the clump. "If you haven't noticed, Kayip, the gunfire has fallen silent. There are no screams anymore, the only people I've seen running past there," he pointed to the open, hinge-broken door, "have been mutant revolutionaries. We won."

Sylvaine opened up Marcel's leg, gently folding pieces back into place, and fixing broken pistons. After a few more minutes of work, her on the leg, Marcel on Kayip, the monk spoke again.

"Roache is still out there," Kayip said. "This is not his only nest."

"Well he's not welcome in Huile, I can tell you that," Marcel said.

"He has friends in the Wastes," Kayip said. "Raiders."

"So he knows a few cog-loose bandits." Marcel shrugged.

Kayip grabbed Marcel's arm. "Not a few. Not a few." He held it, tense, eyes locked. "He is not done, Marcel. He will plan something; it is in his nature. I know evil is still to come." He kept the gaze for several seconds, before dropping it, and laying back.

"It'll be okay," Marcel said, a slight tremor in his voice. "We won here. Desct will make contact with Phenia, or maybe some local Resurgence town, and if Roache tries something, we'll have a UCCR army on his ass."

"Where is Desct anyway?" Sylvaine said. "If he won, shouldn't he be calling people together, sending a message out?"

Marcel glared at her a moment with an anger that surprised her, and must have surprised him, since he caught himself and shook the grimace off his face. "He's just... Probably negotiating with City Hall," he said.

"Yeah," Sylvaine replied, turning back to the leg. "I'm sure something like that."

The already broken door was pushed aside as four mutants walked in, two dragging large sacks, the other two armed. The foremost held a large bludgeon made from a bit of an autocar axle, the second, Sabyn, had found himself a rifle. He jogged over to Sylvaine and produced a small glass cylinder from his pocket.

"This the kind of thing you were looking for?"

"Yes!" Sylvaine took the diminutive æther-oil tank. She picked out the last pieces of glass from the old one in Marcel's leg and laid in place its replacement. "This one's a bit larger than ideal, but..." She sucked in her breath and focused, morphing and molding the pipework, "it should be fine." The leg kicked suddenly, as if in agreement.

Sabyn nodded, then began distributing medical supplies. Sylvaine passed the now mostly functional leg to Marcel, who, to his credit, first worked at applying the newly scavenged ointment onto Kayip's wounds. This the man did flinch at.

"Well, it's as good as it'll ever be," Marcel muttered.

He finished wrapping the bandages, after which Sylvaine helped him reattach his leg. Kayip lifted himself up, and then caught Marcel, whose leg gave way as he stood.

"Shit," Sylvaine said, "are you okay?"

"I'm good. Good." Marcel caught his balance, and with some assistance took some steps. "Just a little loose-feeling is all."

"Well, I had to make some workarounds," Sylvaine admitted, "but it should be, if anything, better. A lot of gunk had built up between those gears, and I don't think that was Verus's doing."

Marcel's face displayed a hint of red. "No good engineers in Huile for fix-ups."

It would have required little more than a corner mechanic, but Sylvaine didn't press the point. The mutant medics were quick at work applying whatever treatments they could manage with the new bandages, bottles of rubbing alcohol, scalpels, and sutures. One of the scavengers who stood in the middle of the hurry attempted to show off some of his looted treasures, to the annoyed indifference of the busy medical workers.

"Found a whole bunch of aurem coins in this one guard's drawer." He shook a bag at a Gualter who simply ignored him as he stitched up an unconscious mutant's belly, "had some old photographs too. I tossed them, but there was this one back room, had a lot of great stuff, a full voxbox, couldn't lug that obviously, and this coat and hat." He pointed to his headwear, which appeared to be some blue, dust-covered Principate officer's cap.

"Oh, and this!" The man pulled a rust-tinged pistol from his coat, barrel first.

"Hey, that's mine!" Marcel said, limping over. The mutant watched his approach with indignation and held the weapon close.

"I found it," he said.

"That man blew up the monolith!" Sabyn said from across the room. "Give him the damn pistol."

The mutant scowled, but seeing no support around him, slunk his shoulders and handed the weapon back to Marcel.

"Thanks," Marcel said. "Was wondering where Verus was keeping it. And thank you," he addressed Sabyn, who simply nodded and continued inventorying supplies.

Marcel checked the chambers, then messed around with the weapon. "Not working right. Some Lazacorp idiot must have been messing around. Can you—?" Marcel said, before Sylvaine waved him over, rolling her eyes as the man handed her the gun.

Truthfully, it was nice to be useful. She started to unscrew the grip, studying the simple machine below her. For the first time in over a month, she felt a sense of ease. Yes, Roache had escaped, but she was wondering how much that mattered. Marcel might be naïve on some things, but the truth about Lazarus Roache was out, the lies he had built now completely demolished. Whatever hired guns he had left couldn't bail him out of this. As for her own vengeance... the man wasn't dead, but what would his death truly give her at this point?

Sylvaine glanced up at Kayip, who had now joined Marcel in helping to treat the wounded. A mad monk and a private detective who couldn't solve a mystery if it slapped him in the face. Yet, she was grateful that they had both made it through alive and mostly well. This wasn't what she had expected to gain from a quest for revenge, but she was glad she had met them.

She picked through Marcel's pistol. The mainspring was rusted through, hard to see how a Lazacorp goon could be responsible for *that*. Not a problem, she sucked in her breath, focused, and...

Nothing.

Panic flowed through her. The æthermantics wasn't coming, her Knack, had it finally left her? She pushed through every corner of her mind, eyes closed, breath held. She couldn't lose it, not now, not after all she suffered through. Then suddenly the power came rushing out of her, enraged and wild. With a muffled shout she thrust her hand to the floor, sparks flying, concrete chipping.

"You okay?" Marcel called.

"Fine! Almost done!" Sylvaine said. She shut her eyes tight and grit her teeth. A few moments later, with a flash and sigh, the pistol was fixed. She held it up, hoping no one noticed that she was drenched in sweat.

"Thank you," Marcel said, as he grabbed the gun and inspected it.

Sylvaine muttered an empty sound. She had been deluding herself. Roache may have fled the city, but the bastard was still with her, his drug still infused into her blood. She hated the power, but cherished it even more, it humiliated her, but if she lost it she would be nothing. Kayip was right; this wasn't over, not as long as Lazarus Roache lived.

Sabyn walked past, loading a clip into his rifle. Several of his companions were following him out, each one carrying a bludgeon or firearm.

"You doing another supply run, or something?" Marcel asked.

The man nodded. "But not coming back here. Heading to Desct."

"You have seen Desct?" Kayip asked.

"Not exactly," Sabyn said. "Found a runner of his while out. Needs all able and loyal mutants to help with the continued fighting down by City Hall."

"City Hall?" Marcel said, nearly tripping again. "The revolution is won. Why in Inferno is there fighting in Huile?"

Sabyn slung his rifle over his back. "The revolution has spread."

Huile citizens flock the streets as the victorious army of the UCCR marches past battered walls. Despite rumors of a collapse of the Resurgence's assault, the dawn of yesterday's morning arose over a defeated Principate army. Such an incredible rout, in fact, that military experts predict it will force to an end the entire Principate incursion. Details of this stunning victory are still coming in, but early reports suggest a defector from the imperial camp, one Lazarus Roache, provided vital intel on the city's defenses.

"In truth, victory in Huile was always assured," stated General Durand. "The Principate rarely attempts attacks over the Atsols for this very reason, they inevitably must retreat when facing a proud Resurgence army."

The General's words could not have come at a better time for, as this very paper previously reported, undue fearmongering had sparked panic in several northern cities over the past few weeks. Now a sensible calm is certain to return.

"This victory merely makes clear the obvious. The Confederacy will hold strong against all assaults," the General concluded. "The bravery of our soldiers will forever stand as a bulwark for the rights and freedoms that all good Citizens cherish."

As for the lucky city of Huile? "A bright future awaits our freed brothers and sisters!"

Even now reconstruction has begun, soldiers assisting civilian efforts mere hours after victory. Food rations are driven in by the truckload, and plans are being drawn up for new housing projects, agri-factories, and even a trolley line. All this will be funded by extraction of the rich sangleum fields that sit beneath this city.

"Huile will be our diamond in the Border States," announced General Durand. "It will be a beacon of freedom to shine over the Wastes, a bastion of peace and prosperity."

—*Front-page article from the morning edition of The Phenian Post, Eishwind 12th, 1746 AD (After Diedrev).*

Chapter 43

Dying flames ate at the husk of a smashed police autocar, one of many, tossing out a blanket of smoke over the bodies of dozens of mutants and policemen. An uninhumed graveyard stretched from the street up to the walls of Huile. There light poured in through what used to be twenty metres of brickwork, not the light of Huile's streetlamps, nor of apartment windows, but of fire. Marcel staggered forward towards the smashed wall, his slow movement more from shock than his creaking leg.

"Demiurge Desct," he muttered to himself. "What did you do?"

Kayip clutched at his Disc, knee to the ground, whispering some sort of prayer. Sylvaine walked up to the burnt bricks, inspected them with her nails, and sniffed.

"Sangleum," she said, and then gestured to some curved metal scrap on the ground. "Barrels of the stuff. Set off by a clockbomb, maybe two or three clockbombs."

"Clockbombs?" Marcel asked, climbing up the rubble to stare at Audric Avenue, the western edge of Huile. The battlefield extended here, and between the bodies, the blood, the smashed autocars, and burnt viscera Audric Avenue looked no different from its counterparts in Blackwood Row. It resembled how Marcel had imagined, during sweat-drenched nights, what the aftermath of the war had been, sleeping men and women awakening in confused panic, death rising without warning or explanation from the depths of Lazacorp. Except the corpses did not wear military uniforms, but civilian dress.

Marcel staggered on the crumpling stones, leaning on the wall to keep himself up, each glance at the scene beyond hitting him with nausea and a vague ache in his metal leg. He had imagined coming back to the city as a sort of mini triumph, carrying forth the twin banners of justice and peace. Instead he faced a necropolis, lit by on both sides of the wall by flame and choked by smoke.

"Damn it," Sylvaine said, shaking her head. "I *knew* I had built more."

The exposed brickwork exploded a metre from Marcel's head, and he jumped back. Three more gunshots went off, with the flash of gunfire originating from behind a police autocar. Marcel ducked down, pistol out.

"Go fuck yourself, Lazacorp scum!" came a voice.

Marcel squinted and could make out three horn-adorned figures around the autocar, one struggling to extract the engine, one with a dolly at the ready, and one aiming a rifle Marcel's way, horn cracked and blood-caked.

"We're not Lazacorp!" Sylvaine shouted.

Kayip ran up beside them, sword out. Marcel waved him back.

"It's me, Marcel!" he shouted to the mutants.

The dolly-mutant and the gunman started muttering out some rapid debate, while the third tugged out the engine. Marcel peeked around the corner, then ducked back down as a bullet whizzed by his head.

"You can go fuck yourself too, Marcel!" shouted the gunman. The other two hauled the engine onto the dolly and started to push. "This is ours."

"We're not trying to take anything," Marcel shouted. "Where's Desct?"

"That traitorous coward can go fuck himself most of all," screamed the gunman, striking a match. Marcel watched the lit rag of a bottle as it was tossed, landing a few feet short of the wall, spraying burning sangleum. The mutant fired off a few more rounds, and then ran after his two companions southways down the road.

"Should we follow?" Kayip asked.

Marcel shook his head. "We need to get to City Hall." He started up the other direction.

Desct had said he'd keep the fighting to Blackwood Row. Desct had said he'd bring peace. Marcel's chest felt hollow as he stepped over the rubble of Huile. His anger was reaching for a target, but he knew in his gut that whatever happened here hadn't been part of Desct's plan. Desct was not some distant bureaucrat or self-aggrandizing businessman, he knew the pain of injustice firsthand. This bore Celina's mark clear enough, her rage could not be contained, it seemed, to only those who had wronged her.

The three kept low and moved carefully, quick dashes across city blocks after waiting still for Sylvaine's ears to track every potential movement. There were fewer corpses per street corner here, but not by a significant amount, every block seemed to be decorated by at least one dead cop or dead mutant. Or dead civilian. Or many dead civilians. Huile folk lay out in their dozens, dressed in heavy coats, work clothing, but more often simply bedwear. Marcel recognized the face of Miss Dobis, pale and bloodless, body lying flat beneath a smashed windowpane.

He closed his eyes and hurried his step, burning pain spreading up from his cogleg. It had been his job to negotiate. Instead he had stayed behind to save a friend. And now the streets of Huile resembled the wreckage of war.

But then, would his words have even mattered? He wouldn't have made it before the wall was blasted open, he'd have been running into the middle of a riot. Marcel hadn't been able to convince even Lambert, and that was before corpses had been strewn like discarded clothing, in piles along the street.

Occasionally they would be shot at from a shattered window. Most were mere warning shots, but a few bullets whizzed too close to be accidental. They ran past as fast as they could manage, as they did past the open doors to darkened rooms, where Marcel could make out horned figures rummaging through the shadows.

A moan echoed out from around a corner. Marcel snuck forward, Sylvaine and Kayip following.

"I'm back, I'm back," came a woman's halting voice. "We can be together again, Sophia, it'll be like it was. I'm back."

The small courtyard was surrounded with shuttered shops and decorated with blood-drained bodies. Mutants, police officers, civilians, intermingled and still. It looked like a small barricade had been built from café chairs and wide planters, and then demolished. Near the ruins squatted a woman mutant, clothes torn, grasping at a figure beneath her. As Marcel approached it was clear enough that the head the mutant held to her chest was not breathing.

"I know it wasn't you, Sophia," the woman cried. "I know you didn't turn me in. You were waiting for me. You don't have to wait any more," the mutant cried.

Marcel heard a click behind him. He turned and saw that a mutant he took for dead was leaning up on a bullet-ridden autocar, a pistol in his hand. Two more clicks, empty.

"It's me," Marcel said.

The mutant squinted, bullet holes oozing from his stomach. "Oh, you're that... you're one of Desct's Huilian lackeys." He groaned. Marcel recognized the extra eyeball that blinked from the side of his head. He didn't know the mutant's name, but he had seen him among Celina's crowd, silently nodding alongside her during the final meeting. "Well, I would have shot you anyways..." the mutant said, waving the gun, "but no bullets. Wasted them all trying to hit that mad bitch."

"I know you didn't turn me in," the woman muttered to the corpse. "I know it wasn't you, you just didn't know what happened to me. You didn't know to look. I'm back, Sophia, I'm back, and it'll be like it was."

Kayip and Sylvaine caught up, the former muttering a prayer, the later slowly approaching the woman.

"She shot us in the back, you know," the slouched mutant said, "I thought she was one of us, but when she noticed that carcass, she started gibbering. After all we had fought for, all we had survived," he gave a wheezing laugh, which descended into coughs. "A few seconds later, a few quick rifle shots, and we joined the corpses."

"I'm here, Sophia, I'm finally back." The woman rocked as she spoke. Sylvaine tried to tenderly touch the woman's shoulder. She screamed, jumping up and slashing with gnarled claws. Sylvaine fell back on the street, swearing, and the woman glanced around with wide eyes. Her clothes were cut up, gashes oozing from beneath. She ran suddenly, sprinting down the street. The body she left behind, Sophia's body presumably, was marred with crimson, and Marcel noticed a knife clutched tight in her pale hand.

The mutant laughed again. "She killed for some bleeding-out Huile idiot, and how did that idiot repay her? Used her last moments alive to try to stab her savior." He went quiet for a moment, and Marcel though he might have passed, but he coughed again and moaned.

"Why?" Marcel asked, waving to the carnage around him. "You didn't have to attack Huile, it was your city."

"Wasn't my city," the mutant gestured to the limp figures sprawled around him. "Wasn't Adalgar's, or Tatiana's, or Dien's either. Slaves of the Wastes, this city's done nothing but beat us, mutate use, kill us, and then beat again what's left."

"They were innocent," Marcel said.

"They lived in luxury, in ætheric energy that we bled and died to give them." His lips curled in a snarl, he tried to pull himself up, but gave up after a moment. "I didn't come here alone. My own son

428

came to Huile with me, my own flesh and blood was sold with me. But he didn't survive the mutations. He screamed and vomited until there was nothing left inside for him to puke up, and these Huile fuckers didn't lift a finger."

This wasn't what was supposed to happen. Marcel had done the right thing. He had uncovered Roaches lies, struggled, risked his life, sacrificed for the cause. The plan had been clear, the return of justice, of a true freedom to the city. Marcel felt his hand on the grip of his pistol. The urge was there, this mutant had destroyed everything he had fought for, everything he had suffered for, had had friends die for. It would be easy to raise the pistol, flick the trigger, and let his fury finish the man off.

"Perhaps we should go," came Kayip's voice. He walked up with Sylvaine. Marcel released his held breath, and the pistol, before leaning down to the slumped figure.

"We can clean your wounds, try and dress them, quickly," he offered.

The mutant stared at him, a dazed half-smile on his face. "Come on, we both now that's delaying at best. I'm done." He slapped his chest, and winced. "Blood was long coming, you couldn't have stopped it before, and you sure as Inferno can't stop it now. Listen, you can hear it pour."

It was true, Marcel did hear something. He closed his eyes and listened. Footsteps, dozens, no hundreds. Shouts, a discordant angry wail. All echoing down from Viexus Boulevard.

"What happened to Desct?" Marcel asked, turning back to the mutant, but he was silent. The dead man's pistol slid from his hand into the pool that drained from his chest.

Wordlessly, the trio left that massacre grounds and snuck up through side alleys and small streets, cautiously following the voices.

"Mutants?" Marcel asked.

Sylvaine shook her head. "Doesn't sound like it."

They crept out from an alley and could see the movement down the wide boulevard. The men and woman of Huile marched in a mob, bearing rifles, shotguns, and blades, path lit by hand torches, lamps, and actual fire. Poking above the mob swung long poles of glinting metal, frames of axles and bound pipes, each one decorated with a mutilated corpse of a mutant.

"Halt!" A large, crackling voice boomed down from the other side of the street. Running down from the direction of City Hall came policemen and mutants. It took Marcel a moment to realize they were one and the same, mutants dressed in riot gear, or even police caps, holding bayonet-heavy rifles or truncheons. Leading them was one of Desct's comrades. *Calix*, Marcel remembered his name, his twirled right horn, and sparse blond hair giving him away.

"Do not move a step closer," Calix shouted through a bullhorn. "By orders of General Heitor Desct."

General? The absurdity of the title would have been comic to Marcel were the streets not so stained with blood.

The crowd slowed to a standstill, less from the commands and more from the sight of the rifles. Their shouts, however, only increased in ferocity, and Marcel could make out shouts of *"skinsick!" "traitors!" "my child, my child!"* and *"kill the bastards!"*

"Hold. Hold!" Calix commanded.

The crowd started to step forward again, in hesitant waves. Calix gestured and the mutants fired, bullets hitting the ground between the two lines, cracking cobblestone and bursting up dust.

"Return home!" shouted Calix. Several mutants reloaded their carbines and pistols, while others held still their heavier repeater-rifles, sights aimed towards the crowd. "Those who need protection hand over your weapons, and you will be safe and well-treated within the walls of City Hall."

Kayip glanced to Marcel, who bit his lip, and stepped out into the light.

"Hey!" he shouted. Immediately a gunshot went off and a clod of cobblestone shards battered his face.

"Hold! I said hold!" Calix said, running up and grabbing the excited mutant's rifle. Marcel coughed, and patted himself down, relieved to find nothing but muck. "That's Marcel Talwar."

"Marcel!" the mutant commander addressed him with a shout, "quickly, get over here!"

The crowd shouted as well, waving their arms and grisly totems, their voices too confused and contradictory to make an argument.

"Everyone calm down," Marcel shouted back.

"Join us!" said a man from the mob. "These skinsick bastards are trying to murder us all."

"Celina went off mad!" Calix shouted. "We're just trying to restore order."

A woman thrust through the crowd, holding out a bundle of cloth. "They did this to my boy! My child!"

Marcel squinted, and his stomach curled in upon itself. The face of a small child, no more than two, stared back with unfocused eyes, face white, stomach red and open.

The crown started to move forward again, enraged, waving forward their own atrocities, mutant flesh hanging limp above.

"We all need to lower our weapons," Marcel shouted. "This is… a misunderstanding. It was Roache, Lazacorp that set up everything here. Trust me, I'm a Huile citizen, I fought in the war, if we can just talk we can—"

He saw the rifle poke out from behind the weeping woman's shoulder. Then a blast. The mutant closest to Calix was flung back, head splitting in crimson. Suddenly there was a burst of gunfire, from both sides. Marcel leapt back behind the cover of the street corner, as half the mob ran forward, rifles at the ready, charging at the mutants, while the other half broke and fled back.

Marcel stumbled, catching himself on Kayip, unable to think as gunfire echoed. His metal leg burned, and his vision blurred. He grabbed Sylvaine's arm, her fur on edge, her eyes distant.

"The rifles," Marcel said, "use your engineering, melt them down, clog them, something!"

She shook her head, "It's too late."

It had finished in seconds. Several of the mutants lay dead; more clutched at their injuries as their comrades rushed over. The ground before them was covered in bodies of Huile citizens, blood mixing on the ground. A few screamed, and others tried to drag themselves away, to join to the fleeing mob.

Marcel, Sylvaine, and Kayip stepped out slowly. Calix waved them over, embracing each in turn, before tossing out more orders to his band of "police." They ran to tend to the injured, mutants first, but also to those men and women who willingly tossed away their firearms. One elderly man still fought on, turning and firing suddenly as a mutant approached, arm out. The shot missed, and the mutant then unloaded his rifle into the quivering figure.

"Demiurge," Marcel said, watching the scene. "Merciful Demiurge."

Calix's face was as grim. "To be thrust into this, just after victory, after freedom... Come, you'll want to speak with Desct."

Chapter 44

The Banner of the Phoenix lay crumpled on the marble floor, cut by bullet holes. As the city outside screamed, its bird of eternal fire fluttered anemically, caught by drafts of wind from the open doors of the atrium, lit by an erratic arrangement of handtorches. It seemed almost to inflate with slow breaths, each one weaker, collapsing down onto a floor marred by blood and what appeared to be a large, smashed, multi-tiered cake. Party streamers hung limp in the vast hall, a few unpopped balloons wandered aimlessly, as the Phoenix took its last gasps.

The atrium itself was full, throngs of harried mutants ran this way and that. Some seemed to be organizing munitions, others barricading the windows. In the back several guarded a cordoned off area where a few dozen Huile folk sat. Marcel wondered if they were prisoners, but none were chained. A mutant came by with a smile and some shouted words, and a family of four stood still with shock, before running up and embracing him. It seemed at least a few reunions were bloodless.

It was the only sign of joy in the place, more bitter-looking was the line of UCCR bureaucrats led down towards a side hallway. These battered men were held together by handcuffs, bike chains, and ropes, their visages downcast and hateful. Marcel caught the glance of a rotund face through the dim, Lambert's bitter eyes staring towards him. He whispered something, too quiet and distant to hear for sure, but Marcel found himself reading the lips as mouthing "traitor."

Marcel turned his gaze and found Desct, towards whom Calix and Kayip were already marching. The man had changed in the few hours of fighting, out of his workers rags and into an ornate, though ill-fitting, military uniform.

"...remind them that *we* are the new Resurgence government," he said to another armed mutant, "if they are willing to work with us, or at least stand down, then accommodate them as best you can."

"And if not?" his soldier asked.

"It is a bloody night," Desct replied grimly.

"General Desct!" shouted Calix. "I found him."

The man turned, weary face lighting up a bit as he caught sight of Marcel. "You survived!"

"Desct, what in Inferno happened here?" Marcel shouted as he walked over.

The mutant sighed. "The situation had progressed a shit ton further than I anticipated."

"Progressed? Things have gone mad! Have you seen the city? It's worse than the war."

"Let's not spit taur-fucking hyperboles," Desct snapped. "We've been maintaining peace as best as we can. There was always a risk of the Huile police getting involved."

"This is more than a police scuffle," Marcel said.

Desct shook his head. "Celina cared less about emancipation and more for revenge. I knew that from the beginning, but this... I lacked the imagination for this."

"She was supposed to be by the south gate," Kayip said. "Now Roache is gone and free."

"I sent her where I thought she could manufacture the least trouble," Desct said. "I didn't predict she would simply abandon her post and expand the revolution before we even took Blackwood Row."

"Expand the revolution?" Marcel said. "Desct, this isn't a revolution, it's slaughter. Where in our plans did we agree to attack City Hall?"

"Plans change," Desct said, thrusting his fingers into Marcel's chest. "What would you expect to happen once the wall was demolished? I desired peace just as much as you, but once blood had been spilled in Huile, I had no alternative. Celina's bands were looting and killing, and we were viewed as no different, trying to reason gets us fucking gunshots nine times out of ten. If we did not assert control, we would have been shoved back into our cages, or onto the gallows, Marcel, whether by Lazacorp's hand's or Huile's."

Mutants had stopped or slowed to stare. Marcel simply stepped back and crossed his arms, his head lowered. "It wasn't supposed to be like this."

"No shit, Marcel. When was it ever?" Desct said. "Huile should never have fallen under a coup, but we kicked out the Principate, using whatever means necessary. Blackwood Row should never have been the slave-harvesting Inferno-pit that it was, but we did what was needed to end it. This is war, Marcel, just like it was before."

Marcel shook his head, trying to put to words thoughts that refused to cohere. Rage and guilt swirled around and into each other, until he could be sure where one ended and the other began. He didn't know whether to shout, or weep, or vomit, so instead he just kept his silence.

Desct glanced around and waved his soldiers on. "Calix take command. Marcel, Kayip, Sylvaine, let's talk some things over in my office."

His office was what had once been Mayor Durand's, though all decoration had been pushed to the side in a pile, leaving only the desk, some chairs, a few handtorches, and a voxbox jury-rigged to life with an autocar engine.

Desct sat and explained the situation in cold detail. Most of the city was in utter chaos, his forces against Celina's against Huile's militia crowds and the remnants of the police. "Celina preys on them, and they prey on us. We've tried to make peace, and have talked down a few, but most prefer to speak with their rifles," Desct said.

Marcel could only sit and stare at the blank wall behind Desct. They had done everything right, they had won, and yet still the city burned.

"Have you tried contacting other Border State cities?" Sylvaine offered. "Someone Resurgence friendly?"

Desct nodded. "We caught some of the old government officials making frantic calls as we took City Hall. They told their story well enough, barbaric mutant insurgents out for blood. We've tried to clear the air, but to no avail. No one wants to speak with us."

It was Marcel's city; he had chosen to protect it. He had sacrificed his leg for it, he had sacrificed his years, his happiness, because he knew in the end it was the right thing. And now the city burned.

"So you're on your own," Sylvaine said.

"At best." Desct lifted up a steaming mug and drank from it. "Demiurge, I missed coffee. Don't think I'll be sleeping for a good while."

"How are your forces compared to Celina's?" Kayip sat crossed legged on the floor, one hand to his chin, the other massaging his Disc.

"Hard to say for certain," Desct said. "I have a majority, I think, and we're comparatively organized. But I also have people to fucking safeguard. Celina can retreat to any corner of this city without consequence. There are a good number of our brothers and sisters who are not engaged in fighting on any side, simply hiding until this is over, or just fleeing the city. In my heart, I cannot condemn them."

Marcel had been advised to sacrifice, extolled on his nobility, told that he had the power to save the city. All by a man who knew the truth from the beginning.

Sylvaine shook her head. "If you can hold out... I guess it's still a victory. You're free."

"Thrust from chains into the mayor's chair." Desct shook his head and sipped. "Holding out remains a big *if*. Considering the value of the sangleum fields, I wouldn't be surprised if a Resurgence army comes knocking soon. I just don't know whose story they will give credence to."

A man who had used all the ideals of the United Confederacy as mere tools, a man who transformed every just punishment into a personal execution, every freedom earned into more bondage. A man who now walked free from a city he had drained and discarded.

"Who's around?" Desct asked. "As you can imagine I haven't much been following politics. Marcel?"

"Hmm?" Marcel replied.

"Do you know if General Melias's army is still stationed by Quorgon?"

"Oh uh." Marcel shook his head. "I think he moved south for... something. I'm not sure."

"His forces moved to Fim-Niuex, to handle a raider threat," Kayip replied. Desct glanced at him. "I keep my ear to the ground; it is a habit. Though I heard the man had been replaced by General Levair."

"Ah shit," Desct said, slamming the table. "There was a Levair on staff here."

"Was?" Sylvaine asked.

"Worked accounting." Desct wiped off some of the coffee he spilled. "Most of them were keen to hide behind their police force, to give themselves up when the shooting died down. Levair decided to make a last stand with the mayor. Imbecile."

There was a rapid knocking at the door. A mutant woman rushed in, saluting Desct, who stood. The motions of both were imprecise and weary, the night had been a long one.

"Eirena's squad just knocked Celina's gang out of the caravan depot," the woman said.

"Good." Desct nodded. "How many captured?"

"A dozen or so, some killed, most ran," she said. "I'll get the numbers. But Celina was one of those who fled, straight out the main gate, with a couple of 'trucks. Last we saw she was heading south, no sign of turning around."

"Fucking..." Desct caught himself and breathed in. "Congratulate the soldiers and spread the message that Celina has been defeated. Focus Eirena's and Calix's forces and sweep down the eastern wall, I'll be out momentarily."

The woman saluted and ran back out. Desct sipped some more. "So it's headless now," he said, "no easy peace treaty."

"And there is the issue of Roache," Kayip stated.

"Bit late to do anything about him," Desct said. "As much as I'd love to have *his* head."

"It's his fault," Marcel said.

Desct nodded. "Need to consolidate my forces here."

"He's coming back, isn't he?" Marcel asked Kayip.

The monk scratched his chin. "I am unsure on the man's next move."

"But he has raiders as allies. Many of them, that's what you said."

Desct looked to Kayip, who nodded.

"Then we'll need to defend the walls, hold out," Desct said. "If the man returns to reimprison us."

"No," Marcel said. "We have to go after him, strike him down, if we want to protect Huile."

"I need to protect my people," Desct said, "and dispatching them out into the Wastes is not a rational course of action. Even if Roache does comes back, it will be safer behind these walls than out there."

"But if he comes back," Marcel said, "he might give his own story, try to twist the ear of Levair, or whoever else comes by, with his words. He's too dangerous to be left alive."

"I don't know Marcel," Desct rubbed his forehead with two worn hands. "All I can do now is to try and mold this city back into a semblance of sanity and chasing a man across the Wastes does not fit into a strategy of restoring sane fucking order."

"I will go," said Kayip, standing. "I respect your cause, Desct, and hopefully my actions will aid your peace. But it is for my own reasons I must find an end to him."

"We don't have much to offer," said Desct, who stood in turn, "but I'll get what aid I can to you."

"It's not over." Sylvaine sat, eyes downcast.

"Sylvaine?" Kayip asked, offering his arm.

"It's not like I have anything else to do."

The monk nodded. "Then it is decided."

"Marcel?" Desct asked, walking past the pair. Marcel rose from his chair.

"Marcel," Desct said. "I could use you. After all this comes to an end, we'll need someone who can help talk peace. I'll do my utmost, but considering all that's happened, I don't know how my word will be taken."

How strange Desct looked in his uniform. It didn't remind Marcel of the hodgepodge mix of rags and recycled military fatigues they had once worn together as soldiers. This outfit was far too formal, with frilled epaulettes and awkward pretensions. When

Marcel had seen Desct crouched in the storage tank beneath Blackwood Row, he had thought that he had found his friend again, back from the dead, the mutations and filth changing nothing. But Desct wasn't the man he remembered, he had changed, had seen things Marcel never had, suffered cruelties Marcel could never truly understand. The man standing before him was no monster, Marcel could not fairly condemn him for the horrors of the night, but he was also not the Desct he once knew.

Finally Marcel shook his head. "I'm sorry, I can't. I've tried to talk my way out of this, from the very beginning. And it's all gone to shit."

Desct put his hand out. "We are free, Marcel, despite the unfortunate blood spilled, we have still achieved something. Help me protect that."

Marcel stepped back, leaning on the wall, his gaze twitching back and forth in thought.

"We can still save Huile," Desct continued, "truly save it this time. Redeem its transgressions and our own, rebuild it from cobblestone up, to be the refuge of liberty we fought for. It's a mess now, all with sense can see that, but we can clean this mess, make Huile everything that we were once promised. Free and independent, from the Principate, from Lazacorp, from the U-double-CR if it comes to that."

Marcel could stay. He could stay among the ruins of the city; watch the men and woman who once called him a hero hide from his revolution in fear. He could linger in anxiety for the coming judgment of far distant Confederacy officials, men who knew nothing of what happened here, of the atrocities and injustices. He could pass papers with a man who he no longer understood, connected now only by shared trauma and failure. He could sit and wait here, all while Lazarus Roache lived.

"Roache started this," Marcel said "and it won't end as long as he lives. He tricked us Desct, those years ago, tricked me since then. He's twisted the mind of everyone he's talked to, and could be at this moment planning his return. I can't stay here idly, knowing that its merely a matter of time until that bastard comes to destroy it all again. No, while Roache is still alive we can't trust any peace."

Desct's hand finally fell. "Well, if that is your decision, then I can only wish you the best of luck."

Marcel smiled, or produced something akin to a smile. "Don't worry, Desct. We'll be back here soon enough."

Kayip grabbed Desct's shoulder, and nodded. "We will bring you Roache's head. I promise you that, if I can live long enough to find it."

Epilogue

Namter fell.

He fell and he fell. Shapes of shadows flew past, flashes of cities resplendent and in ruin, massive arms the length of the ocean, spheres of everturning celestial gearwork, some mired black, others glistening pure. Through this he fell and he fell and the pain was immense. He was himself, full and impure, and for this he suffered, his mind burning, his body bleeding.

"An Awakener has fallen. An Awakener shall rise."

The voice came in from a world beyond. His world, Namter knew, as swirling visions flung past him, as he was thrown through the ceaseless maelstrom. Verus was gone. Yes, he was still enough of himself to remember that. The old Awakener had betrayed the cause, and though Namter could not understand why it had happened, it had happened nonetheless. That man (for without purpose he was only ever just a man) had perished in the chaos he created, burned in the pyre that he had made out of Blackwood Row. Whatever anguish Namter felt, the truth was that their Awakener had fallen.

And now so was Namter.

"A Brother seeks the Truth. A Brother is Blind. A Brother seeks Redemption. A Brother must Suffer."

Namter did not land so much as find himself suddenly standing. There was no crash, yet he felt such pain as if each bone in his body had been shattered into slivers, skewering out in all directions. He writhed without falling over, he suffered without injury.

"He has Watched and long waited to Serve. Let him wander, let him See."

Around Namter loomed towers with no summits, dark and shattered. Hollowed husks infested with naked forms, men with leech-like features and limbs of metal crawling across a broken cityscape, fighting among themselves or sleeping in nests of bleeding rust.

He cowered, covering his eyes, and yet that did nothing to block the sight. His finger slid into the hole where his right eye should have been. Now there was nothing. It was from this eye of Nothing that his sight flowed in, and such vision could never be shut.

"Let him See. Let him See what mankind has brought to the world, what they have dragged to ruin and rot."

Namter stumbled out into the street. Great bulbous men, with masks of rusting metal and guts of suppurating maggots, walked among him, stumbling by with low groans. Mammoth machines hung above, floating in the crimson maelstrom, poxed with oozing sores. On their sides hung thick chains upon which he could make out the forms of men thrashing.

"May his eyes be opened. If he cannot See, may he be blinded. If he cannot Hear, may he be deafened. If he cannot Feel, may he be Flayed. Let Pain mark his contrition. Let Truth smother him."

It was too much, he wanted to shout, it was too much! He choked on the words, remembering the Oathblood poured into his mouth. He was not breathing back in his world, but drowning.

Creatures flew by, screeching. As they dove, he saw that they were children, winged infants. Each was skinless, aside from the wings, which appeared to be covered in a frame of dried, stitch-worked skin. Their sunken eyes stared with a veiny white, and their fingers were long blades. They cackled and screamed, chasing him down into the winding urban maelstrom. They pursued him down infinite alleys that swung back on themselves and through giant factories where headless crones cut meat from men the size of the world. Figures writhed and wept on the streets, many-faced or no-faced, bodies long and wormlike. Colossal spider-shaped machines spewed black clouds that dissolved the very air around him, leaving floating holes of nothingness.

He ran through the nightmare. He was not ready for this; he was not the Awakener, just a mere Brother, a mere Watcher. If this was the truth, it was beyond him.

"Let him know the price of Hubris. Let him know the price of Ego. Let him know the Sick in the soul of man."

He ran onto a castle of oozing walls, titanic bleeding mechanisms twisting and turning the hallways in an endless mad maze. He stumbled through in seconds that took years, up turning floors of gearwork, past statues of squirming flesh, onto an overhanging balcony.

"I am not ready," he tried to shout, "I am not ready."

"If the Truegods allow it, let him know their Glory. Let him see how it was once. Let him See or let him perish."

He collapsed forward, struggling to take the breaths that he knew were impossible. The pain was beyond the redemptive punishment, beyond even the destruction of the self, but an overwhelming torment from which death seemed no escape. His lungs burned, his veins burned, his heart seemed to pump in flames. He clutched at his right eye socket, where it felt as though a river of boiling blood flowed through, burning him from the inside, melting the flesh from his skull and his soul from his very being, until suddenly...

He could See.

Namter stood at the same balcony, high above the city, but it was not the same balcony, not the same city. His skin, which had just been tearing at in agony, was now soothed. His body was covered in some fabric that was smooth to the touch and showed no signs of stitching. It was clearly never an animal's skin, nor some relative of rubber. The cloth felt almost metallic, yet moved like silk, and glimmered in the light.

The air, which had before been putrid, was now purer than a lake-breezed wind. Each breath felt like life itself. He walked with a lightness over to the edge of the balcony and stared down at a view from the height greater than of the tallest mountain.

Below him was a city, but not the cities of his youth, not the fetid, faux glories of man, not filled with structures of the ego, of places of simple toil and idle comforts. Nor did it resemble the wasteland towns, all ruins and shacks, nor the monotone blocks of Principate cities, or the decadently dressed relics of the Resurgence.

It gleamed white and blue, slender towers of incomprehensible artistry, spires that connected earth to sky. Between them roads, long and serpentine, moving like glistening rivers, crowded but in perfect order. Rolling gardens decorated the landscape, each the size of a forest, organized in perfect symmetry. Inside them stood statues of such majesty and prodigious size that even from this distance they demanded awe.

This was a true City. All others were mere corrupted mockeries.

Men, ants from this height, walked in uncountable crowds. Flocks of winged figures flew beside æroships, tracing lyrics of clouds in the sky as the wondrous machines sung arias from their engines.

Great beings, of beauty beyond measure, walked among the lesser men. They were perfect in features, gleaming, their titanic mass seeming less to walk than to float on the ground, their clothes more marvelous than Namter's own unexplained garments. He found himself weeping at their sight. Whatever lingering doubt he may have had, hiding in the back of his mind, was now banished completely, flung to dust.

445

Namter moaned and gripped the rails, wanting nothing more than to stay in this paradise, even if only to glimpse this one image for all eternity.

"Let him see what we lost, what we threw away with our Betrayal."

The world instantly burst apart into flames, the great city tearing itself apart in a sudden inferno. Namter screamed, clutching at it, willing in to return.

Instead from the inferno, he saw Him. Floating in the void, both beautiful and hideous, flesh torn away to reveal divine blood, which dripped from His Body like rain. Great ribbons of skin floated out from the back of a figure the size of a distant continent.

Namter fell to his knees before his Master, tears draining from him as he stared up at the glory that was The Flayed Prince.

"I am sorry!" he screamed. "I have failed! I have failed." The great Tribute in Huile had burned to ash. His Awakener had betrayed the cause, and Namter could not salvage it, could only run from the fire.

"Let him feel the Agony of a thousand life-times."

He screamed. He screamed not from pain, not from punishment, but regret. A life of regret, millennia of regret, not the personal but the existential, the eternal, more and more and more, unending desperation to return, to serve.

The form of the Flayed Prince grew and grew until Namter was near upon it. The sky was a glorious crimson, and the radiant blood fell down upon him, coating his skin, digging into him like acid, down through the flesh and into his bone. He did not shudder, he did not pull away, he stood and embraced the oncoming torrent

"Let him find redemption in Obedience. Let him find purpose in Service."

"I serve," Namter shouted. "I serve. I serve!"

"Let a new Awakener Arise. Let him bring his Task to a final end."

Namter drowned in the Crimson, the Oathblood flowing into his lungs, and into his veins. He convulsed and writhed, burned

446

away and regrew. Then suddenly, his eye opened. Not the eyes he was cursed with in birth, not the eyes withered by age, not the eyes blinded from childhood by the filth of humankind, but a new one, birthed from a boiling womb of Oathblood.

And with this Eye he saw everything.

There was nothing left. From fields of green and mighty cityscapes now sat only dust. I stood there awhile amidst the desolation, the black-charred trees and the husks of brick and metal that hours before had been my home. I did not weep, I did not scream, I could only stare out at the incomprehensible emptiness before me.

Then, from above, I heard a chirping. A small bird flew down, whether gray of feather or drenched by the dust-thick wind I cannot say. It hopped along the rim a shattered autocar, as it might have tree-branches the day before, chirping. It found there an arm sticking out, clothes torn, flesh burnt. Slowly, then quickly, the bird started to peck at the flesh, nibbling bites, filling its belly fat on carrion.

I knew then that I hadn't witnessed the end. I was standing before a new beginning.

—*"Words of a Wastes Hermit" Author unknown.*

Acknowledgements

There are too many people to thank, for assistance both big and small and smally big.

First off, I want to thank my family. My mother, Susan, and my father, Robert, who have supported me all the way. My sister, Zoe, for being awesome. My wife, Bessy, for always being there, even when my head was a world away. My uncle, John, for first suggesting I write some of this nonsense down. My grandmother, Dolly, for providing for my education, and even more for the example she set in life and in everything.

I also want to thank my professors at CalArts, particularly Janet Sarbanes and my mentor Brian Evenson, who helped shape my novel from what it was into something actually pretty good! Of course, I would be beyond remiss to leave out my fellow CalArts students, who gave amazing notes and inspired me with their work.

I would like to thank the students and instructors of the writing classes I took at UCLA Extension and UC Riverside. I feel an overwhelming gratitude towards my fellow writers in my writing groups, whose feedback has been utterly invaluable. In particular, those who helped with this novel: Forrest, Jared, Marcel (no relation), Andrew, Barton, Corley, Ian, Aatif, Alex, Dom,

Rachel, and Peter. I also want to thank my other beta readers, James and Michaela.

For various assistance and blurbs, thank you to: Brian Evenson (again!), Gary Goldman, David Higgins, Amanda Silver and Rick Jaffa. Also, I want to thank Tiny Fox Press, for believing in me and giving me a shot.

Finally, thank you to everyone else as well, for there are too many people to count who have helped me in indirect ways, or without whom this book simply wouldn't have happened.

About the Author

Noah Lemelson is a short story writer and novelist who lives in LA with his wife and cat. Lover of Science Fiction, Fantasy, New Weird, and "Insert-Noun-Here"-Punk. He received his BA in Biology from the University of Chicago and received his MFA in Creative Writing from the California Institute of the Arts. His favorite monkey is the white-headed capuchin. He is currently writing, or more likely, should be writing.

About the Publisher

Tiny Fox Press LLC
5020 Kingsley Road
North Port, FL 34287

www.tinyfoxpress.com